One Night: Unveiled

Also by Jodi Ellen Malpas

This Man
Beneath This Man
This Man Confessed

One Night: Promised
One Night: Denied

One Night: Unveiled

JODI ELLEN MALPAS

First published in Great Britain in 2015 by Orion Books
an imprint of The Orion Publishing Group Ltd
Orion House, 5 Upper Saint Martin's Lane
London WC2H 9EA

An Hachette UK Company

1 3 5 7 9 10 8 6 4 2

All the characters in this book are fictitious, and any
resemblance to actual persons living or dead
is purely coincidental.

A CIP catalogue record for this book
is available from the British Library.

ISBN (Mass Market Paperback) 978 1 4091 5570 6
ISBN (Ebook) 978 1 4091 5571 3

Typeset by Input Data Services Ltd, Bridgwater, Somerset

Printed in Great Britain by Clays Ltd, St Ives plc

The Orion Publishing Group's policy is to use papers that are natural,
renewable and recyclable products and made from wood grown in sustainable
forests. The logging and manufacturing processes are expected to
conform to the environmental regulations of the country of origin.

www.orionbooks.co.uk

For my partner in crime. Some people are just meant to be in your life. She'll always be in mine. Katie Fanny Cooke, thank you for being there every day. Thank you for letting me be me and loving me for it. Thank you for knowing when I need to be left alone and for pushing me when you know I need to let it all out. Thank you for reading me like a book. Thank you for . . . everything.

Acknowledgements

A while ago, I made my soul on paper available for all to read. The fact that I didn't think anyone would actually read my debut novel, *This Man*, seems a little silly now. And here I am, two years down this amazing road I've found myself on, bracing myself for you all to dive into my sixth novel. I'm not going to question the destiny gods. If my destiny is to take you into my imagination and help you live it through my words, then I'll do it with pleasure for the rest of my days. For all of my devoted followers, thank you for allowing me to wreak havoc on your emotions. As ever, I have a huge amount of gratitude to everyone who works behind the scenes to help bring you my stories, and especially my editor at Grand Central, Leah. *Unveiled* took everything out of me emotionally. I was exhausted, and she was there every moment to help me through the conclusion of Livy and Miller's tale.

Now you get to lose yourself in Miller Hart's world one last time.

See you on the other side.

JEM

xxx

Prologue

William Anderson had been sitting in his Lexus on the corner of the familiar street for over an hour. A whole damn hour and he still hadn't located the strength to get out of the car. His eyes had been rooted on the old Victorian terrace for every painful second. He'd avoided this part of town for over twenty years with the exception of one time. To bring her home.

Now, though, he had to face his past head-on. He had to get out of his car. He had to knock on that door. And he was dreading it.

There were no other options left for him, and boy had he searched high and low in his fraught mind for an out. Nothing. 'Time to face the music, Will,' he breathed to himself, sliding out of his car. Shutting the door softly, he started towards the house, annoyed that he was incapable of steadying his thumping heart. It was vibrating in his chest, echoing in his ears. Each step he took, her face was becoming clearer and clearer, until he was clenching his eyes shut in pain.

'Damn you, woman,' he muttered, shivering.

He found himself outside the house far sooner than he liked, staring at the front door. His poor mind was being blasted with too many bad memories to cope with. He felt weak. It wasn't a feeling William Anderson often experienced because he made sure of it. After her, he made damn fucking sure of it.

Letting his head fall back on his shoulders and his eyes close briefly, he drank in the longest inhale of air he ever had. Then he raised a shaky hand and knocked on the door. His pulse accelerated when he heard footsteps, and he very nearly stopped breathing when the door swung open.

She hadn't changed a bit, except now she must have been . . . what? Eighties? Had it been that long? She didn't look at all shocked, and he didn't know if this was a good thing or a bad thing. He'd reserve judgement until he left here. There was a lot to talk about.

Her now-grey eyebrows raised coolly, and when she started shaking her head mildly, William smiled a little. It was a nervous smile. He was beginning to shake in his boots.

'Well, look what the cat dragged in,' she sighed.

Chapter 1

It's perfect here. But it would be even more perfect if my mind wasn't awash with worry, fear, and confusion.

Rolling onto my back in the queen-size bed, I gaze up at the skylights built into the vaulted ceiling of our hotel suite, seeing soft, fluffy clouds littering the bright blue sky. I can also see skyscrapers stretching up to the heavens. I hold my breath and listen for the now-familiar sounds of a New York morning – car horns, whistles, and the general hustle and bustle are all detectable from twelve floors up. Mirrored skyscrapers close us in, making this building seem lost amid the concrete and glass jungle. Our surroundings are incredible, yet it's not what is making this nearly perfect. It's the man lying next to me in the squidgy queen-size bed. I'm certain that beds in America are bigger. Everything in America seems bigger – the buildings, the cars, the personalities . . . my love for Miller Hart.

We've been here for two weeks now, and I miss Nan terribly but speak to her daily. We've let the city swallow us up and had nothing to do except immerse ourselves in each other.

My perfectly imperfect man is relaxed here. He still has extreme ways, but I can live with that. Oddly enough, I'm starting to find many of his OCD habits loveable. I can say that now. And I can say it to him, even if he still chooses to ignore the fact that he is crippled by obsession in most elements of his life. Including me.

At least there are no interferers here in New York – no one to try to take away his most prized possession. I'm his most prized possession. And it's a title I'm thrilled to have. It's also a burden I'm willing to shoulder. Because I know that the sanctuary we've created here is only temporary. Facing that dark world is a battle hovering on the horizon of our current *almost* perfect existence. And I hate myself for doubting the strength within me to see us through it – the strength Miller is so confident I have.

A mild stirring beside me pulls me back into the lavish suite we've called home since we arrived in New York, and I smile when I see him nuzzle into his pillow on a cute murmur. His dark waves are a mussed mess upon his lovely head and his jaw shadowed by coarse stubble. He sighs and pats around half asleep until his palm feels its way up to my head and his fingers locate my wild locks. My smile widens as I lie still and let my gaze linger on his face, feeling his fingers combing through my hair as he settles again. This has become another habit of my perfect part-time gentleman. He'll twiddle with my hair for hours, even in his sleep. I've woken with knots on a few occasions, sometimes with Miller's fingers still caught up in the strands, but I never complain. I need the contact – any contact – from him.

My eyelids slowly close, soothed by his touch. But all too soon, my peace is bombarded by unwelcome visions – including the haunting sight of Gracie Taylor. I snap my eyes open and bolt upright in bed, wincing when my head gets yanked back and my hair pulled. 'Shit!' I hiss, reaching up to begin the meticulous task of unravelling Miller's fingers from my hair. He grumbles a few times but doesn't wake, and I rest his hand on the pillow before pulling myself softly to the edge of the bed. Glancing over my naked shoulder, I see Miller lost in a deep sleep and silently hope his dreams are serene and blissful. Unlike mine.

Letting my feet find the plush carpet, I push myself up, having a little stretch and a sigh. I remain standing beside the bed, staring blankly out the huge window. Could I really have seen my mother for the first time in eighteen years? Or was it just a hallucination brought on by stress?

'Tell me what's troubling that beautiful mind of yours.' His sleepy rasp interrupts my thoughts and I turn to find him lying on his side, praying hands resting under his cheek. I force a smile, one I know won't convince him, and let Miller and all of his perfection distract me from my inner turmoil.

'Just daydreaming,' I say quietly, ignoring his doubtful expression. I've mentally tortured myself since we boarded that plane, replayed that moment over and over, and my quiet pensiveness has been silently noted by Miller. Not that he's pressed me on it, leaving me certain that he thinks I'm reflecting on the trauma that has landed us in New York. He would be partly right. Many events, revelations, and visions have plagued my mind since arriving here, making me resentful that I can't fully appreciate Miller and his devotion to worshipping me.

'Come here,' he whispers, remaining still with no gesture or encouragement, only his quiet, commanding words.

'I was going to make coffee.' I'm a fool to think I can avoid his questions or concern for much longer.

'I've asked once.' He pushes himself to his elbow and cocks his head. His lips are pressed into a straight line, and his crystal blue eyes are burning through me. 'Don't make me repeat myself.'

I shake my head mildly on a sigh and slip back between the sheets, crawling into his chest while he remains still and allows me to find my place. Once I'm settled, his arms encircle me and his nose goes straight to my hair. 'Better?'

I nod into his chest and stare across the planes of his muscles while he feels me everywhere and takes deep breaths. I know he's desperate to comfort and reassure me. But he hasn't. He's allowed me my quiet time and I know it's been incredibly difficult for him. I'm overthinking. I know it, and Miller knows it, too.

He pulls out of the warmth of my hair and spends a few moments arranging it just so. Then he focuses worried blues on mine. 'Never stop loving me, Olivia Taylor.'

'Never,' I affirm, guilt settling deep. I want to reassure him that my love for him shouldn't be of any concern – none at all. 'Don't overthink.' I reach up and drag my thumb across his full bottom lip and watch as he blinks lazily and shifts his hand to clutch mine at his mouth.

He flattens my palm and kisses the centre. 'It's a two-way street, gorgeous girl. I can't see you sad.'

'I have *you*. I couldn't possibly be sad.'

He gives me a smile and leans forward to plant a delicate kiss on the end of my nose. 'I beg to differ.'

'You can beg all you like, Miller Hart.' I'm quickly seized and pulled onto his front, his thighs spreading so I'm cradled between them. He clenches my cheeks in his palms and reaches forward with his lips, leaving them millimetres away from mine with hot air spreading across my skin. My body's reaction isn't something I can help. And I don't want to.

'Let me taste you,' he murmurs, searching my eyes.

I push forward, colliding with his lips, and crawl up his body until I'm straddling his hips and feeling his mood, hard and hot and wedged under my bum. I hum into his mouth, grateful for his tactics to distract me. 'I think I'm addicted to you,' I murmur, cupping the back of his head in my palms and pulling impatiently until he's sitting up. My legs find their way around his waist and his hands palm my bum, pulling me farther into him while we maintain the smouldering slow dance with our tongues.

'Good.' He breaks our kiss and shifts me back slightly before reaching over to the cabinet and grabbing a condom. 'Your period must be due soon,' he observes, and I nod, reaching to help him, taking it from his hand and ripping the packet open, just as eager to commence worshipping as Miller. 'Good. Then we can get rid of these.' It's rolled on, I'm reclaimed, lifted, and then he clenches his eyes shut as he guides his arousal to my damp opening. I slip down, taking him to the hilt.

My moan of satisfaction is broken and low. Our joining sends every trouble away, leaving room for nothing but unrelenting pleasure and undying love. He's buried deep, holding still, and my head has dropped back as I dig my nails into his solid shoulders for support. 'Move,' I beg, grinding down into his lap, my breath stuttering with need.

His mouth finds my shoulder and his teeth grip gently as he begins guiding me meticulously on his lap. 'Feel good?'

'Better than anything I can imagine.'

'I concur.' His hips drive up as he grinds me down, pulling pleasure from both of our heaving bodies. 'Olivia Taylor, I'm so fucking fascinated by you.'

His measured rhythm is beyond perfection, working us both up slowly and lazily, every rotation edging us closer to explosion. The friction against his groin on the tip of my clitoris when he brings me to the end of each swivel has me whimpering and panting, before my body is journeying back around, relieving the delicious pressure, only briefly, until I'm back at that wondrous pinnacle of pleasure. The knowing in his gaze tells me it's all so very purposeful, the constant slow blinks and the parting of his lush lips only intensifying my desperate condition.

'Miller,' I gasp, dropping my face into his neck, losing the ability to keep myself upright on his lap.

'Don't deprive me of that face, Olivia,' he warns. 'Show it to me.'

I pant, licking and biting at his throat, his stubble scratching at my sweaty face. 'I can't.' His expert worshipping never fails to render me useless.

'For me you can. Show me your face.' His command is harsh and delivered on an upward bolt of his hips.

I yelp at the sudden deep penetration and fly upright again. 'How?' I cry out, frustrated and delighted all at once. He's holding me in that place – the one between torture and other-worldly pleasure.

'Because I can.' He flips me onto my back and re-enters me on a shout of satisfaction. His pace is increasing, and so is the force. Our lovemaking has become harder in recent weeks. It's like a light has switched on and Miller's realised that taking me with a little more aggression and force doesn't make our intimacies any less worshipful. He's still making love to me. I can touch him and kiss him, and he reciprocates, responds, says continuous loving words as if reassuring himself *and* me that he's in full control. It's unnecessary. I trust him with my body as much as I now trust him with my love.

My wrists are seized and held firmly above my head, and he braces himself on his toned forearms, blinding me with the acres of cut muscle on his torso. His teeth are clenched, but I can still detect that mild beam of victory. He's happy. He's delighted by my clear desperation for him. But he's equally desperate for me. My hips rise and begin to meet his firm pumping, our centres clashing as he withdraws and sinks back in, over and over.

'You're clenching around me, sweet girl,' he pants, his wayward curl bouncing on his forehead with each collision of our bodies. Every nerve ending I possess begins to twitch at the onslaught of pressure accumulating at my core. I'm trying desperately to fight it back, anything to prolong the stunning sight of him above me, dripping wet, his face etched in a pleasure so intense it could be confused with pain.

'Miller!' I shout, frenzied, my head beginning to shake but my eyes still holding his. 'Please!'

'Please what? You need to come?'

'Yes!' I gasp, and then suck in air when he pelts forward, pushing me up the bed. 'No!' I don't know what I want to do. I need release, but I need to stay in this faraway place of raw abandon.

Miller groans, allowing his chin to drop to his chest and his fierce grasp to release my wrists, prompting them to shoot to his shoulders. My short nails dig in. Hard. 'Fuck!' he roars, his pace picking up further. This is the hardest he's taken me, but there's no room amid my earth-shaking pleasure to be concerned by it. He's not hurting me, although I suspect I am him. My fingers are instantly aching.

I let off my own little round of expletives, absorbing every pound until he abruptly stops. I feel him swell within me, and then he rears back slowly and pushes forward smooth and slow on a groan. It sends us both tumbling into an abyss of indescribable, wonderful sensations.

I'm taken out by the intensity of my climax, and Miller collapsing to my chest with no concern for his weight atop me tells me he is, too. We're both gasping, both still pulsing and both completely wiped out. That was powerful, frantic love-making that I think may have transformed into fucking, and when I feel hands begin to caress me and a mouth creeping up my cheek, searching for my lips, I know Miller is registering this, too.

'Tell me I didn't hurt you.' He dedicates a few moments to worshipping my mouth, taking it gently, delicately nibbling at my lips each time he pulls away. His hands are everywhere, stroking, skimming, tracing.

My eyes close on a satisfied sigh and I absorb all his slow attention as I smile and muster some waning strength to cuddle him and squeeze some reassurance into him. 'You didn't hurt me.'

He's heavy, resting all over me, but I have no desire to alleviate the weight. We're connected . . . everywhere.

I draw a deep breath. 'I love you, Miller Hart.'

He slowly rises until he's gazing down at me, eyes sparkling, his beautiful mouth tipping at each corner. 'I accept your love.'

I try in vain to narrow my eyes on him in irritation, but just wind up mirroring his amusement. It's impossible not to when his rare smiles are being dished out so willingly and so often these days. 'You're such a smart-arse.'

'And *you*, Olivia Taylor, are such a divine blessing.'

'Or possession.'

'Same thing,' he whispers. 'In my world, anyway.' Each of my eyelids is kissed sweetly before he lifts his hips and slips out of me, sitting back on his heels. Contentment heats my veins and peace spirals in my mind as he pulls me up to his lap and directs my legs around his back. The sheets are a pile of messy material surrounding us and he isn't in the least bit bothered.

'The bed's an awful mess,' I say with a teasing smile as he arranges my hair over my shoulders and slides his palms down my arms until he has my hands.

'My compulsion to have you in bed with me far outweighs any compulsion to have the sheets tidy.'

My smile stretches into a massive grin. 'Why, Mr Hart, did you just admit to a compulsion?'

His head cocks and I flex one of my hands until he releases it, then take my time pushing back his stray wave from his damp forehead.

'You might be on to something there,' he replies, totally composed and with no humour in his tone.

My hand falters in his waves and I watch him closely, searching for that cute dimple. It's nowhere in sight and I look questioningly at him, trying to figure out if he's finally admitting that he suffers terribly from OCD.

'Might,' he adds, remaining poker-faced.

I gasp and jab him in the shoulder, forcing the sweetest sounding chuckle to slip from his mouth. The sight and sound of Miller displaying amusement never fails to mesmerise me. It's without question the most beautiful thing in the world – not just my world but the *whole* world. It has to be.

'I'm inclined to say definitely,' I break in, interrupting his laughter.

His head shakes in wonder. 'Do you realise how hard I find it to accept you're here?'

My smile fades into confusion. 'In New York?' I'd have gone to Outer Mongolia if he had demanded it. Anywhere. He laughs lightly and glances away, prompting me to take his jaw and direct his perfect face back to mine. 'Elaborate.' I raise my eyebrows in authority, pressing my lips together, despite the overwhelming need to join him in his happiness.

'Just here,' he says on a little shrug of his solid shoulders. 'With me, I mean.'

'In bed?'

'In my life, Olivia. Transforming my darkness into blinding light.' His face comes close, his lips ghosting mine. 'Replacing my nightmares with beautiful dreams.' Holding my eyes, he falls silent and waits for me to absorb his heartfelt words. Like many things he says now, I fully understand and comprehend it.

'You could just say how much you love me. That would work.' I purse my lips, desperate to remain straight-faced. It's hard when he's just blown my fallen heart from my chest with such a powerful declaration. I want to push him to his back and demonstrate my feelings for him with a heart-stopping kiss, but a tiny part of me is willing him to take my not-so-subtle hint. He's never said anything about love. *Fascinated* is his word of choice, and I know exactly what he means. But I can't deny my desire to hear those three simple words.

Miller takes me to my back, smothering me with his stubble, kissing every available inch of my screwed-up face. 'I'm deeply fascinated by you, Olivia Taylor.' My cheeks are encased in his palms. 'You'll never know how deeply.'

I surrender to Miller's way and let him completely overwhelm me.

'While I'd love to lose myself beneath these sheets all day with my habit, we have a date.' My nose is nibbled and he's pulling me up from the bed, placing me on my feet and messing with my hair. 'Take a shower.'

'Yes, sir!' I salute him and ignore his eye roll as I saunter off to the shower.

Chapter 2

I'm standing on the pavement outside our hotel, gazing up to the sky. It's part of my daily routine. Every morning I wander down, leaving Miller fussing with something back upstairs, and take up position at the roadside, my head fallen back, staring in wonder up to the heavens. People sidestep me, taxis and shiny black SUVs zoom past, and the chaos of New York City saturates my hearing. I'm held captivated under the spell of the towering glass and metal guarding the city. Just . . . incredible.

There are not many things that can yank me from my raptured state, but his touch is one of those things. And his breath at my ear.

'Boom,' he murmurs, turning me in his arms. 'They don't grow overnight, you know.'

I glimpse up again. 'I just don't understand how they stay upright.' My jaw is clasped and pulled back down. His eyes are soft and amused.

'Maybe you should seek to sate this fascination.'

My neck retracts. 'What do you mean?'

His palm slides to my nape and he starts guiding me towards Sixth Avenue. 'Perhaps you should look into studying structural engineering.'

Dipping out of his hold, I place my hand in his. And he lets me, carrying out the usual flex of his fingers until he has a comfy grip. 'I prefer the history behind the building, not how it was built.' I glance up at him, then let my eyes fall down the length of his tall physique, smiling as I do. He has jeans on.

Lovely, relaxed fitting jeans and a plain white T-shirt. Wearing suits while we're here would be ridiculously inappropriate and I wasn't afraid to tell him so. He didn't argue about it either, allowing me to drag him around Saks for the whole first day we were here. He has no need for a suit in New York; there's no one he needs to fool with his routine as an aloof gentleman. Despite this, though, Miller Hart still doesn't do wandering very well. Or mixing, for that matter.

'So, do you remember your challenge for today?' he asks as we pause at a DON'T WALK signal. His eyebrows are raised as I smile up at him.

'Yes, and I'm all prepared.' I lost myself in the New York Public Library for hours yesterday while Miller took care of some business calls. I didn't want to leave. I'd tortured myself a little by Googling 'Gracie Taylor'. But it was like she didn't even exist. After a few more tries of coming up with nothing, I lost myself in dozens of books, but not all historical architecture books. I took a brief peek at one about OCD, and I found out a few things, like the connection with anger. Miller certainly has a temper.

'And what building did you choose?'

'The Brill Building.'

He frowns down at me. 'The Brill Building?'

'Yes.'

'Not the Empire State or Rockefeller?'

I smile. 'Everyone knows the histories of those.' I also thought everyone knew the histories of most of the buildings in London, but I was mistaken. Miller knew nothing about the Café Royal or the story behind it. Perhaps I've immersed myself a bit too much in the opulence of London. I know everything and I'm not sure if that makes me sad, obsessed, or a damn good tour guide.

'They do?'

I'm delighted by his doubt. 'The Brill Building is more

obscure, but I've heard of it and I think you'll love to hear what I've learned.' The lights change and we begin to cross. 'It has a very interesting history in music.'

'It does?'

'Yes.' I gaze up at him and he smiles fondly. He might seem alarmed by my pointless historical knowledge of architecture, but I know he relishes in my enthusiasm. 'Have you remembered *your* challenge?' I pull him to a halt before he can take us across another road.

My lovely, obsessive man regards me closely. And I grin. He remembers. 'Something about fast food.'

'Hot dogs.'

'That's right,' he confirms, full of trepidation. 'You want me to eat a hot dog.'

'I do,' I confirm, hysterical on the inside. Every day we have been in New York, we've each set a challenge for the other to fulfil. Miller's challenges for me have all been somewhat interesting, from preparing a lecture on a local building to bathing without touching him, even if *he* touched *me*. That was torturous and I failed miserably. Not that he was much bothered, but it lost me a point. My challenges for him have been a little bit childish but perfectly appropriate for Miller, like sitting on the grass in Central Park, eating in a restaurant without precisely aligning his wineglass, and now eating a hotdog. My challenges are all very easy . . . supposedly. He fought through some and failed others, like resisting shifting his wineglass. The score? Eight to Olivia, seven to Miller.

'As you wish,' he huffs, attempting to tug me across the road, but I stand firm and wait for him to turn his attention back to me. He's watching me carefully, his mind clearly racing. 'You're going to make me eat a hot dog from one of those grubby little corner stands, aren't you?'

I nod, knowing he's seen the *grubby little corner stand* only a few paces away. 'Here's one.'

'How convenient,' he mutters, reluctantly following me to the hot dog cart.

'Two hot dogs, please,' I say to the vendor as Miller twitches uncomfortably beside me.

'Sure thing, sweetheart. Onions? Ketchup? Mustard?'

Miller steps forward. 'None.'

'All!' I interrupt, pushing him back and ignoring his gasp of annoyance. 'Lots of it, too.'

The vendor chuckles as he loads the bun with a hot dog and proceeds to pile on onions before squirting lashings of ketchup and mustard across the top. 'Anything the lady likes,' he says, handing me the finished product.

I push it straight to Miller with a smile. 'Enjoy.'

'I doubt it,' he mutters, eyeing his breakfast dubiously.

I direct an apologetic smile to the vendor and take my hot dog, handing him a ten-dollar note. 'Keep the change,' I say, quickly taking Miller's arm and leading him away. 'That was rude.'

'What was?' He looks up, genuinely stumped, and I roll my eyes at his ignorance.

I sink my teeth into one end of the bun and gesture for him to follow suit. But he just looks at the hot dog like it could possibly be the strangest thing he's ever seen. He even turns it in his hand a few times, like looking at it from a different angle might make it more appetising. I remain quiet, enjoying my own, and wait for him to take the plunge. I'm halfway through before he braves a nibble on the end.

Then I watch in horror – which almost matches Miller's – as a big dollop of onions, mixed with a copious amount of ketchup and mustard, slips off the end and splatters down his bright white T-shirt.

'Oh . . .' I swallow hard, bracing for the imminent meltdown.

He's staring at his chest, his jaw clenching, his hot dog quickly tossed to the ground. I'm all tense, my teeth clamped down on my bottom lip to stop me saying anything and stoking the clear irritation coming off of him in droves. He snatches my napkin and starts rubbing frantically at the material, stretching the stain, smearing it in a little more. I cringe. Miller takes a calming gulp of air. Then he closes his eyes and slowly reopens them, focusing on me. 'Just . . . fucking . . . perfect.'

My cheeks puff out, my lip slipping through my teeth painfully as I try my hardest to contain a laugh, but it's no good. I throw my hot dog in the nearby bin and lose control. 'I'm sorry!' I gasp. 'You just . . . you look like the world is going to end.'

Eyes blazing, he clasps my neck and leads me down the street, while I work hard on reining myself in. He won't appreciate it, whether we're in London, New York, or Timbuktu.

'This will do,' he declares.

I look up and see a Diesel store across the street. He quickly guides me across the road, with only three seconds to spare on the pedestrian countdown, no doubt unwilling to even allow the potential of being mowed down delay his mission to be rid of the horrifying stain on his T-shirt. I know for absolutely certain that this would never be his usual store of choice, but his current tarnished condition won't allow Miller to seek out a less casual outlet.

We enter and are instantly bombarded by loud, pumping music. Miller whips off his soiled shirt, revealing miles of sharp muscle to everyone in sight. Lines of definition rise from the waistband of his perfectly hung jeans and drift into stupidly taut abs . . . and then that chest. I don't know whether to cry with pleasure or shout at him for sharing the stunning sight.

Countless female shop assistants trip over themselves to be the first to make it to us. 'Can I help?' It's a petite Asian woman who wins, smiling smugly at her colleagues before dribbling all over Miller.

The mask slips right into place, delighting me. 'A T-shirt, please. Anything.' He waves his hand around the store dismissively.

'Certainly!' She's off, grabbing various garments on her travels, calling behind her to follow, which we do once Miller has settled his palm on my nape. We walk until we're at the back of the store and the sales assistant has reams of material in her grasp. 'I'll pop them all in the changing room and you can call if you need any assistance.'

I laugh, earning me a curious sideways glance from Miller and pursed lips from Miss Flirty. 'I'm certain your biceps need measuring.' I reach down and smooth my palm down his thigh to raised brows. 'Or maybe your inside leg.'

'Sass,' he says simply, before turning his naked chest back to the assistant and riffling through the mountain of clothes in her grasp. 'This will suffice.' He pulls out a lovely casual blue and white checked shirt, with rolled up sleeves and a pocket on each pec. Carelessly yanking off the tags, he slips it on and walks away, leaving Miss Flirty with wide eyes and me following his path to the till. He slaps the tags down, along with a hundred-dollar note, and walks out, fastening the buttons.

I watch him disappear out of the store, Miss Flirty standing to my side, all dumbstruck but still dribbling. 'Um, thanks.' I smile and go after my uptight, ill-mannered part-time gentleman.

'That was so rude!' I exclaim when I find him outside, securing the last button.

'I bought a shirt.' His arms fall to his sides, obviously flummoxed by my scorn. It worries me that he's so unaware of his odd ways.

'It's the way you bought it,' I retort, dropping my head back to look to the heavens for help.

'You mean I told the assistant what I'd like, she found it, I tried it on, and then paid for it?'

My head drops tiredly and I find a familiar impassiveness. 'Smart-arse.'

'I'm merely stating the facts.'

Even if I had the energy to argue with him, which I don't, I wouldn't win. Old habits die hard.

'Do you feel better?' I ask.

'It'll do.' He brushes down the checked shirt and tugs at the hem.

'Yes, it'll do,' I sigh. 'Where to next?'

His palm finds its favourite place on my neck and he turns me with a slight twist of his hand. 'The Brilliant Building. Time for your challenge.'

'It's the *Brill* Building,' I laugh. 'And it's this way.' I divert quickly, causing Miller to lose his hold, and take his hand. 'Did you know that many famous musicians wrote many hits in the Brill Building? Some of the most famous in American music history.'

'Fascinating,' Miller muses, looking fondly down at me.

I smile, reaching up to feel his dark stubbled jaw. 'Not as fascinating as you.'

After a few hours roaming Manhattan and giving Miller a history lesson on not just the Brill Building but also St Thomas Church, we begin to stroll down to Central Park. We take our time, both of us silent as we amble leisurely down the centre of the tree-lined path, benches flanking both sides and peace engulfing us, leaving the concrete chaos behind. Once we've crossed the road that cuts the park in half, dodged all of the runners, and descended the giant concrete stairs to the fountain, my waist is circled with his palms and I'm lifted onto the edge of the giant water feature. 'There,' he says, smoothing down my skirt. 'Give me your hand.'

I do as I'm bid, smiling at his formalness, and let him start leading me around the fountain, Miller still on the ground, his hand lifted to maintain our connection, while I tower above him. I take small paces and watch as he slips his spare hand into the pocket of his jeans. 'How long do we need to stay here?' I ask quietly, returning my eyes forward, mainly to ensure I don't slip off the wall and a little to avoid what I know will be a torn face.

'I'm not sure, Olivia.'

'I miss Nan.'

'I know you do.' He squeezes my hand, his attempt to reassure me. It won't work. I know William has taken on the responsibility of seeing to her welfare in my absence, something that is a worry for me because I still have no idea what he's told my grandmother about his history with my mother and his history with me.

Looking up, I see a little girl skipping towards me on the fountain wall, doing a far better job of looking stable than I am. There's not enough room for both of us, so I make to slip down but gasp when I'm seized and swung around, allowing her to skip on by, before I'm placed back on the raised edge of the fountain. My palms rest on his shoulders while he spends a few quiet moments straightening out my skirt. 'Perfect,' he says under his breath, taking my hand and leading on again. 'Do you trust me, Olivia?'

His question throws me, not because I doubt my answer, but because he hasn't asked this since we arrived. He hasn't spoken about what we've left behind in London, and that has been fine by me. Immoral bastards, someone following me, Cassie going all lunatic on Miller, Sophia warning me off, chains, sex for money . . .

I've surprised myself how easy it has been to bury that somewhere deep within me since being immersed in the chaos of New York – a chaos I'm finding soothing compared to what I could be torturing myself with. I know Miller has been a little baffled by my lack of pressing, but there is something I can't seem to cast aside so easily. Something I can't bring myself to voice, to Miller or even out loud to myself. The only reassurance I needed was that Nan is being taken care of. I'm sensing now is the time that Miller's quiet acceptance of my silence changes.

'Yes,' I answer assertively, but he doesn't look at me or acknowledge my answer. He remains focused forward, holding my hand gently while I follow the curve of the fountain.

'And I trust you to share your troubles with me.' He halts and turns me into him, taking both of my hands and gazing up at me.

I clamp my lips together, loving him more for knowing me so well but hating that it means I'll probably never be able to hide anything from him. I also hate that he feels so obviously guilty for dragging me into his world.

'Tell me, Olivia.' His tone is soft, encouraging. It's desperate.

My eyes drop to his feet, seeing them move in closer. 'I'm being silly,' I say quietly. 'I think all of the shock and adrenaline was playing games with my mind.'

He shifts his hands to my waist and lifts me down, making me sit on the edge of the fountain. Then he lowers to his knees and secures my cheeks in his hands. 'Tell me,' he whispers.

His need to comfort me fills me with the courage to spit out what's been tormenting me since we've been here. 'At Heathrow . . . I thought I saw something, but I know I didn't, and I know it's stupid and impossible and absolutely absurd, and my vision was obstructed and I was so stressed and tired and emotional.' I draw a breath, ignoring his wide eyes. 'It couldn't have been. I know that. I mean, she's been dead for—'

'Olivia!' Miller breaks through my verbal vomit, his blue eyes wide and with a look of alarm on his perfect face. 'What on earth are you talking about?'

'My mother,' I breathe. 'I think I saw her.'

'Her ghost?'

I'm not sure if I believe in ghosts. Or maybe I do now. With no obvious answer, I just shrug.

'At Heathrow?' he pushes.

I nod.

'When you were exhausted, emotional, and being kidnapped by an ex-escort with a terrible temper?'

My eyes narrow on him. 'Yes,' I push through clenched teeth.

'I see,' he muses, glancing away briefly before returning his eyes to mine. 'And this is why you've been so quiet and cagey?'

'I realise how stupid I sound.'

'Not stupid,' he argues quietly. 'Grief-stricken.'

I frown at him, but he continues before I can question his conclusion.

'Olivia, we've been through so much. Both of our pasts have been very much present in recent weeks. It's understandable that you'd be feeling lost and confused.' He reaches forward and rests his lips on mine. 'Please confide in me. Don't let your troubles weigh you down when I'm here to ease them for you.' Pulling away, he smoothes his thumbs across my cheeks and melts me with the sincerity that's shining from his extraordinary eyes. 'I can't see you sad.'

I suddenly feel so very stupid, and with nothing left to say, I close my arms around his shoulders and pull him into me. He's right. It's no wonder my mind's a jumbled mess after everything we've been through. 'I don't know where I'd be without you.'

Accepting my fierce embrace, he inhales into my hair. I feel him locate a lock and start to twist it around his fingers. 'You'd be in London living a carefree life,' he muses quietly.

His sombre statement pulls me from the warmth of his body immediately. I didn't like the words and I definitely didn't like the tone. 'Living a hollow life,' I counter. 'Promise you'll never abandon me.'

'I promise.' He says it without a second's hesitation, yet right now it doesn't feel like enough. I'm not sure what else I can make him say that will convince me. A bit like his acceptance of my love. That wavering is still showing signs and I don't like it. A repeat of him leaving, even if he didn't want to, is still something I live in fear of.

'I want a contract,' I blurt. 'Something legal that says you can't ever leave me.' I realise my stupidly in an instant and I cringe, slapping myself all over Central Park. 'That came out all wrong.'

'I hope so!' He coughs, almost falling to his arse in shock. I might not have meant that the way it sounded, but his clear disgust is like a slap in the face. I haven't given a second thought to marriage, or anything beyond today. There's too much shit blocking dreams of futures and happiness, but now I'm *really* thinking. His clear abhorrence to the idea is making it hard not to. I want to get married one day. I want the kids, the dog, and the cosy family house. I want mess everywhere from children running riot, and I know in this moment that I want it all with Miller.

Then reality crashes down on me. He obviously finds marriage unspeakable. He hates mess, which puts my chaotic family home right out of the picture. And as for the children? Well, I'm not going to ask and I don't think I need to, because I remember that photograph of a lost, grubby little boy.

'We should go,' I say, standing to meet him before I say anything else stupid and have to face another unwanted reaction. 'I'm tired.'

'I concur.' The relief rolls off him in waves. It doesn't help my despondency. Or my hopes for our future . . . once we can finally focus on our happily-ever-after.

Chapter 3

Things have been awkward and tense since we left Central Park. Miller left me to entertain myself when we got back to the suite, choosing to disappear into the office space that leads off the balcony. He had some business to see to. It's not unusual for him to take an hour to make his calls, but it's now been four hours, with no word, appearance, or indication that he's still alive in there.

I'm on the balcony, the sun warm on my face, and I recline back on the lounger, silently willing Miller to emerge from the study. We haven't gone this long without some kind of physical contact since we've been in New York, and I'm craving his touch. I was dying to escape the tense vibes when we returned from our stroll, was quietly relieved when he muttered his intention to deal with some business, but now I'm feeling more lost than ever. I've called Nan and Gregory and chatted idly about nothing in particular, and I've read half of the history book that Miller bought me yesterday, not that I can recall any of the information.

And now I'm lying here – into hour five – twiddling my ring and getting all worked up over our Central Park conversation. I sigh, remove my ring, put it back on again, twist it a few times, and then freeze when I hear stirring from the other side of the office doors. I see the handle shift and snatch my book up, burying my nose in it, hoping to look engrossed.

The doors creak, prompting me to glance up from the random page I opened the book to, and I find Miller standing on the threshold, watching me. His feet are bare, the top button of his jeans undone, and his shirt has been discarded. His dark mop of waves is a dishevelled mess, like he's been raking his hand through the curls. And I know once I seek his eyes out that's exactly what he's been doing. They're brimming with despair. Then he tries to smile, and I feel a million bolts of guilt stab at my fallen heart. Placing my book on the table, I sit up and pull my knees to my chin, wrapping my arms around my legs. The tension is still thick, but having him close again is rekindling my lost serenity. Fireworks crackling beneath my skin, working their way deep, is familiar and comforting.

He spends a few silent moments with his hands resting lightly in his pockets, leaning against the doorframe, thinking. Then he sighs and without a word comes over to straddle the lounger behind me, encouraging me to move forward before he settles, slides his arms over my shoulders, and pulls my back to his chest. My eyes close and I absorb all of him – his feel, his heartbeat against me, and his breath in my hair.

'I apologise,' he whispers, pressing his lips to my neck. 'I didn't mean to make you sad.'

My hands start working in slow circles across the material of his jeans. 'It's OK.'

'It's not OK. If I had one wish,' he begins, working his slow-moving lips up to my ear, 'I'd wish I could be perfect for you. No one else, just you.'

I open my eyes and turn to face him. 'Your wish must have come true.'

He laughs a little and moves a hand to my cheek. 'You must be the most beautiful person God's ever created. Here.' His eyes journey around my face. 'And here.' Then his palm rests on my chest. He kisses my lips tenderly, then my nose, my cheeks, and finally my forehead. 'There's something on the desk for you.'

I instinctively pull away. 'What is it?'

'Go see.' He encourages me to stand before resting back and gesturing towards the doors of the office. 'Chop-chop.'

My gaze flicks from the doors to Miller, back and forth, until he cocks an expectant eyebrow at me, kicking my cautious feet into gear. I pad warily across the balcony, filled with curiosity, feeling blue eyes burning into my back, and when I reach the door, I look over my shoulder. There's a hint of a smile on his perfect face.

'Go,' he mouths, taking my book from the table and flicking through. My lips are clamped together as I make my way to the regal desk, and I release my breath once I'm settled in the green leather chair. But my heart begins to bounce off my breastbone when I see an envelope positioned in the centre, perfectly placed, the bottom square with the edge of the desk. I find my ring and begin to spin it on my finger, worried, cautious, curious. All I see when looking at this envelope is another envelope – the one on Miller's desk in Ice, the one containing the letter he wrote to me when he abandoned me. I'm not sure I want to read it, but Miller put it there. Miller wrote whatever's contained inside, and those two combinations make for one very curious Olivia Taylor.

Scooping it up, I work the seal open, noting the adhesive is still damp. I pull out the paper and slowly unfold it. Then I take a deep breath and brace myself for his written words.

My sweet girl,
I will never do anything less than worship you. Every time I feel you or touch your soul, it'll be etched on that beautiful mind of yours forever – and beyond that. I've told you all of this before. There aren't words in existence that could justify my feelings for you. I've perused the English dictionary for hours looking for them – nothing. When I try to express myself, nothing seems adequate. Yet I know how profound

your feelings are for me. And that makes my reality almost impossible to comprehend.

I don't need to stand before a priest in God's house to validate how I feel for you. Anyway, God never anticipated us when he created love.

There's nothing that could or ever will compare.

If you want to take this letter as my official promise to never leave you, then I'll have it framed and hung above our bed. If you want me to say these words aloud, then I'll do it on my knees before you.

You are my soul, Olivia Taylor. You are my light. You are my reason to breathe. Don't ever doubt that.

Be mine for eternity, I beg you. Because I promise I am yours.

Never stop loving me.

Eternally yours,

Miller Hart

x

I read it again, this time with tears trickling down my cheeks. The words, so elegantly written, hit me harder still, making me truly comprehend Miller Hart's love for me. So I read it again and again and again, each time my heart warming and my love for him intensifying further until I'm an emotional wreck, sobbing all over the posh desk, my face sore and puffy from my relentless tears. Miller Hart expresses himself perfectly well. I know how he feels about me. Now I just feel silly and guilty for faltering . . . for making such a big deal of it, even if I did it silently to myself. But he saw my internal turmoil. And he's acknowledged it.

'Olivia?'

My eyes snap up and see him in the doorway, a distressed look on his face.

'I've made you sad?'

Every aching muscle liquefies, my emotionally exhausted body sinking into the chair. 'No . . . I . . . it's just . . . ' I raise the paper, waving it in the air as I wipe my eyes. 'I can't . . . ' I gather the strength to utter something comprehensible and spit it out. 'I'm so sorry.'

I rise from the chair, forcing my legs to hold me steady, and approach him. My head's shaking a little, angry with myself for making him feel the need to explain when I already know how he feels.

When I'm only a few feet away, his arms open, welcoming me into his embrace, and I practically throw myself at him, feeling my feet leave the floor and his nose head straight for its favourite place. 'Don't cry,' he soothes, tightening his hold. 'Please don't cry.'

I'm unable to speak through my emotion, so I return his fierce cuddle, soaking up every familiar sharp edge of his body against mine. We remain a tangle of limbs for an age, me working hard to gather myself, Miller patient while I do so. He eventually attempts to detach me from his body, and I let him. Then he drops to his knees and tugs me down to join him. That beautiful smile greets me, his hands pushing my hair from my face and his thumbs collecting the tears still escaping my eyes.

He goes to speak but purses his lips instead, and I see his internal struggle to voice what he wants to say. So I speak instead. 'I never doubted your love for me, no matter how you chose to say it.'

'I'm glad.'

'I didn't mean to make you feel shitty.'

His smile stretches and his eyes sparkle. 'I was worried.'

'Why?'

'Because . . .' His eyes drop and he sighs. 'Every woman on my client list is married, Olivia. A blessed ring and a certificate signed by a holy man mean nothing to me.'

His admission doesn't surprise me. I remember William saying loud and clear that Miller Hart struggles with morality. Sleeping with a married woman in exchange for money probably never cost him a scrap of shame – until he met me. I rest my fingertips on his dark jaw and bring his face to mine. 'I love you,' I affirm, and he smiles, but it's in between sadness and happiness. It's light and it's dark. 'And I know how fascinated you are with me.'

'You couldn't possibly know how much.'

'I beg to differ,' I whisper, bringing his letter between our bodies.

He looks down at it and silence falls, only very briefly, before he drags lazy eyes to mine. 'I'll never do anything less than worship you.'

'I know.'

'Every time I feel you or touch your soul, it'll be etched on that beautiful mind of yours forever.'

I smile. 'I know that.'

He takes the letter and casts it aside, then holds my hands *and* my eyes. 'You make my reality so hard to comprehend.'

I suddenly realise he's voicing his written words, and I draw breath to halt him, to tell him it isn't necessary, but I'm hushed when the tip of his finger meets my lips.

'You are my soul, Olivia Taylor. You are my light. You are my reason to breathe. Don't ever doubt that.' His jaw is tense, and even though this is a shortened version of his letter, hearing him speak his declaration hammers it all home more forcefully. 'Be mine for eternity, I beg you.' He reaches into his pocket and produces a small box. 'Because I promise I am yours.'

My eyes are rooted on the tiny gift box, despite the urge to maintain my comfort from keeping our stares locked. I'm too curious. When he takes my hand and places the box in the centre of my palm, I finally rip my eyes from the mysterious leather box and look up at him. 'For me?'

He nods slowly and rests back on his haunches, as do I.

'What is it?'

He smiles, showing a glimmer of that rare dimple. 'I love your curiosity.'

'Should I open it?' My fingers reach up to my mouth and I start to nibble at the tip of my thumb, all kinds of feelings, thoughts, and emotions running riot in my mind.

'I might be the only man who can sate that unyielding curiosity within you.'

I laugh a little, flicking my eyes between the box and Miller's pensive form. 'You spike that curiosity, Miller, so my sanity relies on you sating it, too.'

He matches my amusement and nods at the box. 'Open it.'

My fingers are shaking and emotions are rushing through me as I open the lid. I risk a peek at Miller, finding his blue stare centred solely on me. He's tense. Nervous. And that makes me feel nervous, too.

Slowly, I pull the lid up. And lose my breath. A ring.

'It's diamonds,' he whispers. 'Your birthstone.'

I swallow hard, my eyes running over the length of the thick band that rises to a subtle peak in the centre with a brilliant oval-cut diamond flanked by a teardrop-shaped stone on each side. Smaller stones surround the band, all sparkling beautifully. The white gold is cut, making each encrusted piece look like it's detached from the main diamonds. I've never seen anything like it. 'Antique?' I ask, abandoning the beauty for another beauty. I look up at him. He still looks nervous.

'Art nouveau – 1898, to be precise.'

I smile as I shake my head in wonder. Of course he'll be precise. 'But it's a ring.' I finally steel myself to say the obvious. After today, Central Park, the tension, and Miller's letter, this ring has just thrown me for a loop.

The box is suddenly gone from my grasp and placed to the side. He shifts to his backside, claims my hands, and tugs me forward until I've walked on my knees to between his thighs. I rest back on my haunches again and wait with bated breath for his words. I've no doubt they're going to penetrate deeply, just as his crystal blue eyes are doing right now. He picks the box back up and holds it between us. The sparkles shooting off the exquisite piece are blinding. 'This one here –' he points to the diamond, the centrepiece – 'it represents us.'

My palms cover my face, not wanting him to see the tears building in my eyes again, but I'm not blessed with privacy for long. He takes my hands and guides them to my lap, nodding his handsome head slowly in understanding.

'This one –' he points to one of the brilliant teardrop stones flanking the showpiece diamond – 'is me.' Then his finger drifts across to the matching one on the other side. 'And this one represents you.'

'Miller, I—'

'Shhh.' He places his fingertip on my lips and raises his dark eyebrows in gentle warning. Once he's certain I will fulfil his wish to let him finish, he takes his attention back to the ring, and I can do nothing more than wait for him to finish his interpretation of what this ring signifies. His index finger rests on the teardrop diamond that represents me. 'This gem is beautiful.' The pad of his finger drifts across to the matching teardrop diamond. 'It makes this one brighter. It complements it. But this one, the one that represents us –' he rests his touch on the main gem and drags his gaze up to my stinging face – 'this one is the brightest, most sparkling of them all.' Executing one of his signature lazy blinks, he pulls the antique from the navy-blue velvet cushion, while I continue my internal battle to keep it together.

This perfectly imperfect man is more beautiful than I know he'll ever accept, but I also appreciate that I really do make him a better man – not because I'm trying to change him but because he wants to be better. For me. He holds the ring up and glides his finger across the dozens of tiny stones that stem from the intricate peak. 'And all of these shards of sparkles are those tingling fireworks we create together.'

I expected his words to penetrate me deeply. I didn't expect them to cripple me. 'It's perfect.' I reach up and stroke down his rough cheek, feeling those simmering fireworks begin to ignite within.

'It's not,' he murmurs, taking my hand from his cheek. I watch as he slowly slides the ring onto my left ring finger. 'Now it's perfect.' He drops a lingering kiss onto the ring atop my finger before he nuzzles his cheek into my palm, his eyes closing.

I'm rendered incapable of speech . . . almost. He's just put that ring on my ring finger. On my left hand. I don't want to break the perfection of this moment, but I'm being bombarded by a repeated question. 'Are you asking me to marry you?'

His smile nearly causes me to pass out, his dimple appearing and his rogue wave slipping onto his forehead. I'm taken from my knees and helped to my bottom, my legs being guided around his back as he pulls me in close until we're locked together. 'No, Olivia Taylor, I'm not. I'm asking you to be mine for eternity.'

I can't help the emotion that rips through me. His face, his sincerity . . . his overwhelming love for me. In another pointless attempt to hide my tears, I drop my face into his chest and sob silently to myself while he sighs into my hair and rubs comforting circles into my back. I'm not sure why I'm crying when I feel so happy.

'It's an eternity ring,' he says above me before he encases my head in his hands, silently demanding I look at him before he continues. 'What finger you wear it on is of no importance, and I believe there's another stunning gem holding court on your other ring finger, anyway. I would never suggest you replace your grandmother's ring.'

I smile through my sobs, knowing that isn't Miller's only

reason for placing the ring on my left hand. It's his way of giving just a little piece of what he's figured I'll eventually want. 'I love your bones, Miller Hart.'

'And I'm deeply fascinated by you, Olivia Taylor.' He pushes his lips to mine and completes the perfection of the moment with a perfect, worshipful kiss. 'I have a request,' he says into my mouth between delicate rotations of his soft tongue.

'I'll never stop,' I confirm, allowing him to help me up while he keeps our mouths connected and our bodies close.

'Thank you.' He lifts me to his body, securing me against his chest, and starts to pace to the other door that'll take us into the lounge of the suite. The rug lying in front of the fireplace is cream, soft and plush, and it's where we're heading. Our kiss is broken and I'm settled on my back. 'Wait,' he orders gently, and then strides out of the lounge, leaving me a pile of pent-up desire, my whole body on fire. My eyes fall to my ring, reminding myself of its magnificence, but more of what it signifies. My lips curve into a contented smile, but immediately straighten when I look up and find Miller naked.

He speaks no words as he stalks towards me, his eyes full of promise. I'm about to be worshipped, and something inside tells me it's going to blow all other worshipping sessions into orbit. I can see need seeping from his every naked pore. He wants to follow up his words, his gift, his promise, and his kiss with physical confirmation. Every nerve ending, drop of blood, and muscle within me turns to fire.

Placing a condom to the side of me, he drops to his knees, his arousal already solid and clearly pulsing before my eyes. 'I want my habit naked,' he rumbles, all low and gritty, escalating my wants and needs. Dropping to his elbow so his tall physique flanks my side, he turns my skin to molten when his palm slides beneath the material of my skirt and travels the short distance to my inside thigh.

I try to draw a deep steadying breath but resort to holding

it instead. The smoothness of his palms circling teasingly close to my entrance is torture at its worst, and we're not even out of the gates yet.

'Are you ready to be worshipped, Olivia Taylor?' His finger skims over my knickers softly, making my back snap into an arch and my stored breath rush out fast.

'Please don't,' I beg, nailing him with pleading eyes. 'Please don't torture me.'

'Tell me you want me to worship you.' My skirt is dragged down my legs slowly, taking my knickers with it.

'Please, Miller.'

'Say it.'

'Worship me,' I breathe, lifting my back slightly when he slips his hand under my top to unfasten my bra.

'As you wish,' he agrees quietly, which is obscene, because I know for sure it's what *he* wishes, too. 'Lift for me.'

I rise to a sitting position as commanded, silent and obedient while he shifts to his knees again and pulls my top over my head, then my bra down my arms. They are cast aside carelessly before his palm slips to my upper back and his kneeling frame moves in, causing me to fall to my back again.

He's hovering above me, his body half settled on mine, his eyes sinking into me. 'There's something so amazing that happens every time I look into your eyes.'

'Tell me.'

'I can't. It's beyond my ability to describe it.'

'Like your fascination?'

He smiles. It's a shy smile, making him seem all boyish and cute – a very rare appearance for Miller Hart. Yet regardless of its rarity, it's no smoke screen. It's not fake or a façade. It's real. For me alone, he's real. 'Just like that,' he confirms, swooping down to capture my lips. My hands move to his shoulders and smooth his muscles, both of us humming our happiness as our tongues roll so slowly they're almost unmoving. My head tilts to gain a better connection, my growing need beginning to run away with me.

'Savour,' he says into my mouth. 'We have an eternity.'

His words settle me a little, and I force myself to obey his demand for calm. I know Miller is as eager as I am, yet his strength to maintain his control, to prove he can, blankets that desperation. My bottom lip is nibbled; then the softness of his relaxed tongue licks across my mouth as he rises to his knees again, leaving me squirming under a focused gaze bursting with intention. The hardness of his cock holds me rapt while he negotiates my knees, pulling them up and spreading them. I'm wide open and his stare lingers on the pulsing flesh of my core as he moves between my knees and reaches for the condom. The leisurely pace he adopts, opening, sliding the condom out and onto his erection, is torturous. Demanding he hurry would be pointless, so I throw all of my willpower into waiting patiently.

'Miller.' His name on a plea falls past my lips, and my arms reach up in silent indication for him to come to me. But he shakes his head and links his arms under my knees, moving forward until finally I feel the hot tip of his arousal skim over my centre. I cry out, my eyes clenching shut, my arms flying out to the side and bunching the fur strands of the rug in my fists.

'I want to see all of you,' he declares, nudging forward, stretching me on a hiss. 'Open your eyes, Olivia.'

My head starts shaking, feeling him getting deeper and deeper, every muscle tensing.

'Olivia, please, open your eyes.'

My darkness is bombarded by relentless visions of Miller worshipping me. It's like a slideshow, the erotic images accelerating my pleasure.

'Damn it, Livy!' My eyes fly open in shock, seeing him watching in fascination as he pushes fully into me. His arms are curled under my knees, my lower body elevated and fit snugly to him. His shadowed jaw is rigid, his eyes bright and wild, his hair a wavy mess, his stray wave loose, his lips full, his . . .

Fucking hell! I can feel him throbbing within me, all of my internal muscles wrapping around him, holding tight.

'Earth to Olivia.' His tone is full of sex, drenched in passion, and he follows it up with an exact grind of his body into mine. My mind scrambles, the mental images disintegrating. So I return my focus to his face. 'Keep your eyes on me,' he orders, rearing back, his length slipping from my passage slowly. The lazy friction makes his demand hard to fulfil. But I manage, even when he re-enters painfully slowly. Every one of my muscles engages and works hard to catch his purposeful pace. He rocks into me, each advance pushing air from my lungs and a little whimper past my lips. The sharp edges of his chest are undulating, straining, a light shimmer of sweat budding on his smooth skin. I start to form a steady pattern of breathing while I'm tortured with his expert worshipping skills, the slow, steady pumping of his hips flinging me into pleasure central. Then he starts grinding on each thrust, his chest heaving, his grip of me hardening. My fingers find my hair and pull hopelessly, seeking anything to grip on to with Miller out of reach.

'Fucking hell, Olivia. Watching you fight to hold off gives me a sick satisfaction.' His eyes squeeze shut, his body vibrating.

My nipples start to zing, and my stomach muscles are beginning to ache. As usual, I'm caught in that in-between place. I want to scream for him to push me over the edge, but I also want to delay the inevitable, make this last forever, despite the sweet torture and mind-fucking pleasure.

'Miller.' I writhe, my back bowing.

'Louder,' he demands, firing forward, less controlled. 'Fuck, say it louder, Olivia!'

'Miller!' I scream his name as his last hard thrust brings me right to the brink of orgasm.

He gives a low, strangled moan as he reins in his power and takes us back down to controlled, measured lovemaking. 'Every time I take you, I think it will help quench the desire. But it never does. The minute we're done, I only want you more.'

He drops my legs and falls to his forearms, trapping me under his leanness. My thighs spread farther, giving his body the room it's demanding, and his face comes close to mine, our pants colliding. Our stares lock and his hips roll, inching me closer to the pinnacle of euphoria.

I plunge my hands into his hair and tug on his unruly waves as I squeeze my lower muscles around his cock.

'Fuck, yes! Again.' His eyes glaze over, his primitive tone boosting my boldness. I squeeze again when the tip of his solid length finds the deepest part of me. 'Oh, fuuuck.'

I take some of my greatest pleasure from seeing his chin drop and feeling his body shake with appreciation. Knowing I can render him so vulnerable during these moments fills me with power. He's wide open to me. He's exposed. He's weak and powerful at the same time. I flip my hips up, relishing the sight of him falling apart above me. And I squeeze my hardest around each shaky delivery of his drives. The contours of his perfect face begin to twist and I see wild abandon reflecting from his piercing blues.

'You cripple me, Olivia Taylor. You fucking cripple me.' He rolls over, taking me onto his lap. 'Finish it.' His tone is harsh, full of hunger and desperation. 'Fucking finish it.'

I wince a little at the unexpected shift in position that pushes him to penetrate me the deepest. Strong hands find my thighs and his fingers grip my flesh. I'm completely speared by him, and I hold my breath as I try to accommodate the sheer size of him in this position.

'Move, sweet girl.' His hips jolt upward and I scream, my palms slapping against his chest. 'Now!'

His abrupt shout fires me into action and I begin spinning my hips atop him, ignoring the stabs of pain and concentrating on the flashes of pleasure between them. He's groaning, assisting with the rotations of my hips by pushing into my thighs. I'm well into my stride, watching him watching me as I bring us both closer to the brink of explosion.

'I'm going to come, Olivia.'

'Yes!' I shout, raising to my knees and slamming down. He barks a round of expletives and moves fast, spinning me onto my hands and knees. Grasping my hips, he slams into me on a gratifying shout. 'Oh God! Miller!'

'Yeah, you feel me, Livy? Feel everything I have to give you.' Only a few more powerful yanks of my body until his tosses me over the edge and sees me free-falling into darkness, my body collapsing to the rug and convulsing as my climax slams into me. I'm floating away, feeling the loss of Miller inside of me and his continued curses as he drops to my back, shifting his groin and sliding his cock over the crease of my bum, mumbling and biting at my neck before sliding back into my quivering core. I don't have the brain space through my heady pleasure to be concerned that I climaxed before him. I can feel the dull pulse of his muscled length stroking my walls, slipping in and out leisurely. And then he comes on a torrent of quiet prayers.

Opening my eyes, I stare, panting and heaving, across the cream fur of the rug, attempting to gather cognitive thought. 'You didn't hurt me,' I whisper, my throat sore and scratchy. I know that'll be his first question once he's gathered breath. His animalistic nature, the one he's hidden from me, is becoming addictive. He's still worshipping me.

My arms stretch above my head on a fulfilled sigh as Miller pulls out of me. My shoulder is nipped and kissed, followed by the other; then he's working his way down my spine, licking and nibbling as he goes. My eyes close while he continues with the lazy trail of his lips across my back and down to my bum. His teeth sink in, quite severely, too, but I'm exhausted, unable to yelp or shift to stop him. Once he's had his fill, I feel him crawl up my body and settle over me, his palms sliding up my arms until his hands find mine. He laces our fingers together, pushes his face into my neck, and releases an exhale to match my contentment. 'Close your eyes,' he murmurs.

Then, out of nowhere, music floods the silence. Soft music, with deep meaningful lyrics. 'I recognise this,' I whisper, hearing Miller humming the soothing tune in my mind.

It's not in my mind.

My eyes open and I wriggle until he's forced to lift and I can spin over to see him. He stops humming and smiles at me, twinkling eyes and all, letting the music take over again.

'This song,' I begin.

'I might hum it to you from time to time,' he whispers, almost shyly. 'Gabrielle Aplin.'

'"The Power of Love",' I finish for him as his body comes close to mine and pushes me to my back, his weight settling evenly.

'Hmmm,' he hums.

I'm still buzzing, still quivering, still pulsing.

An eternity of this still couldn't ever be enough.

Chapter 4

My dreams are blissful. They are a repeat of the latter part of yesterday. My sleepy lids flutter open, my waking mind registering him close to me. Very close. I'm curled into his side, totally cocooned in his *thing*.

Carefully and quietly, I lift my left hand and search out my ring, sighing and savouring my mind's insistence to remind me of every word spoken and action played out.

Blissful dreams don't only happen when you're asleep.

Taking the opportunity of Miller's deep slumber, I spend some private time tracing the planes of his chest. He's dead to the world . . . at least most of him is. I watch in fascination as his cock begins to thicken when my touch drifts down to the sharp V stemming from his lower stomach, until it's solid and pulsing, begging for some attention.

I want him to wake moaning in pleasure, so I tentatively start to shuffle down his body and cradle myself between his thighs. They open for me, without the need to push them apart, and I'm up close to his morning erection, licking my lips and mentally preparing myself to send him wild. Reaching forward, I flick my eyes up to his face as I take a gentle hold of the base, watching for any signs of life but finding nothing, just parted lips and still eyelids. I return my attention to the hard length of muscle in my grasp and follow my instinct, my tongue swirling the tip slowly, collecting up the bead of cum that's already building. The heat of his flesh, the smoothness of his taut skin, the hardness beneath, it's all so very addictive and I soon find myself rising to my knees and sliding my lips down the length of him, moaning in indulgence as I work my way back up. My attention is centred solely on the delivery of meticulous licks and kisses. I spend an age soaking up the wonderful feeling of him in my mouth. I'm not sure at what point he starts groaning, but his hands suddenly in my hair alert me to it, and I smile around the slow drives of my mouth as it sheaths him, over and over. His hips start to slowly lift, meeting each of my advances, and his hands guide my head perfectly.

His sleepy mumbles are indecipherable, his voice broken and weak. My hand begins to stroke up and down, mirroring my mouth, doubling his pleasure. His legs shift, his head shaking slowly from side to side. Every muscle touching me has gone rigid, and the swell of him in my mouth tells me he's close, so I increase my pace, my head bobbing, the feel of him hitting the back of my throat pushing on my own pleasure.

'Stop,' he breathes, continuing to push my head onto him. 'Please, stop.'

He's going to come at any moment and this knowledge only encourages me.

'No!' His knee flies up, cracking me in the jaw, making me cry out at the flash of pain it causes. His arousal falls from my mouth as I shoot up, grabbing my face, applying pressure to ease the instant throb. 'Get off me!' He's upright, scrambling back until his back hits the sofa, one knee coming up, his other leg stretched out in front of him. His blue eyes are wide and full of fear, his body sweaty and his chest surging under his clear distress.

My body moves away on instinct, my shock and wariness not allowing me to move in to comfort him. I can't even speak. I'm just watching as his eyes dart around, his palm over his chest in an attempt to ease the palpitations. The pain searing through my jaw is incredible, but my dry eyes won't produce any tears.

I'm on emotional shutdown. He looks like a frightened animal, cornered and helpless, and when his eyes fall down to his groin, mine do, too.

He's still rock-hard. His cock begins to twitch and he groans, his head dropping back onto his shoulders.

Then he comes.

And he whimpers dejectedly.

White liquid spurts up his stomach, across his thighs, seeming to pour from the tip forever. 'No,' he murmurs to himself, his hands raking through his hair, his eyes clenching shut. 'No!' he bellows, slamming his hands down to the floor, making me recoil in shock.

I don't know what to do. I'm still sitting away from him, my hand still clenching my jaw, and now my mind is sprinting. Flashbacks are stamping all over my mind. He's let me take him in my mouth once. It was brief and he didn't come. He moaned his pleasure, assisted me, guided me, but quickly withdrew. The other times I've ventured into that area with my mouth, I've been intercepted. He let me work him with my hand in his office once, and I remember him clarifying that it should only be with my hand. And I also remember him telling me that he doesn't touch himself privately.

Why?

He reaches and grabs a tissue from the box on the nearby table, then sets about frantically wiping himself up.

'Miller?' I say quietly, breaking into the sounds of his rushed breath and mad actions. I can't close the distance, not until he registers I'm here. 'Miller, look at me.'

His arms drop, but his eyes dart everywhere on my body, except to my face.

'Miller, *please* look at me.' I inch forward a little, cautious, desperate to comfort him when he so obviously needs it. 'Please.' I wait, impatient, yet knowing I have to approach this carefully. 'I beg you.'

Tortured blues blink slowly and eventually reopen, seeping into the deepest part of my heart. His head begins to shake. 'I'm so sorry,' he almost chokes, his palm wrapping around his throat, like he's struggling to breathe. 'I've hurt you.'

'I'm fine,' I counter, even though my jaw feels like it needs cracking back into place. I release my hold of it and edge my way closer to him, slowly crawling onto his lap. 'I'm fine,' I repeat, sinking my face into his damp neck, feeling relieved when I feel him embrace the comfort I'm offering. 'You OK?'

He lets out a short spurt of breath, almost laughing. 'I'm not sure what happened.'

My brow wrinkles, realising in an instant that he's going to evade any questions I pose. 'You can tell me,' I press.

The swift detachment of my chest from his and his eyes boring into mine make me feel small and useless. His impassive face isn't helping either. 'Tell you what?'

My shoulders jump up on a little shrug. 'Why such a violent reaction?' I'm uncomfortable under the intensity of him watching me. I'm not sure why when I've been the sole focus of this penetrating gaze since I've met him.

'I'm sorry.' His eyes soften and are quickly laced with concern as he directs them to my jaw. 'You startled me, Olivia. Nothing more.' A smooth palm runs the length of my cheek, then circles gently.

He's lying to me. But I can't force him to share something that will be too painful for him. I've learned that now. Miller Hart's dark past needs to remain in the dark, away from our light.

'OK,' I say, but I don't mean it at all. I'm not OK, and neither is Miller. What I want to do is tell him to elaborate, but instinct is stopping me. The instinct that has guided me since the day I met this confounding man. I keep telling myself that, yet I wonder where I'd be had I not followed all of the natural reactions to him and responses to the situations he's presented me with. I know where. Still dead. Lifeless. Pretending to be happy with my solitary existence. My life may have taken an about-face, been injected with drama to make up for the lack of it in recent years, but I won't falter in my determination to help my love through his battle. I'm here for him.

I've discovered many dark things about Miller Hart, and deep down, I know there are more. More questions are rising. And the answers, whatever they may be, won't make an iota of difference to how I feel about Miller Hart. It's painful for him, which makes it painful for me, too. I don't want to cause him more suffering, and forcing him to tell will do that. So curiosity can go screw itself. I ignore the niggling corner of my brain that's pointing out that maybe, in fact, I don't *want* to know.

'I love your bones,' I whisper in an attempt to distract us from the awkwardness of the moment. 'I love your fucked-up, obsessive bones.'

A full beam breaks the serious expression on his face, revealing his dimple and sparkling blue eyes. 'And my fucked-up, obsessive bones are deeply fascinated by you, too.' He reaches up to feel my jaw. 'Does it hurt?'

'Not really. I'm used to wallops in the head these days.'

He winces, and I realise immediately that I've failed in my endeavour to lighten the mood.

'Don't say that.'

I'm about to apologise when the loud screech of Miller's phone rings in the distance.

I'm removed from his lap and set neatly to the side, and he kisses my forehead as he rises before striding over to the table and scooping it up. 'Miller Hart,' he says with the usual detachment and coldness as his naked body paces towards the study. He has shut the door behind him every time he's taken a call since we've been here, yet this time he leaves it open. I use the gesture as a sign and jump up, following his path until I'm hovering on the threshold, looking at a naked Miller reclined in the office chair, his fingertips working circles into his temple. He looks irritated and stressed, but as his eyes lift and find mine, all negative emotion falls away and is replaced with smiling, shimmering blues. I put my hand up and turn to leave.

'One minute,' he speaks into the phone abruptly and pulls it away, laying it on his bare chest. 'Everything OK?'

'Sure, I'll leave you to work.'

He taps the phone lightly and thoughtfully on his chest, his eyes running slow trails up and down my naked body. 'I don't want you to leave me.' His stare finds mine, and I sense a double meaning to his statement. He cocks his head, and I pad gingerly over to him, surprised by his demand, but not so surprised by the need blooming within me.

Miller looks up at me, a hint of a smile on his face, then takes my hand and kisses the top of my new ring. 'Sit.' He tugs me forward until I land on his naked lap, every muscle I possess tensing when his semi-erect cock wedges itself between my bum cheeks. I'm encouraged to recline, and my back finds his chest, my head nuzzled in the crook of his neck.

'Continue,' he orders down the phone.

I smile to myself and Miller's ability to be so tender and sweet with me and then so obnoxious and curt to whoever is on the other end of the phone. A muscled arm snakes around my waist and holds on tight.

'It's Livy,' he hisses. 'I could be speaking with the fucking queen, but if Olivia needs me, then the queen will have to fucking wait.'

My face bunches in confusion, mixed with a little satisfaction, and I turn to look up at him. I want to ask who it is, but something halts me. It's the muffled sound of a smooth, familiar, very accepting voice down the line.

William.

'Glad we've cleared that up,' Miller huffs, landing a chaste kiss on my lips before nudging my head back into the crook of his neck and shifting in his chair, pulling me even closer.

He falls silent and starts playing idly with a lock of my hair, twisting it repeatedly until it starts to pull at my scalp and I indicate my discomfort with a gentle nudge to his ribs. I can hear the mellow tones of William's voice, yet can't make out what's being said, as Miller unravels the lock before starting to twist all over again.

'Did you establish anything regarding that?' Miller asks.

I know what they must be speaking of, but being here on his lap, listening to his even, detached tone, amplifies that curiosity. I should have stayed away from the study, but now my mind is racing, wondering what William might have found.

'One minute,' he breathes, and I see his hand holding the phone in my peripheral vision fall to the arm of the chair. My hair is released, probably leaving behind a mountain of knots, my cheek clasped in his hand and turned to face him. Staring deeply into my eyes, he clicks a button on his phone and blindly rests it on the desk, never leaving my eyes. He doesn't even break the contact to check where it's landed or to tweak it.

'William, say hello to Olivia.'

I shift nervously on Miller's lap, a million feelings drowning out the serenity I was feeling locked in Miller's hold.

'Hello, Olivia.' William's voice is comforting. Yet I don't want to hear anything he has to say. He'd warned me away from Miller from the moment he knew of our relationship.

'Hi, William.' I quickly turn to Miller and tense my muscles, ready to lift from his lap. 'I'll let you work in peace.' But I go nowhere. Miller slowly shakes his head at me and firms up his grip.

'How are you?' William's question was easy to answer . . . half an hour ago.

'Fine,' I squeak, chastising myself for feeling awkward, but worst of all for acting it. 'I'm just going to make some breakfast.' I make to stand again . . . and go nowhere.

'Olivia's staying,' Miller announces. 'Continue.'

'As we were?' William sounds shocked, and that notches my awkwardness up the scale to plain panic.

'As we were,' Miller breaths, finding my nape and working into my tenseness with firm, purposeful kneads. He's wasting his time.

There's silence down the line, then the odd sound of movement, probably William fidgeting uncomfortably in his big office chair before he speaks. 'I'm not sure—'

'She's staying,' Miller cuts him off, and I brace myself for a counterattack from William . . . but it doesn't come.

'Hart, I question your morals daily.' William chuckles. It's a dark, sardonic chuckle. 'But I've always been certain of your sanity, however in-fucking-sane some of your exploits have been. I've always known you were perfectly lucid.'

I want to jump in to put William straight. There's nothing lucid about Miller when he loses his temper. He's wild, unreasonable . . . a complete, certifiable maniac. Or is he? I slowly turn in his hold to find his face. Piercing blue eyes are immediately singeing my skin. His face, although impassive, is angelic. My mind twists as I try to figure out whether what William is saying could be true. I can't agree. Maybe William hasn't seen Miller touch the kind of rage he has unleashed since he met me.

'I always know exactly what I'm doing and why I'm doing it.' Miller speaks slowly and concisely. He knows what I'm thinking. 'I may lose rationality for a split second, but only for a split second,' he whispers, so quietly William couldn't have possibly heard him. And just like that, he answers another question that I was silently deliberating. 'My actions are always valid and warranted.'

William hears that part. I know this because he laughs. 'In whose world, Hart?'

'Mine.' He turns his attention back to his phone and

tightens his grip on me. 'And now yours, too, Anderson.'

His words are cryptic. I don't understand them, but the fear biting its way up my spine and the long eerie silence that settles tells me to be wary of them. Why did I come in here? Why didn't I head straight for the kitchen and get something to eat? I was hungry when I woke. Not now, though. Now my stomach feels like an empty void filling rapidly with anxiety.

'Your world will *never* be mine.' William's tone is rampant with rage. 'Never.'

I need to leave. This could be one of those times when their two worlds collide, and I don't want to be anywhere near when that happens. The Atlantic between them may mean no physical clash is possible, but just the tone of William's voice, his words, and Miller's vibrating body beneath me is a good enough sign that it still won't be pretty.

'I'd like to leave,' I say, trying in vain to pry Miller's hand from my tummy.

'Stay where you are, Olivia.' My attempts prove fruitless and Miller's unreasonable insistence that I hang around for the unpleasant show sees my sass flying to the surface.

'Let. Go. Of. Me.' My jaw is pulsing, my pissed off eyes stabbing at his straight features. I'm shocked when I'm immediately released. I hastily stand, and not knowing whether to dart out or leave calmly, I begin brushing down my nonexistent clothes while I deliberate my quandary.

'I'm sorry,' Miller speaks up, reaching for one of my busy hands and squeezing it gently. 'Please, I'd like you to stay.'

There's a brief, uneasy silence before William's genuine, amused laugh breaks our private moment, reminding me that he's still technically in the room with us. 'Yes, we're done,' he confirms. 'I apologise also.'

'I don't understand why you want me here,' I confess. This is already too much to process.

'William has been trying to figure out a few things, that's all. Please, stay and hear what he has to say.'

I'm relieved he wants to let me help share the burden, but I'm frightened, too. Nodding a little, I take my place on his lap and allow him to negotiate my body into the position of his liking, which is to the side, my legs dangling over the arm of the chair, my cheek on his chest.

'OK. So, Sophia?'

My blood runs cold, just from the mention of her name.

'She's insisting she never breathed a word to Charlie.'

Charlie? Who's Charlie?

'I believe her,' Miller says. It's a reluctant admission and it surprises me, even more so when William agrees. 'Did you sense any indication that she could have been following Olivia?'

'I couldn't tell for sure, but we all know how that woman feels about you, Hart.'

I certainly know how Sophia feels about Miller, mostly because she was kind enough to tell me herself. She's a former client who fell in love with him. Or became obsessed with him, is more accurate. Miller was worried she'd tried to abduct me. Does she love him that much? Enough to get rid of me?

'Sense anything with Sophia Reinhoff?' William scoffs. 'The only thing I feel when in her presence is cold. You were careless. Taking Livy to Ice was a stupid move. Taking her to your home is beyond that. I bet she's relishing in the knowledge that she can expose you, Hart.'

I cringe, feeling Miller look down at me. I know what's coming. 'Both Olivia and I have played our relationship down. I've only taken Livy to Ice when the club has been closed.'

'And when she turned up without your prior knowledge, did you have her escorted out? Did you remove yourself from her vicinity to lessen the risk of association?' There's humour in William's serious tone. I want to hide. 'Well?' he prompts, despite knowing damn well what the answer is.

'No,' Miller spits the word through a clenched jaw. 'I realise my stupidity.'

'So, what we have is a club full of people who witnessed various incidents involving the aloof, notoriously closed-off Miller Hart losing his rag with a beautiful young woman. Do you see where I'm heading with this?'

I roll my eyes at William's unreasonable need to belittle Miller. I also feel a mountain of guilt settle on my shoulders. My obliviousness to the consequences of my actions and behaviour has accelerated the situation, pushed Miller into a corner.

'It's all being noted, Anderson.' Miller sighs, seeking out my hair again and beginning to twist a lock. Silence falls. It's an uncomfortable silence – one that's just increasing my need to escape the study and leave these two men to continue their surmising of our diabolical situation alone.

It's a long while before William eventually speaks, and when he does, I don't like what he says. 'You must have anticipated the repercussions of your resignation, Hart. You know that's not your call to make.'

I curl into Miller's side, as if making myself smaller and attempting to crawl inside of him might make our reality go away. Not much of my brain space has been dedicated to Miller's invisible chains or the immoral bastards who hold the keys. The ghost of Gracie Taylor has monopolised my mind, and in a weird sense, now that seems so much more appealing than this. This really is reality, and hearing William's voice, feeling Miller's torment, and suddenly being consumed with defeat has flung me to the frontline of anxiety. I'm not wholly certain what will greet us in London when we arrive there, but I know it's going to test me, test *us*, more than ever before.

The sensation of soft lips on my temple brings me back into the room. 'I didn't much care at the time,' Miller admits.

'Do you now?' William's question and the curt delivery clearly indicate there should be only one answer.

'Now I care *only* about protecting Olivia.'

'Good answer,' William retorts sharply, and I look up at Miller, finding him lost in thought, gazing blankly across the study.

I hate that he appears so defeated. I've seen this look too many times, and it worries me more than anything. I feel blind, useless, and with no words of comfort to offer him, I reach up and slide my palm onto his neck, pulling him in tighter to me and pushing my face into the stubble on his throat. 'I love you.' My whispered declaration falls naturally from my mouth, like my instinct is telling me that a constant reinforcement of my love for him is all I have. Reluctantly, I silently acknowledge that it is.

William continues. 'I can't believe you were stupid enough to quit.'

Lean muscles go rigid beneath me in a heartbeat. 'Stupid?' Miller hisses, shifting me on his lap. I can practically feel his emotions heating through our naked contact. 'Are you suggesting I should continue fucking other women when I'm involved with Olivia?' His crass angle makes my face contort in disgust, as do the mental images of belts and—

Stop!

'No.' William doesn't back off. 'I'm suggesting you should never have touched what you can't have. This will all go away if you do the right thing.'

The right thing. Leave me. Go back to London and be the Special One.

I can't hold back the rage that embeds itself deeply within me as a result of William's words, especially if he insists on being such an arsehole. 'He can have me.' My sass fights its way forward, and I wrestle with Miller's hold, sitting myself up, getting as close to the phone as possible, just so he can hear me loud and clear. 'Don't you dare start with this again, William! Don't make me stick a knife in and twist it!'

'Olivia!' Miller yanks me back to his chest, but my defiance injects strength into my slight frame and I bat him away, returning close to the phone. I can hear his exasperation loud and clear, not that it'll stop me.

'I know you're not threatening violence, Olivia,' William says with an edge of laughter in his tone.

'Gracie Taylor.' I say her name through clenched teeth and take no pleasure in the audible inhale of hurt breath that travels down the line. 'Did I see her?' I demand. Miller immediately pulls me back into his chest, and I start prying his hard grip from my limbs. 'Was it her?' I shout, sending my elbow shooting back into his ribs in my frenzy.

'Fuck!' Miller roars, losing his hold of me. I dive for the phone, trying to drink in some air in order to demand an answer, but Miller lunges forward and cuts the call before I get there.

'What are you doing?' I yell, fighting away his grappling hands as he tries to claim me.

He wins. I'm yanked into his body and my flailing arms are locked in a harsh hold. 'Calm down!'

I'm being driven by pure anger, blinded by determination. 'No!' Strength surges through me and I heave upward, violently arching my back in an attempt to escape the clutches of an increasingly concerned Miller.

'Calm. Down. Olivia,' he warns on a quiet hiss in my ear once he's secured me against his naked chest. Our anger is detectable through the combined heat of our skin. 'Don't make me ask you twice.'

My breathing is heavy, my hair a mess of locks falling all over my red face. 'Let go of me.' I struggle to speak clearly through my self-inflicted exhaustion.

Breathing deeply, he pushes his lips into my hair and releases me. I waste no time. I'm up from his lap and running away from my cold reality, slamming the door behind me and not slowing until I land in the en suite of the master bedroom. I slam that door, too. Then I stomp over to the egg-shaped tub and flip the taps on. The anger swirling through me is blocking any instructions from my mind to calm down. I *need* to calm down, but my hate for William and my mental torment over my mother won't allow it. My hands find my hair and yank, the anger transforming into frustration. In an attempt to distract myself, I squeeze some toothpaste onto my brush and scrub my teeth. It's a silly effort to rid my mouth of the sour aftertaste of her name on my tongue.

After spending far more time brushing than is truly necessary, I spit and rinse, then look up to the mirror. My pale cheeks are rosy, a mixture of receding anger and the familiar flush of desire that's ever present these days. But my navy eyes are disturbed. After the horrific events that saw us fleeing London, burying my ignorant head in a bottomless pit of sand has been easy. Now I'm being punished by relentless jolts of realism. 'Lock the world outside and stay here with me forever,' I whisper, losing myself in the reflection of my own eyes. My world slows around me as I brace my hands on the side on the sink, my chin dropping to my chest. Hopelessness is trickling into my overwrought mind. It's unwelcome, but my exhausted mind and body are failing to locate any scrap of resolve amid my emotion. Everything seems impossible again.

On a heavy sigh, I glance up and find the water nearing the top of the bath, but I don't rush over. I haven't the energy, so I slowly turn and drag my dejected body across the room to flip the taps off. Then I step in and sink into the water, resisting the urge to close my eyes and immerse my face. I remain still, staring vacantly across the large room, forcing my mind to blank out. It works to a certain degree. I concentrate of the pleasing tones of Miller's voice, every loving word he's ever spoken to me and every caress of my body. All of it. From the very start to now. And I hope and pray that there is so much more to come.

A light tap on the bathroom door pulls my dry eyes across the room, and I blink repeatedly to moisten them up again. 'Olivia?' Miller's voice is low and concerned. It makes me feel like shit. He doesn't wait for a reply, instead gently pushing the door open and holding onto the handle while he leans on the doorframe and searches me out. He's slipped some black boxers on and I can see a red blotch on his ribs, courtesy of me. When his crystal blues locate me, my guilt multiplies by a million. He tries to smile but ends up dropping his eyes to the floor. 'I'm sorry.'

His apology confuses me. 'What are you sorry for?'

'Everything.' He doesn't hesitate. 'For letting you fall in love with me. For . . .' He looks up at me and takes a slow pull of breath. 'For being too fascinated by you to leave you alone.'

A sad smile forms on my lips and I reach up to collect the shampoo before holding it up to him. 'Will you do me the honour of washing my hair?' He needs to lose himself in some worshipping, anything to steady our shaky world.

'Nothing would give me greater pleasure,' he confirms, his long legs eating up the distance between us. Dropping to his knees at the edge of the bath, he takes the bottle and squirts some in his hands. I sit up and turn my back to him to give him easy access, then close my eyes when I feel his strong fingers push into my scalp. His slow motions and care with me install a glimmer of peace into my worried bones. It's quiet for a while. My head is massaged, I'm gently ordered to rinse, and then he's working conditioner through my waves. 'I love your hair,' he whispers, taking his time to feel it, combing through with his fingers as he hums.

'It needs trimming,' I reply, smiling to myself when his busy fingers halt abruptly.

'Only trimming.' He gathers the wet, slippery masses into a ponytail and twists forever until it's all coiled around his fist.

'And I want to come with you.' Gently pulling back, he tilts and brings my face close to his.

'You want to monitor the hairdresser?' I ask, bemused, shifting in the water, so grateful for his intention to distract me.

'Yes. Yes, I do.' He isn't kidding, either. I know it. I'm kissed lightly on the lips, little soft pecks over and over, until his hot tongue pushes into my mouth and sweeps through lovingly. I relax into his kiss, my eyes closing, my world stabilising. 'You taste so good.'

He breaks our kiss but keeps his face close as he unravels my hair thoughtfully until it's falling down my back and half of the length is splaying in the water. It's grown far too long, now skimming my lower back, but it looks like it's staying that way. 'Let's get this conditioner out of your unruly locks.' He caresses my cheek with his thumb for a few moments before his hands shift to my neck and encourage me to sink into the water. I slide down the tub and close my eyes as I disappear below the depths, my hearing becoming muffled.

Holding my breath is easy. I've done it so many times since meeting Miller, when he's stolen it with one of his worshipful kisses or brought me to climax by teasing me there. With my loss of vision and my hearing compromised, all I can do is feel him. Firm hands are working through my hair, rubbing away the conditioner and rubbing away my helplessness at the same time. But then his hand leaves my scalp and glides down the side of my face to my throat. Then from my throat to my chest. And from my chest onto a swollen mound. The very tip of my nipple tingles with anticipation. It's circled deliciously, and then his touch is drifting across my stomach to my inner thigh. I tense beneath the water, fighting to hold still to preserve my breath. My darkness and silence are heightening my other senses, most significantly, feeling. His finger slips past my quivering lips and slides deeply into me. My hands fly out of the water and clasp the sides of the tub, and I pull myself up fast, needing to grab every gratifying element of Miller worshipping me – namely, his perfect face filled with satisfaction.

I gasp, urgently dragging air into my lungs, and Miller starts to pump lazily. 'Hmmm.' I rest my head back, letting it fall limply to the side so I can watch him pleasure me with his gifted fingers.

'Good?' His voice is rough and his eyes are darkening.

I nod and bite down on my lip, contracting every internal muscle on my mission to seize the flutter of tingles in the pit of my stomach. But I lose my concentration when he pushes his thumb onto my clitoris and begins to work precise, torturous circles into the sensitive nub. 'So good,' I breathe, beginning to pant, my pleasure only multiplying when his lips part and he shifts his position by the side of the tub to get better leverage. Withdrawing slowly, he locks eyes with mine and pushes forward with nothing but satisfaction and victory gushing from every part of him. My body starts to shake. 'Miller, please,' I beg, starting the pointless shaking of my head in despair. 'Please, make it happen.'

My demand doesn't go ignored. He's as desperate as I am to drown out the misery of our time in the study. He leans over the bath, maintaining his deep drives as he clashes our mouths together and kisses me to climax. I bite down on his bottom lip when my orgasm takes hold, probably causing him pain with the pressure of my teeth sinking in, but it doesn't stop him and his determination to fix our spat. I'm being attacked by unforgiving pangs of pleasure, over and over, again and again. My body is shaking violently, making the water splash around me, until I lose my strength and my body goes limp in the water. Now I'm exhausted for a whole different reason and it's far more appealing than my exhaustion of moments ago.

'Thank you,' I splutter through my wheezing breaths, forcing my lids to keep open.

'Never thank me, Olivia Taylor.'

My breathing is heavy and laboured, my body absorbing the after-effects of my satisfying explosion. 'I'm sorry for hurting you.'

He smiles. It's only a small smile, but any glimpse of the beautiful sight is welcome. It's also needed more and more with each passing day. Drawing breath, he slides his fingers out of me and traces over my skin until he's at my cheek. I know what he's going to say. 'You can't hurt me physically, Olivia.'

Nodding my acceptance, I allow him to help me out of the bath and wrap me in a towel. He takes another from the nearby shelf and starts working it through my hair, ridding it of the excess water.

'Let's dry these unmanageable waves.' He takes up position on my nape and leads me to the bed, gesturing me to sit on the end, which I do without complaint, knowing I'm about to have Miller's hands working through my hair while he dries it. The hairdryer is collected from the drawer and he plugs it into a socket, then settles behind me in no time, a leg on either side of me, completely cocooning me with his body. The rush of noise won't allow for conversation, which I'm quite content with. I just relax, close my eyes, and relish in the feel of him massaging my scalp as he blasts my hair with the dryer. I also smile when I imagine the look of fulfilment on his face.

All too soon, the noise dies and Miller is moving in, sinking his face into my fresh hair and locking his arms tightly around my waist. 'You were harsh, Olivia,' he says quietly, almost cautiously. I hate his need to voice this, even if he's entitled to, but I love his need to do it gently.

'I've apologised.'

'You haven't apologised to William.'

I solidify in his hold. 'Since when did you become a William Anderson fan?'

I'm nudged in the thigh with his leg. It's a silent warning to rein in my sass. 'He's trying to help us. I need information and

I can't get it while I'm here in New York.'

'What information?'

'It's not your concern.'

My jaw tenses, my eyes closing to gather my patience. '*You* are my concern,' I say simply, breaking out of Miller's hold and ignoring his audible exhale of weary breath. He's trying to keep his patience, too. I don't care. I grab my hairbrush from the bedside table and leave Miller falling to his back on a quiet curse. My face screws up in annoyance as I stomp into the lounge area, all but throwing myself down to the couch. Taking the brush to my hair, I begin to yank it through the tangles, like in a silly fit of revenge I'm deliberately trying to harm one of Miller's favourite things.

I slip back into despondency, continuously tugging the brush through my waves and getting a sick satisfaction from the discomfort it causes. The sharp stabs of pain are hogging my attention, therefore preventing me from thinking. I even manage to ignore the mild buzz under my skin, working its way deeper with each second that passes. He's close by, but I don't seek him out, instead dead set on ripping my hair from my head.

'Hey!' He halts my hand in its destructive tactics and holds it steady before prying the brush from my clawed fingers. 'You know I have an appreciation for my possessions,' he rumbles, swinging his legs behind me and pulling my hair over my shoulders. His words, however arrogant they may be, go some way to bringing me around. 'This is part of my possession. Don't abuse it.' The soft bristles of the brush meet my scalp and slowly drag through to the ends of my tresses as we're joined by the Beach Boys' "God Only Knows".

Miller's temper refuses to make an appearance, his introduction of such a merry and hard-hitting track emphasising that, leaving my grumpy arse to be grumpy alone. An unreasonable part of me was hoping to spike a bit of that temper so I'd have something to bounce off. 'Why did you hang up on William?'

'Because it got out of hand, Olivia. You're giving me a run for my money in the crazy department. I'm sending you over the edge.' There's despair in his tone. Guilt. Reluctantly, I nod, silently accepting that he's right. It did get out of hand. And he really is sending me over the edge. 'You mentioned Charlie. Who is he?'

He takes a deep breath before he begins. I hold mine.

'An immoral bastard.'

That's it. That's all he says, and my next question, despite knowing the answer, tumbles past my lips as the stored air releases. 'You're answerable to him?'

There's an uncomfortable silence and I brace myself for the reply that I know is coming. 'Yes, I am.'

My head begins to pound mildly with the building of all of those questions I've tossed aside too easily. Miller is answerable to a man named Charlie. I can only imagine what type of character he is if Miller fears him. 'He'll hurt you?'

'I make a lot of money for him, Olivia. Don't think I'm afraid of him. I'm not.'

'Then why did we run?'

'Because I need time to breathe – to think about the best way to handle this. I told you before, it's not as easy as just quitting. I asked you to trust me while I figured this out.'

'And have you?'

'William has bought me some time.'

'How?'

'He told Charlie that he and I had crossed. That he was looking for me.'

My brow meets in the middle. 'William told Charlie you pissed him off?'

'He had to justify why he was in my flat. William and Charlie aren't exactly pals, and neither are William and I. You might have guessed.' He's being ironic, and I huff my acknowledgement. 'Charlie mustn't know about my association with William. It'll give William a headache. I don't like him, but I wouldn't wish a pissed off Charlie on him, no matter how capable he is of taking care of himself.'

My poor mind spirals into meltdown again. 'Where does that leave us?' My voice is hardly decipherable through my fear of what the answer might be.

'Anderson thinks it's best if I return to London. I disagree.'

I sag, relieved. I'm not going back to London if he has to hide me, if he has to continue entertaining these women until he finds an out.

He squeezes me reassuringly, like he knows what I'm thinking. 'I'm going nowhere until I'm certain there's no danger to you.'

Danger? 'Do you know who followed me?'

The brief silence that falls and screams as a result of my question doesn't curb my growing trepidation. He just looks at me as the gravity of our situation grips me in its vicious claws. 'Was it Charlie?'

He nods slowly and the ground tumbles away beneath me. 'He knows you are why I quit.'

He must feel the panic flaring because he drops the brush and turns me around, helping to make me comfy on his lap. I'm locked in his *thing*, but today it doesn't make me feel better. 'Shhh,' he soothes me pointlessly. 'Trust me to deal with this.'

'What other option do I have?' I ask. This isn't a multiple-choice quiz. There is only one answer.

I have no choice.

Chapter 5

Miller spent the rest of the day humouring me, riding the open-top hop-on-hop-off tour bus around New York City. He smiled fondly when I ignored the tour guide, choosing to give him my own rundown of the sights we saw. He listened with interest and even asked me questions that I was quick to answer. He was relaxed when we hopped off to take a wander, and he was willing when I dragged him into a typical deli. The fast pace in which everything is carried out here was a little intimidating when we first arrived, but I'm getting to grips with it now. I ordered fast and paid faster. Then we walked and ate, something else new to Miller. He was awkward but didn't complain. I was delighted but restrained all evidence, like this is *us* every day.

The early morning drama, coupled with our hours of exploring, left me physically unable to hold myself up by the time we make it back to the penthouse. Facing twelve flights of stairs nearly finishes me off, and rather than confronting his fear and utilising the lift, he scoops me up and takes the stairs with my exhausted body draped across his arms. I enjoy the closeness, as usual, only just mustering the energy to cling to him. I can still feel and smell, even if my heavy eyes refuse to remain open. His firmness against me and his signature scent drifting into my nose takes me off to a dreamland to rival the best of dreams.

'I'd love to bury myself inside you right now,' he murmurs, his low, sex-filled timbre pulling my lids open as he lowers me to the bed.

'OK.' My agreement is quick but sleepy. My green Converse are pulled from each foot and set neatly to the side. I only know it's neatly because of the time it takes for him to return to undressing me. He's in a tidying mood, as well as a worshipping mood. My denim shorts are unfastened and dragged down my legs.

'You're too tired, sweet girl.' My shorts are folded and placed with my shoes. I can't locate even the tiniest piece of strength to protest, telling me he's one hundred per cent correct. I'm useless.

He lifts me briefly to pull the covers back, then settles me neatly on the mattress. 'Arms in the air.' He gives me a hint of that cheeky smile before his face disappears, being replaced with the material of my top. My arms only rise because of him lifting my T-shirt and forcing them up, and as soon as I'm free from my bra and knickers, I fall to my back on a sigh and roll onto my front, snuggling down. The heat of his mouth presses into my shoulder for the longest time. 'Take me into your perfect dreams, Olivia Taylor.'

I can't show my agreement, can't even voice my assurance that I will. Sleep claims me and the last thing I hear is the familiar sound of Miller humming.

My dreams *were* sweet, and Miller was there in all of his perfect, relaxed glory. I blink my eyes open, immediately confused by the darkness. I feel like I've been asleep for years. I feel re-energised and ready to take the day on . . . if it was morning. The mattress dips behind me and I feel Miller closing in on me. I want to say good morning, but I think I'm a bit premature. So I shuffle over instead to stick my front to Miller's and push my face into the coarse hair at his throat. Then I inhale and wedge my knee between his thighs.

He accommodates my demand for intimacy, letting me shift and fidget all over him until I'm settled and breathing easy into him. It's comfortably silent, until Miller starts humming "The Power of Love", making me smile. 'You hummed this to me one of the first times we were together.' I press my lips to the hollow void below his Adam's apple and suck briefly before trailing my tongue up to his chin.

'Indeed I did,' he agrees, letting me nibble at his bottom lip. 'You threw my perfect world into total chaos.'

I'm prevented from giving my thoughts on that statement when he moves away and places me on my side before mirroring my new position. It's dark, but I can see his face now that my eyes have adjusted.

And I don't like what I see.

Pensiveness.

Concern.

'What is it?' I back up, my pulse beginning to quicken.

'I need to tell you something.'

'What?' I blurt. I spin over and find the switch for the bedside lamp, and the room floods with a hazy light. I blink back the sudden attack on my eyes, then turn to seek Miller out again. I find him sitting up, his features fretful. 'Tell me,' I push.

'Promise me you'll hear me out.' He takes my hands in his and squeezes. 'Promise me you'll let me finish before you fly into—'

'Miller! Just tell me!' The coldness settling over me accelerates my panic and fear.

His face seems to distort with pain. 'It's your grandmother.'

I lose my breath. 'Oh my God. What's happened? Is she OK?' I try to shake Miller off and go in search of my phone, but I'm held in place by a firm grip.

'You promised to hear me out.'

'That was before I knew it was about Nan!' I shout, feeling my sanity run away with me. I thought I was going to be hit with another obstacle, a piece of Miller's history or . . . I'm not sure what, anything other than this. 'Tell me what's happened!'

'She had a heart attack.'

My world explodes into a million shards of devastation. 'No! When? Where? How do—'

'Olivia, damn it, let me speak!' He's short, but gentle, his eyebrows arching to back up his calm warning.

How can I be calm? He's drip-feeding me information. I open my mouth to fire some choice words at him as my impatience and worry grows, but his hand comes up and silences me and I finally accept that I'll learn more information if I shut the hell up and listen.

'She's OK,' he begins, rubbing circles into the tops of my hands, but nothing will lessen my apprehension. She's ill and I'm not there to take care of her. I've always been there for her. My eyes start to burn with the threat of guilty tears. 'She's in the hospital being cared for.'

'When did it happen?' I choke my question through a sob.

'Yesterday morning.'

'Yesterday?' I shout, shocked.

'George found her. He didn't want to call you and worry you, and he didn't have my contact details. He waited for William to stop by the house. Anderson said he'd let me know.'

I sag with sympathy for old George. I bet he felt lost and helpless. 'When did he call?'

'Late last night. You were in bed.'

'You didn't wake me?' I shake his hands off and shove myself back, away from Miller and his reach.

'You needed to sleep, Olivia.' He makes a play for my hands, but I doggedly knock him away and get off the bed.

'I could've been halfway home by now!' I march to the wardrobe, enraged and astounded that he didn't think Nan's heart attack was a good enough reason to disturb my sleep. I yank the sports bag out of the cupboard and begin stuffing what I can inside. Much of the stuff I've bought since arriving will have to stay. We had planned to buy suitcases, but haven't got around to doing it yet. Now I haven't time to worry about leaving behind hundreds of dollars' worth of clothing.

My frantic packing is disturbed when the bag is taken from my hands and thrown to the floor. My emotions won't remain contained any longer. 'You arsehole!' I scream in his face, then proceed to bash the side of my fist into his shoulder. He doesn't move or reprimand me on it. He's impassive and cool. 'You arsehole, you arsehole, you arsehole!' I strike him again, my frustration building at his unresponsive approach. 'You should have woken me!' Both fists are working now, repeatedly hitting him in the chest. I've lost control of my emotions *and* my flailing body. I just want to lash out and Miller is the only thing in my proximity. 'Why?' I fall into his chest, exhausted and overcome with grief. 'Why didn't you tell me?'

He holds my weak body up, one hand cupping the back of my head, pushing me into him, the other working soothing circles into my lower back. I'm hushed repeatedly, kissed over and over on top of my head until my sobs abate and I'm left snivelling sporadically into his shoulder.

Taking my cheeks, he holds my contorted face in his hands. 'I'm sorry if you feel like I've betrayed you . . .' He pauses, watching me cautiously, and I'm certain it's because he knows I'm not going to like his next words. 'We can't go back to London, Olivia. It's not safe.'

'Don't you dare, Miller!' I try to locate some fortitude, something that'll show him that it's not up for discussion. 'Call William and tell him we're coming home.'

I can see his torment. It's written all over his tight face.

I can't find that fortitude. 'Just get me home!' I beg, brushing away my falling tears. 'Please, take me to my nan.'

I see defeatism crawl across his pained face as he nods faintly. It's a reluctant nod. He hasn't prepared himself to go home. He's being pushed into a corner.

Chapter 6

His palm on my nape has been a constant source of comfort since we left New York. At JFK, on the plane, through Heathrow, every available opportunity to hold me has been taken. It has been needed and welcomed. I've been quite oblivious to our surroundings, not even getting myself worked up each time our passports have been checked. Between gentle kneads of my nape, my mind has only allowed me to think about Nan.

We had time to buy suitcases. Too much time. I told Miller to go buy them himself, but my order was totally ignored. He was right. I would have only moped around the suite, driving myself up the wall if left alone. So we went shopping together, and I couldn't help appreciating Miller's attempts to try to distract me. He asked my opinion on what colour, size, and style of suitcase we should buy, not that my answer counted for anything. After telling him I liked the red, fabric range, I half listened to the reasons why we should buy the graphite, leather Samsonite range.

Once we've collected our new suitcases from baggage arrivals and I've vaguely registered Miller's annoyance at the few scuffs on the leather, we emerge from Arrivals into the cool evening air at Heathrow. I spot William's driver before Miller and quickly make my way over, jumping in the back after giving him a courteous nod. He joins Miller at the back of the car to help load the bags.

Then Miller slips in beside me and rests his hand on my knee. 'My place, Ted,' he instructs.

I lean forward. 'Thank you, Ted, but can you take me straight to the hospital?' I ask it as a question, but there's no choice of answer, and my tone tells Ted that.

Miller's gaze is burning into my profile, yet I won't allow myself to confront him. 'Olivia, you've just got off a six-hour flight. The time differ—'

'I'm going to see my nan,' I grind through a clenched jaw, knowing my tiredness has nothing to do with Miller protesting. 'I'll find my own way there if you'd rather go home.' I see Ted's eyes in the mirror, flicking between me and the road. They'rc smiling eyes. Fond eyes.

Miller makes a point of displaying his frustration with a long, over-the-top sigh. 'The hospital, please, Ted.'

'Sir,' Ted agrees on a nod. He knew it was never up for discussion.

As we break the confines of the airport, my impatience grows as William's driver weaves through the rush-hour traffic on the M25. We find ourselves at a standstill on more than one occasion, and each time I have to fight the urge to jump out and run the rest of the way.

By the time Ted pulls up to the hospital, it's dark and I'm beside myself. I dive from the car before it comes to a stop, ignoring Miller shouting after me. I'm out of breath when I land at the main reception desk. 'Josephine Taylor,' I splutter to the receptionist.

She eyes me with slight alarm. 'Friend or relative?'

'Granddaughter.' I shift impatiently while she starts tapping on her keyboard, throwing the odd frown here and there at the screen. 'Is there a problem?'

'She doesn't appear to be on our system. Don't worry, we'll try another way. Her date of birth?'

'Yes, it's—' I'm halted mid-sentence when my nape is claimed and I'm led away from the reception desk.

'You'll get to your nan a lot faster if you listen to me, Olivia.

I've got the details. I know what ward she's on, the room number, and the directions to get us there.' His patience is clearly wearing thin.

I remain quiet as he steers me down the never-ending tunnel of white, my trepidation mounting with each step. It's eerie, the echoes of our footsteps lingering forever in the hollow space. Miller is quiet, too, and I hate myself for being unable and unwilling to ease his obvious concern for me. Nothing will make me feel better until I see Nan alive and well and throwing some spunk in my direction.

'Here.' His palm on my neck twists gently, prompting me to veer left, where a pair of doors open automatically and a sign saying WELCOME TO CEDAR WARD greets us. 'Room three.' Miller drops his hold, leaving me feeling unstable and weak, and indicates to the second door on the left. My steps falter, my heart refusing to ease up with its steady thumps. The heat of the ward hits me like a sledgehammer and the smell of antiseptic pollutes my nose. A gentle nudge in my back encourages me to take the handle, and after loading my lungs with much-needed air, I turn the knob and push my way into the room.

But it's empty.

The bed is perfectly made, all of the machines neatly tucked away in a corner. There's no sign of life. I feel dizzy. 'Where is she?'

Miller doesn't answer, instead moving past me and halting abruptly, taking in the empty room himself. I'm just staring blankly at the empty bed, everything else around me blurring, including my hearing, which only vaguely registers Miller insisting that this is the correct room.

'Can I help you?' asks a young nurse.

Miller steps forward. 'The lady who was in here, where is she?'

'Josephine Taylor?' she asks. Her eyes are downcast, and I don't think I can take whatever is coming next.

A lump clogs my throat. I reach out and grab Miller's arm, digging my nails in. He responds only by prying my clawed fingers from his flesh and squeezing my hand before bringing it to his mouth.

'You're her granddaughter? Olivia?'

I nod, unable to speak, but before she can answer, I hear a familiar laugh coming from down the hall. 'That's her!' I blurt, yanking my hand from Miller and nearly knocking the nurse off her feet when I barge past. I follow the familiar sound, vibrations rippling through me with each pound of my feet on the ground. I reach a crossroad and skid to a stop when the sound fades to nothing. I glance to the left and see four beds, all with old people asleep.

There it is again.

Laughter.

Nan's laughter.

My head whips to the right, seeing another four beds all occupied.

And there she is, sitting up in an armchair positioned to the side of her hospital bed, watching television. Her hair is perfectly styled, and she's wearing her frilly nightie. I move towards her, drinking in the beautiful sight until I'm standing at the foot of the bed. Her sapphire eyes move away from the television and land on me. I feel like electro probes have shocked me back to life.

'My darling girl.' Her hand reaches for me, and my eyes explode with tears.

'Oh God, Nan!' I make a grab for the curtain that's pulled back by her bed and nearly fall through the damn thing.

'Olivia!' Miller catches my staggering body and quickly steadies me on my feet. I'm all in a fuddle, too many emotions spiralling through me to deal with. He runs a quick scan over me, then looks over my shoulder. 'Fucking hell,' he breathes, every muscle visibly sagging.

He thought it, too. He thought she was dead.

'That's it!' she barks. 'Come in here, causing chaos and cursing all over the place! You'll get me kicked out!'

My eyes bug as my blood begins to warm again. 'Because you haven't caused enough chaos yourself?' I blurt.

Her grin is impish. 'I've been a perfect lady, I'll have you know.'

A scoff comes from behind us, and both Miller and I turn blankly to face the nurse. 'A perfect lady,' she muses, giving Nan eyebrows so high, I can't tell where they end and her hairline begins.

'I've brightened the place up,' Nan retorts, pulling Miller and I back around. She gestures towards the other three beds, all occupied with frail old people, all sleeping. 'I've got more life in me than those three put together! I've not come here to die, I assure you.'

I smile and glance up at Miller, who looks down at me all amused, his eyes twinkling. 'A twenty-four-carat gold treasure.' He blinds me with a full-blown, all-white smile that nearly has me grabbing the curtain again.

'I know.' I grin and virtually dive across the bed into my nan's arms. 'I thought you were dead,' I tell her, relishing the familiar scent of the washing powder she uses, ingrained into the material of her nightie.

'Death seems far more appealing than this dump,' she grumbles, earning herself a little nudge from me. 'Oooh, watch my wires.'

I gasp and jump back, mentally scolding myself for being so careless. She might seem her spunky self, but she's here for a reason. I watch her pull at a line in her arm, grumbling under her breath.

'Visiting hours finished at eight,' the nurse cuts in, rounding the bed to assist Nan. 'You can come back tomorrow.'

My heart sinks. 'But we've—'

Miller's hand on my arm halts my complaint, and he looks to the nurse. 'Would you mind?' He gestures away from the bed, and I watch, amused, as the nurse smiles coyly and leaves the bay, rounding the corner behind the curtains. I raise my eyebrows at Miller, but he just shrugs his perfect shoulders and follows the nurse. He might look drained, but he's still a sight to behold. And he's just bought me some time, so I couldn't care less if the nurse is going to gaze at him all dreamy while he gets the lowdown on Nan's condition.

Feeling eyes studying me, I leave Miller's disappearing back and look down to my spunky grandmother. She looks all mischievous again. 'His buns look even better in jeans.'

I roll my eyes and sit on the bed in front of her. 'I thought you liked a young man to be well turned out.'

'Miller would look delicious in a sack.' She smiles and reaches for my hand, squeezing it in hers. It's a comforting squeeze, which is crazy, given who's the sick one here, but it also abruptly makes me wonder what Nan knows. 'How are you, sweetheart?'

'Fine.' I don't know what else to say, or what I *should* say. Need to know and all that, but does she *really* need to know now? I need to speak to William.

'Hmmm . . .' She eyes me suspiciously, and I shift on the bed, refusing to meet her stare.

I need to change the direction of conversation. 'Didn't you prefer the private room?'

'Don't you start!' She drops my hand and sits back in her chair, taking the remote and pointing it at the TV. The screen goes blank. 'Being stuffed in that room was sending me crackers!'

I glance around at the other beds on a slight smile, thinking Nan's probably been sending *these* poor folks crackers. And the nurse definitely looked like she'd had her fill. 'How are you feeling?' I ask, finding her seated form again, seeing her fiddling with the lines in her arm. 'Leave them!'

Her palms slap the arms of the chair on a huff. 'I'm bored!' she squawks. 'The food is crap, and they're making me piddle in a pot.'

I chuckle, knowing her cherished dignity is being seriously compromised and she's evidently not happy about it. 'Do as you're told,' I warn. 'You're here for a reason.'

'A mild flutter of my heart, that's all.'

'You make it sound like you've been on a date!' I laugh.

'Tell me about New York.'

My laughter is sucked up in a second and I'm back to fidgeting awkwardly as I search my brain for anything to say. Nothing is coming to me.

'I asked you to tell me about New York, Olivia,' she says soothingly, and I chance a glance at her, finding a face to match her tone. 'Not how you came to be there.'

My lips must be white from the force of them pressed together in an attempt to stop my emotion from gushing out on a sob. I couldn't love this woman any more. 'I missed you so much.' My voice is ragged, and I let her pull me into a hug when she reaches for me.

'Darling girl, I missed you terribly.' She sighs, holding me to her squidgy body. 'Although I was kept busy feeding three strapping men.'

I frown into her bosom. 'Three?'

'Yes.' Nan lets me free from her embrace and brushes my blonde mane from my face. 'George, Gregory, and William.'

'Oooh,' I breathe, visions of all three men gathered around Nan's dinner table, tucking into some hearty meals, crawling all over my mind. How cosy. 'You've been feeding William?'

'Yes.' She shows complete indifference with a flap of her wrinkled hand. 'I've been looking after all of them.'

Despite my growing concern at the news that Nan and William have evidently been keeping cosy company, I smile. While Nan's slightly delusional mind thinks she's the one who's been looking after them, I know different. William said he'd take care of her, but even if he wasn't in the picture, I know Gregory and George would do a fine job. But my smile soon recedes when I remember where we are. In a hospital. Because Nan's had a heart attack.

'Time's up.' Miller's soft voice pulls my attention, and I watch as his eyes dull from the lovely, relaxed twinkle into concern.

He gives me a questioning look, which I ignore, shaking my head a little and standing. 'We're being booted out,' I say, leaning down to hug Nan.

She embraces me hard, squeezing some of my guilt away. She knows I'll blame myself. 'Smuggle me out with you.'

'Don't be silly.' I remain where I am, surrounded by Nan, until she's the one to break our clinch. 'Please, be a good girl for the doctors.'

'Yes,' Miller interjects, stepping forward and kneeling down next to me to get level with Nan. 'I've been craving beef Wellington, and I know no other who can make it like you, Josephine.'

Nan visibly turns to mush in her chair, and happiness sails through me. She cups Miller's shadowed cheek and moves in, getting almost nose to nose with him. He doesn't shy away. In fact, he welcomes her tender gesture, placing his hand over hers while she feels him.

I just watch in wonder as they share a private moment in the openness of the ward, everything around them seeming to pale into insignificance as a million words are passed between their locked eyes.

'Thank you for taking care of my baby,' Nan whispers, so quietly I almost don't hear.

I'm biting my lip again as Miller takes her hand and brings it to his mouth, kissing the back tenderly. 'Until there is no breath left in my lungs, Mrs Taylor.'

Chapter 7

I settle in the back of William's car, feeling like the weight of the world has been lifted from my shoulders. There are a million other burdens that should have me crumbling under their pressure, but I can't think past the elation of seeing with my own eyes that Nan is OK.

'My place, please, Ted,' Miller says, reaching over to me. 'Come here.'

I ignore his outstretched hand. 'I want to go home.'

Ted pulls into traffic, and I catch him glimpsing in the rearview mirror, that fond smile gracing his friendly, rugged face. I narrow suspicious eyes on him briefly, even though he's no longer looking at me, then return my attention to Miller. He's watching me thoughtfully, his hand still hovering between us. 'I'm being intuitive here, and I'm going to suggest that when you say "home", you don't mean my place.' His hand drops to the seat.

'Your place isn't my home, Miller.' Nan's traditional terrace house, full of clutter and that familiar, comforting smell, is my home. And I need to be surrounded by all things Nan right now.

Miller's fingers tap the leather seat, his eyes regarding me carefully. I retreat in my chair, wary.

'I have a request,' he murmurs, before reaching across to claim my right hand that's currently spinning my new diamond ring repeatedly on my finger.

'What?' The word rolls from my mouth slowly. Something

tells me he's not going to request me to never stop loving him. He knows how I'll answer that request, and his slightly ticking jaw tells me he's nervous of the answer that I might give to this one.

He starts his own twiddling session of my diamond, thinking hard as he watches his playing fingers, leaving me with a whirling mind, bracing myself for him to voice his wish. It's a long, long, uncomfortable time before he takes a deep breath and his blue eyes lazily crawl up my body until his bottomless pits of emotion sink into me. They steal my breath away . . . make me comprehend very quickly that what he's about to ask means a lot to him. 'I want my home to be your home, too.'

My mouth drops open and my mind blanks. No right words are coming to me. Except one. 'No,' I blurt on a rush of air before I consider wording my refusal a little more considerately. I wince at the clear disappointment that jumps onto his perfect face. 'I mean . . .' My damn brain is failing to load my mouth with anything that could redeem myself, and guilt is instantly crippling me for being the cause of his hurt.

'You are not staying alone.'

'I need to be at home.' My eyes drop, no longer prepared to face the pleading in his intense stare. He doesn't come back at me with an argument, instead sighing and squeezing my little hand in his. 'To Livy's home, please, Ted,' he instructs quietly before falling silent.

I look up to see him staring out the window. He's pensive. 'Thank you,' I whisper, shuffling across the seat to curl into his side. I'm not encouraged or helped and he doesn't welcome me once I'm settled, keeping his eyes on the outside world whizzing past the window.

'Don't ever thank me,' he answers quietly.

'Lock the door,' Miller says, my cheeks cupped in his palms, his worried eyes scanning my face as we stand on the doorstep.

'Don't answer to anyone. I'll be back as soon as I've collected some clean clothes.'

My forehead wrinkles. 'Should I expect visitors?'

The worry disappears in a flash and is replaced with exasperation. After our words in the car, I knew I had scored a victory, but I honestly never expected Miller to so willingly stay here. I want him to, of course, but I wasn't about to test his already fraying patience. I've done that already by insisting I be here and that I be here right this moment. I wasn't prepared to be dragged over to the other side of town so Miller could check his flat and collect some clean clothes. It would have been an opportunity for him to lock me inside. And I've no doubt he would have. But I'm not delusional enough to kid myself that Miller staying here has anything to do with my fraught mind where Nan is concerned.

'Less of the sass, Olivia.'

'You love my sass.' I take his hands from my cheeks and return them to him. 'I'm going to take a shower.' Reaching up on my tiptoes, I kiss his stubbled jaw. 'Be quick.'

'I will,' he breathes.

I pull away and register his evident exhaustion. He looks drained. 'I love you.' I step back until I'm in the hallway and take the door handle.

A strained smile tickles his lips and he shoves his hands into his jean pockets as he starts retreating backwards down the path. 'Lock the door,' he repeats.

I nod my acceptance and slowly shut the door, immediately bolting the locks and putting the safety chain on, knowing he won't leave until he hears them all shift into place. Then I spend too long staring down the long hallway to the back kitchen, waiting for the familiar, comforting sound of Nan pottering around. Of course, it never comes, so I resort to closing my eyes and imagining her there. After standing motionless for an age, I finally convince my depleted body to carry me towards the stairs.

But I pull to an abrupt halt when there's a knock on the front door. With a furrowed brow, I move towards it and go to unbolt the locks, but something halts me. It's Miller's voice telling me not to answer to anyone. I draw breath to ask who it is and quickly stop myself. Instinct?

Stepping silently back from the door, I sneak into the lounge and approach the bay window. My senses are all on high alert. I feel apprehensive, nervous, and I jump a mile when the door is rapped again. 'Fucking hell!' I blurt, probably too loudly. My damn heart bangs relentlessly in my chest as I tiptoe towards the window and peek past the curtain.

A face appears.

'Fuck!' I screech, staggering back from the window. I clutch my chest, heaving shocked breaths while allowing my eyes and mind to register a face I recognise. 'Ted?' I gasp, my face screwing up in confusion. He smiles that fond smile and gives his head a little flick towards the front door before he's gone from view. I roll my eyes and swallow in an attempt to push my heart down from my throat. 'Trying to give me frigging heart failure,' I mutter, making my way to the front door, knowing for sure that he's been here the whole time since Miller left, on lookout.

I unbolt the door and swing it open. A body barrels towards me, and I barely jump out of the way in time. 'Shit!' I cry, pinning myself to the wall of the hallway. My poor heart hasn't yet recovered from the shock of Ted's face at the window.

Miller pushes past me with his suitcase and dumps it at the bottom of the stairs.

'Was Ted keeping guard?' I ask, wanting confirmation. Am I to expect this all the time? My own personal bodyguard?

'Did you honestly think I would leave you alone?' Miller strides past me again, my head turning and following his path until I'm watching his back getting farther away as he stalks down the pathway to Ted, who's closing the boot of the Lexus. 'Thank you.' Miller passes Ted his keys before offering a hand to William's driver.

'Most welcome.' Ted smiles and shakes Miller's hand, then looks past Miller to me. 'Good evening, Miss Taylor.'

'Evening,' I murmur, watching Miller turn and return up the garden path. Ted slides into the driver's seat and is gone in the blink of an eye. Then the world disappears as Miller shuts the front door and secures the locks.

'We need to upgrade security,' he grumbles, turning to find my dumbstruck face. 'You OK?'

I blink repeatedly, looking from the door to him, back and forth. 'There are two bolts, a Yale, a mortise, and a chain.'

'And I still got past it,' he says, reminding me of the occasions when he broke into my home, just to get his *thing*.

'Because I looked out the window, saw it was Ted, and then opened the door,' I retort.

He smiles his acknowledgement to my sass but doesn't retaliate.

'I need a shower.'

'I'd love to join you,' he whispers, low and primal, stepping forward. My arms drop and my blood heats. He takes another step forward. 'I'd love to settle my hands on your wet shoulders and work them over every breathtaking inch of your body until there's only space in that beautiful mind of yours for me.'

He's succeeded already and he hasn't even touched me yet, but I nod anyway and stand quietly until he's before me, lifting me to his body. I wrap around him and my face sinks into his neck as he climbs the stairs and takes us to the bathroom, setting me on my feet once we arrive. I smile and lean over to turn the water on, then begin stripping down. 'There isn't much room,' I say, tossing my clothes into the wash basket one by one until I'm naked.

His head bobs a little on an agreeable nod, and he takes the hem of his T-shirt and pulls it up over his head. The muscles of his stomach and chest roll as a result of the move, keeping my focus on his torso. My tired eyes blink a few times, then drop to his legs when he peels off his jeans. I sigh dreamily.

'Earth to Olivia.' The softness of his tone pulls my eyes to his, and I smile, stepping forward to place my palm on the centre of his chest. After a physically and mentally draining day, I just need to feel him and take my comfort from touching him.

I'm allowed to trace the planes of his chest, my eyes following the slow path I'm making, Miller's head dropped to watch me. I feel his hands rest on my waist lightly, like he's being careful not to disturb my thoughtful motions. My touch drifts up to his shoulders, onto his neck, and across his dark jaw until I'm at his full, mesmerising lips. They part slowly and my finger slips between them, my head tilting a little on a diminutive smile when he bites down lightly.

Then our eyes meet and a million unspoken words collide between us. Love. Adoration. Passion. Desire. Want. Need . . .

I pull my finger free and we both move forward slowly.

And all of those things intensify when our mouths join. My eyes close, my palms slip onto his waist, and my neck is seized in his grasp, holding me secure while he spends an eternity worshipping my mouth. I'm swallowed up and carried off to a place where only Miller and I exist, a place Miller has created for me to run away to. Somewhere safe. Somewhere calm. Somewhere perfect.

His hold of me is so strong, always is, and the power he exudes is mind-bending, but his constant tenderness douses that control somewhat. Yet there is never any mistaking that Miller is always the one driving things. There's no denying he rules my body and heart. He knows what I need and when I need it, and he displays this in every element of our relationship, not just when he's worshipping me. Like when I needed to go to the hospital immediately. Like when I needed to come home and immerse myself in Nan's lingering presence. Like I needed him to remove himself from his perfect world and be here with me.

Our kiss slows, but Miller's hold of me doesn't ease. After nibbling at my bottom lip, then my nose and my cheek, he pulls away and my torn eyes are faced with their usual dilemma. Not knowing which to focus on, my gaze drifts repeatedly from his blistering blues to his mesmerising mouth.

'Let's get you showered, my gorgeous girl.'

We spend a blissful half hour under the hot spray. The space restriction makes it a very intimate shower, although I wouldn't expect it to be anything less, even if we had acres of space. My palms on the tiled wall, I drop my head, my eyes watching the soapy water disappear down the drain while the heavenly sensation of Miller's smooth, soapy palms work into every tired muscle in my body. My hair is shampooed and conditioner smoothed through to the ends. I remain still and quiet the whole time, only moving when he positions me how he needs me. After raining soft kisses over every part of my wet face, he helps me from the tub and dries me off before guiding me to my room.

'Are you hungry?' he asks, pulling the brush through my wet strands.

I shake my head and ignore the slight falter in his movements behind me, but he doesn't argue. I'm placed in bed and he crawls in behind me until our naked bodies are locked tightly together and his lips are performing a lazy dance across my shoulders. Sleep finds me easily, assisted by the low hum of Miller and his heat compressed to every available part of my back.

Chapter 8

A commotion yanks me from my dreams and has me pelting down the stairs at a ridiculous rate. I land in the kitchen, still half asleep, naked and with slightly blurred vision. I blink repeatedly to clear my sight, until I'm staring at Miller, who's standing bare-chested with a box of cornflakes in his hand.

'What's the matter?' he asks, worried eyes scanning my naked frame.

Reality slams into my waking brain, a reality where it's not Nan pottering around the kitchen looking happy and at home; it's Miller looking awkward and out of place. Raging guilt consumes me for being disappointed. 'You startled me,' is all I can think to say, and suddenly very alert, I register my naked form and start backing out of the kitchen. I indicate over my shoulder. 'I'll just get some clothes on.'

'OK,' he agrees, watching me closely as I disappear down the hallway. My sigh is heavy as I take the stairs and my actions subdued as I tug on some knickers and a T-shirt. Once I've made it back downstairs, I find the table set for breakfast and Miller looking even more out of place, sitting with his phone to his ear. He indicates for me to take a seat, which I do slowly while he continues with his call. 'I'll be in around lunchtime,' he says, clipped and to the point before hanging up and setting his phone down. He gazes across the table at me, and I note after only a few seconds of studying him that he's slipping into that emotionless man who repels everyone. We're back in London. All that's missing is his suit.

'Who was that?' I ask, picking up the pot of tea that's steaming in the centre of the table and pouring myself a cup.

'Tony.' His reply is as curt and short as he was with Tony just now.

Dumping the teapot a little heavy-handed to my right, I make quick work of adding milk and stirring, and then watch in astonishment when Miller leans over the table and takes the pot, placing it exactly back in the centre of the table. Then he tweaks it a little more.

I sigh, taking a sip of my tea and immediately wince at the taste. I swallow hard and put the mug down. 'How many tea bags did you put in there?'

He frowns and looks at the pot. 'Two.'

'Doesn't taste like it.' It tastes like warmed milk. I reach over to take the lid off and peek inside. 'There are none in here.'

'I took them out.'

'Why?'

'Because they'd block the spout.'

I smile. 'Miller, a million teapots in England have tea bags steeping inside. The spouts never get blocked.'

He rolls his eyes and sits back in his chair, folding his arms over his naked chest. 'I'm being intuitive here—'

'Miller Hart?' I cut in, reining in my smirk. 'Never.'

His tired look only increases my amusement. I can tell he's relishing in my playfulness, even if he's refusing to reciprocate. He continues. 'And I'm going to suggest that you're insinuating my tea-making skills are lacking.'

'Your intuition is correct.'

'Thought so,' he mutters, collecting his phone from the table and pressing a few buttons. 'I was trying to make you feel at home.'

'I *am* at home.' I wince when he shoots an injured look in my direction. I didn't mean that how it sounded. 'I—'

Miller puts the phone to his ear. 'Have my car ready for nine,' he orders.

'Miller, I didn't—'

'And make sure it's spotless,' he continues, flat-out ignoring my attempt to explain.

'You've taken it—'

'And that means the boot, too.'

I pick up my mug, just so I can slam it down. And I do. Hard. 'Stop being childish!'

He recoils in his chair and cuts the call. 'I beg your pardon.'

I laugh a little. 'Don't start with the begging, Miller. I didn't mean to upset you.'

His forearms meet the table and he leans in. 'Why won't you stay with me?'

I look into his pleading eyes and sigh. 'Because I need to be here,' I reply, seeing no understanding developing, so I go on in the hopes of making him comprehend. 'I need to have things ready for when she comes home. I need to be here to take care of her.'

'Then she can come and live with us,' he counters immediately. He's serious and I'm shocked. He's prepared to expose himself to the potential of another person, besides me, screwing up his perfect home? Nan will send Miller into obsessive meltdown. She might be ill, but I'm under no illusion that she won't seize control of Miller's household. It would be anarchy. Miller would never cope.

'Trust me,' I laugh. 'You really don't mean that.'

'I do,' he retorts, wiping my smile from my face. 'I know what you're thinking.'

'What?' I'd love him to confirm my thoughts, because if he does that, we're halfway to an admission.

'You know what.' His eyes are warning me. 'I'd feel more at ease if you're at my place. It's safer.'

It takes every ounce of my remaining patience not to show

my exasperation. I should have expected this. I refuse to be chaperoned and guarded. Meeting and falling in love with Miller Hart might have given me freedom, awakened me, and ignited a desire to live and feel, but I'm also aware that there could now be an element of constraint attached to my newfound freedom. I'm not going to let that happen. 'I'm staying,' I assert with utter finality, making Miller's whole body go lax in his chair.

'As you wish,' he breathes, closing his eyes and looking to the heavens. 'Fucking sass.'

I smile, loving the sight of Miller so exasperated, but loving his easy acceptance even more. 'What are you doing today?'

His head drops, one eye narrowing on me suspiciously. 'You're going to refuse to accompany me, aren't you?'

My smile widens. 'Yes. I'm going to go see Nan.'

'You can come to Ice with me first.'

'No.' I shake my head slowly. I expect Cassie will be there and I'm not up for looks of disdain or words that'll likely reduce me to dust. I have better things to do than get involved in a territory battle, and nothing will delay me getting to Nan.

He leans forward, jaw ticking. 'You're testing my fucking patience, Olivia. You are coming and you *will* accept.'

I will? I know why he's trying to lay down his rules, but the arrogant manner in which he's doing it has my sass exploding before I can tell myself to be reasonable. My palms meet the table and I move in fast, making Miller retreat in his chair. 'If *you* want to keep me as a possession, then you'll lay off on the arsehole behaviour! I'm not an object, Miller. Having an appreciation of your *possession* doesn't mean you get to boss me around.' I stand, sending my chair skidding back on the floor. 'I'm going for a shower.' My feet make quick work of removing me from the simmering anger emanating from Miller as a result of my insolence. He just couldn't stop, and there's only so long I can humour him.

*

I take my time showering and dressing, and I'm surprised when I get downstairs and find Miller's gone. But not so surprised when I find the kitchen smelling like it's been attacked by antibacterial spray and looking like it's been doused in sparkle dust. I won't complain, though, because it means I can get to the hospital without delay. Snatching up my bag, I swing the front door open and dart out while fishing my keys from my satchel.

'Oh!' I yelp, bouncing off a chest and staggering back. I collide with the front door as it meets the frame, smacking my shoulder blade. 'Shit!' My hand instinctively reaches over my back and rubs away the sharp stab of pain.

'In a rush?' Strong fingers wrap around my forearm and hold me in place.

I drag irritated eyes up a suited frame, knowing what I'm going to be confronted with once I venture past the neck. And I'm right. William. My mother's ex-pimp/my self-appointed guardian angel. 'Yes, so if you'll excuse me.' I go to sidestep him, but he shifts with me, blocking my path. Biting my tongue and taking a calming breath, I square my shoulders and lift my chin. He's not in the least bit fazed. It doesn't sit well. My sass is getting hard to uphold. It's exhausting.

'In the car, Olivia.' His tone irritates the hell out of me, but I know that refusing will get me nowhere.

'He made you come here, didn't he?' I don't believe it! The sneaky bastard!

'I see little point in denying it,' William confirms my thoughts and gestures towards his car again, where Ted is standing holding the back door open, that smile ever present on his rugged, friendly face.

I return his smile, then quickly revert to furious when I swing my eyes back onto William. 'If you chew my ear off, then I'll do a bunk!'

'A bunk? You mean leave?' William laughs. 'Chewing ears, doing bunks. Whatever next?'

'A foot up your annoying arse,' I mutter, stomping past him. 'I'm not sure whether you and Miller have noticed, but I'm an adult!'

'Miss Taylor.' Ted nods, and my aggravation falls away in an instant as I slip into the back.

'Hi, Ted,' I chirp, ignoring the look of disbelief that William throws in his driver's direction, followed by the shrug of Ted's shoulders as he brushes it all off. I couldn't be stroppy with him if I tried. He has a calming aura surrounding him that seems to rub off on me. And to think this guy drives like a demon.

Settling back in my seat, I wait for William to slide in the other side while I swivel my ring, looking out of the window. 'I was planning on visiting Josephine this morning anyway,' he says.

I ignore him and take my phone from my bag to text Miller.

I'm mad at you.

I don't need to elaborate. He knows William is the last person I want to be with. I click SEND and go to toss my phone back into my bag, but William catches my hand and I look up to see him frowning. 'What's this?' he asks, tracing over my diamond ring.

Every defence mechanism I have flies up. 'Just a ring.' Oh, this should be fun. I pull my hand away, annoyed that my other hand instinctively hides it from his prying eyes. I don't want to hide it. From anyone.

'On your left ring finger?'

'Yes,' I snap, mildly aware that I'm pressing his buttons. I'm leading him down a merry path, when I could quite easily put his obviously racing mind to rest. I'm not explaining. He can think what he likes.

'You're marrying him?' William pushes, his tone getting impatient at my continued disrespect. I'm a brave girl, but I'm also a very pissed off girl. Fleeing from London again is becoming more tempting by the second, except this time I'll be kidnapping Nan from the hospital and taking her with me.

I maintain my silence and look down at my phone when it pings the arrival of a text.

What have I done to make you mad, sweet girl?

I scoff and drop my phone back into my satchel, not prepared to irritate myself further by entertaining his ignorance with a reply. I just want to see Nan.

'Olivia Taylor,' William sighs, humour starting to dilute his annoyance. 'You never fail to disappoint.'

'What's that supposed to mean?' I swing to face him, finding a mild smile on his handsome face. I know exactly what he means, and he said it to draw a reaction, to snap me from my moody silence. He's succeeded. Now I'm still moody, but I'm far from silent. 'Ted, could you pull over, please?'

William shakes his head and doesn't bother to voice his counter-command to his driver. He doesn't need to. Ted's clearly not as brave as me . . . or, most definitely, has more respect for William Anderson. I look to the mirror and see that smile again. It seems to be a permanent fixture on his face.

'Why's he always so happy?' I ask as I return my eyes to William, genuinely interested.

He's regarding me thoughtfully, his fingers drumming the door where his arm is resting. 'I think perhaps you might remind him of someone.' He speaks quietly, almost cautiously, and I recoil in my chair when I register what he means. Ted knew my mother? I frown, thinking hard. Should I ask? I open my mouth to speak, but it snaps closed just as quick. Would I even want to see her if it turns out she is alive? My answer comes to me quickly with hardly any thought behind my reasoning. I don't question it.

No. I wouldn't.

The hospital is hot and stuffy, yet my feet still move fast down the corridor, keen to get to Nan. William is pacing steadily beside me, his long legs seeming to keep up easily. 'Your friend,' he says, out of the blue, making my steps falter. My mind falters, too. I don't know why. I know who he's talking about. 'Gregory,' he clarifies, as if he is in any doubt of who I think he is referring to.

My stride catches up again and I keep my focus forward. 'What about him?'

'Nice chap.'

My forehead wrinkles at his observation. Gregory is a very nice chap, but I sense William isn't simply intending on heading down a road of flattery. 'He is a very nice *chap*.'

'Ambitious, smart . . .'

'Wait!' I skid to a halt and throw disbelieving eyes at William. Then I laugh. Uncontrollably. I'm in pieces. The distinguished, suited man is rendered speechless and wide-eyed as I fall all over the hospital corridor, tittering to myself. 'Oh God!' I chuckle, wiping under a leaking eye as I glance up at William. He's looking around us, clearly uncomfortable. 'Nice try, William.' I march on my way, leaving William tentatively following behind. He really is desperate. 'Sorry to disappoint you,' I call over my shoulder, 'but Gregory is gay.'

'He is?' His stunned reply makes me turn on a smile, keen to see the formidable William Anderson's surprise. Not much fazes him. But this has, and I'm rolling in the delight it has brought me.

'Yes, he is, so you can save your breath.' I should be fuming at his continued efforts to put me off Miller, but my enjoyment won't allow it. Miller, however, won't take it too kindly if he gets wind of William's relentless interfering.

Leaving William to regain his composure, I rush into the ward, heading straight to the bay where I know Nan to be. 'Good morning!' I chirp, finding her sitting in her chair, adorned in a floral dress, her hair styled perfectly. There's a tray on her lap and she's poking at what looks like an egg sandwich.

Unimpressed old navy eyes beat down my breeziness in a flash. 'Is it?' she grumbles, sliding the tray onto the table.

My heart sinks as I take a seat on the edge of her bed. 'You're in the best place, Nan.'

'Pfft!' she sulks, brushing her perfect curls off her face. 'Yes, if I were dead, but I'm perfectly well!'

Not wanting to be condescending, I force my eyes not to roll. 'They wouldn't keep you here if they thought you were perfectly well.'

'Do I look like that?' She swings an arm out and points her wrinkled finger to the old dear in the opposite bed. My lips straighten, not knowing what to say. No, she looks nothing like the poor woman who's dozing across the way, her mouth dropped open. She really does look dead. 'Enid!' Nan hollers, making me jump. 'Enid, dear, this is my granddaughter. Remember I told you?'

'Nan, she's sleeping!' I hiss, just as William rounds the corner. He has a grin on his face, no doubt after hearing the spunky Josephine causing havoc.

'She's not sleeping,' Nan argues. 'Enid!'

I shake my head and look to William again with pleading eyes, but he just maintains that amused smile, shrugging his shoulders. Both of us cast a sideways glance when coughing and spluttering emanates from Enid's direction, and I find her heavy eyes looking around, bewildered.

'Yoo-hoo! Over here!' Nan waves a deranged arm in the air. 'Put your glasses on, dear. They're on your lap.'

Enid pats around on the covers for a few moments, then slips her glasses on. A gummy grin materialises on her pasty face. 'Sweet thing,' she croaks, before her head falls back, her eyes close, and her mouth drops open again.

I make to stand, alarmed. 'Is she OK?'

William chuckles and joins me on the bed in front of Nan. 'It's her medication. She's fine.'

'No,' Nan jumps in. '*I'm* fine. *She's* on her way to the pearly gates. When are they releasing me?'

'Tomorrow, or maybe Friday, if the consultant agrees,' William tells her, bringing a hopeful smile to her face. '*If* the consultant agrees,' he reinforces with a certain look of knowing.

'Oh, he'll agree,' she replies, too confidently, her hands resting in her lap. Then silence falls and her navy eyes travel between me and William a few times, curiosity rife on her round face. 'How are you two?'

'Very well.'

'Fine.' My answer clashes with William's, and we both look out the corner of our eye at each other.

'Where's Miller?' she goes on, pulling our attention back to her demanding presence.

I keep silent now, thinking William will answer again, but he remains quiet, leaving me to speak up. There's a tension between us, and Nan's clearly picking up on it. We're not helping matters in the slightest. I don't want her to worry about anything other than getting well. 'He's at work.' I start faffing with the water jug on the cabinet beside her bed, anything to instigate a conversation change. 'Shall I get you some fresh water?'

'The nurse did it before you arrived.' She's speedy with her reply, leaving me redirecting my attention to the plastic beaker sitting next to it.

'Clean cup?' I sound hopeful.

'Done.'

I deflate and confront her curious face. 'Do you need any clean clothes or underwear? Toiletries?'

'William saw to that yesterday morning.'

'He did?' I throw a surprised look at William and get flat-out ignored. 'That was thoughtful.'

The strapping man rises from the bed and dips to kiss my grandmother's cheek, and she accepts on a fond smile, lifting her hand and patting William's arm. 'Do you still have plenty of credit?' he asks.

'Oh yes!' Nan scoops up a remote control and points it at the television. It springs to life and Nan settles back in her chair. 'Marvellous piece of equipment! Did you know I can watch any episode of *EastEnders* from the last month at the touch of a button?'

'Incredible,' William agrees, flicking his smile to me.

I'm stunned into silence as I watch Nan and her daughter's ex-pimp converse like family. William Anderson, the lord of the underworld, doesn't look like he's shaking in his boots right now. And Nan doesn't look like her spunk is about to be unleashed on the man who sent her daughter away. What does she know? Or what has William told her? They don't look like there has ever been any animosity or bad feelings between them. They look comfortable and cosy. I'm confused.

'I'd best be off now.' William's soft announcement breaks into my conflicting thoughts and puts me back in the stifling hospital ward. 'Be good, Josephine.'

'Yes, yes,' Nan huffs, waving him away with a flap of her hand. 'If they set me free tomorrow, I'll be an angel.'

William laughs, his liquid grey eyes sparkling affectionately at my beloved grandmother. 'Your freedom banks on it. I'll pop in later.' His tall body turns to me and his smile widens at my evident bemusement. 'Ted will be back to collect you once he's dropped me at the Society. He'll drive you home.'

The mention of William's establishment halts my instinct to refuse as flashbacks of the opulent club start to creep to the front of my mind, making me clench my eyes shut in an attempt to halt them. 'Fine,' I mutter, standing and plumping the redundant pillow on the bed so I don't have to confront the stern look that's pointed at me for any longer than I have to. The chime of my iPhone is timed perfectly, allowing me to re-focus my attention on seeking out my mobile once I'm done toying with the pillow.

It's polite to answer someone when they ask you a question.

I should just go home and escape to the sanctuary of my bed, where no one can find me or aggravate me. 'Olivia, sweetheart, are you OK?' Nan's concerned question leaves me no option but to force a smile.

'I'm fine, Nan.' Dropping my phone carelessly without replying, I disregard the further reprimands my ignorance will likely spike and make myself comfortable on the bed again. 'So, home tomorrow or Friday, then?'

Relief floods me when Nan's concern slips away instantly before she launches into a rundown of why she can't wait to escape this 'hellhole'. I endure a whole hour of it until George arrives and I leave Nan filling him in on her grievances after I've had a recap of them myself. I'm not certain of many things at this point in my life, but I know for sure I wouldn't want to be a nurse on Cedar Ward right now.

Just before leaving Nan and George, I receive a text message from an unknown number, advising me that my car awaits when I'm ready to go home. But I'm not ready to go home, and I also know that Ted will have had strict orders from William to take me nowhere else. I also know that no amount of sweet talk or smiles will convince William's driver to do otherwise.

'Baby girl!'

I swivel on my Converse and virtually squeal when I see Gregory jogging towards me, the familiarity of my best friend in his grubby combats and tight T-shirt eliminating every tortured thought currently plaguing my mind.

He seizes me and swings me around, prompting another high-pitched squeal. 'God, it's so good to see you.'

'And you.' I cling to him tightly and let him squeeze me happy. 'Are you going to see Nan?'

'Yeah, have you been?'

'I left her with George. She might be allowed home tomorrow.'

Gregory detaches me from his body and holds me in place by the tops of my arms. Then he narrows guarded eyes on me. I don't know why. I haven't said or done anything to be suspicious of. 'What's up?' he asks.

'Nothing.' I immediately chastise myself for avoiding his eyes.

'Of course,' he retorts sarcastically. 'Because watching you run away and then having the pleasure of a few heavies ram-raid Miller's flat was all a figment of my imagination. You've got *nothing* to be worried about.'

'Heavies?' I home right in on Gregory's reference to what Miller prefers to call the immoral bastards.

'Yeah, quite an experience.' He takes my hand and links it through his bent arm as he starts to lead me towards the exit.

'You never mentioned anything on the phone all of the times we spoke.'

'Livy, whenever we've spoken since you disappeared to New York, it's been mindless chitchat. Don't pretend you wanted it any other way.'

I can't argue with him, so I don't. I had no interest in hearing what went down once Miller and I had left, and still, deep down, I don't, yet the mention of heavies is piquing my curiosity.

'Mean-looking sons of bitches.' Gregory only heightens that curiosity, along with adding a mountain of trepidation, too. 'Your man William – master of the frigging drug world – handled them like they were kittens. He didn't even break into a sweat when one tapped the holster of a gun. A fucking gun!'

'A gun?' I gasp, my heart jumping into my throat.

Gregory takes a cautious look around us, then diverts us down another corridor, out of the earshot of other hospital visitors. 'You heard me. Who *are* these people, Livy?'

I retreat a few steps back. 'I don't know.' I can't feel guilty for lying. I'm too worried.

'Well I do.'

'You do?' My eyes are wide and I'm frightened. William surely hasn't told Gregory. Please say he hasn't told Gregory!

'Yes.' He comes in closer and has a quick peek each way to check our privacy. 'Drug dealers. Miller works for the heavies, and I bet he's in all kinds of shit now.'

I'm horrified. I'm stunned. I'm not sure whether letting Gregory believe Miller's involved with drug dealers is better than the truth. Gregory has one thing right, though. Miller *does* work for the heavies. 'Right,' I breathe, desperately searching for something else to say and finding nothing, but it's fine because Gregory continues before my silence is noticed.

'Olivia, not only is your man a psychotic, OCD-suffering, ex-homeless, ex-hooker/escort, but he's also a drug dealer!'

My back falls against the wall and I look up to the harsh lighting, not even blinking back the powerful light when it burns my retinas. I'm banking on it burning away my troubles, too. 'Miller isn't a drug dealer,' I say calmly. It would be so easy to fly off the handle right now.

'And that Sophia bird, I haven't figured out who she is yet, but she can't be good news. I mean –' he laughs – 'kidnap?'

'She's in love with Miller.'

'And poor Nan,' Gregory goes on. 'She welcomed William to her dinner table like they were old friends.'

'They are.' I reluctantly acknowledge that I should perhaps find out how friendly they are, but I'm also mindful that Nan is delicate, and stirring up old ghosts would be stupid. I drop my head on a sigh, not that he notices. Gregory is well into his stride, keen to get his conclusions out there.

'He was there every day when you were . . .' He finally pulls up, his neck recoiling on his wide shoulders. 'They are?'

'He knew my mother.' I know those words will begin an outburst of questioning, so I hold my hand up when he draws breath. 'Miller does work for those people and they won't let him quit. He's trying to find a way.'

He's scowling. 'What's that got to do with the Godfather?'

I can't help but smile at his quip. 'He was my mother's pimp. He and Miller's boss don't get along. He's trying to help.'

He can't hide his wide eyes. They're like saucers. 'Fuuuuuck . . .'

'I'm tired, Gregory. I'm tired of feeling so frustrated and helpless. You're my friend, and I'm asking you not to enhance it.' I sigh, all of those feelings magnifying anyway, simply because of my own admission. 'I need you to be my friend. Please, just be my friend.'

'Well, damn,' he murmurs, dropping his head in shame. 'Now I just feel like a hundred tonnes of first-class shit.'

I want to ease his obvious guilt, tell him he doesn't need to as long as he quits right here, yet the strength to do that is nowhere to be found. I push my back from the wall and drag myself towards the exit. I might be highly pissed off at Miller, yet I also know he's the only one who can comfort me.

A tentative palm slides onto my shoulder and his legs match my pace. But he says nothing, probably too scared to send me further into despondency. I look up at my best friend as he pulls me a little closer, but he remains focused forward. 'Aren't you going to see Nan?'

He shakes his head with a rueful smile. 'I'll Skype her on that fancy television. She gets all excited.'

'It has Internet?'

'And a phone, but she likes seeing me.'

'Nan's been using the Internet?'

'Yep. A lot. William's been constantly topping up her credit. Must have cost him a fortune in the past few days. She's hooked.'

I laugh. 'How's Ben?'

'We're getting there.'

I smile, delighted by this news. It can mean only one thing. 'I'm glad. Have you got your van?'

'Yes. You want me to take you somewhere?'

'Yes, I do.' I smile and snuggle deeper into his chest. I'm not going with Ted. 'Can we go to the bistro, please?'

Chapter 9

Gregory's phone starts ringing as he pulls up around the corner from the bistro, and he lifts his arse from his seat to rummage through the pocket of his trousers as I open the door.

'I'll call you later,' I say, leaning across to peck his cheek. He frowns down at the display. 'What's the matter?'

'Hold up.' He signals for me to wait a moment by holding up one finger as he answers. 'Hello.' Relaxing back in my seat, my hand resting on the handle of the open door, I watch as he listens intently for a few seconds. Then he seems to shrink into his seat. 'She's with me.'

I cringe, wince, and grit my teeth all at once, then instinctively dive from the van and shut the door, my feet working fast to carry me across the road. I should have anticipated a search party after leaving Ted waiting for me at the hospital and ignoring numerous calls from Miller *and* William.

'Olivia!' Gregory shouts.

I pivot when I'm safely on the other side of the road, seeing him shaking his head at me. I shrug guiltily, but only because I neglected to advise Gregory that Ted was waiting for me under William's instruction. I didn't intentionally drag him into the centre of locking horns.

Raising my hand in a little wave, I turn my back on my friend and slip down a side street that'll take me to the bistro. But I'm cringing all over again when my fancy iPhone starts chiming "I'm Sexy and I Know It" from my satchel. 'Damn,'

I mutter, pulling it out, howling on the inside at my choice of ringtone for my best friend.

'Gregory,' I say, maintaining my determined stride.

'You devious sod!'

I laugh and check the traffic before crossing the road. 'I'm not devious. I just didn't tell you I had a driver for the day.'

'Damn it, Olivia! William isn't happy, and I've just had Mr Screw-Loose call me, too.'

'Miller?' I don't know why I asked. Who else could Mr Screw-Loose be?

'Yes. Jesus, baby girl! When did being your friend become a hazardous job? I fear for my spine, my bones . . . my fucking pretty face!'

'Chill out, Gregory.' I jump when a car horn honks at me and put my hand up in apology as I make it to the pavement. 'I'll check in with them both now.'

'Make sure you do,' he grunts.

This is ridiculous, and I'm now weighing up the lesser of two evils. My self-inflicted solitary life was a little stifling but far easier to deal with, as it was me, myself, and I who controlled the reins. No one else. I feel like Miller awakened me, set me free, just like he's said, yet now he's trying to take away that sense of freedom, and I'm beginning to resent him for it. Gregory's supposed to be on my side. I'll be damned if they're dragging my best friend over to the dark side. 'Whose friend are you?'

'Huh?'

'You heard me. Whose friend are you? Or have you and William become bosom buddies since I've been away?'

'Funny, baby girl. Very funny.'

'I'm not trying to be funny. Answer the question.'

There's a brief pause followed by a long pull of breath. 'Yours,' he says as he exhales.

'I'm glad we've cleared that up.' I frown as I hang up on

Gregory, then check left and right before I cross the road to the bistro. My steps are light across the tarmac, almost skipping as I come closer to my place of work. I'm smiling, too.

'Olivia!'

The bellow, laced with dread, has me stopping in the middle of the road and swinging around. I hear car horns and more shouts of horror.

'Olivia! Move!'

I'm confused, looking around frantically, trying to figure out where and what the commotion is. It's then I see a black four-wheel drive coming at me. Fast. My mind is giving me all of the right instructions.

Move!

Run!

Get out of the way!

But my body is ignoring each and every one of them. They're in shock. I'm frozen. A sitting target.

All of the sound around me is drowned out by the repeated demands in my mind. The only thing I'm focused on is that car coming closer and closer and closer.

The screeching of tyres is what finally yanks me from my trance, then the pounding footsteps on tarmac. I'm rugby-tackled from the side and sent crashing down to the pavement. I'm stunned back to life by the impact, but my landing is soft. I'm disoriented. Confused. Then I'm suddenly moving, but not by my own volition, and I'm soon sitting up with Ted crouching in front of me. Where did he come from? I left him at the hospital.

'You're gonna get me sacked, girl,' he says, scanning my face quickly before checking my body for injuries. 'Fuck's sake,' he grumbles, helping me up.

'I'm . . . sorry,' I stammer over my words, totally shaken, while Ted brushes me down with constant huffs and puffs of irritation. 'I didn't see the car.'

'You weren't supposed to,' he mutters quietly, but I heard him loud and clear.

'Did someone purposely try to run me down?' I ask, dazed and motionless before him.

'Maybe a little warning, but let's not jump to conclusions. Where are you going?'

I indicate blindly over my shoulder to the bistro across the street, unable to tell him with words.

'I'll wait here.' He shakes his head as he pulls his phone from his pocket, giving me serious eyes that dare me to give him the slip again.

I turn on shaky legs, willing some solidity into them before I present myself to my work friends and they have a chance to suspect something is wrong. But something is very wrong. Someone may have just tried to mow me down, and if I take all of the worry that Miller has expressed in recent days, I can only conclude that the heavies, the immoral bastards, whatever you want to call them, are to blame. They're sending a message.

The smell and sounds of the bistro are familiar. It almost makes smiling easy.

'Oh my God! Livy!' Sylvie dives across the bistro, leaving endless customers with wide eyes as they follow her path to me. I remain where I am for fear of her crashing into the door if I move. 'It's so good to see you!' Her body collides with mine, knocking the wind right out of me.

'Hi,' I cough, but I'm frowning again when I catch sight of an unfamiliar face behind the counter of the bistro.

'How are you?' Sylvie steps back, her hands still on my shoulders, her pink lips pursed as she scans my face.

'I'm fine,' I say, no matter how much I'm not, distracted by the girl behind the counter tackling the coffee machine like she's been here for years.

'I'm glad,' Sylvie says, smiling. 'And Miller?'

'He's good,' I confirm, suddenly feeling awkward, my feet

shifting nervously. A surprise holiday, that's what she thinks. After our ups and downs, Miller whisking me off to have some quality time was a perfectly feasible excuse for my sudden absence. Del sounded surprised when I called him to let him know I'd be off for a week, yet he gave me his blessing and told me to have a nice time. Problem is, it's been more than a week.

My phone sings from my hand, and I'm again assessing the merits of not having one at all. Concealing the screen from Sylvie's prying eyes, I silence my phone. It's either Miller or William, and I still don't want to talk to either one.

'So how are things here?' I ask, using the only diversion tactic I have.

It works. Her shiny black bob swishes when she shakes her head on a tired exhale. 'Stupidly busy, and Del's catering for more events than ever.'

'Livy!' Del appears at the swing door to the kitchen, quickly followed by Paul. 'When did you get back?'

'Yesterday.' I smile awkwardly, a little embarrassed that I didn't let him know. But it was all so sudden, and Nan consumed my mind from the moment Miller told me about her heart attack. Everything else was so inconsequential, including my job. Now that I'm here, though, I can't wait to get started again, once I ensure Nan has fully recovered.

'It's great to see you, darling.' Paul winks before returning to the kitchen, leaving Del wiping his hands on a tea towel. He casts a sideways glace to the girl, who's now handing a coffee to a waiting customer, then looks back at me with an embarrassed smile. I feel self-conscious all of a sudden – uncomfortable and out of place. 'I didn't know when you'd be back,' he starts. 'And we were run off our feet. Rose here inquired about vacancies and she fell right into it.'

My heart sinks into my Converse. I've been replaced, and by the look on Del's guilty face and the sound of his sorry voice, he doesn't plan on reinstating me. 'Of course.' I smile, feigning indifference to within an inch of my life. I can't blame him. I was hardly reliable in the weeks running up to my disappearance. As I watch Rose load the filter contraption of the coffee machine, an unreasonable sense of possessiveness seeps into me. The fact that she is performing the task with ease and with one hand when she reaches to grab a cloth isn't helping. I've been replaced, and worst of all, I've been replaced by someone more competent. I'm injured, and I'm exhausting every modicum of strength not to let it show.

'It's fine, Del. Honestly. I never expected you to keep my job open for me. I didn't think I would be gone for so long.' Looking down at the phone in my hand, I see Miller's name flashing up at me but I ignore it, forcing my smile to remain fixed on my face. 'Anyway, Nan's being released from the hospital tomorrow, so I need to be at home to take care of her.' It's ironic. All that time I used Nan as an excuse to keep me away from the big wide world so I could look after her, and now she really does need my help. And I really want to be in the big wide world. I feel untold guilt for allowing a little resentment to simmer deep within me. I'm beginning to resent everyone and everything. The people who are giving me freedom are the people snatching it away from me.

'Your grandmother's ill?' Sylvie asks, sympathy etched all over her face. 'You never said.'

'Oh, Livy, honey, I'm so sorry.' Del moves towards me, but I back away, feeling my emotions taking hold.

'It was just a scare, nothing major. They're discharging her tomorrow or Friday.'

'Oh, that's good. You take care of her.'

I smile as Sylvie rubs my arm. All of this empathy is unbearable. I need to escape. 'I'll see you,' I say, throwing a little wave to Del as I back out of the bistro.

'Make sure you keep in touch,' my ex-boss calls before returning to the kitchen and resuming business as usual – business as usual that doesn't include me anymore.

'Take care, Livy.' Sylvie looks guilty. She shouldn't. This isn't her fault, and in an attempt to ease it for her, to make her see I'm cool, I paste a huge smile on my face as I curtsy.

She laughs, turns on her biker boots, and sashays back to the counter, leaving me to shut the door on my old job and the people I became so fond of. My feet are heavy as they carry me across the pavement, and when I finally look up, I see a waiting car and Ted holding the back door open. I slide in without a word, the door shuts, and Ted's up front in no time, pulling into the afternoon London traffic. My low mood is obvious, as expected, yet I seem to have a taste for lowering it further.

'You knew my mother.' I utter the words quietly and get only a nod in response. 'I think she's back in London,' I say casually, like it's of no consequence if she is.

'I have instructions to take you home, Miss Taylor.' He ignores my observation, quickly telling me that Ted is going to remain tight-lipped – if, indeed, there's anything to know at all. I hope there's nothing to know, which begs the question why I'm digging at all. Nan will never cope.

I concede easily to Ted's coolness. 'Thank you for saving me,' I sigh, showing my white flag in the form of some gratitude.

'Anytime, Miss Taylor.' He keeps his eyes on the road, avoiding my stare in the rearview mirror.

Gazing blankly out the window, I watch the big, wide world go by as an even bigger black cloud descends, blanketing my favourite city in a gloomy darkness that matches my current state of mind.

Chapter 10

July 17 1996

Peter Smith

Investment Banker
46 – boring by name, wild by nature. The older man again. Married, but clearly not getting what he craves. I think he might crave me now.

Date one: Dinner at the Savoy

For starters, the best lobster salad I've tasted, but I'll reserve judgement until I've eaten at the Dorchester. For main, fillet steak and some well-aimed coy looks. For dessert, a tiramisu, rounded off with a diamond bracelet. Of course, I showed my gratitude in the penthouse suite before I slipped out. I think I might see this one again. He can do incredible things with his tongue.

I snap my mother's journal shut and toss it onto the couch next to me, annoyed with myself. Why am I putting myself through this again? Nothing I'll find could possibly make me feel better. I remember William once saying that she wrote this journal to torture him. And amid my own self-pity, I feel a little bit of sympathy for the man who's currently adding to my misery. She really was a wicked woman.

Plumping one of Nan's frilly cushions, I rest my head back, close my eyes, and try my damn hardest to blank my mind and relax. My hardest isn't enough, but I'm distracted when I hear someone come through the front door, then urgent footsteps approaching down the hall. Even before I open my eyes, I can picture the expensive leather shoes and the bespoke suit. Someone has his armour back.

Sure enough, there's Miller – in all his suited glory – standing on the threshold of the lounge. His dark waves are in disarray and despite his impassive face, his piercing blue eyes harbour fear.

'You bought more suits,' I state quietly, remaining reclined on the couch, regardless of the fact that I'm desperately craving his attention and touch.

His hand rakes through his hair, pulling the wayward wave off his forehead, and he sighs his relief. 'Just a few.'

Just a few? I bet he's replaced each and every one of the masks that I shredded.

'Del gave my job to someone else.'

I see him sag. He didn't think it appropriate for me to be working in a cafe, yet I know for sure he would never have forced me to stop. 'I'm sorry.'

'It's not your fault.'

He strides forward until he's towering over me, his hands resting lightly in his trouser pockets. 'I was worried about you.'

'I'm a big girl, Miller.'

'You're also my possession.'

'And I'm also a person with a mind of my own.'

He fails to prevent his lips from pursing in mild annoyance. 'Yes, a mind that overthinks, and not too clearly right now, either.' He crouches by the sofa next to me. 'Tell me your troubles, sweet girl.'

'You mean aside from the fact that someone tried to mow me down today?'

His eyes flash danger as his jaw sets, and I think for a moment that he might put it down to my lack of attention. But he doesn't speak, telling me everything I need to know.

'Everything.' I don't hesitate to go on. 'Everything is wrong. William, Nan, Gregory, my job.'

'Me,' he breathes, reaching for my cheek. The warmth of his skin on mine has my eyes closing and my face nuzzling into his touch. 'Don't give up on me, Olivia. I beg you.'

My chin trembles and I take his hand and tug my demand for his *thing*. He doesn't deny me, even though he's kitted from top to toe in the finest clothes money can buy, and he's only just bought them. His warm body comes down on mine and the softness of his lips finds my neck. I don't need to affirm my promise with words, so I let my body do the talking and cling to him everywhere.

I find that peace.

I find the serenity.

I find a familiar deep comfort that can be found nowhere else. Miller wreaks havoc on my mind, body, and heart. And he chases it away just as well.

We're still in the same position an hour later. We've not spoken, just happy to be together. It's dusk. Miller's new three-piece suit must be a crumpled mess, my hair has been twisted into various knots, and my arms have drained of blood, leaving pins and needles prickling at my skin.

'Are you hungry?' he asks into my hair, and I shake my head. 'Have you eaten today?'

'Yes,' I lie. I'm not up for food, my stomach won't take it, and if he tries to force-feed me, I might shoot him down with my waning sass.

He pushes himself up until he's braced on his forearms, gazing down on me. 'I'm going to put something casual on.'

'You mean you're going to put your shorts on.'

His eyes twinkle, his lips twitching. 'I'm going to make you feel comfortable.'

'I'm already comfortable.' My mind is invaded by images of a perfect bare chest on that one night. One night that has evolved into one lifetime. The one night when I thought I'd only get twenty-four hours but hoped for more. Even now, amid this nightmare, I don't regret accepting Miller's offer.

'*You* may be, but my new suit isn't.' A disgruntled look is thrown down his torso as he lifts his body from mine. 'I'll be quick. And I want you naked when I get back.'

I offer a demure smile as he backs out of the room, his eyes flicking to my figure in a silent prompt. His fiery gaze virtually burns the material from my body and the internal fizzing transforms into full-on scorching fire bolts. Then he's gone, leaving me worked up and with nothing to do other than as I'm bid, so I slowly strip down.

By the time I've cast my clothes aside, pulled the woollen throw down over me, and flicked the TV on, Miller is back, except he hasn't got his shorts on. He has nothing on. My appreciative eyes are riveted, my body aching for his attention. He stands before me, his strong legs slightly spread, his eyes lowered. His beauty defies the imaginable. He's the finest of masterpieces. He's incomparable. He's my possession.

'Earth to Olivia,' he whispers. I confront his penetrating eyes and watch, totally rapt, my lips parting to give me much needed air, as he blinks lazily. 'I've had a stressful day.'

Join the club, I think as I lift my hand and he takes it. I expect him to bring his body down to me, but I'm pulled from the couch, the woollen throw tumbling to the floor at my feet. He takes my hand around to my back and applies some pressure, pulling me into his chest. We're touching. Everywhere.

'Are you ready to de-stress me?' His hot breath spreads across my cheeks, heating them further. 'Are you ready for me to take you to that place where nothing exists, only us?'

I nod and let my lids fall shut when his spare hand slides onto the back of my head and his fingers start combing through my hair.

'Come with me.' His grip shifts to my nape and I'm turned and led from the room. We only make it halfway up the stairs, and I'm prevented from going any farther when he slides his hands onto my hips and tugs back gently. 'Brace your hands on a step.'

'On the stairs?' I look over my shoulder, seeing nothing but hunger pouring from every sharp edge of his being.

'On the stairs,' he confirms, reaching forward to take my hands and guide them to where they need to be. 'When we're old and grey, there'll be nowhere that I haven't worshipped you, Olivia Taylor. Comfortable?'

I nod my acceptance, hearing the ripping of a foil packet. I use the time it takes Miller to sheathe himself to try and prepare. He's tracing my back, his delicate touch drifting lightly over every piece of my exposed skin. My breathing is challenged. I'm soaking wet and trembling in anticipation, every troubled thought twisting my mind being chased away under his touch and attention. He is my escape. I am his. This is all I have. His attention and love. It's the only thing getting me through this.

Flexing my hands on the step and shifting my feet, I drop my head and watch as my hair tumbles to the carpet, and when I feel the hardness of his tip meet my opening, I hold my breath. He spends a few torturous moments circling a palm on my bottom, then tracing the line of my spine before he's back at my bum, separating my cheeks. My eyes clench tighter still as his finger makes a lazy path over my anal passage, the unaccustomed sensation advancing my shakes. I'm vibrating. My whole body is quivering. His cock is still held against my core, and with the added sensation of his finger teasing my other entrance, I'm left silently begging for penetration. In either place. 'Miller,' I breathe, moving my grip to the edge of the step to brace myself.

His soft touch slides down and back up over my passage,

pausing over the tight ring of muscle. I tense automatically, and he hushes me as his touch drifts down to my drenched core. I push back, attempting to gain some friction and failing when he withdraws his touch and takes my hips. He advances slowly, stealing my breath as his hard, muscled length slips into me; then he hisses, his grip tightening severely to the point of pain. I whimper, a mixture of unthinkable pleasure and mild pain that throws stars into my darkness. Miller throbs within me and every internal muscle I possess utterly dominates me. I'm a slave to the sensations. I'm a slave to Miller Hart.

'Move,' I demand, dragging my limp head up and gazing to the ceiling. 'Move!'

A sharp inhale resonates from behind me, his fingers flexing on my hips. 'Becoming quite the demanding lover, aren't you?' He remains still, and I attempt to thrust back, but find no benefit, only his hold locking me in place. 'Savoured, Olivia. We do this my way.'

'Fuck,' I whisper hoarsely, searching deep for some calm and control. I'm being held in no-man's-land, helpless and unable to generate the friction my body needs. 'You always say you never make me do anything you know I don't want to.'

'Huh?'

If I wasn't so focused on my current desperation, I'd laugh at his genuine confusion.

'You don't want to be worshipped?' he asks.

'No, I don't want to be held in limbo!' There's no calm to be found anywhere. I've given up trying to locate any. 'Miller, please, just make me feel good.'

'Oh shit, Olivia!' He rears back painfully slowly and hovers there, now only a fraction within me. He's still, but his ragged panting matches mine, and I know he's struggling to maintain his control. 'Beg me.'

My teeth grit and I fly back, shouting my satisfaction when he hits me deep and hard.

'Fuck, Olivia!' He removes himself, leaving me whimpering quiet pleas. 'I can't hear you.'

I feel defeated, my scrambled mind frantically searching for the simple words I need to meet his demand.

'Beg!' His shout shocks me, and I feebly attempt to shoot back again. But I'm trapped, helpless in his hold as his tall, powerful frame remains poised behind me, waiting for me to fulfil his harsh request. 'I've asked twice,' he puffs, his breathing laboured. 'Listen to me, Olivia.'

'Please.'

'Louder!'

'Please!' I shout, and follow it up with a scream when his hips fire forward, harder than I was expecting. I focus my attention on tightly moulding every internal muscle around him, making the friction when he withdraws out of this world. My arms straighten to steady me, just as he plunges deep again, and my chin drops to my chest lifelessly.

'I'm watching my cock lose itself inside of you, sweet girl.'

Everything aligns, sending me to that faraway place of utter bliss. We establish a steady tempo after a few more drives; our bodies are again in tune and gliding effortlessly together. He's persistently groaning and mumbling incoherent, pleasure-filled words while sustaining his meticulous pace. I'm in awe of his control, yet mindful it's something he struggles with. I lift my head and look over my shoulder, finding every mesmerising trait that I love: parted, moist lips; a tight, shadowed jaw; and when he rips his rapt attention away from his arousal slipping in and out of me, the package is complete and I'm staring into gleaming, sharp blues eyes.

'Do you always struggle?' I ask my question on a wisp of air as he thrusts smoothly forward.

He shakes his head lazily, knowing what I'm referring to, and grinds deeply into me. 'Not with you.'

The strength I need to keep my head turned to look at him

vanishes and I return forward, letting a knee rest on the step when my legs begin to wobble. His plunges are constant. And the pleasure is endless. My arms bend and my forehead meets the step. Then I feel the warmth of his chest blanket my back, forcing my body flush to the stairs. We remain locked together until Miller is lying the length of me and he continues wreaking havoc on my senses, his lips now in perfect position to dance lightly across the top of my back.

'Shall we?' he asks, just as my arm flies out and my hand wraps around one of the balustrades on the stairs.

'Yes.'

His rhythm increases yet remains controlled, and I squeeze my eyes shut as a switch flicks and my orgasm is suddenly charging forward. There's no holding it back, especially when Miller's teeth clamp down on my shoulder and he jolts forward unexpectedly.

'Miller!' My body temperature is increasing by the second, my skin starting to burn.

'That's it, Livy.' Forward he snaps again, flinging me into his realm of indescribable pleasure. 'Scream my name, gorgeous girl.'

'Miller!'

'Fuck, that sounds good.' He hits me with another hard but controlled advance of his hips. 'Again!'

Everything around me blurs – vision, hearing. 'Miller!' I reach the pinnacle and burst in a hazy fog of stars, my focus set solely on riding out the delicious waves of pleasure ruling me. 'Oh God!' I pant. 'Oh God, oh God, oh God!'

'I concur,' he gasps, lazily grinding into me. 'I *fucking* concur.'

I'm reduced to a useless mass of twitching body parts, trapped beneath him, relishing in the continuous throbbing of his cock held deep inside of me as he finds his own climax. My knuckles are numb and white from my grip of the balustrade, I'm heaving and wheezing, and I'm drenched. I'm perfect.

'Olivia Taylor, I think I'm addicted to you.' His teeth graze my shoulder, dropping delicate kisses between light bites, and he grabs and tugs my hair, forcing my head up. 'Let me taste you.' I let him take everything from me as we remain stretched out on the stairs, the roughness of the carpet on my damp skin only mildly registering in my blissed-out mind. He sucks my bottom lip into his mouth and applies a little pressure with his teeth before pecking his way to my cheek.

My worn-out muscles protest, trying defiantly to cling to him when he carefully slides out of me. I'm helped to turn around and positioned on a step, Miller kneeling in front of me. The concentration on his flawless face holds my attention while he spends a few silent moments arranging my hair over my shoulders. He doesn't pass up the opportunity to twiddle a few strands. His eyes catch mine. 'Are you real, sweet girl?'

I reach forward on a smile and pinch his nipple, but he doesn't wince or yelp. He returns my smile and leans in to kiss my forehead affectionately. 'Come on. Let's go be vegetables.' He pulls me to my feet and guides me back down the stairs by my nape.

'Have you ever watched television?' I ask as Miller makes himself comfortable on the sofa, ready to veg. I can't imagine Miller watching television, just like I can't imagine him doing most normal things. He reclines and gestures for me to join him, so I lie on his chest, face tucked neatly under his chin, my body falling between his thighs when he spreads them.

'Would you like to watch television?' he asks, taking my hand and bringing it to his mouth.

I ignore that he hasn't answered my question and reach for the remote control with my spare hand. The screen jumps to life, and I immediately smile when I'm confronted with Del and Rodney Trotter. 'You must have watched *Only Fools and Horses*.' It's a national treasure!

'Can't say I have.'

'Really?' I blurt, swinging my astonished face up to his. 'Just watch it. You'll never look back.'

'As you wish,' he agrees quietly, beginning to knead lovely firm circles into my nape. 'Anything you wish.'

I'm only watching the television, not hearing any of the banter, as my mind wanders to a place where Miller's words were true. Anything I wish. I compile a mental list of things I'd wish for, smiling when I feel the vibrations of a suppressed laugh beneath me. My part-time, refined gentleman is amused by the antics playing out on the screen before us, and the normalcy of that fills me with contentment, no matter how trivial it is.

And then the moment is shattered by the sound of Miller's phone ringing in the distance.

A few easy movements has me minus one Miller beneath me and immediately resentful of his phone. 'Excuse me,' he mutters as he carries his naked body from the room. I watch as he disappears, smiling at the vision of his butt cheeks tensing and swelling with his long strides, then curl onto my side and retrieve the woollen throw from the floor.

'I have her,' he virtually growls, walking back into the room. I roll my eyes. There's only one other man who would be asking where I am, and I have no desire to face him and his displeasure over my AWOL performance today. I wish my fraudulent gentleman wouldn't make me sound like a possession all of the time, or, as the case might be now, a felon. I look to the end of the couch when he rests his arse on the edge, the contentment of a few moments ago vanished. 'I was busy,' he hisses, then follows it up with a flick of his eyes to mine. 'Is that all?'

My resentment multiplies, and it's now held solely for William Anderson. It seems to have become his life goal to make my life as difficult and as miserable as possible. I'd love to snatch the phone from Miller's angry grasp and spit a few choice words down the line.

'Well she's with me, she's safe, and *I'm* done explaining, Anderson. We'll reconvene tomorrow. You know where to find me.' He tosses his phone down, all bristly and worked up.

'Who was that?' I ask, smiling when Miller gapes at me.

'Really, Olivia?'

'Oh, lighten up,' I breathe, swinging my legs off the sofa. 'I'm ready for bed. Coming?'

'I might tie you down.'

I recoil a little, frantically batting away the rapid influx of images that are dancing at the front of my mind, reminding me. Belts.

Miller visibly winces when he catches the unmistakable horror on my face. 'So you don't knee me in the balls,' he rushes to clarify. 'Because you're a terrible fidget in bed.' An awkward hand sweeps through his waves as he stands.

Humour chases away the flashbacks. I know I'm an awful fidget in my sleep. My bedcovers come morning are proof. 'Have I caught you in the crown jewels?'

He frowns. 'The what?'

'Crown jewels.' I smile. 'Balls.'

His hand comes towards me, but I keep my eyes on a face full of exasperation, relishing the fact that he's trying his utmost not to fuel my sass. 'Many times. Elbows in my ribs, knees in my balls, but they're a small price to pay for having you in my arms.'

I take his hand and let him pull me to my feet. 'I'm sorry.' I'm not sorry at all. I'd give anything to be a fly on the wall so I could watch my night-time shenanigans and Miller fighting to cope with them.

'I've already forgiven you, and I'll forgive you again tomorrow morning.'

I chuckle quietly but halt in the blink of an eye when the sound of a harsh knock at the door cuts into our light repartee. 'Who's that?' I ask, my eyes swinging to the window. My sass receives the proverbial equivalent of a douse of petrol to a spark. If William's made a special trip to express his displeasure personally, then my sass might burst into uncontrollable flames.

Miller's gone in a flash, taking the woollen throw with him, and I'm left butt-naked and alone in the lounge. I didn't like the anxious vibes emanating from him before he left. Not at all. Creeping on my tiptoes to the door, I peek down the hallway, seeing he's wrapped the throw around his waist and secured it by tucking the edge in, but he's still far from decent. So when he opens the door and steps out without a word or concern for his semi-naked body, my mind goes into overdrive. And then I catch a glimpse of shiny ebony locks before the door clicks shut.

My sass explodes into angry flames. 'The cheeky bitch!' I gasp to no one in particular, going in pursuit of Miller but pulling to a sharp halt when I allow the fact that I'm naked to worm past the anger. 'Shit!' I turn and sprint into the lounge, locate my clothes, and yank them on. I fly towards the source of my anger at a dangerous rate and wrench the door open, coming face-to-face with Miller's naked back, but I'm far too consumed by fury to appreciate it. I push him aside and let my angry eyes punch holes into Cassie's perfect frame, ready to hurl a torrent of verbal abuse her way.

Except she's not perfect today, and the shock of her pitiful state halts me dead in my tracks. She's pasty, almost grey in complexion, and the designer clothes she usually wears are nowhere to be seen. She has on black sweatpants and a dull grey roll-neck jumper. Hollow eyes cast away from Miller and fall onto me. Despite her personal crisis, it's clear she still has nothing but contempt where I'm concerned.

'Good to see you, Olivia.' There's not a scrap of sincerity in her tone.

Right on cue, Miller's palm finds my neck and begins a vain

attempt to rub my irritation away. I shrug him off and square my shoulders. 'What are you doing here?'

'Livy, go inside.' His grip is back on my neck and trying to turn me. He can forget it.

'I asked her a question.'

'And it's usually polite to answer, right?' Cassie retorts, full of smugness.

A red mist starts to descend. He doesn't only use that term with me? I've never thought about it, but now, having it thrown in my face by this lunatic bitch, it's all I can focus on. He sounds like an arrogant prick when he says it, yet the feeling of betrayal is there. And it's unwarranted and silly. All I can see in my mind is Cassie draped over Miller all those times, and then quickly I have a flashback of Miller's office and her lashing at him with sharp fingernails while she screamed, deranged.

'Cassie,' Miller warns, still attempting to direct me away from what could potentially be eruptions.

'Yeah, yeah,' she huffs on an over-the-top roll of her eyes.

'Will you quit?' I snap at Miller, shaking him off. 'After what she did to you last time, when she attacked you, do you truly expect me to go inside?'

'What about what he did to me?' Cassie blurts. 'The bruises have only just faded!'

'Then you shouldn't behave like an animal,' I hiss in her face as I step forward, fully aware that she wasn't the only one, and the other animal is beginning to bristle next to me.

'For fuck's sake,' Miller mutters, pulling me back to his side. 'Cassie, I told you earlier we'll deal with this tomorrow.'

'I want to deal with it now.'

'Deal with what?' I ask, my irritation flaring. 'And how the hell do you know where I live?' I look up at Miller. 'Did you tell her?'

'No.' He grits his teeth, his blue eyes now full of aggravation. 'No one knows I'm here.'

I throw my arm out in the general direction of Cassie. 'She does!'

'Olivia!' Miller shouts, pulling me back into him. I hadn't realised I was moving forward. Jesus, I feel like the devil has taken over my mind and body. I feel dangerous.

'Why is she here?' I shout. That's it. I've lost it. The shit-fest of today, of the past few months, in fact, has finally caught up with me. It's all going to spill out of me right now and Cassie is going to cop the lot.

'I came to apologise,' she says indignantly.

'What?'

'We said tomorrow,' Miller pipes up, pointing a finger in her face while he keeps a tight hold on me. 'I told you earlier to wait until tomorrow. Why the hell can't you just fucking listen for once?'

'Are you sorry?' I ask.

Her scowling eyes sink into me, then turn to Miller. 'Yes.'

'For what?' I press.

'For the way I've treated you.' She turns to me slowly. There's still no trace of genuineness. She's here because she doesn't want to lose Miller. She hates that he's leaving her behind, that he's leaving their dark world to find his light.

'He's mine now.' I pry Miller's hand from my arm and step forward. 'Body and soul, mine.' I ignore the pang of trepidation that arises as a result of the mild doubt Cassie is blatantly trying to conceal. I'm Miller's light, but in the same breath, I comprehend fully that he is a certain kind of darkness to me. But it's irrelevant. There is no me or him; there is only us. 'Do you understand?' She stares at me, and Miller remains quiet in the background, allowing me to have my say.

'I understand.'

I hold her stare for an age, not willing to be the one who backs down. I don't blink either. Eventually, it's Cassie who drops her gaze, and with that silent submission, I turn on my bare feet and leave them on the doorstep behind me.

I've nearly made it to the top of the stairs when I hear the front door close. 'Olivia.' His placid call of my name tears at my heartstrings and I turn, keeping a steadying grip on the banister. 'She needs out, too. I'm not leaving her behind. We've been stuck in this world together; we'll be leaving together.'

'Does she *want* out?'

'Yes,' he affirms as he steps forward. 'I can't see you sad.'

I shake my head. 'Impossible.'

'I've shut the door. That's it. It's just us in here now.'

'But the world is still outside, Miller,' I say quietly. 'And we need to open that door and face it.' I escape, leaving him downstairs in turmoil.

He needs his *thing* as much as I do, and I hate myself for depriving us both of it.

Chapter 11

Miller didn't deprive us of our *thing*. He joined me in bed within minutes and moved in close. I wanted to deny him, to hurt him for hurting me – even if he didn't do it directly. But I didn't move away from his delicious heat, my own need for solace outweighing the need to punish him.

He remained wrapped around my whole body the entire night, limiting my ability to wriggle and fidget, so we woke in the exact same position come morning. We didn't speak a word while we lay there as the sun rose. I knew he was awake because my hair was being twisted and his lips were pressing into my neck. Then his fingers drifted down my thigh and found me ready and willing for some worshipping. I was taken from behind, our bodies spooned, and there was still no murmur of words, just consistent laboured breathing. It was peaceful. It was calm. And we both came in unison on breathy gasps.

I was hugged fiercely while Miller bit into my shoulder, jerking within me, then released and pushed to my back before he settled on me. He still didn't speak and neither did I. My hair was swept from my face and our burning gazes held for an eternity. I think Miller said more through that intense look than he ever could have with words. Not even the elusive *I love you* would have told me what I saw in his eyes.

I was captivated.

I was under his potent spell.

He was speaking to me.

After ghosting his lips delicately over mine for a few

moments, he peeled himself away from me and went for a shower while I tangled myself in the sheets, thoughtful. His goodbye was a tender kiss in my hair and a drag of his thumb across my bottom lip. Then my phone was swiped from the bedside table and he played with it for a while before placing it in my hand and kissing each of my eyelids before he left. I didn't question him, letting him leave before I glanced down to find my Internet open on YouTube and Jasmine Thompson on the screen. I pressed Play and listened carefully while she sang "Ain't Nobody" to me. I lay there for a long time after she'd finished and the room fell back into silence. After finally convincing myself to get up, I showered and spent the morning cleaning the house, listening to the song on repeat.

Then I went to see Nan. I didn't protest when I found Ted outside. I didn't complain when he shadowed me all day. I didn't bite William's head off when I found him leaving the hospital on my arrival. I didn't retaliate when Gregory gave me another ticking off for implicating him in my crimes. And I didn't ignore any of Miller's text messages. But I *did* sag under the wave of disappointment when the consultant visited Nan and told her that she wasn't being discharged until tomorrow – something to do with sending her home with the right medication. She, of course, kicked up a stink, but not wanting to bear the brunt of a Nan-style tongue-lashing, I kept quiet the whole time.

Now I'm home, it's past nine, I'm sitting at the table in the kitchen, and I'm longing for the familiar scent of a hearty, stodgy meal. I can hear the low hum of the television from the lounge, where Ted has set up base, and I've heard the frequent sound of his mobile phone before he answers promptly and speaks in a low whisper, no doubt assuring either William or Miller that I'm here and I'm fine. I've made him endless cups of tea and chatted idly about nothing in particular. I even gently broached the subject of my mother again and got nothing, only a sideways glance and Ted's observation that I look just like her. He's told me nothing that I didn't already know.

My phone rings. I look down at the table where it's laid and raise surprised eyebrows when I see Sylvie's name flashing up at me.

'Hey,' I answer, thinking I've masked my hopelessness well.

'Hey!' She sounds out of breath. 'I'm running for the Tube but wanted to call you as soon as possible.'

'Why?'

'A woman came into the bistro earlier asking after you.'

'Who?'

'Don't know. She left pretty quick when Del asked who was asking.'

My back straightens in my chair, my mind racing. 'What did she look like?'

'Blonde, stunning, very well dressed.'

My heart catches up with my mind and commences to sprint. 'Around forty?'

'Late thirties, early forties. Do you know her?'

'Yeah, I know her.' My palm finds my forehead and my elbow rests on the table. Sophia.

'Rude cow,' Sylvie spits indignantly, and I huff my agreement, but what the hell is she doing tracking me down?

'What did you tell her?'

'Not much, just that you no longer work at the bistro. Who is she?'

I take a deep breath and sink back into my chair, injured at Sylvie's reminder that I no longer have a job. 'No one important.'

Sylvie laughs through her exertion – an insulted, disbelieving laugh. 'Sure,' she says. 'Anyway, just thought you should know. I'm at the station so my reception is gonna die any moment. Swing by next week. It would be nice to see you.'

'I will,' I agree, though there is no mistaking the lack of

enthusiasm in my voice. Stupidly, I don't want to see my replacement handling the coffee machine with precision or delivering the shop's famous tuna melts.

'Take care, Livy,' Sylvie says softly, and then cuts the call before I can give my assurance that I will. That reply wouldn't have been any more convincing than the previous agreement to swing by sometime.

I go to dial Miller but freeze when an unknown number illuminates my screen. I stare at my phone in my hand for a long, long while, trying to fathom the deep-seated sense of anxiety riddling me, telling me not to answer.

Of course, I ignore it and go right ahead and connect the call. 'Hello.' I sound timid and nervous. I am, yet I don't want whoever's on the other end of this call to know that, so when I get no response, I repeat myself, this time clearing my throat and forcing confidence into my tone. 'Hello?' There's nothing, no reply, no sound in the background. I draw breath to speak again, but I catch a familiar sound and end up holding the air that I've just inhaled. I hear words. A familiar voice with a foreign accent, all husky and low.

'Miller, darling, you know how I feel about you.'

I swallow my breath and battle to prevent myself choking on it.

'I know, Sophia.' Miller's reply is soft and accepting. It makes me feel nauseous.

'Then why have you been avoiding me?' she asks, equally as gentle. My mind is quickly building up the scene on the other end of this line. And I really don't like what I'm picturing.

'I needed a time-out.'

'From me?'

My bum lifts from the chair until I'm standing, waiting for Miller's response to that. I hear him sigh, and I definitely hear the chink of glass on glass. He's pouring a drink. 'From everything.'

'The other women, I accept. But do not run away from me, Miller. I'm different, yes?'

'Yes,' he agrees without hesitation. None whatsoever. My body develops the shakes, my heart is pounding in my chest, and my racing mind is making me dizzy.

'I missed you.'

'And I you, Sophia.'

The bile shoots from my stomach to my throat and an invisible grip wraps around my neck, choking me. I cut the call, not needing to hear any more. I suddenly can't breathe, overcome by fury. And yet, I'm perfectly calm as I pop my head around the lounge door to find Ted at the window, his suited body relaxed in his standing pose. He's pretty much been in the same position since we got home.

'I'm going to soak in the bath,' I tell his back, and he looks over his shoulder, smiling at me warmly.

'Will do you good,' he says, returning to face the window.

I leave him on watch and go upstairs to get dressed. I'm trying to think straight, trying to recall Miller's words to Sophia, Sophia's words to me, Miller's words to me *about* Sophia. It's all gone, leaving a mammoth void in my mind to conjure up plenty of other thoughts – none of which I like. I knew she was different, someone to be more wary of. I slip on some skinny jeans and a satin camisole. I avoid my Converse, stepping into my black stilettos instead. A ruffle of my hair to bring out the waves and a dusting of powder finishes me off. Then I grab my purse, creep down the stairs, and wait for my moment to slip out the door unnoticed. My moment comes in the form of a call on Ted's mobile. He turns his back to the window and starts to pace around the lounge, talking quietly. Letting myself quietly out the door, I set off with absolutely no urgency. The anger is dominating me. So why on earth do I feel so calm?

*

The doormen are holding court at the entrance to Ice, armed with their clipboards, causing me an immediate predicament. The moment one of them clocks me, I'll be reported to Ice HQ and Tony will be in pursuit. I *really* don't need that. Resting my back against the wall, I run through my limited options . . . and come up with none. I'm not daft enough to think the doorman won't recognise me, so aside from a convincing disguise, I'm not getting in that club without warning bells going off.

My whole being was so full of purpose from the moment I disconnected that call. One obstacle has chased away that fortitude and left a little room for sensibility to take hold. I allow myself to consider the consequences of my intended actions for a moment, and I actually begin to comprehend the danger I'm putting myself in, but then a commotion from across the road snaps me from my deliberating and pulls my attention to the entrance. A group of four men with their girlfriends are all ranting, and the doormen are clearly trying to pacify the rankled group. It doesn't seem to be working, and my back pushes away from the wall when the scene moves to a whole new level of disturbance. One of the women steps up to a doorman, screaming in his face, and his hands come up in a gesture to suggest she should calm down. His attempt has the opposite effect and within a second, four men are all diving on him. My eyes widen at the chaos unfolding. It's anarchy. Yet I quickly register that this could be my only opportunity to slip in undetected.

I hurry across the road, being sure to keep as close to the wall as possible. I make it into the club unnoticed. I know exactly where I'm going now, and I walk with steady, even paces, my earlier calmness and purpose returning the closer I get to Miller's office. But now I'm confronted with another obstacle. My shoulders sag. I'd forgotten about the keypad code required to enter Miller's office. I didn't think this through properly at all.

What now? The element of surprise won't work if I have to

knock, and he'll see me on the camera before I get to the door anyway. 'Idiot,' I mutter. 'Fucking idiot.' Taking a deep breath, I straighten my camisole and close my eyes for a few seconds in an attempt to gather my wits. I feel relatively calm, yet anger still burns in my gut. *Damaging* anger. It's all contained, although that may change once I face Miller.

I'm standing in front of the door, under the watch of the camera, before I've even instructed my legs to carry me there, and I'm knocking it calmly in quick succession. As I knew they would, Miller's eyes widen in alarm when he throws the door open, but in the blink of an eye, he has that impassive mask back in place. I begrudgingly note how spectacular he looks. But his jaw is tight, his eyes warning, and his chest is heaving.

He steps out and pulls the door behind him, swiping his hand through his hair. 'Where's Ted?'

'At home.'

His nostrils flare and he whips his phone out, dialling urgently. 'Get your fucking driver here,' he spits down the line, before punching in a few more buttons and taking the phone back to his ear. 'Tony, I won't ask how the fuck Olivia got past you.' He's whispering, but the hushed tone doesn't eliminate the authority. 'Come and get her, and watch her until Ted arrives. Don't let her out of your sight.' He stuffs his phone in his inside pocket and hits me with blazing eyes. 'You shouldn't have come here, not when things are so delicate.'

'What's delicate?' I ask. 'Me? Am I the delicate thing you don't want to break or upset?'

Miller leans into me, slightly lowering his frame to get our faces level. 'What are you talking about?'

'You think I'm fragile and weak.'

'I think you're being forced to deal with things that are beyond your ability, Olivia,' he whispers, making it plain and clear. 'And I haven't got a fucking clue how to make it less painful for you.'

Our stares hold for the longest time, mine lifting to maintain our connection when he straightens up, rising to his full height. The agony in his expression nearly floors me.

'Are you trying to send me over the edge?' he whispers, not coming closer to comfort me. I need his *thing*, so I move in, but he steps back, shaking his head in warning. Realisation dawns fast, and I glance up at the security camera above the door. She's watching us.

'Why is she here?' My voice is even and strong.

'Who?' Miller's face is guarded and guilty. 'No one's here.'

'Don't lie to me.' My chest begins to puff under the strain to breathe through my anger. 'How much did you miss her?'

'What?' He checks over his shoulder again, and I seize the opportunity, using his momentary lapse in focus to push past him. 'Olivia!'

I land in his office less ladylike than I would have hoped, but I soon find my composure, flicking my hair over my shoulder and tucking my purse under my arm. Then I smile as I cast my eyes to where I know she'll be. I'm not wrong. Reclined in Miller's office chair, legs crossed, wearing a cream trench coat and drawing on a long, slender cigarette, is Sophia. The air of superiority suffocating me is potent. She's smiling slyly, looking at me with interest. It's only now I wonder how she got my number. It's inconsequential. She wanted to pull me from my hiding place and she's succeeded. I've played right into her hands.

'Sophia.' I make sure I'm the first to break the painful silence, and I also ensure I hold my own. 'It looks like you beat me to him this evening.' I detect two things the moment I finish speaking – Sophia's mild surprise because I can see it plain and clear in the slight parting of her red lips, and Miller's unease multiplying by a million, because I can feel him twitching behind me. 'I'll just help myself to a drink before I leave.'

My high heels carry me across to the drinks cabinet and I pour myself a tall, straight vodka.

'Sweet girl, I'm not stupid.' Sophia's haughty tone makes my confidence vanish.

I close my eyes and try to steady my trembling hands, and when I'm sure I've reined in my shakes, I take the glass and turn to face my spectators. I'm being regarded carefully by both parties – Sophia thoughtful, Miller nervous – as I slowly bring the highball to my lips. 'I'm not sure what you mean.' I swig the whole glass back and gasp before filling it again.

The tension in the room is palpable. I look across to Miller, only mildly registering condemnation on his face. I swig my second glass and slam it down, making him physically flinch. I want Miller to feel what I'm feeling. I want to take that resilient part of him and hurt it. It's all I know.

'I mean,' Sophia starts confidently, looking at me with a slight curve on her red lips, 'you're in love with him and you think you can have him. You can't.'

I don't deny her conclusion. 'Because *you* want him.'

'I have him.'

Miller doesn't argue with her or put her straight, and when I look at him, I see that there is no intention to. I can't even locate the sensibility to convince myself that there must be good reason, so pouring another shot of vodka for good measure, I saunter across to him. He's standing like a statue by the door, hands in pockets, clearly brimming with aggravation. He looks at me with the expressionless, emotional beauty that captured me in the first place. It's rife. His defence mechanism is on lockdown. I stop before his tall, motionless form and gaze up, noting the slight pulse of his dark stubbled jaw. 'I hope you're happy in your darkness.'

'Don't fucking push me, Olivia.' His mouth barely moves, his words hardly audible, but they are loaded with threat . . . which I totally ignore.

'See you around.' I slam the door behind me and navigate the maze of corridors urgently, finding the stairs and taking them two at a time while knocking back my third vodka, eager to get to the bar and maintain the numbness that the alcohol has incited.

'Livy?'

I look up and see Tony and Cassie standing at the top of the stairs, both frowning down at me. I have nothing to say to either of them, so I bypass them and round the corner to the main club.

'Livy,' Tony calls. 'Where's Miller?'

I swing around, finding both of their expressions have morphed into worry. And I know why. 'In his office,' I say, walking backwards so as not to delay my escape. 'With Sophia.' Tony curses and Cassie looks genuinely worried, but I don't waste time evaluating the cause for their concern. My overwhelming need to stake my claim is there, but so is the need to hurt Miller after hearing that call and Sophia state with such confidence that Miller belongs to her. I know he doesn't, he knows he doesn't, but his lack of input and the memory of him telling her he missed her has fired me up.

Weaving my way through the crowd, the powerful beats of NiT GriT's "Prituri Se Planinata" assaulting my hearing, I arrive at the bar and slam down my empty glass with a twenty. 'Vodka and tonic,' I demand. 'And a tequila.' My order is delivered hastily, my change just as fast, and I'm throwing back the tequila immediately, followed closely by the vodka. The liquid burns its way down to my stomach, making me close my eyes and feel out my throat. It doesn't deter me, though. 'Same again,' I shout once he's done with the guy next to me. The numbing of everything – my mind, my body, my heart – is intensifying with every swig of alcohol, the feeling of misery slipping away fast. I like it. A certain sense of detachment is building.

I lean against the bar and cast my eyes across the club. My gaze drifts over the hordes of people, taking my time, my drink poised at my lips, wondering whether my lack of urgency to lose myself amid the crowds and wreak havoc on my part-time gentleman's sanity is my subconscious telling me not to be rash, that I need to stop drinking, sober up and think hard about what's happening and why.

Maybe.

Probably.

Undoubtedly.

I may be on my way to a drunken stupor, but I can still appreciate that dormant reckless gene that had me willingly seeking out my mother's clients and lowering myself to a level that I can't bear to accept. Feeling the familiar fizzing of internal fireworks, my eyes dart around the club less casually now, more panicked, and I catch sight of him stalking towards me.

Oh shit. Any notion I had that Miller wouldn't rein me in under the circumstances has just been dramatically crushed. He looks homicidal, and I'm clearly the sole focus of his anger.

He makes it to me, his lips straight, his eyes dark, and takes the drink from my hand. 'Never serve this girl again,' he barks over my shoulder, keeping his eyes on me.

'Yes, sir,' comes a timid reply from behind.

'Get out,' Miller breathes down on me. He's barely containing himself. A quick flick of my eyes over his shoulder confirms Sophia is standing across the club, chatting with a man, but her eyes are rooted firmly in our direction. Interested eyes.

My shoulders square of their own volition and I reclaim my drink from behind me. 'No,' I whisper before taking a sip.

'I've asked once.'

'And I've told you once.'

He reaches for my glass again, but I pull away and attempt

to escape by dipping past Miller. I don't get far before Miller's grip on the top of my arm stops me. 'Let go.'

'Don't cause a scene, Olivia,' he says, snatching the drink from my hand. 'You are not staying in my club.'

'Why?' I ask, unable to stop him from pushing me on. 'Because I'm interfering with your *business*?' I'm yanked to a stop and swung around.

He pushes his face to mine, so close I'm certain it could look like he's kissing me from afar. 'No, because you have a fucking nasty habit of letting other men taste you when you're pissed off with me.' His eyes drop down to my mouth, and I can tell he's fighting the urge to tackle it – to taste me. His hot breath on my face burns away some of my anger, making way for another heat. But he pulls back, face straightening as he takes a step away from me. 'And I won't think twice about breaking them in half,' he whispers.

'I'm really pissed off with you.'

'So am I.'

'You said you missed her. I heard it, Miller.'

'How?' He doesn't even deny it.

'Because she called my phone.'

His breathing deepens. I can see it and I can hear it. I'm claimed and swung around, being pushed on harshly.

'Trust me,' he spits. 'I need you to trust me.'

He shoves me roughly through the crowd as I try to desperately cling to my faith in him. My legs are unstable and my mind even more so. People are watching us, standing back and moving aside as they throw inquisitive looks at us. I spend no time studying their faces . . . until I clap eyes on a familiar one.

My eyes fix on the man, my head turning slowly as we pass to maintain my view. I know him, and by the look of recognition on his face, he knows me, too. He smiles and moves to intercept us, leaving Miller no option but to stop. 'Hey, no need to escort the young lady out,' he says, tipping his drink to

Miller. 'If she's too intoxicated, I'll happily take responsibility of her.'

'Move.' Miller's tone is deadly. 'Now.'

The guy shrugs mildly, unaffected, or simply unbothered by the threat lacing Miller's words. 'I'll save you the hassle of ejecting her.'

My eyes drop from his intent stare, thinking hard. Where do I know him from? But then I flinch and step back when I feel my hair being played with. The cold chills creeping onto my neck tell me it's not Miller indulging in the feel of my wild blonde. It's the stranger.

'Feels just like it did all those years ago,' he says wistfully. 'I'd pay just for the pleasure of smelling it again. I've never forgotten this hair. Still turning tricks?'

All breath is sucked from my lungs when realisation sucker punches me in the stomach. 'No,' I gasp, moving back and colliding with Miller's chest.

The heat and tremors firing off him and soaking into me are all indicative of psychotic Miller, yet the focus I need to appreciate that danger is being sucked up by unrelenting flashbacks – flashbacks I've managed to push to the back of my mind. I can't now. This man has awakened them, brought them thundering forward. They make me grip my head with my hands, make me wince and shout in frustration. They won't go. They're attacking me, forcing me to witness a mental re-run of encounters from my past that I've wrestled to the dark, hidden place at the back of my mind for so long. Now they've been set free and nothing can stop them from charging forward. Memories are circulating repeatedly, burning into the back of my eyes. 'No!' I shout, my hands shifting to my hair and yanking, knocking the stranger's grip from my strands.

I feel my body cave under the shock and distress, every muscle giving up on me, yet I don't fold to the floor, and that is because the vice-like grip on my upper arm is holding me up. I'm numb to my surroundings, everything dark from my clenched eyes, everything silent from my mental lockdown. But that doesn't rid me of my awareness to the ticking bomb holding on to me.

He's gone from beside me in the blink of an eye, leaving me crumbling to the floor from my lack of support. My palms slap the hard ground, sending shock waves up my arms, and my hair tumbles around me. The sight of my golden tresses pooling in my lap makes me feel sick; it's all I can see, so I throw my head up and choke on nothing when I face the stomach-turning sight of Miller in psychotic action. It's all in slow motion, making every bloodcurdling collide of his fist to the guy's face repulsively clear. He's relentless, repeatedly striking his victim over and over, roaring his rage as he does. The music has stopped. People are screaming. But not one person steps forward to intervene.

I sob, wincing constantly as Miller continues to rain punches into the man's face and body, spraying blood everywhere. There's no fight in the poor guy. He isn't being given any opportunity to fight back. He's completely helpless.

'Stop him!' I scream, catching sight of Tony to the side, looking on with dread on his rough face. 'Please, stop him.' I drag myself from the floor with some determined effort. No one in their right mind would try to intervene. I painfully accept that, and when the focus of Miller's rage collapses lifelessly to the floor and Miller still doesn't relent, starting to kick him in the stomach, I succumb to my need to escape.

I can't watch anymore.

I run away.

I'm sobbing as I fight my way through the crowds, my face stinging and swollen from my tears, not that anyone notices. Everyone's attention is still on the mayhem behind me, the sick arseholes unable to tear their eyes away from the gruesome scene unfolding. I stagger and stumble, distraught and disorientated, to the entrance of Ice. Making it to the pavement outside, I cry gut-wrenching tears, my body shaking uncontrollably as I frantically search out a cab to take me away, but my opportunity to escape is lost when I'm grabbed from behind. It's not Miller; I know that much. There are no fireworks or burning need rising within me.

'Inside, Livy.' Tony's troubled voice sinks into my ears and I'm on the move with not a hope of fighting him off.

'Tony, please,' I beg. 'Please, let me go.'

'Not a fucking chance.' He guides me to the stairs that lead down to the maze under Ice. I don't understand. Tony hates me. Why would he want me to stay when Miller needs to focus on *this world*? A world that's now all too clear.

'I want to leave.'

'You're going nowhere, girl.'

I'm being pulled and pushed around corners, down corridors. 'Why?'

The door to Miller's office is opened and I'm pushed inside. I turn to face Tony, finding his stocky body heaving, his jaw tight. A finger comes up and points in my face, making me recoil slightly. 'You're not leaving, because when that maniac has finished beating that man to death, he's gonna be asking for you. He's gonna want to see *you*! And I'm not risking him going in for round two when he can't find you, Livy! Stay where you fucking are!' He walks out, slamming the door ferociously, leaving me standing in the middle of Miller's office, eyes wide, heart thundering.

There's still no music coming from the club above. I'm alone and useless in the bowels of Ice, with only stark silence and Miller's stark office for company. 'Arhhhhhhhhhhh!' I scream in a delayed reaction to Tony's tactic, my hands delving into my treacherous blonde and wrenching aimlessly, like I can pull the events of the past half hour from my head. 'I hate you!' My eyes wince shut from the physical pain I'm causing myself, the tears kicking in again. I don't know how long I spend pointlessly wrestling with myself, it feels like eons, and it's only physical exhaustion and a sore scalp that make me stop. I whimper as I turn in circles, my mind a riot, unwilling and unable to let any cognitive thought settle and calm me. It's only the sight of Miller's drinks cabinet that pulls the futile whirling of my body to a stop.

Alcohol.

I run over and clumsily pull a random bottle from the throng of others, sniffling and choking on my emotions as I unscrew the cap and tip it to my lips. The instant scald of the alcohol on my throat works wonders at burning away the focus of my thoughts, leaving me gasping and wincing at the discomfort and potent taste.

So I drink some more.

I gulp it all down until the bottle is empty and I'm hurling it across Miller's office in a temper, annoyed and deranged. My eyes fall onto the masses of other bottles and I randomly select and swig, turning and staggering over to the bathroom. I collide with the wall, the door, the frame, until I'm propped up against the vanity unit and staring at a mess of a woman in the mirror. Tears black with mascara are streaming down my flushed cheeks, my eyes are glazed and haunted, and my heavy blonde hair is an array of tangled waves, framing my pale face.

I see my mother.

I look at my reflection with utter contempt, like it's my arch-enemy, like it's the thing I hate most in the world.

Right now . . . it is.

Lifting the bottle to my lips, I glug down more alcohol while holding my own eyes. Then I take a deep breath and stumble over to Miller's desk. I pull drawers open, swipe my hands through the precisely placed items within, messing up his perfectly neat arrangements, until I find what I'm looking for. I gaze down at the shiny metal as I flex my hand around the handle, taking sporadic sips from the bottle while I think.

After staring blankly at my find for an eternity, I stand and wobble back to the bathroom, slamming the bottle down on the counter. I look up at myself, noting an expressionless face, and bring my hand to my head. Clenching a massive chunk of hair, I open the scissors and snap them shut around my locks, leaving me with a handful of blonde and a scraggy section of hair that's half the length it once was. Strangely, stress seems to flow out of me. So I grab another section and hack it off, too.

'Olivia!'

I let my drunken head flop to the side where I find Miller at the doorway of the bathroom. He's a wreck. His dark waves are a chaotic mess, his face and collar are splattered with blood, his suit is ripped, and he's wet through. His chest is heaving, but I'm unsure whether it's a result of exertion or if he's shocked by what he's found. My expression remains straight, and it's only now, when I'm seeing the horror on his notoriously impassive face, that I remember all of the times he's warned me never to cut my hair.

So I pull at another section and take the scissors to it, chopping away manically.

'Olivia, fuck, no!' His body flies towards me like a bullet fired from a gun and his hands start to grapple with me.

'No!' I scream, twisting away, holding on fiercely to the scissors. 'Leave me! I want it gone!' I throw my elbow back into his ribs.

'Fuck!' Miller yells. His teeth are clenched, the pain clear in his tone, yet he refuses to give up. 'Give me the fucking scissors!'

'No!' I haul myself forward, finding myself suddenly free, and swing around wildly, just as Miller comes at me. My hands fly up instinctively, my body going into protective mode, and his tall, lean body collides with me, knocking me back a few paces.

'Fuck!' he roars, and I open my eyes, finding him on his knees before me. I step back some more as I watch him slap a palm over his shoulder. My wide eyes look down at the scissors in my grasp and I see thick red liquid dripping from the blades. I gasp and my grip immediately releases, letting them tumble to the floor at my feet. Then I collapse to my knees as I watch him shrug off his suit jacket on a few winces until I'm confronted with a white shirt soaked in blood.

I gulp back my fear, my remorse, my guilt. He rips his waistcoat open, followed in quick succession by his shirt, sending buttons popping and flying in all directions. 'Shit,' he spits, inspecting his wound – the wound I'm responsible for. I want to comfort him, but my body and mind are on shutdown. I can't even speak to apologise. Hysterical cries are tumbling from my lips as my shoulders jerk and my eyes are so full of tears, I struggle to see him anymore. My intoxication isn't helping my distorted vision. It's unquestionably a good job. Seeing Miller injured and bleeding is bad enough. Knowing I'm the cause for his pain is bordering unbearable.

And with that thought, I haul myself to the toilet and throw up. It comes and comes, the alcohol still strong and burning my mouth as my hands brace on the seat and my stomach muscles twist and knot. I'm a mess – a frail, wretched soul. Hopeless and living in hopelessness. A cruel world. And I can't cope.

'Jesus fucking Christ,' Miller mumbles from behind me, but I'm too remorseful to chance turning and confronting my wrongs.

My forehead meets the toilet seat when my retching finally subsides. My head is pounding, my heart is aching, and my soul is broken.

'I have a request.' Miller's unexpected calm words fuel the after-effects of my breakdown, prompting the tears to redevelop and burst from my eyes. I keep my head where it is, mainly because I haven't the strength to lift it, but also because I'm still too much of a coward to face him. 'Olivia, it's polite to look at me when I'm talking to you.'

I shake my head and remain in my hiding place, ashamed of myself.

'Damn it,' he quietly curses, and then I feel his palm on my nape. He doesn't gently encourage me out. He yanks me, not bothering to be gentle. It doesn't matter. I can feel nothing. He grabs each side of my face and jerks me forward, but I drop my eyes to the sliver of naked, blood-stained flesh peeking through his open shirt and waistcoat. 'Don't deprive me of that face, Olivia.' He wrestles with my head until I lift my eyes and his sharp features are close enough to focus on. His lips are straight. His blue eyes are wild and bright, and the hollows in his cheeks are pulsing. 'I have a fucking request,' he grits. 'And you'll fucking fulfil it.'

A little sob escapes and my whole body sags in my kneeling position, but his hold of my head keeps me up. The few seconds before he speaks feels like an eternity. 'You won't *ever* stop fucking loving me, Olivia Taylor. Do you fucking hear me?'

I nod in his hold as he scans my wreck of a face and moves in closer, getting forehead to forehead with me. 'Say it,' he breathes. 'Now.'

'I won't stop,' I choke through a sob.

He nods against me and I feel his hands slide to my back and tug me forward. 'Give me my *thing*.' There's no softness to his command, but the instant calm that descends as the heat of his body starts to blend with mine is all I need. Our bodies collide and we cling to each other like life itself could end if we let go.

It might.

The cracks in our existence are gaping wide open now. There's no hiding from the cruel reality we need to face. The chains. Escaping them. Being on the brink of despair as we face our demons. I just hope we clear those cracks when we leap and don't fall into the blackness.

Miller hushes me repeatedly as I shake in his arms, the tightness of his hold not reducing the vibrations in the slightest. 'Don't be sad,' he begs, his voice now taking on a softer edge. 'Please, don't be sad.' He pries my clawed hands from his back and holds them between us, searching my tear-stained face as I sniffle and judder.

'I'm so sorry,' I murmur feebly, dropping my eyes to my lap to escape his lovely face. 'You're right. I can't cope with this.'

'There is no *you* anymore, Olivia.' His fingertips grip my chin and lift until I'm facing eyes full of determination. 'There's only *us*. We deal with this together.'

'I feel like I know so much yet so little,' I confess, my words broken and raspy. He's shared so much with me, some voluntarily, some he was forced, but there are still so many blanks.

My perfect part-time gentleman inhales a weary breath and blinks slowly as he brings my hands to his mouth and pushes his lips to the back of each. 'You possess every part of me, Olivia Taylor. For all of the wrongs I have done and all that I am yet to do, I'm asking for your mercy.' His eyes sink into me beseechingly. I have forgiven him for all that I know, and I will forgive him for all that I don't. The wrongs he has yet to do? 'Only your love will see me through this hell.'

My bottom lip starts to quiver, the lump in my throat growing rapidly. 'I'll help you,' I vow, flexing my hand in his grip until he releases me. I reach up, my movement a little disorientated, until I feel his rough cheek. 'I trust you.'

He swallows hard and nods mildly. Determination slowly creeps onto his emotion-soaked face and into his telling eyes, bringing my detached, fraudulent gentleman back into the room. 'Let me get you out of here.' His body lifts fluidly to full height and he helps me to my feet. The change in position sends blood rushing to my head and I stagger a little. 'Are you OK?'

'I'm fine,' I answer, swaying on the spot.

'You're right,' Miller says matter-of-factly, like I should know exactly what he's talking about. I can't frown my confusion because all of my focus is being used to stop myself face-planting to the floor. 'Alcohol doesn't suit you.' My nape is taken, along with my arm, and I'm led on wobbly legs to the couch in Miller's office. 'Sit,' he orders, helping me down. He kneels before me and shakes his head as he reaches for my ruined waves. His fingers comb through what's left of my hair, the pain clear on his handsome face. 'Still beautiful,' he murmurs.

I attempt a smile but struggle, knowing he's devastated, and glance past him when his office door swings open. Tony stands there for a few moments, taking in the situation. He looks set to burst under pressure. Miller slowly stands and turns, sliding his hands into his trouser pockets. They just stare at each other, Tony silently assessing his boss and then me. I feel small and stupid under his watchful eyes and in an attempt to shy away and hide the result of my meltdown, I pull my hair from my face and use the tie on my wrist to secure it in a messy knot.

'What's the situation?' Miller asks, reaching up to his shoulder and flinching a little.

'The situation?' Tony blurts on a sarcastic huff of laughter. 'We have a fucking mess, son!' He slams the door and stalks over to the drinks cabinet, quickly pouring a scotch and downing it. 'I've a half-dead bloke out there and crowds of people wondering what the fuck just went down!'

'Damage control?' Miller asks, taking a shot of scotch himself.

Tony laughs again. 'Do you have a time machine? Shit, Miller, what the fuck were you thinking?'

'I wasn't thinking,' he spits, making me shrink into the couch, like the root cause of this mess might not be noticed if I make myself small. A flick of Tony's stressed eyes in my direction confirms I've failed in my endeavour. My unreasonable need to hurt Miller has resulted in the bloodbath up in the club and it has confirmed Sophia's suspicions about the true nature of our relationship. 'No, you weren't. Story of your life, son,' Tony sighs. 'You don't go all ape-shit on a guy over a woman who's a bit of fun!' He reins in his exasperation and frowns, reaching forward to pull Miller's shirt aside. 'A puncture wound?'

Miller shrugs him off and places his glass down. I'm stunned when he actually tweaks its position before he starts to pull at his shirt. 'It's nothing.'

'Did he have a knife?'

'It's nothing,' Miller repeats slowly, leaving Tony tilting his bald head questioningly. 'Has Sophia gone?'

'Oh, she's got her hooks in you deep, my boy. Don't question her loyalty to Charlie. She's his fucking wife!'

My teary eyes widen. Sophia's Charlie's wife? And she's in love with Miller? Charlie holds the keys to Miller's chains. Does he know Sophia's in love with his Special One? I didn't think this web of corruption could get any more tangled.

Tony attempts to gather himself, taking another drink and bracing his hands on the side of the cabinet, head dropped. 'Our corrupt lives are fucking real, boy, and attached to our arses for as long as we breathe.'

'It doesn't have to be like that.' Miller is quiet in his retort, almost uncertain of his own claim. It makes my stomach turn.

'Wake up, son!' Tony casts his empty glass aside and grabs the tops of Miller's arms, making him wince, not that Tony acknowledges it. 'We've been over this time and time again. Once you're in this world, there's no escaping. You don't get to leave when it suits you. You're in it for life or you don't have a life at all!'

I cough on nothing as I absorb Tony's frank clarification. Sophia said it, Miller confirmed it, and now Tony's reinforcing it. 'Just because he doesn't want to fuck for money anymore?' I pipe up, unable to hold back.

Miller looks across at me and I expect to be ordered to keep quiet, but I'm stunned to find he looks to Tony, like he wants an answer to my question, too.

Getting involved with Miller Hart will be his demise.

It's not as easy as just quitting.

The consequences will be shattering.

Chains. Keys. Life debt.

I'm about to force my body to stand, an attempt to appear stable and strong, when the door opens again and Sophia breezes in. The intense, difficult atmosphere multiplies by a million. I sit back in my seat while she casts her eyes around, giving everyone in the room a moment of her beady eyes' time as she draws on her cigarette. I'm even more wary when Cassie appears, too, her perfection reinstated, but she's looking worried and cautious.

Sophia saunters over to the drinks cabinet and pushes her way between Miller and Tony, and neither man objects. They step back and give her the room she's demanding to pour herself a drink. She takes her time, her posture and actions screaming supremacy, then turns to face Miller. 'Quite a violent reaction for someone who's supposedly only fucking her.' Sophia's European accent makes the threat in her tone almost sexy.

My eyes close briefly, guilt digging their hateful claws into me again. I'm so fucking stupid. One eye peeks carefully, finding Miller looking down at her, his expression blank, his body deathly still. His time hiding me is up. His time to think of the best way to deal with this is up.

Because of my rash actions.

'I only ever make love to that woman.' He looks at me, nearly crippling me with the love in his eyes. I want to run into his arms, stand by his side and face her together, but my useless muscles are failing me again. When Miller returns his eyes to Sophia, the coldness of his blank expression returns instantly. 'I only ever worship her.'

The shock on her face is obvious. She's trying to conceal it, taking a sip of her drink and then a puff on her cigarette to assist, but I can see it crystal clear from all of the way over here.

'Do you let her touch you?' she asks.

'Yes.'

Her breathing increases, a little anger now surfacing through the shock. 'Do you let her kiss you?'

'Yes.' His jaw ticks, his lip curling into a snarl. 'She can do whatever the hell she wants with me. And I'll accept it all willingly.' He leans into her. 'I'll even fucking beg for it.'

My heart explodes into a million shards of badly timed contentment, making my already unstable mind dizzier. Sophia is rendered speechless, taking quick, frantic sips of her drink and pulling on her cigarette in between. Her powerful composure has been obliterated by Miller's confession. She suspected this, so it shouldn't be a shock. Or did she underestimate the situation? Think it was something in nothing?

How very wrong she was.

Remaining a quiet spectator to the events unfolding, I cast my eyes over to Tony and see raw dread on his face. Then I look to Cassie and see shock that equals Sophia's.

'I can't protect you from him, Miller,' Sophia says calmly, though the edge of irritation is still so very apparent. She's warning him.

'I never for a moment expected you to, but know one thing. I'm no longer at your beck and call. We're leaving,' Miller declares, moving away from Sophia. He's coming at me fast and determined, but I haven't a hope of making it to my feet. I'm a shaking mess. His hand extends towards me and my eyes flick up to his, seeing hard reassurance in his blues. 'Do you think there will be sparks?' he whispers, his mouth seeming to move in slow motion, his eyes sparkling and raining strength and hope all over me. I accept his offering, keeping our stares locked while he pulls me to my feet. Reaching to my hair, he pushes a few strands behind my ears gently, then scans my face. He's in no rush. There's no urgency to remove us from the horrific situation. He's simply content with making me melt before him under the penetrating effect of his eyes. He kisses me. Softy. Slowly. Meaningfully. It's a sign, a declaration. And I can do no more than accept. 'Let's go home, sweet girl.' My nape is claimed and I'm guided to his office door, the anxiety beginning to drain from me with the knowledge that we'll soon be gone from here – away from this cruel world. For tonight, we can shut the door. And I hope tomorrow never comes so we don't have to open it.

'You'll regret this, Miller.' Sophia's even tone halts Miller in his tracks, subsequently halting mine, too.

'My life up to this point has been one big regret,' Miller states clearly, his voice even. 'Livy is the only good thing that's happened to me, and I have no fucking intention of letting go of her.' He slowly turns, taking me with him. Sophia has restored her air of superiority, Tony still looks pensive, and when I look at Cassie, I see tears in her eyes as she watches Miller. I study her for a few moments, and she must feel my stare burning into her because she flicks a glance at me.

She smiles.

It's not a smug smile, hardly even there, in fact. It appears to be a sad smile of recognition, but after a few seconds, I realise it's a comforting smile. Then she nods very slightly and substantiates my thoughts. She comprehends it all.

Sophia laughs wickedly, snapping both mine and Cassie's attention back to her couture-decorated frame. 'I could stop all of this in a heartbeat, Miller. You know that. I'll tell him she's gone. She's nothing to you.'

I'm insulted, but Miller remains calm. 'No thank you.'

'It's a phase.'

'It's not a phase,' Miller counters coldly.

'Yes, it is,' Sophia retorts confidently, waving a condemning hand at me. Her reproachful eyes stab at me harshly, making me shrink a little. 'You know only one thing, Miller Hart. You know how to make women scream with pleasure, but you don't know what it means to really *care*.' She smirks. 'You're the Special One. You. Only. Know. How. To. Fuck.'

I wince, resisting my overwhelming temptation to put her straight, but I've done enough damage already. The reason Sophia is standing here, oozing self-righteousness, is because of me. The reason Miller is bleeding next to me is because of me.

I can feel Miller building up into maniac mode. 'You have no idea what I'm capable of. I worship Olivia.' His voice quivers under the anger fizzing beneath his cool exterior.

Her face screws up in disgust and she steps forward. 'You're a fool, Miller Hart. He'll never let you walk away.'

He explodes.

'I love her!' he roars, knocking every person back in the room. 'I fucking love her!' Tears burst from my eyes and I fall into his side. He immediately grabs me and pulls me close. 'I love her. I love everything she stands for and I love how much she loves me. It's more than *you* love me. It's more than any of you claim to love me! It's pure and light. It's made me feel. It's made me want more. If any fucker tries to take her away from me, I'll fucking kill them.' Pulling up for a second, he gathers a long breath. 'Slowly,' he adds, shaking beside me, clinging to me tightly, like he's afraid someone will try right now. 'I don't care what he says. I don't care what he *thinks* he can do to me. It'll be him sleeping with one eye open, Sophia, not me. So tell him. Fucking run to him and confirm what he already knows. I don't want to fuck for a living anymore. Tell him I don't want to line his pockets anymore. You're not holding me to ransom. Miller Hart is out of the game. The Special One has quit!' He withdraws and takes a few moments to suck in another calming gulp of air, while everyone looks at him, shocked. Including me. 'I love her. Go to him. Tell him I love her. Tell him

I'm Olivia's now. And tell him if he even *thinks* about touching a hair on her precious head, it'll be the last thing he ever does.'

We're on our way out before I can gauge what we're leaving behind, although I can imagine perfectly well. I can't even process his violent declaration. His arm is draped around my shoulder, and it feels warm and comforting, but it goes nowhere near the sense of belonging that I feel when he has his signature hold of me. I wriggle free of him, making him look down at me, totally perplexed as we keep up our pace, and move his hand to the back on my neck. Then I coil my arm around his tight waist. He breathes a sigh of acknowledgement, returns his focus forward, and marches on.

The music is back, pumping through the speakers at every turn, but the elite clientele are far from back to normal. Crowds of people are gathered everywhere, huddled close, obviously discussing the earlier scene involving the club owner. It makes me think of something. 'Do all of these people know who you are?' I ask, feeling eyes begin to bore into us from every direction of the club as we emerge from the stairs.

He doesn't look at me. 'Some,' is his straight, one-word answer, telling me he knows what I'm talking about, and it isn't the fact that he owns this establishment.

The evening air collides with my body, sending instant shivers bolting through me. I snuggle farther into Miller's side and catch the eye of one of the doormen. His mean face straightens as he watches Miller escort me from the premises and across the road where Miller's Mercedes is parked. As I'm guided to the passenger door, I glance across to the front of the club, seeing the guy who Miller has just beaten to within an inch of his life being bundled into a taxi by another bouncer. I'm suddenly *very* worried. 'He needs treatment,' I say. 'The doctors will ask questions.'

The door is opened and I'm gently pushed to the seat. 'Those types of people don't want the police involved in their affairs,

Olivia.' He pulls my seat belt across and buckles me up. 'You've no need to worry.' He plants a light kiss on my head and pushes the door shut, then pulls his phone from his pocket and makes a brief call as he rounds the car.

Those types of people.

This world.

It's very real.

And I'm in the centre of it.

Chapter 12

The alcohol and exhaustion have caught up with me. My head is woozy and my legs are like jelly. As we're walking through the lobby of his building, Miller scoops me into his arms and marches on. 'Where you should be,' he whispers, pushing his lips to my temple.

My arms twine around his neck and my head rests on his shoulder, my eyes closing, finally relenting to my tiredness. My weak request to be taken to Nan's was refused. I didn't argue. He needs calm, and I know his flat, with me inside of it, will bring him closer to achieving that.

Until we open the door again tomorrow morning.

The black shiny door welcomes us and is soon opened and kicked softly closed, locking the world outside. My eyes remain shut as I'm carried onward, the familiar clean smell of my surroundings settling me further. It's not the fond scent of Nan's house, but I'm happy to be here with Miller.

'Can you stand for me?' he asks, turning his face into mine. I nod and ease up on my grip, letting him gently place me on my feet. The concentration of his face holds me rapt as he undresses me slowly and carefully. All of the usual habits are here with us – the clothes being folded before he puts them in the laundry basket, his soft lips parted just so, his eyes swimming with emotion. Once he's seen through his task, he looks to me in silent demand, so I step forward and begin to slowly strip him down, even folding his blood-stained suit before placing it in the basket, despite it being more at home in the bin. Seeing past the puncture wound and blood to allow my eyes to indulge in his perfection is impossible. His hands are covered in red stains, his chest, his jaw. I'm uncertain as to which blood belongs to Miller and which to the guy who appeared so unexpectedly from my sordid past. His timing couldn't have been worse, though I doubt Miller's reaction would have been any less violent had he materialised on any other occasion.

I reach up and gently prod around the site of the wound with my fingertip, trying to gauge whether it needs professional attention.

'It doesn't hurt,' he says quietly, taking my hand away and placing it over his heart. 'This is my only concern.'

Smiling a little, I step into his chest and lift myself to his body, wrapping my limbs around him, absorbing him. 'I know.' I murmur into his neck, savouring the feel of his overgrown waves tickling my nose and his harsh stubble on my cheek.

Strong hands slide onto my bum and his lean legs stride towards the shower. My back is pushed up to the tiles the moment we enter and he pulls back, denying my face the warmth of his neck. 'I just want to clean us,' he says, a slight frown on his face.

'Elaborate.' I'm delighted when I see his lip tip at one corner, his eyes developing a shimmer of playfulness.

'As you wish.' He reaches over and flicks the shower on, and the instant warm water rains down on us. His hair flattens on his head and the blood on his chest starts to pour away.

'I do.'

He nods a little and reaches behind him to push my thighs from his waist before doing the same with my arms. I'm on my feet, my back resting against the wall, watching Miller closely. His palm meets the wall by my head and he leans in, his nose a millimetre from mine. 'I'm going to glide my hands over every curve of your perfect body, Olivia. And I'm going to watch while you writhe and fight to contain your desire for me.' His fingertip traces a burning path down my wet hip, onto my thigh. I'm struggling for control already, and he knows it.

I rest my head back, parting my lips to gather more air.

'I'm going to pay extra special attention just here.' Heat radiates through me when he strokes tenderly back and forth over my pulsing centre. 'And here.' His head drops to my chest and he sucks a tingling nipple into the warmth of his mouth.

I hold my breath and hit my head against the wall behind me, fighting my natural instinct to seize him, feel him, kiss him.

'Tell me how it feels,' he orders, clamping his teeth onto my nipple, sending a sharp shot of pain down to my core while his fingers glide back and forth, constantly and calmly. My backside flies back in a lame attempt to escape the intense sparks of pleasure, but I wind up thrusting my hips forward, keen to capture the sensations and make them last forever.

'Good.' My voice is nothing but a husky, pleasure-fuelled gasp.

'Elaborate.'

I start to shake my head, unable to fulfil his demand.

'Do you want to touch me?'

'Yes!'

'Do you want to kiss me?'

'Yes!' I cry out, going to place my hand over his to increase the pressure on my clit, but finding the willpower from God knows where to stop myself.

'Then take it all.' It's a demand, and only a second later, I'm attacking his mouth and my frantic hands are all over him. He bites my lip, so I bite him back, making him growl. 'Do what the fucking hell you like to me, sweet girl.'

So I grab his cock and squeeze. It's hard. It's hot. He throws his head back and yells, his fingers working faster over my pulsing nerves, bringing me closer and closer, encouraging my own hand to fly over his shaft.

'Shit!' he gulps, and drops his head, his face contorting, his jaw tense, every feature razor sharp. My budding climax accelerates under the power of his eyes drilling into me and I begin to thrust my hips forward to meet his strokes.

He follows suit.

We watch each other as we bring each other to a head, me crying out constantly, Miller panting in my face. Drops of water are forming on his dark lashes, making his already heated eyes glisten wildly.

'It's coming,' I shout, trying to concentrate on seizing the pleasure that's about to send me dizzy while ensuring I maintain my strokes so Miller gets his release, too. 'It's coming!'

It's all very urgent – my feet shifting to stabilise me, Miller pushing his body farther into me, our mouths clashing and working frantically. 'Fucking come, Olivia!'

I do. His command sends me wild. I bite his tongue, dig my nails into his flesh, and squeeze his cock hard, feeling it throbbing harshly in my hold.

'Ooooh, shiiiit,' he groans, going limp and collapsing against me, pushing me into the wall. I feel the heat of his essence hitting my tummy even through the heat of the water. 'Just hold it,' he pants. 'Don't let go.'

I do as I'm bid, working him slowly down as I thrust my hips gently against his hand, my heart racing, my mind focused only on getting through my blitz of pleasure. He's pinning me to the wall with his tall body and his face is buried in my neck. Our breathing is laboured and broken. Our hearts are clattering, bashing together from our compressed chests. And our worlds are perfect.

But just in this moment.

'I've not touched us with any soap,' he pants, rolling his fingers around my flesh, then slowly pushing into me. My eyes close and I squeeze my muscles around him. 'Yet I feel we're cleaner already.'

'Take me to bed.'

'And give you my *thing*?' He nips at my throat and then sucks gently, nips and sucks.

I smile through my exhaustion and release my hold of his semi-erect cock, moving my arms to circle his shoulders. I muscle my face into his, until he's forced to free my throat, and locate his lips. 'I want every part of you touching me,' I mumble past his lips. 'Don't let go of me all night.'

He groans and deepens our kiss, squashing me farther into the wall. The fluidity of our tongues circling softly together is effortless. I could kiss Miller Hart forever, and I know he feels the same. 'Let me wash us down.'

My sense of loss is palpable when he pecks my lips and locates the shower gel. 'Let's see how fast you can do that,' I tease.

He pauses from squirting the gel into his palm and flicks me a knowing look. 'I like taking my time with you.' The bottle is replaced in its rightful spot and he begins working some suds up in his palms. Standing before me, he breathes hot air into my face, then performs one of those lazy blinks of his blistering blue eyes. 'You know that, Olivia.'

I hold my breath, slam my eyes shut, and brace myself for his hands. They start at my ankles – slow, tender rotations, swirling away the dirt of today. My mind spaces out as I absorb his heated touch leisurely working up my legs. No rush. And I'm happy with that.

'What happens now?' I finally ask the question I've been avoiding since we left Ice. We're together, locked up safely in Miller's flat, but it can't stay this way forever.

'I expect Sophia will be relaying to Charlie everything I said.'

'Does Charlie know that Sophia is in love with you?'

He laughs lightly. 'Sophia doesn't have a death wish.'

'Do you?'

He breathes in deeply and holds my eyes. 'No, sweet girl. Now I have a fierce passion to live. You've given me that passion and not even the devil will stop me from having my eternity with my someone.'

I reach up and cup his cheek. 'Is Charlie the devil?'

'He's close,' he whispers.

'And have you figured everything out?'

'Yes.' He sounds confident.

'Will you tell me?'

'No, baby. Just know that I'm yours and all this will be gone very soon.'

'I'm sorry for making this harder.' I say no more. He knows what I mean.

'Knowing I have you at the end makes it easy, Olivia.' Very tentatively, he reaches forward and pulls the tie loose from my hair, almost wincing when my once epic long hair only just falls past my shoulders. 'Why?' he whispers, combing through carefully, keeping his eyes on the hacked strands.

'Don't.' I drop my head, feeling so incredibly remorseful, but not because I'm going to miss my masses of uncontrollable blonde but because I know Miller will miss them more.

'How would you feel if I shaved my hair off?'

My head flies up, horrified. I love his hair. It's longer now, the waves, when dry, all tousled and flicking out at his nape haphazardly and my favourite wayward curl that falls naturally onto his forehead . . . No, no, he can't.

'I'm being intuitive here,' he breathes in my face. 'And I'm going to suggest that by the look on your face, it would hurt deeply.'

'Yes, it would.' I can't deny it, so I don't. His beautiful hair is a part of this beautifully perfect man. Ruining any part of that would hurt. 'But I wouldn't love you any less,' I add, wondering where he's going with this.

'Neither I you,' he murmurs, 'but you should know that I'm

forbidding you to ever cut it again.' He takes the shampoo and squeezes some on my head.

'I won't,' I assure him. I don't think I'll ever pick up any scissors again after what I've done, and I mean to Miller, not to my hair. His hands delve into my remaining locks and my eyes fall to the puncture wound on his shoulder.

'I don't just mean you.'

I'm suddenly frowning at his chest, but he turns me to face the wall so I'm unable to show him my confusion. 'What do you mean?' I ask as he works my hair into a lather.

'Ever,' he says short and sharp – no elaboration. I'm turned back and positioned under the spray so he can rinse.

'Ever what?'

He doesn't look at me, just continues with his task, unaffected by my perplexity. 'I forbid you to ever have your hair cut again. By anyone.'

'Ever?' I blurt, shocked.

A straight face falls to mine. I know that face. He's adamant. He's adding my hair to his list of obsessive ways. He may have surrendered a few, but he's going to make up for them with others . . . like my hair. 'That's what I said, isn't it?' He's deadly serious. 'I realise it might sound unreasonable, but that is what I want, and I'd like you to accept.'

I'm stunned by his arrogance, though I really shouldn't be. I've encountered it plenty of times before. 'You can't demand what I do with my hair, Miller.'

'Very well.' He shrugs nonchalantly and sweeps some shampoo through his waves before rinsing himself. 'Then I'll have all of mine shaved off.'

My eyes widen at his threat, but I soon rein in my exasperation, knowing one thing and one thing for sure. 'You love your hair as much as I do,' I declare confidently . . . smugly.

Some conditioner is passed through the waves he loves so much, casually and quietly, while I remain propped up against the shower wall, matching his arrogance. He dips under the showerhead, washing it all out before sweeping it back neatly. My smile increases. He's thinking hard about this, and when he's taken a deep breath, he confronts my amusement. His hand meets the wall by my head, his face coming close to mine. 'Are you prepared to risk that?' His lips ghost over mine, and I turn my face away cockily.

'Maybe.'

I feel the heat of his skin meet my breasts from his quiet laugh that has his chest expanding. 'OK,' he breathes into my ear. 'I *promise* to shave my hair off if you so much as look at a hairdresser.'

I pull in a shocked gush of air and turn my face back to his, finding high, daring eyebrows. 'You wouldn't.'

'Try me.' His lips push to mine and I'm momentarily blind-sided by his worshipful mouth. 'There are many things I've changed since I've fallen in love with you, Olivia Taylor.' He nibbles at my lip and my heart soars with happiness. 'Don't think I won't fulfil that promise.'

He loves me. I didn't pay much attention when he bellowed it at Sophia at Ice – either not believing it or not processing it. But now the words resonate through my core, filling me with warmth. 'I don't care,' I announce. 'You've just told me you love me. Do whatever you like.'

He laughs. He actually laughs, head thrown back, eyes glistening madly, body shaking uncontrollably. I'm rendered incapable of anything. Even breathing. I watch in silent wonder at my beautiful man falling apart before me, shaking my head, close to tears. 'Olivia,' he coughs, picking me up and cradling me in his strong arms. 'I'm always telling you that I love you.'

'No, you don't,' I object. 'You say *fascinated*.' We make it to Miller's gigantic bed and I'm placed neatly on top. I begin wriggling my way beneath the sheets while he rids the area of cushions, placing them in the chest at the foot of the bed.

'I may not use the words, but it's there – every time I look at you.' He slides into bed and settles his lean physique on top of me, spreading my thighs and making himself comfy between them. He looks down at me on the tiniest of smiles. 'It's written all over you,' he whispers, dropping a kiss on my confused forehead. 'I write it with my eyes on a different part of your body every time I look at you.' He kisses his way down to my lips and his tongue plunges deep. The irony of my contentment after such a traumatic day is making my head spin. I'm being constantly tossed from utter elation to total despair. 'And I've written it on you physically.'

My brow furrows through my smile as he continues to work my mouth lovingly. But then realisation kicks in. 'In your studio,' I mumble against his lips. 'You wrote it on my tummy with red paint.' I remember it well, and I also remember him smearing it before I could catch a glimpse.

'Correct.' He pulls back and gazes down at my smiling face. He's feeling me everywhere, but right now, with those incredibly hypnotising, sharp blue eyes, he's touching my soul. 'I'll love you until there's no breath left in my lungs, Olivia Taylor.' He locates my hand and brings my diamond to his lips. 'For eternity.'

I smile. 'It's not long enough.'

'Then beyond that, too,' he whispers.

Chapter 13

He is, indeed, clinging to me in the morning when I come to. He is still cradled between my thighs, his head nuzzled as far into my neck as it will go, his arms lying on each side of my head, encasing me. I bury my nose in his hair and breathe him into me, my fingertips tracing the sharp, defined muscles of his back for an age.

It's another day. A new day. It's a day that I have no desire to face. But while I'm trapped beneath Miller, safe and happy, I don't have to worry. So I close my eyes again and sink back into semi-consciousness.

It feels like *Groundhog Day*. My eyes peel open and I do a quick assessment of my surroundings. Everything is exactly how it was when I closed my eyes before. Both times. My mind is at risk of wandering off to all thoughts horrid, when it very abruptly occurs to me that it's Friday.

Nan!

I'm urgent but cautious in pushing Miller from my confined frame, ignoring his sleepy grumbles when he rolls to his back. '*Thing*,' he groans, blindly grabbing at my escaping body. 'Livy.'

'Shhhh,' I hush him, and pull the covers over his naked physique, dropping a pacifying kiss on his long stubble. 'I'm just going to call the hospital.'

At that, he relents and tosses himself onto his front, his arms slipping beneath the pillow where his head lies. Leaving Miller dozing, I dash out of the bedroom on the hunt for my phone, and I'm soon put through to Cedar Ward.

'It's Josephine Taylor's granddaughter,' I say, making my way to the kitchen. 'I was told she could come home today.'

'Oh yes!' the nurse practically screeches, like she's relieved to confirm it. 'Her consultant will make his rounds early afternoon, so I expect to have her discharge papers by three-ish. Say four to be on the safe side.'

'Great!' Excitement flies through my waking brain. 'And she has all of her medication?'

'Yes, darling. I've sent down the prescription to the pharmacy here at the hospital. It should be back by the time she leaves. She must take it easy for a while. And we'll have to schedule a follow-up appointment.'

'Thank you.' I lower myself into a chair at Miller's table and exhale my relief, thinking Nan *taking it easy* might be easier said than done. I have a challenge on my hands, and no doubt weeks of the notorious Taylor girl sass flying my way.

'So very welcome. She's certainly lightened up this dull place for the past few days.'

I smile. 'But you won't miss her, eh?'

The nurse lets out a sharp shot of laughter. 'Actually, I will.'

'Well, you can't keep her,' I declare quickly. 'I'll be there at four.'

'I'll let her know.'

'Thank you for your help.'

'My pleasure.' She hangs up and I sit alone in the quiet kitchen, unable to contain my joy. Maybe today won't be so bad after all.

I jump up and decide to make Miller breakfast, but I need to do something before I can crack on. I want it to be perfect and there's only one way I can achieve that. I dash into the bedroom and dive on the bed, making Miller's sleeping body jerk atop the mattress. He shoots up, alarmed, his wonderful hair a wild mess, his eyes sleepy. 'What's going on?'

'I need you for a moment,' I tell him, taking his arm and tugging. 'Come on.'

His sleepy eyes aren't so sleepy anymore. They're loaded with craving. A calculated, superfast move has him removed from my grip and me yelping as he flips me to my back and straddles my tummy, pinning my arms above my head. 'I need *you* for a moment.' His voice is rough and low and sexy as hell. 'Shall we?'

'No,' I blurt before I can think to control my insulting, and quite stupid, decline.

'I beg your pardon!' He's understandably thrown.

'I mean soon. I want to make you breakfast.'

Blue eyes narrow a little and his face comes closer. 'In my kitchen?'

I roll my eyes. I fully expected the uncertainty I'm currently being faced with. 'Yes, in your kitchen.'

'If you're making me breakfast, then why do you need my help?'

'I need five minutes.'

He regards me for a few moments, considering my request. He won't decline. I've made him curious. 'As you wish.' He lifts and pulls me from the bed. 'And what is my sweet girl planning on preparing me for breakfast?'

'That's not your concern.' I allow him to guide my naked body back to the kitchen, ignoring his mild huff of amusement at my sass.

'What would you have me do?' he asks as we enter. I don't miss him scanning the clear space, like he's making a mental note of everything's position in case it's moved while I'm let loose in his perfect space. It's silly. He knows *exactly* where everything is.

'Lay the table,' I order, standing back, delighting in the frown that wriggles its way onto his brow. 'Please.'

'You want me to lay the table?'

'Yes.' I may be able to pull off the perfect breakfast, but there's not a chance in hell I'll get the table right.

'OK.' He looks at me dubiously and makes his way to the drawer where I know the knives and forks to be. The rolling of every muscle in his back gives me a perfect view while I remain static, but I get the best view when he's on his way back to the table – his face, those eyes, his thighs, chest, tight waist . . . hard cock.

I shake my head, determined not to be distracted from my plan. I study him pottering around the space, flicking curious eyes at me every now and then while I stand silently to the side and let him work his magic.

'Perfect,' he says, gesturing to the table with a sweep of his arm. 'Now what?'

'Go back to bed,' I say, making my way to the fridge.

'When you're naked in my kitchen?' he almost laughs. 'Wrong.'

'Miller, please,' I swivel on my bare feet as I take the fridge door handle, finding him almost scowling at my back. 'I want to do something for you.'

'I can think of many things you can do for me, Olivia, and none of them involve you being in my kitchen.' His back straightens and he casts his eyes around thoughtfully. 'Or maybe . . .'

'Go back to bed!' I'm not submitting on this.

His head drops with his shoulders on a mighty sigh. 'As you wish,' he mutters, backing out of the kitchen. 'But I can't sleep without you, so I'll just be lying there thinking of what I'm going to do to you after you feed me.'

'As you wish,' I retort on a sickly sweet smile, bowing my head as I do.

Miller fights to prevent his smirk through his affronted state and disappears, leaving me to crack on. First thing I do is take the chocolate and strawberries from the fridge – no natural, fat-free yogurt in sight. Next, I race to break up the cubes, melt the chocolate down, hull the strawberries, and wash them.

Then I turn to face the dressed table, seeing everything in its rightful position . . . or the position that Miller says is correct. I nibble on the inside of my mouth as I consider it all, thinking I'm certain I could get this right if I strip the table down and redress it. Maybe I'll take a photo. I bob my head on an agreeable, private nod, giving myself a mental clap on the back. But then an even better idea comes to me and I hotfoot it over to the drawers and start opening and closing, being sure not to upset the contents as I work my way down the unit. I freeze the second I clap eyes on Miller's journal. It's screaming at me again. 'Shit,' I curse, forcing myself to shut the drawer, close it away where it's supposed to be.

I eventually find what I'm searching for.

Actually, I don't.

I find something better.

I remove the cap and stare down at the nib of the Sharpie, concluding very fast that this will most certainly work better than a regular ballpoint pen. 'Right.' I take a deep breath and pad over to the table, running my eyes over each accurately placed piece. My head cocks as I tap the end of the pen on my bottom lip. The plates. That's as good a place as any to start.

Placing my fingers in the centre of the porcelain, I hold it in place and proceed to draw around the plate, smiling as I do. 'Perfect,' I announce to myself, standing back and eyeing the rest of the table. I'm way too proud of myself, and it's obvious on my crafty face. I do them all – each and every single thing on the table. It all gets circled with the Sharpie, perfect lines everywhere marking the perfect place for that piece of dinnerware.

'What the fucking hell!'

I swing around at the sound of the distressed voice, armed with my Sharpie, and in a ridiculously stupid attempt to conceal exhibit A, I hide the Sharpie behind my back, because there are a million other people in Miller's flat who could have been responsible for the defacing of his table. The look of horror on his face is like a reality check. What the hell have I just done? His eyes are wide and disbelieving as he carries his naked body to the table, his mouth agape as he scans the area. Then he picks up a plate and looks at the circle. Then a glass. Then a fork.

I chew madly on the inside of my cheek, bracing myself for the imminent meltdown. His bare arse hits the chair and his hand delves into his hair. 'Olivia.' Disturbed eyes lift to mine. He looks like he's seen a ghost. 'You've scribbled all over my table.'

I look to the table and lift my thumb to my mouth, transferring my chewing to my thumbnail. This is silly. It's a table. Anyone would think someone had died. On an exasperated sigh, I throw the Sharpie to the side and approach the table, where Miller is back to lifting items to see if I really have marked everything. I'm not sure whether to confirm it or leave him to continue examining to discover it for himself. 'I've made our lives easier.'

He looks at me like I've grown horns. 'Really?' He drops a plate and I smile when he pokes it roughly until it's within the guidelines. 'Please, elaborate on that.'

'Well . . .' I take a seat next to him and think of how I can word it so he'll appreciate it. Now *I'm* being silly. This is Miller Hart. My obsessive fruitcake. 'Now I can lay the table so there's no risk of your sweet girl screwing up your –' I purse my lips – 'particular ways.'

'Sweet girl?' He looks at me incredulously. 'You are far from sweet, Olivia. Right now you're akin to the fucking devil! Why would . . . what the . . . Oh, Jesus, look at it!' He waves his arm around aimlessly, then drops his elbows to the table and buries his face in his palms. 'I can't look.'

'Now I can set the table just how you like it.' I avoid saying *need*. This is how he needs it. 'It's the lesser of two evils.' Reaching over, I take his hand so his head is no longer supported and he has to look at me. 'Either I constantly fuck it up, or you just get used to this.' I indicate the table on a smile. This may be an overreaction, but it's one time. He'll grow to accept the outlines. The alternative is a mini seizure each time I set the table. It's a no-brainer to me.

'*You* are the only evil thing around here, Olivia. Just you.'

'Look at it as art.'

He scoffs at that suggestion and shifts my grip so *he* now has hold of *me*. 'It's a fucking mess, that's what it is.'

My body sags in my chair, and I catch him looking at me out of the corner of his eye, all sulky. Over a table? 'Is it replaceable?'

'Yes,' he grumbles. 'Good fucking job, too. Wouldn't you agree?'

'Well, *I'm* not replaceable, and I'm not spending a lifetime with you, constantly worrying whether I've put a stupid plate in the right place.'

He recoils at my harshness, but *come on*! I've been more than accommodating with his obsessive habits. Yes, he's eased up on a few, but there's still work to do, and since Miller refuses to openly admit he suffers severely from obsessive-compulsive disorder, and point-blank refuses to see a therapist, then he'll just have to get used to my way of helping him. And helping myself at the same time, too.

'It's no big shakes.' He forces indifference to within an inch of his life.

'No big shakes?' I ask, laughing. 'Miller, your world is currently experiencing an earthquake of epic proportions!' He virtually snarls, increasing my amusement. 'Now –' I stand and pull my hand free – 'do you want breakfast, or are you going to refuse, since you didn't witness me making it how you like it?'

'There's no need for insolence.'

'Yes, there is.' I leave my grumpy man at the table to fetch my bowl of melted chocolate, hearing him muttering and shifting crockery. 'Oh,' I breathe, looking down into the bowl that resembles nothing like the delicious dark puddle of chocolate that Miller created.

Picking up the wooden spoon, I have a little poke and lose my grip of the handle when the spoon gets suck in the semi-hard goo. I'm pouting when my body lights up, and I know it's because he's on his way over to investigate. The heat of his chest meets my back and his chin falls to my shoulder. 'I have a request,' he speaks right into my ear, making my shoulder rise and my head push into his face in a vain attempt to halt the tingles that have started to assault my body.

'What?' I reclaim the spoon and try to stir.

'Please don't make me eat that.'

My whole body deflates, disappointment replacing the tingles. 'What did I do wrong?'

The spoon is taken from my hand and left to rest in the bowl before he turns me in his arms. All dismay has vanished. Now I'm the butt of his amusement. 'You spent too long vandalising my table, so the chocolate has set.' He's smug. 'I'm afraid there will be no licking chocolate from body parts.'

I really am hopeless. I realise it's silly, given that I've just wrecked his table in the process, but I wanted to do this trivial thing, because it isn't so trivial in Miller's world. 'I'm sorry,' I sigh, letting my forehead drop onto his chest.

'You're forgiven.' His arms curl around my back and he presses his lips to the top of my head. 'How about we abandon breakfast for today?'

'Fine.'

'We'll veg. All day. Then have brunch.'

I cringe. I knew that would be his plan. Lock us away to

protect me from his world. There's no way, not when Nan's coming home today. 'I'm picking Nan up from the hospital at four.'

'I'll collect her,' he offers, but I know exactly what he's doing. There's no way I'm going to be kept from Nan. 'And I'll bring her back here.'

'We've been over this. She needs to be in her own home, in her own bed, with everything she knows around her. She won't like it here.' I break away and head from the kitchen, not prepared to allow him to even try and talk me down. It'll be a waste and will result in a row. After last night, I expect he'll be unbearably protective.

'What's wrong with here?' he asks, insulted.

I swing around, a little mad that he would be so obtuse where Nan is concerned. 'Because it's not home!' I spit, and a small part of me is wondering if he truly does want me here polluting his flat with my messy ways or if he's so desperate to keep me from harm's way that he'll even torture himself by having me and Nan permanently here.

The hurt is visible instantaneously, and I snap my mouth shut before I twist the knife some more. 'I see,' he says coldly.

'Miller, I—'

'No, it's fine.' He walks past me, ensuring he doesn't touch me. I feel like all kinds of shit as I let my back fall to the wall and gaze up to the high ceilings of his flat. I've hurt his feelings. He's trying to help. He's worried about me, and I'm being a total bitch.

Reaching up and pinching the bridge of my nose, I groan my frustration before I go after him. 'Miller,' I call, watching his back disappear into the bedroom. 'Miller, I didn't mean to hurt your feelings.'

He's yanking all of his bedsheets into place when I enter, being rough and stroppy. 'I said it's fine.'

'Clearly,' I sigh, my arms falling lifelessly to my sides. I'd go over and help, an olive branch in the form of Miller-style tidying, but I know I'll only piss him off further when I get it all wrong.

'You don't want to live here.' He plumps the pillows and glides careful palms across the top. 'I accept that. I don't have to like it, but I accept it.' The silk runner is practically tossed onto the bed and he starts pulling and huffing it into position. I watch silently, a little surprised by his juvenile, stroppy behaviour. He's pissed off. Not angry or looking on the brink of psychotic, just plain slighted. 'Fuck it!' he shouts, grabbing at the perfected sheets and tossing them across the bed. He collapses to his arse on the edge and throws his hands into his hair, breathing heavy. 'I want you in my arms every night.' He looks up at me, his eyes pleading. 'I need to keep you safe.'

I pad over to him, his eyes following me until I'm looking down at him. He spreads his thighs, giving me room to move in. My hands rest on his shoulders, his on my bottom. Looking up at me, he sighs and swallows hard, then lets his forehead fall to my tummy. My hands climb the sides of his neck and thread into his hair.

'I realise I sound needy and demanding,' he whispers. 'It's not just because I'm worried. I've got so used to waking up with you and falling asleep with you. You're the last thing I see before I close my eyes and you're the first thing I see when I open them. The thought of not having that doesn't sit well with me, Olivia.'

I immediately comprehend his issue. We've not been separated for weeks. New York was a constant carousel of worshipping, *things*, and indulging in each other. We're back to real life now. I smile sadly, unsure of what to say or do to make him feel better. Wild horses won't keep me away from Nan. 'She needs me,' I murmur.

'I know.' He looks up at me and tries his hardest to bless me with one of his smiles. Tries. The worry awash his features won't allow it to push through. 'I wish I could control my need for you.'

I do and don't want him to control that need. 'Need for *me* or need to ensure my safety?' I ask, because that's what matters here. I'm well aware of what's beyond Miller's front door.

'Both.'

I nod my acceptance of his answer and pull in a steady lungful of air. 'You have always promised never to make me do something you know I don't want to do.'

He clenches his eyes shut and purses his lips. 'I'm beginning to regret that.'

My lips stretch into a smile. I know he does. 'This isn't an argument you'll win. The only solution is you coming to stay with us.'

His eyes snap open, and I rein in my grin, knowing the issue here. 'How am I supposed to worship you at your grandmother's house?'

'You managed just fine the other day.' I raise my eyebrows, loving his blues darkening before my eyes as he obviously mentally runs through our encounter on the stairs. On a slight scowl, he applies pressure to my bum and hauls me forward.

'She wasn't in residence.'

'You make her sound like royalty!'

'Well, isn't she?'

I huff my agreement and bend to get our faces level. 'I've given you your options, Mr Hart. I'm going home with Nan. Would you do me the honour of joining me?' I'm delighted when his eyes win a bit of sparkle and his lips twitch terribly.

'I will,' he mutters, trying to be grumpy when I know his illusive playfulness is fighting to break free. 'It'll be pure hell, but I'll do anything for you, Olivia Taylor, including vowing to refrain from touching you.'

'You don't need to do that!'

'I beg to differ,' he says calmly, standing and lifting me to his waist. My ankles lock around his lower back as my face screws up in displeasure. 'I'm not about to disrespect your grandmother.'

'She threatened to sever your manhood, remember?' I remind him, hoping to rid his conscience of this silly matter.

His brow furrows beautifully. I'm getting him. 'I concur, but now she's ill.'

'Which means she'll struggle to catch you.'

He loses the battle to contain his amusement and blinds me with one of his heart-stopping smiles. 'I love hearing you scream my name when I make you come. That's not going to be possible. I don't want your nan thinking I have no respect for her and her home.'

'Then I'll whisper it in your ear.'

'Is my sweet girl's sass coming out to play?'

I shrug nonchalantly. 'Is the man I love pretending to be a gentleman again?'

He inhales sharply, like I've shocked him. I'm not buying it. 'I'm offended.'

I lean in and bite the end of his nose. Then I lick a slow, wet trail up to his ear. I can feel his heart rate increase under my chest. 'Then teach me a lesson,' I whisper, low and seductively into his ear before I bite down on his lobe.

'I'm under obligation to do so.' In a fast string of expert moves, he shifts his grip and flings me onto the bed.

'Miller!' I squeal as I coast through the air, my arms flailing in shock. I land in the centre of his huge bed, gasping through my laugh as I attempt to win my bearings. I find him, standing at the edge of the bed, still and calm, looking at me like I'm his next meal. My heavy breathing rockets and I shift, trying to sit myself up as he watches me, his eyes all hooded and oozing desire.

'Come to me, sweet girl,' he says, his voice rough. It increases my heart rate further.

'No.' I shock myself with my refusal. I want to go to him. Desperately. I don't know why I said that, and judging by the mild surprise creeping onto his face, Miller's shocked, too.

'Come. To. Me.' He spells out each word, warning lacing his low tone.

'No,' I whisper teasingly, edging back a little, distancing myself from him. This is a game. A hunt. I want him badly, but knowing how badly he wants *me* is upping the ante, increasing our desire to a point that's difficult to cope with . . . which makes the catch and kill so much more satisfying.

Miller's head tilts and his eyes twinkle. 'Playing hard to get?'

I shrug and glance over my shoulder to plot my escape. 'I don't feel like any Miller-worshipping right now.'

'That's a preposterous claim, Olivia Taylor. I know it and you know it.' He steps forward and gazes down at the apex of my thighs. 'I can smell how ready you are for me.'

I wither on the spot, clenching my thighs shut, shifting in a vain attempt to hold off the want ripping through me. 'I can *see* how ready you are.' I centre my attention on his cock, visibly pulsing before my eyes.

He reaches over to the bedside cabinet and slides a condom out slowly, takes it to his lips slowly, and rips it open with his teeth slowly. Then he watches me as he slides it down his hard shaft. That look is debilitating enough. It turns my blood into molten lava and my mind to mush.

'Come. To. Me.'

I shake my head, wondering why the hell I'm resisting. I'm about to explode. I keep my eyes on his, watching for his next move, seeing him widening his stance a little. I creep back some more.

A mild shake of his head, knocking his curl into place, and a minute curve of his mouth catapults my need. My whole damn body is visibly vibrating. I can't control it. And I don't want to. Anticipation is sending me crazy with desire, and it's my entire fault. He purposely, threateningly jerks forward and watches with amusement as I jump back on a little gasp. 'Play all you like, Olivia. I'm going to be buried inside of you within ten seconds.'

'We'll see,' I counter cockily, but before I can anticipate his next move, he's barrelling towards me. Fast. 'Shit!' I yelp, and spin over, crawling to the edge of the bed urgently, but he grabs my ankle and yanks, spinning me to my back. I'm panting in his face as he cages me in with his body, breathing down on me, steady and controlled.

'Is that the best you can do?' he asks, scanning my face until his eyes land on my lips. He moves in and as soon as I feel the softness of his flesh brush over mine, I fly into action, catching him off guard. He's on his back in a nanosecond, me straddling his waist, my palms holding his wrists over his head.

'Always be on your guard,' I breathe into his face before nibbling teasingly on his bottom lip. He groans, pushing his hips up into me, trying to capture my lips. I deny him, making him growl his frustration.

'Touché,' he quips, rocketing up and taking me back to beneath him. I make a feeble attempt of grabbing at his shoulders, but my hands are intercepted and pinned down. He's smug, a sanctimonious grin on his otherworldly face. It heightens my sass *and* my desire. 'Sweet girl, give up.'

I yell my frustration and throw everything I have into getting free. My body shoots up and over, but the feeling of free-falling hijacks my sense of determination. 'Shit!' I screech as Miller stealthily spins to his back, just before we come to land on the floor with a thud. There's no shock or distress from him, and he's only at the disadvantage for a split second before it's me on my back again. I yell at myself, allowing the frustration to consume me. I also ignore the suspicion that he's relenting willingly, letting me feel like I'm getting somewhere, before he regains the power.

He's gazing down at my heated face, his eyes wild with passion, one hand holding both of mine over my head. 'Never act out of frustration,' he whispers, dipping and taking the tip of my nipple between his teeth. I scream, totally ignoring his advice. I'm so frustrated! 'Miller!' I yell, and pointlessly writhe beneath him, tossing my head from side to side as I strive to deal with the pleasure attacking me from every possible angle. 'Miller, please!'

His bite drags across my sensitive nub, driving me wild. 'You wanted to play, Olivia.' He kisses the tip and spreads my thighs by wrestling his knee between them and forcing them apart. 'Are you regretting that?'

'Yes!'

'So now you have to beg me to stop.'

'Please!'

'Sweet girl, why do you try to deny yourself of my attention?'

My jaw tightens. 'I don't know.'

'Neither do I.' His hips shift and he rams forward, spearing me to maximum. 'Jesus!'

His shock invasion catches me by surprise but doesn't make the full satisfaction any less gratifying. My internal muscles grab on to him with everything they have and I squirm to free my wrists from his iron hold. 'Let me hold you.'

'Shhh,' he hushes me as he braces his torso up on his arms, keeping me locked beneath him. 'We do it my way, Olivia.'

I moan my despair, throwing my head back and arching my back violently. 'I hate you!'

'No, you don't,' he retaliates surely, rearing back and hovering on the edge of my passage, teasing me. 'You love me.' He pushes forward a little. 'You love what I can do to you.' Forward a little more. 'And you love how it feels.'

Bang!

'Fuck!' I scream, hopeless under his hold and helpless to his forceful attack. Not that I'd stop it. Not in a million years. I crave his power. 'More,' I gasp, relishing in the delicious ache he's spiking.

'It's polite to look at someone when you're speaking to them,' he gasps, slowly pulling out.

'When it suits you!'

'Look at me!'

I throw my head up and my eyes open on an angry yell. 'More!'

'Hard and fast? Or soft and slow?'

I'm too desperate for soft and slow. I'm way past soft and slow, and I don't even think Miller's demand to savour it will assist. 'Hard,' I pant, lifting my hips sharply. 'Really hard.' I have no qualms, no fear or concern. I have his full devotion, his love and care, whether he fucks me or worships me.

'Oh fucking hell, Livy.' He pulls out, leaving me slightly confused and ready to object, but then I'm spun onto my hands and knees and my waist is grabbed harshly. I gulp, appreciating the depth that Miller can achieve from this position. Oh God, and hard, too? 'Tell me you're ready.'

I nod, pushing my backside into him, longing for that deepness. He doesn't hang around. There's no easing gently in. He crashes forward on an ear-piercing bellow, sending me into a dazed euphoria of toe-curling pleasure. I scream, my hands balling into fists on the carpet, my head thrown back in despair. He's merciless, barking on each pound forward, his fingers clawing into the soft flesh of my hips. The carpet feels rough on my bare knees – Miller is being uncharacteristically rough with me, yet the slight discomfort and unforgiving power of his body hitting mine doesn't deter me. It has me begging for more instead.

'Harder,' I mumble weakly, letting Miller take full control, the strength to meet his punishing blows failing me. All I can focus on is the pleasure consuming me, taking over every single part of me.

'Christ, Olivia!' His fingers flex and dig back into my flesh. 'Am I hurting you?'

'No!' I blurt, suddenly worried he'll ease up. 'Harder!'

'Oh, you fucking dream.' His knees widen, pushing my legs farther apart, and his pace accelerates, our bodies clashing loudly. 'I'm going to come, Olivia!'

My eyes close and all breath leaves my lungs as my mind empties, too. I'm in a dark, silent world, where my only purpose is basking in the attention that Miller delivers. There's nothing else to steal my focus, nothing to distract me or ruin our precious time together. It's just us – my body and his body doing incredible things.

The pleasure is rising. Each collide of his body with mine is pushing me towards utter rapture. I want to speak, tell him how he's making me feel, yet I'm rendered mute, unable to utter a word, only whimpers of despair and pleasure. I feel the pinnacle of his climax looming. He's expanding within me, and a mighty roar snaps me back into the room. My orgasm takes me by surprise, and I cry out as it rips through me like a tornado. Every muscle I own engages, except my neck, which leaves my head dropping limply between my arms. Miller's sharp thrusts accelerate once more to carry him over the edge, and he yanks my stiff body onto him. 'Arhhhhhhhhhhhhh!' he bellows, and strikes with a force that's only comprehensible if you're on the receiving end of it. And I am. The sharp flash of pain that sears through me, mixing with the spikes of pleasure bubbling deep in my groin, takes everything out of me. 'Fucking hell,' he breathes, locking us together and holding us joined. I'm ready to collapse. Miller is the only thing supporting me, and when he unclaws his fingers from my hips, I lose that support, flopping to my front on the floor, heaving and gasping.

The coolness of the carpet on my cheek is welcome as I watch Miller fall to his back next to me, his arms falling limply above his head, his chest expanding violently. He's soaking wet, the taut flesh of his chest glistening from sweat. If I had the energy, I'd reach over and stroke him, but I'm useless. Completely incapacitated. But not enough to close my eyes and deprive them of the stunning sight of Miller post-climax.

We both remain sprawled across the carpet for an eternity. My ears are being invaded by consistent and drawn-out gasps of breath. Finally mustering some strength from somewhere, I drag my arm across the carpet and brush my fingertip down his side. It glides easily, assisted by the dampness of his hot skin. His head drops to the side until his eyes find mine and exhaustion runs away, leaving behind some scope for talking. But he beats me to it.

'I love you, Olivia Taylor.'

I smile and put all of my effort into crawling on top of him, settling my body all over his, sinking my face into the comfort of his neck. 'And I'm quite fascinated by you, too, Miller Hart.'

Chapter 14

'Let's see, then.' He's waiting on the pavement outside the salon, and I can tell he's extremely anxious. He's fidgety, looking unreasonably stressed by the potential of my new haircut. I was delivered to the salon with strict instructions to trim minimal amounts, although Miller took it upon himself to reiterate those instructions to the hairdresser and only left when I forced him to, seeing how nervous he was making her feel with his curt orders. Miller watching over her probably would have landed me with something worse than I already had. My once long, wild waves are now smooth and glossy and bouncing just below my shoulders. Bloody hell, even *I'm* nervous. I reach up and run my fingers through them, thinking how silky they feel, while Miller regards me carefully. I wait. And wait. Until I blow out my exasperation on an impatient exhale.

'Say something!' I order, hating the scrutiny I'm under. It's not rare for him to study me so closely, but the intensity isn't welcome right now. 'Don't you like it?'

He slips his hands into the trouser pockets of his suit, thinking hard. Then he closes the distance between us and drops his face into my neck as soon as he makes it to me. I tense. I can't help it, except it's not his closeness. It's his quietness. After a long inhale, he speaks. 'I don't need to tell you that I was a little worried about the potential of losing any more.'

I huff a cynical burst of laughter at his understatement. 'A little?'

He pulls away and hums thoughtfully. 'I sense sarcasm.'

'Your senses work well.'

He gives me a wicked smile and moves in, locking his arm around my neck and pulling me in. 'I love it.'

'You do?' I'm stunned. Is he lying?

'I really do.' Pushing his lips to my head, he takes another long inhale. 'It'll look even better when it's all mussed up and damp.' His fingers thread through and grip hard, pulling at my scalp. 'Perfect.'

It's silly how relieved I am. Really silly. 'I'm glad you like it, although if you didn't, I'd have something to say. She followed your instructions to the word.'

'I should hope so.'

'You made her nervous.'

'I was entrusting my most treasured possession to her. She *should* be nervous.'

'My hair is *my* possession.'

'Wrong,' he counters quickly and confidently.

I roll my eyes at his impertinence but refrain from challenging him. 'Where to now?' I ask, taking his wrist to check the time. 'We're too early for Nan.'

'Now we have to pay someone a visit.' He clasps my neck and leads me towards his Mercedes. Worry grips me. I don't like the sound of that.

'Who?'

Miller turns an almost apologetic expression onto me as I look up at him. 'I'll give you three guesses.'

Everything deflates. I don't need three. 'William,' I sigh.

'Correct.' He doesn't give me an opportunity to object. I'm guided into his car and the door shuts firmly before he strides around the front and gets in. 'I really do love your hair,' he says softly as he settles in his seat, like he's trying to pacify me . . . ease me.

My focus remains straight ahead as I weigh up the merits of

doing a bunk. I don't want to see William. I don't want to face his disapproval, his smug arrogance. Miller knows it, and he doesn't make me do things that he knows I don't want to do. Yet I fear on this occasion his promise will be broken. It doesn't stop me from trying, though. 'I don't want to come.' I turn to look at him, finding thoughtfulness riddling his face.

'Tough luck,' he whispers as he starts the car and pulls away, leaving me gulping down courage.

Miller has come to depend on William for information. I know Miller doesn't like it, and I know William doesn't like it. *I* definitely don't like it. But regrettably, it seems none of us has a choice. My eyes close and remain that way during the entire journey. Neither of us speak, the silence cutting the close air around us. It's awkward. It's painful. And it makes the drive drag out forever.

When we've reached our destination, I can sense Miller's tension. The atmosphere seems to freeze, sending every muscle in my body rigid. They're not even within sight of each other yet, but all of the invisible animosity is already rife. It's making my skin prickle and my pulse quicken. I feel like I'm walking willingly into the lion's den with a steak strapped to my chest.

'Open your eyes, Olivia.' Miller's placid tone strokes my skin and I find myself peeling my lids open, even though I have no desire to see what will be outside of the car. But I keep my gaze on my lap, noting my eternity ring spinning wildly on my finger, courtesy of my own unconscious fiddling. 'And look at me,' he orders.

Before I can obey, my nape is clasped and twisted until I'm facing him. I root my eyes to Miller, knowing what I'll see beyond him if I cast my eyes past him.

The Society.

William's club.

'Better,' he says, reaching over with his spare hand and arranging my new hair just so. 'You know William Anderson isn't my favourite person,' he declares, 'but he cares for you dearly, Olivia.'

I choke on nothing and open my mouth to argue, to tell him that all of William's actions are spiked by his guilt. He couldn't save my mother so he's trying to cleanse his soul and save me, but I get a palm laid neatly on my lips to shut me up before I start.

'If I can accept his help, then you *certainly* can.'

My face twists in defeat behind his palm, my eyes narrowing slightly. The mild curve of his lips tells me exactly what the next words from his perfect mouth will be.

I'm bang on the money.

'Sass,' he breathes, moving his hand fast and replacing it with his mouth. The touching of our lips does everything I've come to expect and I find myself unbuckling my seat belt while I return his kiss. I quickly find my way across the car to his lap. 'Hmmmm,' he hums, helping me get comfortable while our tongues find perfect synchronisation. He's loading me with the strength I'll need to face William, to walk into the Society.

'Come on. Let's get this over with.'

Moaning my objection, I make it as tricky as possible for Miller to detach me from his mouth and open his door. He cocks his head in instruction for me to jump out, which I do on an audible grumble, slipping from his lap and finding myself on the pavement sooner than I'd like. I do everything to avoid looking up. I faff with my dress, flick my new hair over my shoulders and pull it back to my front, and then accept my bag when it appears by my side. My lungs collect air slowly and I finally locate the strength to face the building before me.

Years of anguish seem to creep up my body from the concrete at my feet and suffocate me. The air grows thick, making breathing challenging. And my eyes burn from the visual reminder of my tainted past. The building is just how I remember it – the giant limestone bricks, the original giant stained-glass windows, the smooth curved concrete steps leading up to gigantic double doors that'll take me into William's world. Glossy black metal railings guard the frontage, with gold spikes at the tip of each rod, making it seem grand and opulent, but with an edge of danger. A gold plaque fixed to one of the pillars flanking the entrance states in large bold letters THE SOCIETY. I stare blankly at the doors, feeling more vulnerable than ever before. This is the centre of William's world. This is where it all began, when a young woman stumbled boldly into the unknown.

'Olivia?'

I shake myself from my reverie and cast a sideways glance at Miller, seeing him looking down at me. He's trying to conceal his apprehension . . . and failing. It's pouring from those eyes, yet I'm unsure whether his unease is because of where we're heading or because I'm falling fast into despondency. 'The last time I was here, William sent me away for good.'

Miller's lips straighten and misery to equal mine plagues his features.

'I never wanted to see this place again, Miller.'

His misery doubles and he moves in to take me in his *thing*. It's the perfect hiding place. 'I need you with me, Livy. I feel like I'm constantly balancing on the edge of a black hole that'll swallow me up and take me back to complete darkness with one slight wrong move.' His palms skate up my back until they're cupping the sides of my head. He pulls me from my hiding place and finds my eyes. I hate the hint of defeatism I can detect there. 'Don't give up on us, I beg you.'

A light switches on in response to Miller's plea, and I mentally pull my sorry self together. Miller Hart isn't a weak man. I'm not mistaking his confession as weakness. He's not. I'm simply a chink in this confounding man's tight armour. But I'm also a strength, because without me, Miller wouldn't have entertained the thought of escaping his life of debasement. I've given him the reason and strength to do it. I mustn't make it harder for him than it already is. My history is exactly that – in the past. Gone. It's Miller's history preventing us from moving forward. We need to remedy that.

'Let's go,' I say evenly, defying the lingering apprehension that's still rooted deep. I take the steps steadily and with purpose, me leading Miller for once, until I'm being blocked from proceeding farther by the ominous double doors. I'm astounded when Miller reaches over and punches in the keypad code from memory. What in the world?

'You know the code?'

He shifts uncomfortably. 'Yes,' he answers, flat and with utter finality.

'How?' I splutter. I'm not accepting any of the usual signs that tell me the subject is exhausted. It isn't. William and Miller despise each other. There's no good reason why he would know the code that can grant him access to William's establishment.

He halts in his attempt of shifting me and starts fiddling with his suit jacket sleeves, brushing each down. 'I've stopped by one or twice.'

'Stopped by?' I laugh. 'What for? Cigars and laughs over a mature whiskey?'

'There's no need for insolence, Olivia.'

I gape at him, not needing to correct him or ask what the topic of conversation was during those visits. I bet there have been some quite colourful words exchanged. Yet my damn curiosity won't allow me to shut the hell up. 'What for?' I watch as his lids perform a lazy, patience-gathering blink. His jaw is tight, too.

'We may not like each other, but when it comes to you, Anderson and I rub along just fine.' His head cocks, expectantly. 'Now, let's go.'

I feel my bottom lip curl in condemnation, but I follow through on his order, bristling from head to toe.

The grand entrance hall of the Society gleams with elegance.

The original wooden floor is clearly still polished weekly and the décor, although now cream and gold instead of deep red and gold, is opulent. It's dripping in money. It's luxurious. It's magnificent. But all of the lovely décor now just seems like a disguise – something to fool people from seeing what this building truly represents and what happens here. And who frequents this posh establishment.

Preventing my eyes from familiarising themselves with my surroundings any more, I push on, begrudgingly knowing where I'll find William's office, but Miller grabs my upper arm, swinging me around to face him. 'The bar,' he says quietly.

My bristling returns. It's unwarranted and unnecessary, but I can't help it. I hate that I know this place, probably better than Miller. 'Which one?' I retort, harsher than I mean to. 'The Lounge Bar, the Music Bar, the *Mingle* Bar?' He drops my arm and his hands slide into his trouser pockets as he regards me closely, clearly wondering if the sass is going to subside any time soon. I can't confirm that. The farther into the Society I venture, the more I can see my sass getting harder to control. All of Miller's words outside are suddenly forgotten. I can't remember them. I *need* to remember them.

'The Lounge Bar,' he responds calmly, and signals to the left with a sweep of his arm. 'After you.' Miller is taking all the sass I'm throwing his way without retaliation. He's not biting. He's calm, cool, and aware of the irritation flaring within his sweet girl. On the longest gulp of air I'm ever likely to take, I yank some reason from God knows where and follow Miller's gesturing arm.

It's busy but quiet. The Lounge Bar, just as I remember, is almost tranquil. Plush velvet armchairs litter the space, suited bodies reclined in many, all with tumblers of dark liquid grasped in their palms. The lighting is dim, the chatter quiet. It's civilised. Respectful. It defies everything William's underworld signifies. My nervous feet cross the threshold of the double doors. I can feel Miller behind me, my body's natural reaction to his closeness ever present. I'm simmering but unable to enjoy the usual delicious sensations of internal sparks because of the exquisite surroundings that are torturing my wrought mind.

A few heads turn as we make for the bar. They recognise Miller. I can tell because of the surprised expressions replacing the initial curiosity. Or do they recognise me? I quickly rein in my disturbing thoughts and push on, finding myself at the bar fast. I can't think like that. I *mustn't* think like that. I'll be dashing for the exit any moment if I don't halt these thoughts. Miller needs me with him.

'What can I get you?'

I direct my attention to the impeccably turned out barman and immediately blurt my order. 'Wine. Whatever you have.' My bum drops to one of the leather barstools as I gather every reasonable fibre of my being in an attempt to calm myself down. Alcohol. Alcohol will help. The barman nods acceptingly and begins making my order while he looks on to Miller in question.

'Scotch. Straight,' Miller mutters. 'The best you have. And make it a double.'

'Chivas Regal Royal Salute, fifty years old. It's the very best, sir.' He indicates a bottle on a glass shelf behind the bar and Miller grunts his acceptance, but he doesn't take a stool next to me, choosing to remain standing by my side, scanning the bar and nodding to a few inquisitive faces. *The best they have.* No one pays for drinks at the Society. The obscene membership fees cover it. And Miller will undoubtedly know this. He's making a private point. He remembers William messing with his perfectly neat drinks cabinet and helping himself to a drink. He's on a silly revenge fit. Is this rubbing along just fine?

A glass of white wine is placed before me and I immediately

swipe it up, taking a long healthy glug as a huge frame appears behind the bar from nowhere. Glancing to my right with my glass suspended in mid-air before me, I take in the ominous presence of the giant man. Blue eyes, so pale they resemble clear glass, cut through the relaxed atmosphere like a machete, and his shoulder-length black hair is slicked back into a tight ponytail. Everyone is aware of him, including Miller, whose hackles seem to have risen and are currently stabbing at my back. I remember him – I could never forget – but his name is stuck on my tongue. He's William's first in command. He's well turned out, but his tailored suit does nothing to dilute the evil vibes emanating from every pore.

I sit back on my stool and take a nervous sip of my wine, trying to ignore his presence. Impossible. I can feel those mirror-ball eyes slicing into my flesh. 'Olivia,' he all but growls, making me take in a steadying breath of air, and Miller bristles into the realms of taking leave of his senses. He's now pushed up against my back and virtually vibrating on me.

I can't speak. I can only just swallow, sending more wine down my throat fast.

'Carl,' Miller utters quietly, instantly reminding me of his name. Carl Keating. One of the scariest men I've ever met. He's not changed one bit – not aged . . . not lost his frightening aura.

'We weren't expecting you,' Carl says, taking the empty tumbler from the barman and flicking his head in command, sending him away without the need to verbalise his order.

'Surprise visit.' Miller's retort is full of arrogance.

Carl places the glass on the marble counter of the bar before he turns and takes down a black bottle from the shelf that's embellished with an intricate gold plate. 'The good stuff.' He raises his black eyebrows as he holds the bottle up and pulls the gold stopper from the top. I shift uncomfortably on my stool and risk a peek over my shoulder to Miller, dreading what I'll find. His stoic expression and heated blue eyes, boring right into Carl, do nothing to lessen my unease.

'Only the best,' Miller speaks clearly, never letting his focus waiver.

I blink slowly on a quiet hitch of breath, my shaky hands taking my glass back to my lips. I've been in some painful situations of late, and this is right up there with the best of them.

'Nothing but the best for the Special One, yes?' Carl smiles cunningly to himself as he pours a few fingers.

I cough over my wine, slamming the glass down before I drop it. He's playing a dangerous game and he knows it. Miller's chest heaving, buzzing, burning against my back tells me he could explode at any moment.

Carl passes the glass over and holds it in mid-air, rather than placing it on the bar for Miller to take, then wiggles it slightly . . . teasingly. I wince on a little jump when Miller's hand flies out and viciously swipes it from his clasp, making the mean beast grin evilly. He's getting a sick thrill from poking Miller and it's beginning to get under my skin. Miller drains the alcohol in one smooth gulp before he smashes the glass down and licks his lips slowly, a slight curl developing at the side of his mouth. His eyes remain locked on Carl the whole time. The animosity batting between these two men is making me dizzy.

'Mr Anderson wants you in his office. He'll join you shortly.'

My neck is taken before Carl's words fully sink in, and I'm on my feet and being led away from the bar before I can finish the rest of my much-needed wine. The anger pouring from Miller is potent. I'm nervous enough just from being here. All these bad feelings aren't assisting. The pounding of Miller's expensive shoes on the polished floor is ricocheting around my head, the walls closing in around me as the corridor swallows us up.

And then I see the door – the one I staggered towards the last time I saw it. The intricate door handle seems to swell before my eyes, enticing me in, showing me the way, and the wall lights seem to dull the farther we progress. The light buzzing of the posh club is fading into a muffled fuzz of quiet sound behind me, my poor mind being hijacked by relentless, painful memories.

My eyes are set on the handle, and I see Miller's hand extend in slow motion and take hold, pushing it down and opening the door. He shoves me through quite firmly. I never thought I'd see this room again, but before I have time to absorb it, I hear the sound of the door close and I'm being whirled around and taken with conviction. I gasp, caught off guard, and stagger back in shock. Miller's kiss is hungry and urgent, but I accept it, grateful for being spared the chance to take in my surroundings.

Our mouths are clashing repeatedly as we consume each other. Then he's at my neck, my cheek, my shoulder, and returning to my mouth. 'I want you here,' he growls, beginning to step forward, encouraging me to move back until I feel hard wood at the back of my legs. 'I want to fuck you right here, make you scream in ecstasy and come all over my aching cock.' He lifts me and places me on the desk behind us, my dress pushed to my waist as he continues to attack my mouth. I know what he's doing. And I couldn't care less. This is the refuelling of strength I need.

'Do it,' I gasp, reaching up and pulling at his hair. Miller growls into my mouth as he unbuckles his belt and rips his trousers open before returning his hands to me and yanking my knickers aside. Our kiss is broken and my eyes drop to his groin. His cock is twitching eagerly, begging for me to come to it.

'Move forward,' he instructs hoarsely, sliding his spare hand to my bum and tugging impatiently as he stares down at himself slowly stroking his arousal. 'Come to me, sweet girl.'

I shift a little, placing my palms flat on the desk behind

me, being sure to never let my eyes stray from his perfect face – being sure not to allow myself a reminder of where we are. The moist head of his cock skims my centre, making me hiss and tense. The strength required to keep my eyes open nearly finishes me. He's rolling the tip of his erection in painful circles, around and around on my flesh, still using those familiar teasing tactics, despite his earlier urgency.

'Miller!' My hands ball behind me, my teeth gritting.

'Do you want me inside you, Olivia?' He flicks his eyes from his groin to my flushed face, teasing my opening. 'Do you?'

'Yes.' I circle my legs around his waist and use them as leverage, yanking him towards me. 'Yes!' I choke, the instant, deep penetration robbing me of breath.

'Oh fuck! Livy!' He withdraws slowly, watching himself emerge from my passage, his jaw pulsing. Then he looks up at me as he holds still and his blue eyes visibly darken, his grip on my thighs flexing . . . preparing. I wait for it, holding his purposeful gaze as it comes closer to me until his suit-covered torso is leaning over me and our noses are nearly touching. Yet he remains poised at my entrance, only the very tip of him submerged. I don't move. I remain still and patient under his close studying of me, panting in his face, so desperate for movement, but just as desperate to let Miller lead the way, knowing it's exactly what he needs.

Now.

Here.

Me.

Our eyes are stuck. Nothing will pull them apart. And when he slowly closes the small remaining gap between us and kisses me tenderly, I still don't lose his blues. I keep my eyes wide open and so does he. His kiss is brief but loving. It's worshipful. 'I love you,' he whispers, returning upright, still never allowing his gaze to wander.

I smile, keeping myself braced on one arm and using the

other to reach forward. I skim his bristly cheek with my fingertip as he continues to regard me closely.

'Put your hand back on the desk.' His instruction is soft but firm, and I fulfil it without delay. I know full well what his intention is. I can see it past the softness of his eyes. Desperate hunger.

He takes a deep breath, making his chest expand beneath the material of his suit.

I take in air, too, holding it, preparing, silently willing him on.

Beautiful, lush lips straighten and his head shakes slowly in wonder. 'I love you so, so much.'

Then he pounds into me on a guttural bark.

I scream, my lungs bursting and allowing every scrap of air I've contained to escape. 'Miller!'

He freezes against me, holding us close, filling me to the maximum. Just that one powerful pound of his body into mine has us both gasping for breath. There's so much more to come, so I gather the depleted air and take the few seconds he's giving me to prepare for his attack as he twitches and jerks within me.

It happens faster than I anticipated. I get a few seconds of painful torture as he pulls out of me slowly before he totally lets loose. He's unforgiving. Our bodies smash together over and over, creating the most wonderful sounds and sensations – our shouts of mind-bending pleasure saturating the large office, the feel of us both uniting sending me to that place beyond pleasure. My mind spaces out and my focus remains solely on accepting his brutality. I'm sure there will be bruises when we're through, and I don't even care.

I want it harder. Faster. I'm craving more. More Miller. I bunch his suit jacket in my fists and hang on for dear life. Then I push my mouth to his and tackle his tongue. He needs to know I'm OK. He wants to fuck me but worship me. He wants the things that make us *us*. Touching. Tasting. Loving.

'Harder,' I shout into his mouth, just so he knows I'm fine with this. I'm loving it. Everything about it – the strength of him, his merciless taking of me, his claiming of me, where we are . . .

'Oh sweet Jesus, Livy.' His mouth moves to my neck. He bites and sucks, my head falls back as my hold of him moves to his shoulders, and he doesn't falter one . . . little . . . bit. The speed of his advancing hips picks up a gear. Or two. Could possibly be three. 'Fuck!'

'Oh God!' I yelp, feeling the rush of blood hurling to my centre. 'Oh God, oh God, oh God! Miller!' My hearing is muffled, my mind distorted, and I finally give up and close my eyes, leaving me blind, too. Now all I have is feeling. Lots of feelings. 'I'm coming!'

'Oh yes! Come for me, sweet girl.' His face emerges from my neck and he tackles my mouth, impatiently pushing his tongue past my lips when I fail to open up to him. I'm too focused on the orgasm powering forward. It's going to blow my world into pieces.

I begin to panic when I get stuck at a point of no return, yet not seeming to be able to capture my release. I tense everywhere. I'm rigid in his arms, only moving because of Miller's control of our bodies. He strikes me over and over, yanking my body onto his while our mouths attack each other violently. But it won't happen. I can't get there, and my frustration explodes. 'Fucking harder!' I yell in desperation. 'Make it happen!' I reach up and boldly yank at his hair, making him shout as he hammers forward.

But he stops. Abruptly. My rage only multiplies by a million when he smirks at me. He's watching me gasp unevenly all over him, feeling me squeeze him within me. He's ready to explode, too. I can see it past the smug satisfaction of his gaze. But I'm not sure if that satisfaction is because he has me going out of my mind or because he has me on William's desk.

The sheen of sweat glistening on his brow diverts my attention there momentarily . . . until he speaks, pulling my eyes back to his. 'Say I'm yours,' he orders quietly.

My pounding heart pounds harder. 'You're mine,' I tell him with one hundred per cent conviction.

'Elaborate.'

He's holding me on the cusp of orgasm, holding us tightly together, his groin pushed against my sex the only thing keeping me there. 'You. Belong. To. Me.' I spell it all out for him, loving the glint of gratification that replaces the smugness. 'Me,' I affirm. 'No one else gets to taste you, feel you –' I cup his cheeks with my palms and press my lips to his, biting down a little before licking my mark – 'or love you.'

A long moan emanates from my part-time gentleman. A happy moan. 'Correct,' he murmurs. 'Lie back, sweet girl.'

I comply willingly, releasing his face and dropping to my back as I look up at him. He smiles, that glorious, dizzying smile, then circles his groin deeply and slowly, pushing me instantly over the edge. 'Ooooh,' I sigh, and close my eyes, my hands delving into my blonde and holding my head as it shakes from side to side.

'I concur,' Miller moans, shuddering above me before quickly pulling out and resting his length on my stomach. It's only then that I realise he's not wearing a condom.

He comes all over my tummy, his cock pulsing as it releases, and we both watch quietly.

I don't need to say what we both know. There was no room in his consumed mind to think of protection when he pushed me into William's office. He was thinking only of marking what's his in the office of one of his nemeses.

Perverse? Yes. Do I care? No.

He slowly lowers his body over mine and pins me to the desk, seeking out that place on my neck he loves, nuzzling lovingly. 'I'm sorry.'

The small smile that tickles my lips is probably as perverse as Miller's unreasonable actions. 'It's . . .'

The slamming of a door resonates through the room, cutting me short, and Miller's face slowly lifts from my neck until he's staring down at me. The calculating smile that slowly graces that lovely mouth of his makes me bite my lip to prevent mirroring it.

Oh, God help us!

'You arsehole.' William's rich voice is loaded with venom. 'You fucking immoral arsehole.'

My eyes widen as the enormity of our situation bashes past the sick satisfaction I'm feeling. Although Miller's sly grin remains firmly in place. He dips and kisses me chastely. 'It was a pleasure, sweet girl.' He lifts from my body, keeping his back to William to conceal me as he fastens his trousers. He smiles down at me, and I know it's his way of saying not to worry. He pulls my knickers into place and arranges my dress, which is a good job because I'm arrested by anxiety, unable to make myself decent. Then he pulls me from the desk and steps to the side, exposing me to the potent anger pouring from William's powerful frame.

Oh shit, he looks homicidal.

William's lip curls in disgust. He's physically shaking. And now I am, too. Not Miller, though. No. He ignores the rage and calmly pulls a chair out and turns me, pushing my unresponsive body onto the seat. 'My lady,' he says, making me cough at his continued arrogance. He has a death wish. He must.

I stare blankly forward and start nervously spinning my diamond on my finger, and in my peripheral vision, I see Miller making an over-the-top meal of smoothing his suit down before he takes a chair next to me. I cast him an edgy glance. He smiles. And he winks! He actually winks, making my hand shoot to my mouth as I start to snort all over the place. I try so hard to contain my giggles, try to disguise my laugh as a coughing fit. It's such a waste of energy. There's nothing funny about this situation. There wasn't before Miller violated me on William's desk, and there most definitely isn't now. We're both in big, big trouble. Double than what we were before we arrived.

I remain stiff and pipe down when I hear the sound of footsteps closing in, while Miller makes himself comfy, relaxing back, resting his ankle on his knee and sliding his hands down the arms of the chair. William rounds the desk, pulling my wary eyes in their sockets to follow his path. The atmosphere is just . . . horrible.

Lowering slowly to his chair, keeping pissed off grey eyes on a blasé Miller, he finally speaks. But William's words stun me.

'Your hair's different.' He turns to me, taking in my new hair, which is most likely a sexed-up mess now. My face feels damp, my body still buzzing.

'I had it cut,' I reply. Now that he's turned his contempt onto me, I can feel my sass igniting.

'By a hairdresser?'

My body starts to shift awkwardly. This isn't good. People usually have their hair cut by a hairdresser – it goes without saying – so the fact that he's asked doesn't sit well. 'Yes.' I'm not lying. I *did* have my hair cut by a hairdresser . . . the morning after I hacked it off myself.

William's hands form a steeple in front of his mouth as he watches me continue to fidget and avoid his eyes. I'm soon spared his glacial stare and words, though, when he turns them onto Miller. 'What the fuck were you thinking?' He's injected some heat into his tone now, and I chance a glance at him, wondering if he's questioning what he's just found or what he undoubtedly knows of last night's events at Ice.

Miller clears his throat and reaches up to casually dust his shoulder down. It's an indifferent act and meant to be. He's pushing William's buttons, and while I'm guilty of doing this on many occasions, I'm not sure now would be the time. I contained my sass . . . just. Miller needs to rein his impudence in, too. 'She's mine,' he says, looking up to William. 'I'll do with her as I please.'

I shrink in my chair, astounded by his pure egotism at such a delicate time. He's the one who claims we need William's help, so why the hell is he being such a twat? Rub along just fine? Sure! I know he has a strange way with words. I've come to accept it, but that statement is clearly designed to rile William further, and when I brave a peek at my mother's ex-pimp and see steam virtually bursting from his ears, it's very obvious, *very* quickly, that he's succeeded.

William shoots up from his chair and smashes his palms down on the table, leaning forward, his face twisted with anger. 'You're a fraction away from being crushed, Hart! And I'm putting myself in the middle of this fucked-up situation to make sure that doesn't happen!'

I fly back in my chair to put as much distance between me and William – a vain attempt to dodge the violent vibes shooting from his heaving body. This situation is getting more unbearable by the second. Miller slowly rises from his seat and mirrors William's pose. It's about to get worse. I'm not mistaking Miller's calm, fluid move as a sign of control. His ticking jaw and wild eyes say otherwise. I'm frozen and useless while these two powerful men have a face-off.

'You know as well as I do that I can and *will* break every bone in each of their parasite bodies.' He practically whispers the words in William's face, his shoulders pulsing steadily . . . almost calmly. 'Make no mistake, I won't think twice, and I'll be laughing my way through it.'

'Fuck!' William curses, his hand flying out and grabbing Miller's shirt at his throat, bunching it tightly and pulling him closer. I jump up in shock, yet I don't shout at them to stop. No words are forming.

'Let . . . go . . . of . . . me.' Miller speaks slowly and concisely, his tone dripping in ferocity. 'Now.'

Both men hold still for what seems like forever, until William curses again and shoves Miller back before plummeting to his arse and dropping his head back to look up to the ceiling. 'You've really fucked up this time, Hart. Sit down, Olivia.'

My bum meets the chair fast, not prepared to cause further problems, and I look to Miller, watching as he straightens out his shirt and fiddles with the knot of his tie before taking a seat. I feel a stupid sense of relief when he reaches over and takes my hand, squeezing tightly, his way of telling me he's fine. He's in control. 'I assume you're referring to yesterday evening.'

A sarcastic laugh spills from William's mouth and his head drops, his eyes flicking between me and Miller. 'You mean as opposed to you marking what you think is your territory in my office?'

'What I *know*.'

Oh, good God! 'OK, stop!' I shout, swinging my exasperation onto Miller. 'Just cut it out!' Both men retreat in their chairs, surprise evident on their annoyingly handsome faces. 'Enough of the macho bullshit, please!' I yank my hand free from Miller's, but he quickly reclaims it, bringing it to his mouth and resting his lips on the back, kissing it repeatedly.

'I'm sorry,' he says sincerely.

I take a deep breath, then direct my attention on William, who's regarding Miller closely, thoughtfully. 'I thought you'd accepted there's no breaking us,' I say, noticing Miller halt with the continuous rains of kisses he's applying to the back of my hand. After William helped us flee London, I was certain there would be no more interfering on his part.

He sighs, and I feel my hand being lowered into Miller's

lap. 'I'm constantly having an argument with myself on this, Olivia. I can see love when it's staring me in the face. But I can also see disaster when it's staring me in the face. I haven't got a fucking clue what to do for the best.' He clears his throat and looks at me all apologetically. 'Excuse my language.'

I let out a sarcastic puff of air. Excuse his language?

'Where do we go from here?' William goes on, ignoring my bemusement and looking to Miller.

Yes, let's get this done with. I look at Miller, too, making him shift uncomfortably in his chair. 'I still want out,' Miller says, clearly uncomfortable under two sets of watchful eyes, yet his declaration is delivered with a load of determination. Determination is good. Although I've silently concluded that it isn't enough.

'Yes, we've established that. But I'll ask you again, do you think they'll let you walk away?' It's a rhetorical question. It requires no answer. And it doesn't get one. So William continues. 'Why did you take her there, Hart? Knowing how delicate things are, why?'

I seize up. Every guilty muscle in my body solidifies as a result of that question. I can't let him take the flak for that one. 'He didn't take me,' I whisper, ashamed, feeling Miller's hold of my hand tighten. 'Miller was at Ice. I was at home. I had a call on my phone. Unknown number.'

William frowns. 'Go on.'

I gulp down some courage and look at Miller out of the corner of my eye, catching a soft, loving expression. 'I could hear a conversation and I didn't like what I heard.' I wait for the obvious question but gasp when William says something else instead.

'Sophia.' He closes his eyes and inhales warily. 'Sophia-fucking-Reinhoff.' His eyes open and land on Miller with a bang. 'So much for playing down your relationship with Olivia.'

'Miller did nothing,' I argue, leaning forward. 'I was the one who caused this situation. I went to the club. I tipped Miller over the edge.'

'How?'

My mouth snaps shut and I'm far back in my chair again. He won't want to hear this any more than Miller wanted to see it. 'I . . .' My face heats under William's expectant look. 'I . . .'

'She was recognised.' Miller steps in, and I know it's because he'll be blaming this part on William.

'Miller—'

'No, Olivia.' He cuts me off and leans forward a little. 'She was recognised by one of your *clients*.'

The regret that invades William's face fills me with guilt.

'I watched as some slime ball tried to claim her from me, offered to take care of her.' He's beginning to tremble, the reminder re-stoking his anger. 'Tell me, Mr Anderson, what would you have done?'

'Killed him.'

I recoil in response to William's short, menacing reply, knowing for certain he absolutely means it.

'Well, I spared him –' Miller relaxes back in his chair – 'just. Does that make me a better man than you?'

'I believe it might,' William replies, no hesitation and with complete honesty. For some reason, I'm not surprised.

'I'm glad we've cleared that up. Now, let's move on.' Miller shifts in his chair. 'I'm getting out, I'm taking Cassie with me, and I'll tell you exactly how.'

William regards him carefully for a while, and then both men turn to me. 'You want me to leave?'

'Wait in the bar for me,' Miller says coolly, showing me a face that I've fast become familiar with. It's his I'm-not-budging face.

'So, you only brought me in here to fuck me on his desk?'

'Olivia!' William scolds me, pulling my contemptuous glare from Miller to him for a few moments. He's returning my glare, and if I wasn't so slighted at the moment, I'd snarl at him. But I accept I can be of no help here. In fact, everything that has brought us to now only confirms that I'm a hindrance, but I'm pissed off for . . . everything. For feeling helpless, for being difficult.

Standing quietly, I turn my back without another word and escape the tension, shutting the door quietly behind me. I walk numbly down the corridor, navigating my way to the ladies' washroom, ignoring the fact that I know exactly which way to go. I disregard the looks of interest being thrown at me by men, women, and staff on my way. It's hard, but I succeed, the knowledge of what further state of hopelessness the looks could cause giving me the necessary strength to do so.

Once I've used the toilet, washed my hands, and stared at myself blankly in the mirror for an age, I make tracks to the Lounge Bar and settle on a barstool, quickly ordering a glass of wine – anything to focus on except what may be going down in William's office.

'Madam.' The barman smiles, sliding my drink across to me.

'Thank you.' I take a long swig and cast my eyes around the bar, grateful that Carl is no longer here. A quick look at my phone tells me it's only noon. It feels like this morning has been dragging out over years, but the thought of seeing Nan and taking her home in a few hours lifts my tired mood.

I feel myself relax under the peaceful surroundings of the bar and my continuous sips of wine . . . until that feeling – the one I haven't felt since before we left for New York – is suddenly bombarding me. Chills. Prickling chills jumping onto my shoulders, and then the raised neck hair joins them. Reaching up and stroking the back of my neck, I glance to the side, seeing nothing unusual, only men sipping from tumblers, talking quietly, and a woman seated on the stool next to me. I brush off the tingling sensations and sip some more.

The barman approaches, smiling as he passes to attend to the lady. 'Hendrick's, please,' she orders, her soft, husky voice dripping with sex, just how I remember most of William's women sounded. It's like they've taken lessons in perfecting the art of verbal seduction, even something as simple as ordering a drink sounding erotic. Despite the reminder, I smile to myself, and I have no idea why. Maybe because I know for sure that I never sounded like that.

I take my wine to my lips, watching as the barman pours and passes the lady her glass before turning my back slightly to get the entrance of the bar into view, waiting for Miller and William to appear. How long will they be? Are they still alive? I try to stop worrying, finding it easy when all of those unwanted sensations return, making me turn slowly, automatically.

I find the woman facing me, her glass held lightly in her dainty fingers.

Fingers like mine.

My heart catapults up to my head and explodes, scattering millions of memories into a haze that floats before me. The visions are clear. Too clear.

'My baby girl,' she whispers.

Chapter 15

The smash of my glass as it drops from my lifeless hand and clashes with the floor doesn't even rip our eyes apart.

Sapphire on sapphire.

Sorrow on shock.

Mother on daughter.

'No,' I whimper, falling to my feet from the stool and backing away on unstable legs. 'No!' I whirl around to escape, dizzy, shaking and breathless, but crash into a huge chest. I feel strong palms circle my upper arms, and I look up to find Carl assessing my distraught face with worried eyes. It only confirms that what I think I just saw is real. The evil guy looks apprehensive – a look that doesn't suit him at all.

Tears burst from my tortured eyes as he holds me in place, anxious vibes shooting from his big body into me. 'Fucking hell,' he growls. 'Gracie, what the fuck are you playing at?'

The mention of my mother's name injects life into my numb body. 'Let me go!' I scream, and buck in Carl's hold, distressed and panicked. 'Please, let me go!'

'Olivia?' Her voice seeps into the corners of my mind, prompting a barrage of lost memories to attack me. 'Olivia, please.'

I hear her voice from when I was a small child. I hear her humming lullabies, feel her soft fingers stroking my cheek. I see her back for the last time walking out of Nan's kitchen. It's all confusing me. Her face has spiked it all. 'Please,' I beg, turning my welling eyes up to Carl, my voice trembling, my heart choking me. 'Please.'

His lips straighten and every possible emotion plays like a camera roll across the evil guy's face – sorrow, sadness, guilt, anger. 'Fuck,' he curses, and I'm suddenly being pulled behind the bar. He smashes his fist on a concealed button behind a shelf full of spirits, and the whole building is suddenly screaming, alarm bells ringing so loudly around us, making everyone jump up from their chairs. The hype of activity is instant, and the unbearable sound is strangely soothing. He's drawing the attention of everyone, but I know he wants just one man here.

'Olivia, baby.'

I feel an electric shock fly through my body as her soft touch meets my arm. It has my small frame bucking again in Carl's hold, except this time I manage to free myself.

'Gracie, leave her!' Carl roars as I bolt from behind the bar, my legs instantly numb from the speed I've achieved so quickly. I can think of nothing except escaping. Get out of here. Run away. I make it to the bar door and take the corner quickly, just catching her coming after me, but then William appears from nowhere and blocks her.

'Gracie!' William's tone is oozing threat as he fights to hold her back. 'You stupid woman!'

'Don't let her go!' she yells. 'Please, don't let her go!' I can hear the anguish in her voice, see the terror on her beautiful face as it disappears from my view when I round the corner. I can see it. But I don't feel it. I can only feel my own hurt, anger, confusion, and I can't cope with any of it. I return my focus forward and pelt for the doors that'll take me away from this hellhole, but I'm suddenly not moving anymore, and the sensation of my legs working but the door not coming any closer takes a while to sink in past the distress consuming me.

'Olivia, I'm here.' Miller's soothing words are whispered quietly into my ear, but however hushed they are, I hear him perfectly over the screaming alarms and frantic activity around me. 'Shhhh.'

I whimper and turn, throwing my arms around him and holding on for dear life. 'Help me,' I sob into his shoulder. 'Take me away, please.' I feel my feet leave the ground, feel myself held secure against his chest.

'Shhhh.' He cups the back of my head, pushing my face into the comfort of his neck as he starts to pace away. His strides are purposeful. I can feel the panic in me beginning to subside, just from being immersed in his *thing*. 'We're leaving, Olivia. I'm getting you away from here.'

My dead muscles come to life under his fierce hold of me and his calming tones, and I squeeze my appreciation, no words forming to voice it. I'm vaguely aware of the blaring sirens cutting abruptly, but I'm more than aware of footsteps pounding behind us. Two pairs of pounding feet. And neither are Miller's.

'Don't take her away from me!'

I swallow hard and push my face farther into Miller's neck as he ignores my mother's demand and marches on.

'Gracie!' William's bellow dilutes the stamping of feet, making Miller's stride falter slightly, but my head shaking into him soon kicks him back into top gear. 'Gracie, damn it! Leave her!'

'No!'

We're suddenly jerked to a stop and Miller growls, swinging around to confront my mother. 'Let go of my arm,' he hisses, his tone bursting with the same level of threat that I've heard him use on others. The fact that this woman is my mother is of no consequence to Miller. 'I won't repeat myself.' He remains still, obviously waiting for her to let go rather than yanking himself from her grip.

'I'm not letting you take her.' Gracie's resolute voice puts the fear of God in me. I can't face her. I don't *want* to face her. 'I need to talk to her. Explain so many things.'

Miller begins to pulsate against me, and it's in this moment I fully comprehend my situation. He's looking at my mother. He's looking at the woman who abandoned me. 'She'll talk to you when *she's* ready,' he says quietly, but there's no mistaking the warning laced in his words. '*If* she's ready.'

I feel his face turn into the side of my head and his lips push into my hair, breathing in deeply. He's reassuring me. He's telling me I'm going to be doing nothing that I don't want to do. And I love him so much for it.

'But I need to talk to her now.' Determination is rife in her tone. 'She needs to know—'

Miller loses it in the blink of an eye. 'Does she look ready to talk to you?' he roars, making me jump in his arms. 'You abandoned her!'

'I had no choice.' My mother's words are shaky, her emotion obvious. Yet I feel no empathy, and I wonder right now if that makes me inhuman. Heartless. No, I have a heart, and it's pounding in my chest right now, reminding me of *her* cruel actions all those years ago. My heart has no room for Gracie Taylor. It's too consumed by Miller Hart.

'We all have choices,' Miller says, 'and I've made mine. I'd walk through the bowels of hell for this girl, and I am. You didn't. *That's* what makes me worthy of her love. *That's* what makes me deserve her.'

My sobs return full force as a result of his admission. Knowing he loves me fills the emptiness within me with pure, powerful gratitude. Hearing him confirm that he thinks he's worthy of my love makes it all overflow.

'You self-righteous arsehole,' Gracie seethes, that Taylor sass flying up to support her.

'Gracie, darling,' William pipes up.

'No, Will! I left to prevent her from being subjected to the depravity I faced. I've skipped from country to country for eighteen years, killing myself on a daily basis that I couldn't be with her. That I couldn't be a mum! I'll be damned if he's going to strut into her life and toss every painful moment I've endured all these years to shit!'

That statement registers loud and clear through my crippling agony. Her pain? Her fucking pain? My need to jump from Miller's arms and slap her face sends me momentarily dizzy with anger, but Miller pulls a long, steady breath of air and flexes his arm around my waist, distracting me from my intention. He knows. He knows what those words have done to me. He shifts a palm to the back of my leg and tugs in a sign for me to respond, so I wrap my thighs around his waist in acknowledgement, and maybe for my mother's benefit.

This is all I need. He's not giving me up and I'm not letting him go. Not even for my mother.

'She's *mine*,' Miller states coolly, calmly, and confidently. 'Not even *you* will rob her from me.' His almost unreasonable promise fills me with hope. 'Take me on, Gracie. I fucking *dare* you.' He turns and strides out of the Society, me coiled around him like a scarf – a tightly knotted scarf that will never be undone.

'You have to let go now,' Miller murmurs into my hair when we reach his car, but I answer only by squeezing him tightly and moaning into his hair. 'Olivia, come on now.'

Sniffing back my subsiding tears, I peel my wet face from his neck, keeping my eyes on the sodden collar of his crisp white shirt. My makeup has rubbed off on it. There's mascara and pink blush mixed and embedded into the expensive material. 'It's ruined,' I sigh. I don't need to see him to know a frown has just appeared on his handsome face.

'It's fine,' he replies, confusion rich in his tone, confirming my previous thought. 'Here, jump down.'

I relent and detach myself from his tall frame with his assistance, then stand before him, eyes dropped, not wanting to face his perplexity. He'll demand an elaboration on my nonchalance. I don't want to elaborate, and no amount of demanding will make me. So it's simply easier to avoid his probing stare. 'Let's go get Nan,' I practically sing, pivoting and making for the passenger side, leaving Miller behind, unquestionably confused. I don't care. As far as I'm concerned, what just happened never happened. I slip into the seat and shut the door, making fast work of getting my belt on. I'm dying to get to Nan, desperate to take her home and start helping with her recuperation.

I ignore the heat of his eyes on me when he slips in beside me, choosing to reach forward and flick the stereo on instead. I smile when M83's "Midnight City" blasts from all of the speakers. Perfect.

After a good few seconds have passed and Miller still hasn't started his car, I finally pluck up the courage to face him. I smile brighter. 'Chop-chop.'

He barely contains his recoil. 'Livy, what . . .'

I reach up and push my fingertips to his lips, immediately shutting him up. 'No *them*, Miller,' I start, tracing my way to his throat when I'm certain he'll let me continue without interruption. His Adam's apple rolls under my touch when he gulps. 'Just *us*.' I smile and watch as his eyes narrow in uncertainty, his head moving from side to side slowly. Then he returns my smile with a small one of his own and takes my hand to his mouth and kisses it tenderly.

'Us,' he confirms, broadening my smile. I nod my thanks and reclaim my hand, getting comfortable in the leather seat, my head dropped back, my eyes staring up at the ceiling. I do an incredible job of centring my thoughts on one thing and one thing alone.

Nan.

Seeing her lovely face, listening to her spunky words, feeling her squidgy body when I take her in a fierce hug, and relishing in the time I'll get to spend with her while she's recovering. It's my job. No one else's. No one else gets the pleasure of all of those things. Just me. She's mine.

'For now I'll respect your request,' Miller muses as he turns the engine over, and I look out the corner of my eye to see him doing exactly the same to me. I quickly divert my stare forward, ignoring his words *and* his look, which tells me I'm not going to be basking in ignorance for long. I know this, but for now I have the perfect distraction and I'm going to throw myself into it completely.

The hospital is horribly hot and stuffy, but crazily a source of calm. My feet march on with resolve, like my body has cottoned on to my ploy and is assisting me in reaching the object of my distraction plan without delay. Miller hasn't said a word since we pulled away from the Society. He's left me to my thoughts, which have been blocking anything that may tarnish the elation I'm depending on once I lay my eyes on my grandmother. His palm is wrapped securely around my nape as he walks beside me, his finger kneading softly into my flesh. I love how he knows what I need, and I need this. Him. And Nan. Nothing else.

We round the corner into Cedar Ward, and I immediately hear the distant cackling of Nan, making that elation I was depending on soar. My pace picks up, eager to make it to her, and when I enter the bay of beds where I know her to be, every lost piece of me clicks right back into place. She's sitting in her chair, fully dressed in her Sunday best, with her huge carpetbag resting on her lap. And she's hooting bursts of laughter at the TV. I relax under Miller's hold and stand watching her for the longest time, until her old navy eyes pull from the screen and find me. They're all watery from her laughter, and she reaches up and brushes the hysterical tears away from her cheeks.

Then her smile disappears and she scowls at me, making my

delight run and hide and my happy heart quicken, but now in worry. Does she know something? Is it written all over my face? 'About time!' she squawks, aiming the remote control at the screen and zapping it off.

Her harshness restores that happiness in a second, and my fears that she may know something is off disappear. She must never know. I refuse to risk her health further. 'I'm a half hour early,' I say, taking Miller's wrist and lifting it to look at his watch. 'They said four.'

'Well, I've been sitting here getting a numb arse for the past hour.' She frowns. 'Have you cut your hair?'

'Just a trim.' I reach up and pat it down.

She goes to stand, and Miller disappears from my side quickly, taking the bag from her and offering his hand. She pauses and looks up at him, her irritation being replaced with an impish grin. 'Such a gentleman,' she gushes, laying her wrinkled hand in Miller's. 'Thank you.'

'You're welcome,' Miller replies, bowing as he helps her up. 'How are you feeling, Mrs Taylor?'

'Perfect,' she answers surely, steadying herself on her feet. She's not perfect at all; she's a little wobbly on her feet, and Miller's quick flick of his eyes to me tells me he's noticed it, too. 'Take me home, Miller. I'll make you beef Wellington.'

I scoff my thoughts on that and glance to my right when the ward nurse appears with a paper bag. 'Your grandmother's medication.' She smiles as she hands it to me. 'Your grandmother knows what pills and when, but I also went over it with her son.' The nurse blushes.

'Her son?' I blurt, my eyes widening.

'Yes, the lovely man who's here twice a day every day.'

I swing around and find Miller looking as confused as I am and Nan smirking from ear to ear. She bursts into a helpless fit of giggles, bending slightly as Miller holds her arm. 'Oh bless you, dear. He's not my son.'

'Oh . . .' the nurse says, now joining Miller and me in the confusion department. 'I assumed . . . well, I just assumed.'

Nan gains a little composure and straightens out, rolling her eyes and threading her arm through Miller's. 'William is an old family friend, dear.'

I'm scoffing again but rein it in when Nan throws an inquisitive look my way. An old family friend? Seriously? My mind is sprinting, yet I do an incredible job of preventing my mouth from blurting questions left, right, and centre. I don't want to know. I've just left the old family friend back at the Society, holding back my mo— 'Are you ready?' I ask, keen to put this little misunderstanding to rest.

'Yes, Livy. I've been ready for an hour,' she bites back, her lips pursing as she turns her sour eyes onto the nurse. 'This is my granddaughter's boyfriend,' Nan announces, louder than necessary, like she's showcasing him to the whole ward – the proverbial trophy on her arm. 'Handsome bugger, isn't he?'

'Nan!' I gasp, blushing on Miller's behalf. 'Stop it!'

The nurse smiles and backs away slowly. 'Bed rest for a week, Mrs Taylor.'

'Yes, yes.' She dismisses the nurse and nods to Miller. 'He has great buns.'

I choke, Miller chuckles, and the nurse burns bright red as her eyes fight to drop in the area of Miller's buns, but I'm saved from my grandmother's crafty behaviour when my mobile starts singing from my bag. Shaking my head in total exasperation, I rifle through and locate it, immediately freezing when I see William's name illuminating my screen.

Reject.

I shove it back in my bag and swing a wary look to Miller's cheery face when his phone starts shouting from his inside pocket. His smile drops as he catches my look and registers the ringing of his phone. I shake my head subtly, hoping Nan doesn't catch the silent messages passing between Miller and

I, then get mighty mad when he drops Nan's bag and slowly reaches for his inside pocket. I silently scream at him to leave it, firing continuous looks of warning across the bed, but I'm flat-out ignored and he connects the call. 'Would you?' he asks, indicating for me to take over his hold of Nan.

Trying my hardest not to screw my face up in disgust, because I know Nan's watchful eyes are passing between us, I approach slowly and replace Miller's arm with my own. 'Important call?' Nan asks suspiciously. I should have known nothing gets past her.

'You could say that.' Miller drops a chaste kiss on my forehead in a pathetic attempt to pacify me, and Nan sighs dreamily as she watches Miller's tight buns walk away. 'Yes,' Miller greets down the line as he disappears around the corner.

I'm pouting. I can't help myself, and I resent Miller for not being able to do what comes to me too easily. Bury my head in the sand. Ignore it. Carry on like nothing shitty has ever happened.

'Are you and Miller OK?' Nan's concerned croak breaks through my racing mind and puts me firmly back where I want to be.

'Perfect,' I lie, forcing a smile and collecting her bag from the floor. 'Are you ready?'

'Yes!' she grumbles, exasperated, before slapping a smile back on her age-worn face and turning towards the bed opposite hers, forcing me to turn with her. 'Bye, Enid!' she shouts, stirring the poor old lady from what looks like a deep sleep. 'Enid!'

'Nan, she's snoozing!'

'She's always bloody snoozing. Enid!'

The old dear's eyes slowly open until she's staring around, a little bewildered.

'Over here!' Nan yells, raising her hand and waving it above her head. 'Cooooeeee!'

'For God's sake,' I grumble, my feet starting to move when Nan begins trotting across the ward.

'Don't use the Lord's name in vain, Olivia,' she warns, dragging me alongside her. 'Enid, dear, I'm going home now.'

Enid gives us a gummy smile, making a small laugh of sympathy slip from my mouth. She's so frail and clearly not with it. 'Where are you going?' she croaks, attempting to sit up but giving up on an exhausted sigh.

'Home, dear.' Nan gets us to the side of Enid's bed and shuffles from my hold so she can take her hand. 'This is my granddaughter, Olivia. Remember? You met her before.'

'I did?' She turns inspecting eyes on me and Nan turns to follow her stare, smiling at me when she has me in view. 'Oh yes. I remember.'

I smile as both ladies hold me in place with old, wise eyes, feeling a little uncomfortable under their studying stares. 'It was nice to meet you, Enid.'

'You take care, duck.' She pulls her hand from Nan's with some determined effort and grasps at air before me, prompting me to give her what she's looking for. I rest my hand in hers. 'He'll be perfect,' she says, making my head cock in question. 'He'll be perfect for you.'

'Who will?' I ask on a nervous laugh, flicking my eyes to a serious-looking Nan. She shrugs and turns back towards Enid, who's drawing a laboured breath of air, ready to enlighten us, but she says no more, dropping my hand and falling back into a deep sleep.

I bite my lip and resist the urge to tell a sleeping Enid that he's already perfect for me, however weird her surprising claim is.

'Hmmm.' Nan's thoughtful hum drags my attention back to her. She's watching Enid sleeping with a fond smile. 'No family,' Nan says, spiking immediate sadness within me. 'She's been here for over a month and not one person has visited. Can you imagine being so alone?'

'No,' I admit, contemplating such loneliness. I may have cut myself off from the world, but I was never lonely. Never *alone*. Miller was, though.

'Surround yourself with people who love you,' Nan says to herself, yet the intention for me to hear is obvious, although her reason for such a statement isn't. 'Take me home, sweetheart.'

I waste no time gesturing my arm for Nan to slip hers through and start a slow, easy walk to the exit. 'Are you feeling OK?' I ask, just as Miller rounds the corner, his luscious lips displaying a hint of a smile. He isn't fooling me. I caught the stressed eyes on his impassive face before he spotted us.

'Here he is!' Nan sings. 'All suited and booted.'

Miller relieves me of Nan's bag and takes up position on the other side of her, offering his arm, too, which she takes on a happy smile. 'The rose between two thorns,' she titters, forcing us both closer to her with a surprisingly firm tightening of her arms. 'Toodle-oo!' she shouts at the nurse's station as we pass. 'Farewell!'

'Goodbye, Mrs Taylor!' They all laugh as we escort my grandmother from the ward, and I smile my apology to the team of medical staff who've endured days of her sass. I'm not really that sorry, only for not being the one on the constant receiving end of that Taylor sass.

It takes us a while, but we eventually make it out of the hospital, Miller and I both happy to amble along, while Nan has to be constantly held back from virtually sprinting from the place she's seen as a prison for the duration of her stay. I haven't looked at Miller once in the twenty minutes it's taken us to make it to his car, though I've felt his eyes directed at me across Nan's head on more than one occasion, probably gauging my thought process. If Nan wasn't between us, I'd tell him exactly what my thought process is and save him the trouble.

It's simple. I don't care and I don't want to know. Whatever he and William may have spoken about, whatever plans they've made, I don't want to know. The fact that Miller is probably fully armed in the knowledge department isn't in the least bit piquing my curiosity as to what that knowledge might be. I have, however, silently concluded that William knew Gracie Taylor was here and he chose not to tell me. I'm not sure whether that should make me angry with him or grateful.

'Well, would you look at Mr Swanky Pants!' Nan laughs when Miller opens the back door of his Merc for her and swoops his arm in guidance – all gentlemanly. He's taking Nan's delusional conclusion that he's always such a gent and playing on it. But I'll let it pass, if only to keep that incredible smile gracing her face. I toss him slightly narrowed eyes, fighting to prevent matching his amusement as he helps Nan lower to the seat. 'Oh, I say!' she gasps, getting comfy on the backseat. 'I feel like royalty!'

'You are, Mrs Taylor,' Miller replies as he shuts the door, hiding the satisfied blush that's just crept onto her cheeks. Now that Nan's out of the way, it's just me and Miller, and I seriously dislike the thoughtful look on his face. Where's all the impassiveness gone? I love and hate all of these facial expressions. 'William would like to speak to you,' he whispers, quite wisely, too, given Nan's a mere foot away, albeit behind a closed door.

I'm quickly on my guard. 'Not now,' I hiss, knowing that I probably mean never. 'Right now I have one priority.'

'I concur,' Miller agrees without delay, surprising me. He moves in and dips to get our faces level. Reassuring blue eyes haul me into their safety and comfort, make my arms twitch at my sides. 'Which is why I told him you're not ready.'

I give up fighting to keep them by my sides and throw them over his shoulders in gratitude. 'I love you.'

'We established that long ago, sweet girl,' he whispers, pulling back to get my face in view. 'Let me taste you.'

Our mouths meet and my feet leave the ground, our tongues falling into a beautifully delicate pace of swirling, each of us nipping at each other's lips when we pull back, time and time again. I'm lost, consumed, oblivious to our very public surroundings . . . until a sharp rapping jolts me back to the here and now and we both pull apart. Miller huffs a quiet, disbelieving shot of laughter as we turn towards the window of his car. I can't see Nan's face – the blacked out windows are preventing it, but if I could, I know she'd be pushed up against the glass, grinning.

'A treasure,' Miller mutters, releasing me and straightening me out before beginning on himself. It's been some time since he's fixed his suit, but he's making up for it now, taking a good minute to pull and smooth every part of him into place while I watch on a smile, comforted by one of his finicky ways, even reaching up and dusting off a piece of lint that he's missed. He smiles in response, reaches for my nape, and pulls me forward, planting a kiss on my forehead.

Rap rap rap!

'Give me strength,' he mumbles against my skin, then releases me and turns a scowl onto the window of his car. 'Beautiful things should be savoured, Mrs Taylor.'

Nan's answer to that is another round of taps on the window, prompting Miller to bend and get up close to the window, his scowl still firmly in place. My amusement increases when he raps right back. I hear Nan's gasp of shock, even through the closed door, not that it has any effect on my part-time gentleman. He raps again.

'Miller, behave,' I laugh, loving the irritation flaming in him under my grandmother's pesky behaviour.

'She really is royal.' He straightens and slips his hands into his pockets. 'A royal . . .'

'Pain in the arse?' I finish for him when he pulls up, guilt jumping onto his face.

'Sometimes,' he agrees, making me laugh. 'Let's get her ladyship home, shall we?' He nods towards the other side of the car and I follow his instruction, taking myself to the passenger side and jumping in the back with Nan.

When I've got my seat belt on, I look across and find her fiddling with hers, so I lend a hand and secure it for her. 'There,' I say, resting back in my seat and watching as she takes in the sumptuous interior of Miller's posh car. She reaches up and presses a button that puts a light on, then turns it off again. She fiddles with the air-con buttons between the footwells, humming her approval. She pushes a button that sends her window down, then pushes it again to close it back up. Then she finds an armrest between us and pulls it down, sliding the runner back to reveal cup holders. Old, amazed navy eyes fly up to mine and she forms an O with her marshmallow lips. 'I bet the queen's car isn't as posh as this.' Her comment should make me laugh, but I'm too busy flicking nervous eyes to Miller in the rearview mirror, trying to gauge his reaction to all this messing of his perfect world.

He's staring at me, his jaw tight, and I return that smile awkwardly, mouthing 'sorry' on a bunched up face. His lovely head shakes from side to side, tousling up his waves as he virtually screeches out of the parking space. I conclude very quickly that he wants to get this journey over with as soon as possible and limit the time my dear grandmother has to screw around with his perfect world. God forbid if she could reach the temperature controls up front. I inwardly laugh. And he wanted to move her into his flat? Holy shit, he'd have a seizure every five minutes!

There are continuous hoots of glee coming from Nan as Miller zips and weaves through the London traffic, but her excitement dulls to nothing when she catches sight of my left hand as it reaches up to rest on the seat in front of me. I realise what's holding her attention straightaway. She reaches across the car and takes my hand, pulling it towards her and studying it quietly. I can do nothing more than let her, bracing myself for her reaction. I turn pleading eyes up to the rearview mirror and find Miller watching intermittently between keeping an eye on the road.

'Hmmm,' she hums, rubbing across the peak of my ring with the pad of her thumb. 'So, Miller, when are you marrying my beautiful granddaughter?' Her raised grey eyebrows are quickly on me, despite the question being directed at Miller, and I shrink into the leather seat. He better think of something quick-sharp, because I haven't the foggiest idea of what to tell her. I need her to stop looking at me like that. My cheeks are flaming red-hot and my throat is closing off under the pressure, making speech impossible. 'Well?' she prompts.

'I'm not.' Miller's short, sharp response makes everything die inside. He has no problem telling my spunky nan, and while I understand him, I'm not sure she will. She's old school.

'Why ever not?' She sounds offended, almost angry, and I consider the possibility of her reaching forward and smacking the back of Miller's head. She probably would. 'What's wrong with her?'

I'd laugh if I could find air to draw breath. What's wrong with me? Everything!

'That ring is a sign of my love, Mrs Taylor. My eternal love.'

'That's all good and well, but what's it doing on her wedding finger?'

'Because your beautiful ring holds position on her right hand and I wouldn't be so disrespectful as to ask her to replace what's been in her life for longer than me.'

I swell with pride and Nan stutters her astonishment. 'Can't we just swap them?'

'Are you trying to marry me off?' I ask, finally finding some words.

'So?' she huffs, her nose put firmly out of joint, not even

Miller's respectful explanation diluting her displeasure. 'You plan on living in sin forever?'

Her absent-minded choice of word resonates deeply, and I find mine and Miller's eyes locked together in the mirror, mine wide, his wary.

Sin.

There are so many sinful things she's unaware of, things that my poor mind is struggling to deal with. I wouldn't have exposed her to it before, no matter how sassy and spunky she might be, and I'm most certainly not exposing her to it now. Not with her being so delicate after her heart attack, though you'd never know it. Being hospitalised for the past few days seems to have injected even more sass into her Taylor bones.

Miller returns his eyes to the road, and I remain tense in my seat, but Nan keeps expectant eyes on my OCD-suffering, ex-prostitute, notorious male ex-escort . . .

I sigh. My mind hasn't the strength to even mentally list the endless sinful things that Miller was.

'I plan on worshipping your granddaughter for the rest of my life, Mrs Taylor,' Miller says quietly, yet Nan's wistful coo indicates she heard it perfectly, and that might just be good enough. It is for me, and though I constantly tell myself no one else matters, Nan's approval really does. I think I have it. I'll just have to keep telling myself that her lacking knowledge is of no consequence, that her opinion wouldn't change in the least bit if she knew every sordid detail.

'Home sweet home, my lady.' Miller breaks into my stray thoughts as we pull up to Nan's house. I notice George and Gregory on the pavement outside, both men sitting on the low wall at the end of our front garden, both men looking apprehensive. I haven't the time or energy to waste on worrying about Miller and Gregory in such close proximity. They just better behave.

'What are they doing here?' Nan grumbles, making no

attempt to get out, instead waiting for Miller to open the door for her. She's not fooling me. She's loving all of the special treatment, not that she doesn't get it under normal circumstances. 'I'm not an invalid!'

'I beg to differ,' Miller retorts firmly, offering his hand, which she takes on a little scowl. 'Less of the sass, Mrs Taylor.'

I chuckle to myself as I get out of the car and join them on the pavement, hearing Nan huffing and puffing all over Miller. 'The cheek!'

'Olivia's certainly learned from the best of them,' he grumbles, giving Nan up to George when he steps forward, a worried look all over his old round face.

'How are you feeling, Josephine?' George says, taking Nan's arm.

'I'm fine!' She accepts Georges arm, indicating her need for support, and lets him lead her up the garden path. 'How are you, Gregory?' she asks as she passes him. 'And Ben?'

He's told her? I look to my friend, as does Miller, as does George. Four sets of eyes are all resting on Gregory, spiking a string of uncomfortable shifting movements to play out before us. His boots scuff the concrete, he flicks us all wide eyes, and we all just stand staring at the poor guy, waiting for his reply. He coughs. 'Um, yeah, fine. We're fine. How are you, Nan?'

'Perfect,' she replies in an instant, and nudges George on his way. 'Let's make some tea.'

Everyone jumps back into action and follows Nan and George towards the house, but I quickly take over the lead so I can open the front door, allowing them all to pass as I hold it open. The deep inhale that she takes as she's helped over the threshold and absorbs the familiarity of her home fills me with bliss that could rival the wonderful place that Miller takes me to when I'm the sole focus of his attention. And that's some mighty blissful place. Having her home, seeing and hearing her sass, it's all stamping out other more challenging matters that I'm currently doing anything to avoid dealing with.

Gregory wanders in, giving me a cheeky wink that escalates my happiness, followed by Miller, who takes over my hold of the door and nods for me to continue. 'Such a gentleman,' I tease, turning to see Nan now guiding George to the kitchen at the back of the house, when she should be settling on the couch or maybe even going to bed. This is going to be hard work. She's impossible! On a roll of my eyes, I make chase, set on nailing down a few rules, but a sharp slap of my arse stops me dead in my tracks. The sting is instant and I reach to rub the soreness away as I whirl around, finding Miller pushing the door closed.

'Ouch!' Ouch? I have no other words. Miller Hart – my man whose manners put royalty to shame, just slapped my arse? Not patted. Slapped. And a stinger of a slap, too.

A perfectly straight face slowly turns to me, and he inhales as he smoothes down his suit, taking his usual ridiculous time and care, while I remain totally dumbfounded before him, waiting for . . . something . . . anything.

'Give me something!' I blurt, still rubbing at my backside.

He finishes up perfecting his perfect suit, then sweeps his perfect hair from the goddamn perfect face. His eyes darken. My legs cross in my standing position. 'Another one?' he asks casually, a glint of mischief in his beautiful eyes.

I take a deep breath and hold it, biting at my bottom lip furiously. What's gotten into him? Is Nan rubbing off on him?

'What I'd actually like to do is sink my teeth into that gorgeous, cute arse.'

All breath leaves my lungs and sexual anticipation devours me. The bastard. He has no intention whatsoever of finishing what he's started. But that doesn't zap my craving or my need. Damn him!

He nears, slowly, like he's on the prowl, my eyes following him until he's breathing down on me. 'Sweet Nan isn't in any fit state to be brandishing a carving knife.' He wiggles a suggestive eyebrow. It's probably the most unlike-Miller action of all the unlike-Miller actions I've experienced as our relationship has grown. I can't help myself. I fall to pieces before him, but he doesn't recoil in offense like I expect him to. He starts laughing, too, and while my desperate desire for him has faded somewhat, the overwhelming happiness coursing through me is a good compromise.

'Don't be so sure.' I chuckle as he takes my waist and turns me in his arms, starting to guide me down the hall with his chin resting on my shoulder. 'I think her sass has multiplied as a result of all that medication.'

He pushes his mouth to my ear. It has me closing my eyes and soaking up every delicious piece of him touching me. 'I concur,' he whispers, nibbling at my lobe.

I don't need to fight the flames of desire from my veins because they turn to flames of madness the moment we fall into the kitchen and I catch Nan filling the kettle at the sink. 'Nan!'

'I tried!' George gasps, throwing exasperated arms into the air as he sits. 'She's having none of it!'

'Me too,' Gregory interjects, just to put me firmly in the picture, his arse dropping to a chair at the kitchen table. He looks over at me, shaking his head. 'I'm not up for a verbal beating down. I've had enough physical ones.'

Guilt plagues me for a split second as a result of my best friend's curt quip, before I'm reminded of my grievance when the kettle clatters against the edge of the sink. 'For God's sake!' I shout, zooming across the kitchen when she totters slightly. Miller's in quick pursuit, and I hear the scraping of two chairs, indicating Gregory's and George's quick movements. 'Why can't you just listen?' I yell, anger and worry all mixing together, making me shake as I hold her.

'Stop fussing!' she barks, trying to bat my grappling hands away. 'I'm no invalid!'

It takes every modicum of strength not to scream my frustration at her, and I turn my helpless eyes to Miller, surprised to see annoyance rife on his lovely face. His lips straighten, which would usually be cause for concern, but right now I'm silently willing him to help rein in my stubborn grandmother.

'Here,' he mutters impatiently, removing the kettle from her hands and slamming it down before taking possession of Nan. 'You will sit, Mrs Taylor.' He guides a bewildered Nan past a stunned George and Gregory and sits her in a chair. She's looking up at Miller from her seated position with wary eyes as he towers over her, daring her to defy him. She's speechless, her mouth dropped open in shock. Miller drags in a long, calming pull of breath, hitches up his trousers slightly at the thighs, then lowers to his haunches before her. Nan's eyes follow him down until they're level. She remains silent, and so do the rest of us.

'You will do as you're told,' Miller begins, quickly raising a hand and placing a finger over her lips when she inhales, ready to fire back some sass. 'Nuh-uh-uh,' Miller cuts in firmly. I might not be able to see his face, but I can see the slight warning cock of his head, and I know for sure she's also being held in place with equally warning eyes. Miller slowly, carefully removes his finger and she immediately purses her lips indignantly.

'Quite the bossy man, aren't you?'

'You have no idea, Mrs Taylor.'

Nan's eyes flip to mine, searching for . . . I don't know what, but I know I'm giving her something, even if I'm trying my hardest not to. My cheeks are flushing furiously. I damn them to hell for letting me down and shift under her curious gaze.

'Mrs Taylor,' Miller says quietly, saving me from further probing eyes when she returns her attention to him. 'I'm quite familiar with the Taylor sass.' He jabs a thumb over his shoulder in my general direction, making me want to announce that it's only utilised in special circumstances. But I refrain. Wisely. 'I've become quite accustomed to it, in fact.'

'Bully for you,' Nan mutters, raising her nose in the air insolently. 'What you gonna do? Spank me?'

I cough to conceal my laugh, as do George *and* Gregory. She's a gem!

'Not my style,' Miller replies flippantly, not biting to her sass. It only spikes more huffiness from Nan and snickering to the point of tears from the rest of us. This is just priceless, and I desperately avoid George's and Gregory's eyes, knowing they'll have me doubling over should I catch a glimpse of their own amusement.

'Do you know how much I love your granddaughter, Josephine?'

That soon brings all of the uncontrollable tittering to a rapid halt, and Nan's face softens in an instant. 'I have a good idea,' she says quietly.

'Well let me confirm it for you,' Miller says formally. 'It hurts like hell.' I freeze and watch Nan's face over Miller's shoulder practically burst with happiness. 'Right here.' He takes her hand and lays it over his suit jacket. 'My sweet girl has shown me how to love, and that just makes me love her all the more. She's everything to me. Seeing her hurt or sad, it cripples me, Josephine.'

I remain quiet in the background, just like Gregory and George. He's speaking to her like they're alone. I don't know what this has to do with Nan being obedient, but he seems to be in his stride and I trust it has some relevance.

'I know that feeling,' Nan murmurs, forcing a sad smile. I could cry. 'I've felt that before.'

Miller nods and reaches up to brush a stray grey curl from her forehead. 'Olivia is besotted with you, dear lady. And I'm quite fond of you, too.'

Nan gives Miller a shy smile and claims his hand. I've no

doubt she's squeezing it hard. 'You ain't so bad yourself.'

'I'm glad we've cleared that up.'

'And you have good buns!'

'So I'm told.' He laughs, leaning in and kissing her cheek. I crumble on the inside with happiness, when I should probably be rolling on the floor with laughter as a result of her cheeky remark.

Miller's never had anyone. Now he not only has me, but he has my nan as well. And the extent of his appreciation is suddenly so palpable. He loves Nan, too. On a different level, of course, but his feelings for her are strong. Very strong, and he's proved it in every word and action since we've returned from New York.

'Now –' he stands, leaving Nan seated, looking all content and dreamy – 'Olivia is going to tuck you into bed. I'll help Gregory make tea, and George is going to deliver it to your room.'

'If you insist.'

'I do.' Miller looks across to me, giving me an interested look when he catches my watery eyes. 'Chop-chop.'

I mentally pull myself together and collect Nan from her chair, eager to escape the presence of my beautiful man before he has me wailing all over the kitchen. 'OK?' I ask as she takes slow steps out of the kitchen, up the corridor towards the stairs.

'Never better,' she answers with total sincerity, tugging painfully at my heartstrings. My contentment is soon stolen and replaced with dread because no matter how far down I bury it in my head, there's one thing that I can't hide from her forever.

Gracie Taylor.

I'm struggling to come to terms with it myself. Nan would never cope.

'He'll marry you one day,' she muses to herself, snapping me from my wandering, agonising thoughts. 'You mark my words,

Olivia. I've never felt love so rich and pure in my eight decades of life.' She takes the stairs gingerly, me following and holding her from behind, my mind in a whirlwind of conflict – indescribable happiness and overshadowing sadness. 'Miller Hart loves you to death.'

Chapter 16

It takes me over an hour to tend to Nan, and I relish every moment, from helping her bathe to tucking her into bed. I dry and brush her hair, help her slip on her frilly nightie, and plump her pillows before helping her climb in. 'I bet you're loving this,' she muses quietly, patting down the bedding around her. She's sitting up, her grey curls perfectly swishing around her shoulders as she gets cosy.

'I like looking after you,' I admit, refraining from tagging on the end that I prefer looking after her when she really doesn't need it. I want her well, back to normal. She may have regained her spunk, but I'm not delusional to think that makes her fully recovered.

'You needn't think I'll allow you to slip back into that empty world you chose to hide in before Miller came along,' she tells me, keeping her attention on the sheets. I pause with my fussing and watch as she looks at me from the corner of her eye. 'Just so you know.'

'I know,' I appease her, ignoring the dash of doubt nibbling at the corner of my mind. It would be easy to hide again, rather than deal with all of the challenges ahead.

'I've told you before, Olivia,' she continues. I don't like where this conversation is heading. 'Falling in love is easy. Holding on to it is special. Don't think I'm silly enough to believe everything is perfect. I see a besotted man. I see a besotted girl.' She pauses. 'And one thing I can see even clearer than that are the demons Miller Hart is harbouring.'

I lose my breath.

'I can also see his desperation. He can't hide from me.' She watches me closely. I'm still holding my breath. 'He's depending on you, my darling girl. Help him.'

A light rapping at Nan's bedroom door startles me and I rush across her room to open the door, my mind racing, the need to escape making me panic. I find George looking slightly reluctant as he balances a tray of tea in his hands. 'OK, Olivia?'

'Yes,' I squeak, standing back to give him access.

'Is she up for visitors? I have tea.'

'Take me dancing, George!' Nan yells from behind me, making George grin.

'I'll take that as a yes.' George slips in, his grin widening when his eyes find her, all neat and tidy in her bed. 'You look spectacular, Josephine.'

I'm surprised not to hear a scoff or sarcastic retort. 'Thank you, George.' Nan taps the bedside table in a signal for him to set the tray down, which he does promptly and carefully. 'Let's see if his tea is up to scratch.'

'No one makes tea like you, Josephine,' George says happily, popping a sugar into each teacup.

I observe them for a few moments as I hover at the doorway, smiling when I catch Nan smack the back of George's hand and George laugh delightedly. He's happy to have her home, and though she'll never admit it, she's as equally happy with George back under her roof. The role reversal may bring on more bickering than usual between the two of them.

'I'll be downstairs,' I say, backing out of the room, but neither acknowledges my announcement and Nan continues to give George precise instructions as he attempts to make the tea to Nan's standards. He's attempting in vain. No one makes tea like Nan.

Leaving them to their comedy act, I take off down the stairs, relieved to be out of Nan's radar, soon finding myself in the kitchen, where Miller is leaning against the worktop and Gregory is slumped in a chair. Both men look at me as I enter. I'm under close scrutiny, but while I'm uncomfortable, it's a relief not to find them at each other's throat. That relief soon fades when I take all of the anxious vibes being thrown my way and conclude why Miller and Gregory look so apprehensive.

Miller's told him about my mum. Every defence mechanism loads, locks, and gets ready to fire at whoever decides to hit me with their thoughts first, but after a long painful silence and neither man has spoken, I take the situation into my own hands.

And bury my head a little farther.

'She's settled and George is with her.' I head for the sink and plunge my hands into the soapy water. 'She seems quite bright, but she needs to stay in bed for a week or so.' I wash and place the few dirty mugs on the drainer and then swirl my hands around in the sink, vainly trying to locate something else to wash. 'She's going to be hard work.'

'Olivia?' Miller's footsteps approach behind me. My eyes close and I give up blindly grappling in the water for nothing. 'I think you're done.' He takes my hands from the sink and starts to dry them with a tea towel, but I shrug him off and grab a dishcloth.

'I should wipe the table down.' I slap the sopping material on the table, making Gregory shift back. I don't miss the cautious look he tosses over my shoulder in Miller's direction. 'I need to keep the house spic-and-span.' My hand works furiously across the pristine wood, wiping up a mess that isn't even there. 'She'll only moan or try to clean up herself.'

Strong hands wrap around my wrists and hold them still. 'Enough.'

My eyes climb his bespoke suit, up his neck, and onto his shadowed jaw. Blue eyes are sinking into me. Sympathetic eyes. I don't need sympathy. I need to be allowed to get on with things.

'I'm not ready,' I whisper, swallowing down the lump forming in my throat, my eyes begging him to let me be.

'And I don't want to expose you to more pain.' He pries the cloth from my hand, folding it neatly, while I silently thank him and breathe in some composure. 'I'm staying here tonight, so I'll need to pop home and collect some things.'

'OK,' I agree, busying myself by brushing down the front of my sundress.

'Yeah, I should be going,' Gregory pipes up, standing and putting his hand out to Miller, who accepts immediately, nodding sharply. It's a silent message – something to reassure my best friend.

Their polite exchange at any other time would be so satisfying to see. Not now, though. Now it's like they've teamed up as a last resort . . . to deal with the fragile waif. I can't help the wave of resentment I feel. This is just a show. They're not being courteous because they know it's what I would really love, for them both to be friendly and actually like each other. They're acting like this for fear of tipping me over the edge.

Gregory approaches and pulls me into a hug that I struggle to return. I suddenly really do feel fragile. 'I'll call you tomorrow, baby girl.'

I nod and break out of his hold. 'I'll see you out.'

'OK.' His reply is drawn out, and he moves to the kitchen door, raising his hand to Miller in goodbye.

I don't see Miller's response, or whether any more exchanges are passed because I'm halfway up the hallway.

'She's a firecracker!' George laughs, and I look up to see him plodding down the stairs. 'But exhausted. I've left her to have a kip.'

'Are you going, George?'

'Yes, but I'll be back tomorrow at noon sharp. I have my

orders.' He reaches the bottom of the stairs on a huff, his big chest pulsing from the exertion. 'You look after her,' he says, giving my shoulder a little squeeze.

'I'll take you home, George.' Gregory appears, waving his keys. 'As long as you don't mind sharing a seat with a few tools.'

'Ha! I shared space with far less desirable things during the war, lad.'

Gregory passes me on a strained smile and opens the door for George. 'You can tell me all about it on the way home.'

'It'll make your toes curl!'

They're both off up the garden path, George rabbiting about his war days, Gregory laughing tightly every now and then in response. I close the door, shut the world outside, but soon realise that I can't shut my mind down. I'm fooling myself. Being here, smelling our house, knowing Nan is safe upstairs and Miller is floating around in all of his perfection, isn't working as I'd hoped. Nan's shockingly accurate conclusion has only added to it.

The distant ring of my mobile makes me moan, and I make no rush to go in search of it. Anyone who I would like to talk to is either here or just this moment left. I pad back to the kitchen, finding no Miller. Locating my bag, I rummage through it until I find the source of the persistent sound. I hit Reject and notice six missed calls, all from William. I turn it off and toss it to the side, glowering at it.

Then I go in search of Miller. I find him in the lounge, seated on the edge of the couch. He has a book in his hands. A black book. And he's engrossed in the pages.

'Miller!'

He visibly jumps and the book snaps shut as I hurry over and swipe it from his hand. 'Where did you get this?' I ask angrily, holding it behind my back, hiding it . . . ashamed of it.

'It was tucked down the side of the couch.' He points to the edge, provoking a mental image of me dumping it on the sofa when I last tortured myself by reading a passage. How could I be so careless?

'You shouldn't have read it,' I spit, feeling the horrid thing burning my hands, like in a weird sense, it's coming back to life. I shake that wayward train of thought away before it takes too much more of my attention – undeserved attention. 'Reminiscing, were you?' I ask. 'Reminding yourself of what you're going to be missing?' I regret my vicious attack before Miller's face twists with hurt, even more so when that hurt morphs into anger. That was unnecessary and spiteful. I didn't mean it at all. I'm lashing out, being unreasonable and cruel to the wrong person.

He slowly rises to his full height, his face falling into his signature impassiveness, and busies himself by pulling at his jacket sleeves before straightening his tie. I'm shifting on my feet, searching my brain for something to redeem myself. There's nothing. I can't take that back. 'I'm sorry.' I drop my head in shame, resisting the urge to toss the book into the fire.

'You're forgiven,' he retorts with zero genuineness, striding past me.

'Miller, please!' I reach out to grab his arm, but he dodges me, stealthily removing himself from my reach. 'Miller.'

He swings around, physically knocking me back when his fierce eyes land on me. His jaw is pulsing, his chest expanding fast. I wilt under every hard-cut plane of his face and telling sign of his current state of mind. He points directly at me. 'Never throw that in my face again,' he warns, beginning to shake before me. 'Never! Do you hear me?' He storms out, slamming the door behind him, leaving me immobilised by his raw fury. It's never before been directed solely on me with such intensity. He looked like he could smash something to pieces, and while I'd put my life on him never laying a finger on me, I fear for anyone else who may cross his path right now.

'Fuck!' I hear him curse, and then his stamping shoes get

closer again. I remain where I am, silent and still, until he's bursting through the door of the lounge. That finger is pointed at me again, and he's shaking more than before. 'You'll stay here. Understand?'

I don't know what happens. Something triggers under his order and I find myself up in his face before I can weigh up the pros and cons of retaliation. I knock his hand out of the way. 'Don't tell me what to do!'

'Don't push me, Olivia.'

It doesn't matter that I don't plan on going anywhere and leaving Nan alone. This is principle. 'Fuck off!'

He clenches his teeth. 'Stop being so fucking difficult! You'll stay here!'

I see red, then blurt something that surprises me as much as it clearly surprises Miller. 'Did you know?'

Miller's neck retracts on his shoulders, a scowl settling. 'What?'

'Did you know she was back?' I shout, thinking how well he handled the situation. There was no shock. He fell straight into comfort mode, like he was prepared for it. 'When I thought I was losing my mind and you talked me down, did you know?'

'No.' He's adamant, but I don't believe him. He'll do anything to lessen my hurt. No one's speaking. Ted's shirked me, William has avoided me at all costs until now – now that I know for sure – and Miller virtually threw the phone off his desk to cut the call when Gracie's name was mentioned. And then I'm thinking about the call from Sylvie, the one telling me about the woman looking for me. Her description. It matches Sophia perfectly, but it also matches my mother. Clarity is a wonderful thing.

Blood burns in my veins. 'You told William to keep it from me, didn't you?'

'Yes, I fucking did!' he yells, startling me. 'And I'm not fucking sorry!' Firm palms cup my face, almost aggressively, and squeeze tightly, his nose meeting mine, his eyes penetrating me deeply. 'I. Didn't. Know. What. To. Do.'

I can't speak; his grip won't allow my mouth to open. So I nod, feeling emotion take hold – all of the stress, worry, and fear ripping through my vulnerable being. He was trying to shield me from more hurt.

'Don't leave.' He scans my face, his gaze drifting everywhere, and though it's an order, I know he wants my acknowledgement. I nod again. 'Good,' he says simply, then smashes his lips onto mine and gives me a forceful kiss.

When he releases me, I step back and blink myself back to life, just catching his back disappearing out of the room.

The door closes loudly.

Then I cry like a baby, trying to suppress the sound so I don't wake Nan. It's silly; if she was to wake up, then she would have by now after that brief shouting match and the slamming of a few doors. My pathetic choked sobs won't rouse her.

'Everything OK, Miss Taylor?'

I look up, seeing Ted in the doorway of the lounge. 'Fine.' I rub at my eyes. 'Tired, that's all.'

'Understandable,' he says softly, making me smile a little.

'You knew she was back, too, didn't you?'

He nods, dropping his eyes. 'Not my news to share, sweetheart.'

'So you did know her.'

'Everyone knew Gracie Taylor.' He smiles, keeping his eyes on the floor, like he's scared I might press for more should he give me eye contact. I'm not going to. I don't want to know.

'You'd better take up position.' I indicate over my shoulder when he looks up at me, his rugged face a little surprised. 'I'm sorry for going AWOL again.'

He chuckles. 'You're safe. That's the main thing.' He strides across the room and finds his position at the window, and I observe for a while, remembering his skilful driving.

It pushes me to press him. 'Have you always worked for William?'

'Twenty-five years.'

'What did you do before?'

'Military.'

'You were a soldier?'

He doesn't answer, just nods, telling me he's done talking with me, so I leave Ted and drag my weary bones up the stairs to the bathroom, hoping a hot shower will soothe my aching mind and heart while it's soothing my aching muscles. The different elements of pressure on each of us are becoming too much, both of us trying to shoulder everything. We're going to give way under the strain soon.

After flipping the shower on, I stand before the sink, staring at my washed out face, seeing dark circles under my hollow eyes. Only a century's sleep and waking to find every burden gone will remedy it. I sigh and open the mirrored cupboard, cursing when a load of cosmetics tumble from the shelves and clatter into the sink. 'Shit,' I grumble, scooping up pots and tubes one by one and placing them back. I'm nearly done, only the Tampax left to . . .

Tampax.

I stare at the box, my tongue thickening in my mouth. Tampax. I'm late. I'm never late. Not ever. I don't like the feel of nervousness beating in my chest or the pulsing of blood in my ears. I try to calculate when my last period was. Three weeks ago? Four weeks ago? I hadn't gotten it in New York. Shit.

I dash for my bedroom, finding the empty box of the morning-after pill, and pull the pamphlet out, fiddling with clumsy fingers to unfold the paper until it's laid flat on my bed. Chinese. German. Spanish. Italian. 'Where's the fucking English?' I yell, turning it over and slapping it on the bed. I spend the next twenty minutes reading piles and piles of small print. Nothing sinks in, though. Nothing except the success rate. There's no guarantee. Some women become pregnant – a small amount, but some, nevertheless. All of the blood drains from my head. I come over all light-headed and the room begins to whirl. Fast. I collapse to my back and stare up at the ceiling, feeling hot, cold, sweaty, choked. 'Oh fuck . . .'

I don't know what to do. I'm blank. Totally stumped. My phone! I spring to life and run downstairs to the kitchen. My shaky hands won't co-operate, my stupid fingers not hitting the buttons I'm telling them to. 'Damn it!' I stamp my foot, then stand motionless, pulling in some reasonable amount of air into my suppressed lungs. I let it all stream out calmly and start again, successfully pulling up my calendar. I go over the days time and time again, counting more than I'd hoped, thinking maybe amid the madness of my life just lately, I may have made a colossal error. I haven't. Each time I count, I come to the same calculation. I'm a week late. 'Fuck.'

I flop against the worktop, spinning my iPhone in my grasp. I need a chemist. I need to know for sure. This meltdown might be completely unnecessary. Glancing across the kitchen, I note it's past eight. But a twenty-four-hour pharmacy will be open. My legs are in action before my brain, and I'm off up the hallway, but when my brain kicks in, I'm soon halted in my task of pulling my denim jacket down from the coat stand.

'Nan.' My body deflates. I can't leave, no matter what the emergency. I wouldn't be able to live with myself if anything happened and I wasn't here. Plus, Ted is keeping watch. There's only so many tongue-lashings he'll put up with as a result of my Houdini-like behaviour before he realises I'm not worth the bother and quits.

Releasing my coat, I collapse onto the bottom step of the stairs and drop my head in my hands. Just when I thought I couldn't be any more hopeless, I have something else to add to my never-ending list of shitty things to deal with. I don't want to deal with any of them. I want to curl into a ball and have Miller surround me in his *thing*, protect me from this godforsaken world. His beautiful, comforting face pops into my mind's eye, sending me somewhere near to that safe place. Then it drifts into the anger that was all too evident before he stormed out.

He's not speaking to me, and if he is, then I'm sure I won't want to hear what he has to say. I groan and rub my palms into my face, trying to scrub away . . . everything. I'm an idiot. A first-class, A-rated, top-notch fool. A deluded fool who should face up to everything going on around her and find that renowned Taylor-girl sass to deal with it. Where has that easy, peaceful life gone? Miller's right. I don't have the ability to cope.

Chapter 17

My dreams are dreams. I know this because everything is perfect – me, Miller, Nan . . . life. Content to remain immersed in my illusory world, I snuggle down farther, moaning my comfort and hugging my pillow. Everything is bright. It's all so very light and colourful, and though I'm aware that I'm being held in a false sense of security, I don't wake myself. I'm hovering on the edge of sleep and consciousness, pushing myself to fall further into my dreams – anything to delay facing my reality. I'm smiling. Everything is perfect.

Gracie Taylor.

She joins me in my dreams, leaving her mark, making it impossible to shake out once I wake.

Everything is suddenly dark.

Everything is dull.

'No!' I shout, angry that she's encroached on the only tranquillity to be found in my troubled world. 'Get out!'

'Olivia!'

I shoot up, gasping, and whip my head around, searching for him. Miller's sitting next to me in his boxer shorts, his hair wild, his eyes worried. My shoulders sag, a mixture of relief and annoyance – the relief that he's here, the annoyance that I'm awake and alert. I'm back in the real world. I sigh, reaching up to brush my hair from my face.

'Bad dream?' He moves in and crowds me, gathering my body into his arms and cradling me in his lap.

'I can't tell the difference,' I whisper into his chest, making his movements falter slightly. I'm totally honest with him. I can't define between my nightmares and reality and he needs to know, although it's a given that he's fully aware of my current turmoil, because he's sharing it with me. Or most of it. I'm very quickly even more awake and alert as I recap on last night after he left. I could be pregnant. But something else more important blocks my worry. 'Nan.' I go to move from his hold, panicked.

'She's fine,' he soothes, tightening his hold of me. 'I've helped her downstairs to the couch and given her breakfast and her medication.'

'You have? In your underwear?' Images of Miller waiting on Nan in his boxers are suddenly all I can see. I would have loved to be a fly on the wall for *that*. I bet she milked him dry of patience while staring at his buns.

'Yes.' He drops a light kiss on the back of my head and inhales deeply, taking in a soothing hit of my hair's scent. 'You need rest, too, sweet girl. I came back and found you asleep on the stairs.'

I begin prying myself from his arms but soon give up when his arms lock tighter. 'Miller, I need to see Nan.'

'I told you. She's fine.' He wrestles with me until he has me where he wants, straddling his kneeling lap. I take immense comfort in him fussing with my hair, and even more when I spot his wayward curl misbehaving, calling for me to give it some attention. I sigh and push it away from his forehead, cocking my head in wonder as I refresh my memory of all of Miller Hart's beautiful traits. I go over them all – the ones I can see and the ones I can't. 'I need you more right now,' he whispers, making my tracing fingers falter on his naked chest. '*Thing*,' he demands quietly. 'Please.'

I seize him in my arms, cocooning him in all of me, my face seeking out the comfort of his neck as he locks his palm on my nape, holding me in place. 'I'm sorry,' I mumble pathetically. 'I'm sorry for being so hateful.'

'I've already forgiven you.'

I let the few building tears trickle silently from my eyes and soak into his neck, remorse crippling me. He's been nothing but loving, protective, and supportive, to both me and Nan. I'm inexcusable. 'I love you.'

He pulls me from his chest and takes his time wiping under my eyes. 'And I love you.' There's no code or alternative words or actions. It's delivered simply. 'I can't see you sad, Olivia. Where's the sass I love so much?'

I smile, thinking he really probably doesn't mean that. 'I've run out,' I admit. Too much energy is required to be sassy or spunky or whatever he wants to call it. I feel zapped of life, the only scraps of it I have left reserved to care for Nan and ensure Miller knows how much I love him. Everyone else can go to hell.

'No, you haven't. You've temporarily lost it, that's all. We need to relocate it.' He gives me one of those lovely smiles, lighting my darkness slightly. 'I need you strong by my side, Olivia.'

My sorrow-soaked mind gives way to guilt. He's being strong for me. He's by my side through my own traumatic issues. I need to do the same for him. We've still yet to deal with Miller's problems – my problem, too, because there is only *us*. But Gracie Taylor has added a whole new dimension to our screwed-up world. And now my late period.

'I'm here for you,' I affirm. 'Always.'

'I sometimes wonder.'

My guilt multiplies by a million. *Pull it together.* That's what I have to do. These problems aren't going away, and no amount of ignoring them will make them disappear either. 'I'm here.'

'Thank you.'

'Don't thank me.'

'I'll always be grateful for you, Olivia Taylor. Eternally. You know that.' He takes my hand and kisses my diamond.

'I know.'

'Jolly good.' I'm kissed chastely on my nose, my lips, one cheek, then the other, before he's pecking his way down my neck. 'Time for a shower.'

'Would you do me the honour of joining me?' I grip his hair in my hands, smiling when he pauses and slowly pulls from my throat.

'Worship you in that tiny shower?'

I nod, delighted at the playful twinkle springing into his sharp blue eyes.

His lips pout. It's the most beautiful sight. 'How long would it take your grandmother to get from the lounge to the kitchen, find her most lethal carving knife, and make it upstairs?'

I grin. 'Under normal circumstances, a minute flat. *Now*, I guess a good ten minutes, if at all.'

'Then we're good to go.'

I laugh as he scoops me into his arms and starts striding quickly for the door. I so need this. 'You don't want to disrespect Nan,' I remind him.

'What she doesn't know won't hurt her.'

I smile, delighted. 'We have to be quiet.'

'Noted.'

'You can't make me scream your name.'

'Noted.'

'We have to listen for Nan.'

'Noted.' He virtually breaks down the bathroom door and kicks it closed behind him, defying every *noted* he's just noted. I'm placed on my feet, the shower is flipped on, and with a lack of clothes on me and Miller's yummy tight hips graced only in his yummy tight boxers, it's a mere second before *both* of us are naked. 'In.' He cocks his head in signal, an element of urgency to his approach. I'm not in the least bit bothered.

My desperation is growing with each painful second that he refrains from touching me. I step into the bath, under the hot spray, and wait.

And wait.

And wait.

He's just staring at me, his eyes journeying slowly up and down my dripping nakedness. But I don't feel uncomfortable. Instead, I use the time to drink in every perfect piece of him, musing silently, thinking that perhaps he becomes more perfect with each day that passes. His obsessive habits are showing signs of abating, albeit sporadically, or maybe I've just become accustomed to things that were so glaringly obvious before. Or maybe we're meeting somewhere in the middle and *neither* of us are noticing. Probably because we are so consumed in each other, and when we're not, we're tackling obstacles. But I do know one thing for sure. The only thing that's indisputable.

I'm crazy in love with Miller Hart.

My eyes work their way from his perfect toes, up his perfectly shaped legs, until I'm locked on his perfectly hard cock. I could go farther, lose myself in the rest of him – his sharp abs, his firm pecs, those strong shoulders . . . his flawless face, lips, eyes, and finally the perfect waves of his perfect hair. I could. But I don't. I'm too riveted by the centre of his perfection.

'Earth to Olivia.' His rough voice contradicts the soft tone. I finally allow my eyes to indulge in the rest of him, in no rush to make it to the stunning blues that captured me so completely the first time I encountered him. 'There she is.'

I smile and reach for him. 'Come to me.' My order is delivered on a breathy gasp, laced with desperation. My hand is taken gently and our fingers shift and play for a few moments, each of us watching, before Miller entwines them, locking them together. He steps into the tub and crowds me, leaving me no option but to back up until my skin's pressed against the coldness of the tiles. He's towering over me, his eyes sinking into the deepest part of me.

He lifts our joined hands and pushes them into the wall above my head, then slides his spare palm to the back of my thigh, tugging firmly. I oblige, lifting until my leg is locked around his waist, pulling us together. Miller's lips part, prompting mine to follow suit, and he dips, getting us nose to nose. 'Tell me what you want, sweet girl.' His hot breath spreads across my face, turning the heated desire running riot through my veins into flaming need.

'You.' I push my demand with a gasp and close my eyes when his mouth descends to mine.

He takes what's his.

Chapter 18

Nan looks well. But the sight of her sitting all prim and quiet at the kitchen table, her palms around a cup of tea, has taken me a little aback. I'd expected to find her pottering around the kitchen, despite being told to take it easy. Nan's never been good at doing what she's told.

'Morning,' I chirp, sliding onto a seat next to her and helping myself to the pot of tea.

'I wouldn't bother,' Nan retorts to my greeting, no *morning* or *hey*.

'Wouldn't bother with what?'

'The tea.' She turns her nose up at her mug. 'Tastes like gnats' piss.'

The teapot clatters against the cup I'm attempting to pour into, and Miller laughs from across the kitchen. I cast a sideways glance, finding him looking divine in a three-piece suit, this one charcoal grey, his shirt pale blue, his tie matching his shirt. He looks delicious, all groomed, and by the looks of things, ready for work. Perfect. I find his eyes and smile. 'Twenty-four-carat gold treasure, right here.'

I'm taking the piss. He knows it but disregards my sarcasm and joins us at the table. 'You're too kind, Mrs Taylor.'

'How was your shower?' she fires back, and the damn teapot clashes with the cup again, so hard I'm certain I must have cracked the porcelain. I swing my wide eyes in her direction, finding that impish grin tickling her lips. The minx!

'*Hot*.' Miller drags the single word out forever, and now I'm swinging my even wider eyes across the table to him. I knew it. He's fighting a grin. These two are intolerable when put together, getting a thrill from winding each other up. But they are also beautifully loving towards each other.

'You should've had Olivia in to show you how to work the temperature knob.' Back my head goes to Nan. She's toying with the handle of her mug, fiddling thoughtfully, playing all naïve. Double minx!

'I did,' Miller replies casually, mirroring Nan's fiddling fingers with his own mug.

'I knew it!' Nan gasps. 'You little devil!'

I give up with the head-swinging business. Neither is taking any notice of my evident shock and my neck's hurting. I sit back in my chair and let them play their game, a warmth filling me to the brim. Seeing her so alive and vivacious is doing wonders for my current frame of mind.

Miller flashes Nan a stunning smile, bashing down her attempt at a scornful look, and he shrugs. 'I'm sorry, Mrs Taylor. I can't apologise for loving her to the point it's painful when I'm not touching her.'

'Little devil,' she repeats quietly, her curls swishing around her ears when she shakes her head. 'You little bloody devil.'

'Are we done winding each other up?' I ask, reaching for the cornflakes. 'Or should I settle in for the show?'

'I'm done,' Miller says, taking the liberty of pouring the milk on my flakes. 'And you, Mrs Taylor?'

'Yes, all done.' She takes a sip of her tea and winces. 'You're a dreamboat, Miller Hart, but you can't make tea for shit.'

'I concur,' I add, lifting my cup to him and screwing my face up. 'It's bad. So, so bad.'

'Noted,' he grumbles. 'I've never claimed to be an expert tea maker.' That mischief creeps back onto his face, making me put my cup down slowly, warily. 'Ask me about worshipping,' he suggests.

I cough all over my flakes, drawing Nan's immediate interest.

'Hmmm,' she hums, drilling old navy eyes into me. 'What's worshipping?'

I refuse to look at her, centring my attention on my bowl.

'I'm very good at it,' Miller declares cockily.

'You mean sex?'

'Oh, give me strength!' I grab my spoon and plunge it into my bowl, taking a huge mouthful of my breakfast.

'I call it worshipping.'

'So you really do worship the ground she walks on,' Nan asks on a smile.

'Oh, I really do.'

I'm dying on the spot, praying for divine intervention to save me. Impossible. Both of them. 'Please stop,' I beg.

'OK,' they say in unison, grinning like a pair of idiots across the table at each other.

'Good. I need to go to the supermarket.'

'But I like doing the shopping,' Nan whines, an episode of the sulks on the horizon. 'You'll get it all wrong.'

'Then write me a list,' I counter, solving the problem in an instant. 'You're not leaving this house.'

'I'll take you, Olivia.' Miller reaches over and shifts the sugar bowl a fraction to the right, then the milk a tad to the left. 'And it isn't up for discussion,' he adds, flicking me a warning look.

'I'll be fine,' I say, not backing down. I don't care what tone he uses or what looks he flashes. 'You can stay and watch Nan.'

'I need to go to Ice.'

I look at him, knowing he doesn't mean to actually do any work.

'I don't need watching, for the love of God!' Nan squawks.

'I beg to differ!' I snap. It's bad enough being rubbed up the wrong way by Miller. Nan can quit while she's ahead.

'She's right, Mrs Taylor. You shouldn't be alone.'

I'm delighted when I see Miller flash Nan a warning look that matches the one he's just aimed at me, and even more delighted when she doesn't kick up a stink. 'Fine,' she mutters, 'but you can't keep me prisoner forever.'

'Just until you're feeling fit,' I appease her. I show my appreciation for Miller's support with a quick squeeze of his knee under the table, which he ignores, surprising me.

'I'll take you shopping,' he says again, standing from the table and collecting some breakfast things.

That appreciation vanishes in the blink of an eye. 'Noooo, you're staying with Nan.'

'Noooo, I'm taking you to the supermarket,' he bats back, unaffected by the warning that was rampant in my order and intended to be. 'I've spoken to Gregory. He'll be here soon, as will Ted.'

I deflate in my chair. Nan snorts her annoyance but remains quiet, and Miller nods his approval at his own announcement. He's got it all worked out. This isn't good. I can't buy a pregnancy test with Miller tailing me.

Shit . . .

After giving Gregory the rundown on Nan and ensuring all her pills are laid out so he doesn't need to bother with instructions, I'm guided to Miller's car by my nape and placed neatly in the passenger seat. He seems a little tetchy after taking a call while I spoke with Gregory, all signs of the easy-going man at the breakfast table gone. As ever, it's like he was never with me in the first place and while the gaps in his signature aloofness are becoming more frequent, his usual habits are muscling their way back. I sense fiddling with the temperature controls won't be disregarded today, so I let the window down instead. Miller puts the stereo on, killing the difficult silence, and I sit back and let Paul Weller keep me company. I call the house twice en route, each time hearing Nan in the background squawking something about being a whittle arse. She'll just have to tolerate the fuss.

I start forming a plan in my head, plotting and scheming trying to figure out how best to get a few moments alone in Tesco so I can buy what I need to either put my mind at rest or send it into a faster tailspin. There's only one way.

After Miller parks and we've collected a trolley, we get swallowed up in the chaos of Tesco. We make our way up and down the aisles, me armed with the list that Nan wrote, Miller looking all stressed. I can only conclude that the chaos of our surroundings is the cause. There are abandoned trollies everywhere and the shelves are a royal mess. I inwardly laugh, having a mental bet with myself that he's fighting the urge to tidy all the shelves. But when his mobile rings from his inside pocket and he takes it out and scowls harder at the screen before rejecting the call, I think maybe it's not just the pandemonium of Tesco that's bothering him. I don't ask who's calling him because I don't want to know, and, in fact, I'm still mentally plotting our separation.

'I need to get Nan some bits from the toiletries aisle,' I say, feigning casualness to within an inch of my life. 'You take this and get the last few bits.' I hand him the list that I've cunningly added some items to – items at the opposite end of the supermarket.

'We'll go together,' he replies without hesitation, scuppering my plan.

'It'll be quicker if we separate,' I say offhand. 'I can see you hate being here.' I tactically use his discomfort to my advantage and head off before he can come back at me, glimpsing over my shoulder to check he's not in pursuit. I find him staring down at the list with the biggest scowl of all.

Rounding the corner, I take off fast, looking up at the signs above the aisles to find what I'm looking for. It's only a few moments of scurrying until I land in the correct aisle and I'm staring at box after box of pregnancy tests – all locked away in individual Perspex outer boxes – a stupid security measure. 'Great,' I grumble, reaching for the first that guarantees a rapid and accurate result. Flipping it over, I scan the print as I start to walk away, but gasp when I collide with something.

'Sorry!' I blurt, the box tumbling from my hand. The plastic casing creates a deafening clatter when it meets the floor, the box jumping around at my feet. And another pair of feet, too. Feet I don't recognise. I don't like the chill creeping up my spine, nor the sense of vulnerability that suddenly engulfs me.

'My apologies.' The man's voice is posh and he's wearing an expensive suit. He's bending down to pick up the box before I can register his face, and he spends a few seconds resting on his haunches, looking at the pregnancy test, spinning it in his hand repeatedly while humming his interest. I haven't seen his face yet, only the back of his head as he remains crouched at my feet. I definitely don't recognise the grey-flecked hair, yet something is screaming that *he* knows *me*. He had every intention to be in this aisle with me – the aisle mainly full of women's toiletries. I may be in a busy supermarket, people everywhere, but I can feel danger thick in the air around us.

The stranger lifts his face as he rises. His eyes are bordering black and harbouring all sorts of unspoken threats. He has a scar that runs from the centre of his right cheek all the way down to the corner of his mouth, and his thin lips curve into a fake smile, deepening it. It's a smile that's intended to lead me into a false sense of security.

'I believe this is yours.' He hands me the box, and I will my hands to stop shaking when I take it. I know I've failed in my attempts when he raises a sharp eyebrow, still keeping a hold of the box as I accept, probably absorbing my trembles.

My eyes drop, no longer able to meet the harshness of his

stare. 'Thank you.' I gulp back my fear and sidestep him, but he moves with me, blocking my path. I clear my throat, anything to get the strong assertiveness I'm desperately searching for and that I desperately hope fools him. 'Excuse me.' I step to the other side this time, and so does he, letting out a little chuckle.

'We don't seem to be going anywhere fast, do we?' He moves in, getting way too close to my personal space, doubling my fretfulness.

'No,' I agree, attempting again to dodge him and, yet again, getting blocked. Taking a deep breath, I reluctantly lift my eyes until they meet his face. He's the epitome of evil. It's screaming from every single fibre of his ominous being, and it has me wilting on the spot. He smiles down at me and reaches out, taking a stray tendril of my hair and twirling it in his fingers. I freeze, immobilised by terror.

He hums thoughtfully . . . darkly . . . sinisterly. Then he dips and brings his mouth close to my ear. 'Sweet girl,' he whispers. 'We finally meet.' I jump back on a gasp, my hand flying to my hair and brushing away the traces of his breath while he remains slightly dipped, a malevolent sneer pulling at the edges of his thin lips as he regards me closely.

'Olivia?' I hear my name being spoken in the distance, unease in the familiar tone, and watch as the stranger straightens and casts his eyes over my shoulder, that smirk widening. Spinning on the spot, every breath leaves my lungs when I see Miller striding quickly towards me, his face straight but a wealth of emotion in his clear eyes – relief, fear, caution . . . anger.

'Miller,' I breathe, energy surging through my dead muscles and firing my legs into action, taking me a few paces forward until I'm hiding in his chest, my arms bunched between our bodies. He's quivering. Everything about this situation is shrieking hazard.

Miller's chin is resting on the top of my head, one arm

holding me tightly against him, and there's a stone-cold silence amid the hype of activity around us, like we're stuck in a bubble and no one except the three of us are aware of the peril and hostility polluting the supermarket air. I don't have to look to know he's still behind me; I can feel his presence as well as I can feel Miller trying to squeeze some comfort into me, and the hardness of Miller's tense muscles against me is a clue. So I remain concealed in my comfort zone.

It feels like a lifetime before I feel Miller relax a little, and I chance a peek, looking over my shoulder. The man is strolling down the aisle, his hands resting casually in his trouser pockets, browsing the shelves like he frequents the supermarket daily. But just like Miller, he looks out of place.

'Are you OK?' Miller asks, placing me at arm's length and scanning my blank face. 'Did he touch you?'

I shake my head, thinking it very unwise to tell him anything that could set my human bomb ticking. I don't think I need to, anyway. Miller knows that man and he knows what I've just encountered without my confirmation. 'Who is he?' I finally ask the question that I really don't want to know the answer to, and if I go by the pained look on Miller's face, it's clear he doesn't want to tell me. Or confirm it. He's *the* immoral bastard.

I'm not sure whether Miller sees me make my silent conclusion or whether he simply doesn't want to settle it, but my question goes unanswered and he's quickly pulling his phone from his pocket. One push of a button and a few seconds later, Miller's talking down the line. 'Time's up,' he says simply, before hanging up and making a grab for my hand.

But he pauses his urgent string of movements when something catches his attention.

Something in my hand.

Every defeated bone in my body gives up on me. I make no attempt to hide what I'm holding. I make no attempt to conjure up an excuse. He's blank, just gazing down at the box for the longest time before he eventually lifts empty blues to my watery eyes. 'Oh Jesus fucking Christ,' he exhales, the tips of his thumb and index finger meeting his forehead, his eyes clenching shut.

'I don't think the morning-after pill worked.' I choke over my words, knowing I don't need to elaborate and that he won't demand it.

His hand rakes through his waves, pulling them all back from his face, and his cheeks puff out, adding to the display of shaken actions. 'Fuck!'

I flinch as a result of his curse, my earlier terror being replaced by nerves. 'I didn't want to say anything until I was sure.'

'Fuck!' Miller seizes my nape and pushes me towards the end of the aisle, where I find our full trolley waiting. He chucks the box in carelessly, takes the handle of the trolley with his free hand, and starts leading us to the checkout.

My movements are automatic, my muscles working without instruction, maybe appreciating the delicate situation or maybe noting Miller's explosive mood. I'm placing things on the conveyor belt at the checkout, quiet and wary, as Miller repositions everything according to how it should be. Leaving him to it, I go to the other end and begin packing the bags, but I'm spared that task, too, when Miller takes up position beside me and begins to remove and repack everything. So I stand like a spare part while he does his thing. His jaw is a constant source of ticking, his hand movements fast but ever precise as he shoves our buys into carrier bags before dumping the full ones in the trolley. He's trying to restore some calm into his crumbing world.

After paying a dopey-eyed cashier, the trolley and I are reclaimed and we're being pushed on firmly until we escape the confines of the bustling supermarket. But Miller's unease doesn't lessen, though I'm uncertain of the main cause now – me and my shocking revelation or that creepy man and his unnerving surprise visit.

At that thought, my eyes start darting everywhere.

'He's gone,' Miller says to the open air before him, just as we reach his car. 'Get in.'

I do as I'm bid without complaint, letting Miller load the boot of his car alone. It's not long before we're speeding out of the car park and joining the main road, the atmosphere unbearable, but there's no escaping it. 'Where are we going?' I ask, suddenly worried that he's no intention of taking me home.

'To Ice.'

'But Nan,' I argue quietly. 'You can take me home first.' I've no desire to accompany Miller to Ice. I'd rather commence with my favourite pastime of late and wedge my head a bit farther into the sand.

'Wrong,' he fires back resolutely, leaving no scope for negotiation. I know that tone. I know this behaviour. 'We haven't got time to fuck about, Olivia.'

'Taking care of Nan isn't fucking about!'

'Gregory will take care of her.'

'*I* want to take care of her.'

'And *I* want to take care of *you*.'

'What does that mean?'

'It means I haven't got time for your sass right now!' He pulls a hard right and screeches down a side street. 'None of this is going away unless I make it.'

My heart rate slows. I don't like the determination that's written all over his hard features or lining his gravelly voice. I should be feeling a sense of relief that he's full of fortitude to fix things. Problem is, I'm not sure how he intends to do that, but the little voice in my head is telling me I might not like it. And where will he start, anyway? Give me five minutes and I'll produce a list of the shit to be dealt with, but then we go back to our original problem: What takes priority? Something tells me that my suspected pregnancy won't be at the top of that list. Nor will the appearance of my mother.

No. Everything is telling me that our encounter with the ominous guy in the supermarket is reigning supreme on our list of shit. The immoral bastard. The man who Miller has been hiding me from. The man who holds the key to Miller's chains.

Chapter 19

It's the first time I've seen Ice completely empty.

Miller lifts me onto a stool and spins me to face the bar before making his way around and grabbing a sparkling tumbler from one of the glass shelves. He slams it down with force, seizes a bottle of scotch, and pours the glass to the brim. Then he downs the lot, gasping, his head falling back. Slowly, he turns and collapses back against the counter, looking down at his empty glass.

He looks defeated, and it scares the hell out of me. 'Miller?'

He concentrates on his glass for a while before tortured blue eyes finally meet my gaze. 'The guy in the supermarket. That was Charlie.'

'The immoral bastard,' I say, willingly showing my understanding. He's exactly who I feared he was, yet my conclusion of the man, having been told about him by Miller, doesn't do him justice. He's terrifying.

'Why won't he just let you quit?' I ask.

'When you owe Charlie, you're indebted for life. If he does you a favour, you pay forever.'

'He got you off the streets years ago!' I blurt. 'That doesn't justify your lifelong commitment to owing him. He made you a prostitute, Miller! And then promoted you to the *Special One*!' I nearly fall from my stool as a result of the sudden anger bubbling in my gut. 'This isn't right!'

'Hey, hey, hey.' He swiftly discards his empty glass and slaps a palm on the bar as leverage to flip himself over to my side. He clears it with ease and finesse, his feet landing silently in front of me. 'Calm down,' he placates me, cupping my hot cheeks and pulling my face up to his, scanning my welling eyes. 'Nothing about my life has been right, Olivia.' Spreading my thighs with his knees, he moves in close, lifting my face farther to accommodate him towering over me so our eyes can remain locked. 'I'm too fucked up, sweet girl. Nothing can help me. Me and my club are gold mines for Charlie. But it isn't only my profitability and the convenience of Ice for his dealings that dictates things. It's the power trip, too. It's principle. Show weakness and the enemy will have you by the bollocks.' He breathes in deeply as I take it all in. 'I've never considered quitting because I've never had reason to,' Miller goes on. 'He knows that. And he knows if I were to ever walk away, there would be good reason.' His lips straighten and his eyes blink lazily, an action I usually find comforting, spellbinding. Not today, though. Today it's just adding to my trepidation because that slow blink, accompanied by another deep inhale, is an attempt to gather the strength he needs to utter his next words. When he drags his lids open, I hold my breath, bracing myself. He's looking at me like I'm the most precious thing in his universe. Because I am. 'They will eliminate that good reason,' he finishes quietly, punching the breath from my lungs. 'One way or another, he wants you out of my life. I haven't been acting like a neurotic lunatic for nothing. I belong to him, Olivia. Not you.'

My poor brain explodes under the pressure of Miller's brutal explanation. 'I want you to be mine.' I utter the words mindlessly. There's no thought behind them, just desperation. Miller Hart is unobtainable, and not only because of the guarded exterior he holds firmly in place.

'I'm working on it, my gorgeous, sweet girl. Believe me, I'm working fucking hard on it.' He presses his lips to the top of my head, inhaling me into him, getting a dose of the strength that he siphons off me. 'I have a request.'

I don't vocalise my confirmation to the request that I know is coming. I need to hear it. 'Anything.'

He picks me up from the stool and sits me on the high bar, like he's placing me on the proverbial pedestal. Then he muscles in between my thighs and looks up at me, circling my waist with his big hands. My fingers brush through his waves, all the way through the top until I'm kneading the back of his neck. 'Never stop loving me, Olivia Taylor.'

'Impossible.'

He smiles a little as he drops his face into my chest and moves his hands around to my back, pulling us closer, blending us together. I stare down at the back of his head, stroking comfort into him. 'How sure are you?' he asks out of the blue.

My stroking hands pause as I muster the might to face another one of our shocking revelations. 'Sure,' I reply simply, because I am. Just like everything else, I can't and shouldn't be hiding from this.

He slowly releases me and holds the test out, watching as my eyes flick between him and the box. 'Sure isn't good enough.'

I reach and take it tentatively.

'Go.'

I say nothing as he lifts me down, and leave him at the bar pouring another drink. I follow my feet to the ladies' room and brace myself for the confirmation in black and white. My actions are mindless, from entering the stall to exiting it. I try to ignore the few minutes' wait I've read it takes to give me the result and spend that time washing my hands, also trying to ignore the possible reaction I'm likely to get from Miller. At least now he's aware there's a possibility. But will that lessen the shock? Will he even want it? I slam a lid on those thoughts before they run away with me. I don't expect him to be dancing on the ceiling over the pending confirmation of my pregnancy. There's no room for celebration in our lives.

Turning the test over, I stare down at the tiny window. Then I wander out of the restroom and back into the main club, where I find Miller waiting, tapping the bar. He looks up at me. He's expressionless. Once again, I can't fathom a bit of his thought process. So I hold the test up, watching as his eyes flick to it. He won't be able to see from all the way over there, so I murmur one word. 'Positive.'

He deflates before my eyes, making my stomach turn. Then he cocks his head, silently demanding I go to him. I'm cautious, but I do, reaching him in a few strides. I'm lifted onto the bar and his body moves in, his head resting on my chest, his palms sliding onto my bottom.

'Is it wrong for me to be delighted?' he asks, shocking me. I honestly expected a Miller-style meltdown. Because my sole focus has been on my own shock, plus what I thought would be a negative reaction from Miller, I've not stopped and considered the potential of being happy by this news. I've seen it as being another thorn in our side – another pile of shit to deal with. Miller, on the other hand, sounds like he's seeing it from a whole other perspective.

'I'm not sure,' I admit aloud, when I only meant to silently wonder. Can we be happy about this amid all the darkness? Is he seeing brighter light? My world has become just as dark as Miller's, and I can only see more gloom on the horizon.

'Then I'll tell you.' He lifts his head and smiles at me. 'Anything you bless me with I see as a gift, Olivia.' A smooth palm strokes my cheek. 'Your beauty to look at.' He scans my face for an eternity before slowly dragging his hand down to my chest and tracing wide circles around my breast. My breath hitches, my spine lengthening. 'Your body to feel.' He tries to pull back his smile as he takes a glimpse up at me. 'Your sass to deal with.'

I bite my lip through my budding desire and refrain from telling him that, ultimately, he is the source of my sass.

'Elaborate,' I demand unreasonably. He's made himself pretty clear already.

'As you wish,' he agrees without hesitation. 'This –' he plants a kiss on my tummy, humming as he does – 'is another gift you're giving me. You know I fiercely protect what's mine.' He looks up at me, and I lose myself in the sincerity of his telling eyes. 'What's growing inside of you is mine, sweet girl. And I'll destroy anything that tries to take it away from me.'

His strange way with words, his way of articulating his feelings, it's irrelevant now because I'm fluent in Miller's language. He couldn't have put it any more perfectly.

'I want to be a perfect daddy,' he whispers.

Happiness sails through me, but through that bliss, I reach the very solid conclusion that Miller was referring to Charlie. It's Charlie he'll destroy. He knows about me. And he saw me with a pregnancy test in my hand. I'm a good reason for Miller to walk away, even more so now. Charlie eliminates good reasons. And Miller will destroy anything that tries to take me away from him. Frighteningly, I know he's perfectly capable.

Which means Charlie is on death row.

A loud rapping brings me around, whipping my head in the direction of the club entrance.

'Anderson,' Miller mutters, his mask slipping into place, our happy moment being cut too short. He breaks away from me, giving my thigh a little squeeze before he strides off . . . and my sass appears from nowhere and bites me on the arse.

'Why's he here?' I ask, slipping from the bar to my feet.

'To help.'

I don't want to see him. Now I know for sure she's in London and he hasn't got Miller holding him back, he'll want to talk about her. I don't want to. Suddenly feeling claustrophobic in the mammoth space of Ice, I pace around the bar until I'm staring up at rows and rows of the hard stuff. Burn the anger away. That's what I need to do. I reach up and snatch down a bottle of vodka, mindlessly unscrew the cap, and pour myself a triple. But when the cold glass meets my lips, I don't tip the contents down my throat, mainly because my mind is distracted by a mental image.

An image of a baby.

'Damn,' I sigh, slowly taking the glass back down to the bar. I just stare at it, swivelling it around gently until the clear liquid is still. I don't want it. Alcohol has served a purpose of late – a silly attempt to blank my woes. Not anymore.

'Olivia?' Miller's questioning tone pulls my tired body around, revealing my hopeless face . . . and the glass. 'What are you doing?' He steps forward, uncertainty creeping onto his face as he flicks his eyes from me to the glass.

Guilt joins my hopelessness and I shake my head, full of remorse for even pouring the damn thing. 'I wasn't going to drink it.'

'Damn straight you weren't.' He strides around the bar and viciously swipes the glass from my hand before throwing the contents down a sink. 'Olivia, I'm dangling off the edge of insanity already. Don't give me the nudge that'll tip me.' His warning is stern and serious, yet the soft expression suddenly rife on his face defies every word of that command. He's pleading with me.

'I wasn't thinking,' I start, wanting him to know that I poured that drink in a blind temper. I've barely been given the opportunity to let this news sink in. 'I've no intention of drinking, Miller. I would never harm our baby.'

'What?'

My eyes widen in response to that shocked yell, and Miller virtually snarls.

Oh. My. God.

I don't turn around and face the enemy. If there's any scrap of sass within me, it'll be stripped down to nothing with a look of disgrace or the delivery of some scornful words. So I keep my guarded eyes on Miller, silently begging him to take the lead. There's nothing right now that can shield me from William Anderson, except him.

The long silence that stretches becomes painful. I'm mentally willing Miller to be the one to break it, but I close my eyes tightly when I hear William draw breath, accepting that it'll be him instead. 'Tell me what I'm thinking is wrong.' I hear a soft thud and see William collapsing to a barstool in my mind's eye. 'Please, tell me she's not.'

The words *I am* bubble in my throat, along with *and so what?* But they remain exactly where they are, defiantly refusing to put themselves out there. I'm mad with myself, mad that I'm rendered useless when I want to be wielding some bravery and unleashing it on William.

'She's pregnant.' Miller's chin rises, his shoulders squaring. 'And we're ecstatic.' He's *daring* William to continue.

William dares, though.

'For fuck's sake,' Anderson spits. 'Of all the stupid shit you could pull, Hart.'

I wince, not liking the slow-building heaving motions of Miller's chest. I want to join him, stand united, yet my damn body refuses to take me to him. So I remain with my back to William while my mind continues its assessment of the perilous situation looming.

'We agreed that if Charlie didn't have anything concrete on Olivia already, he would soon. Soon is now.' He reaches me and links an arm around my neck, encouraging me into his embrace. 'I said if he even breathed near her, it would be the last thing he did. He just breathed near her.'

I can't see him, but I know William will be matching Miller's hostility. The frosty vibes are crawling all over my exposed back.

'We'll discuss this later.' William dismisses it too easily. 'But for now you keep this between us.'

'He knows.' Miller's confession draws a shocked gasp from behind me, but he continues before William can interrogate him. 'He found Olivia buying a pregnancy test.'

'Oh Jesus,' William mutters, tensing my shoulders. Miller catches my reaction and moves his palm to my neck. 'You don't need me to tell you that you've just doubled his ammo.'

'No, I don't.'

'What did he say?'

'I don't know. I wasn't there.'

'Where the fuck were you?'

'Being sent on a treasure hunt.'

I bite my lip and nuzzle farther under Miller's chin, feeling so guilty and even more stupid. 'He was friendly.' My words are muffled against Miller's suit jacket. 'Or trying to be. I knew he was bad news.'

William lets out a snap of sardonic laughter. 'That man is friendly like a poisonous snake. Did he touch you?'

I shake my head no, certain I'm doing the right thing by keeping that little piece of my encounter with Charlie to myself.

'Did he threaten you?'

Again, I shake my head. 'Not directly.'

'Right.' William's tone has taken on an edge of decisiveness. 'Now's the time to stop thinking and start doing. You don't want to go to war with him, Hart. If it's not too late already. Charlie only knows how to win.'

'I know what needs to be done,' Miller states.

I don't like the sense of William tensing behind me, nor the increased thump of Miller's heartbeat under my ear.

'Not an option,' William says quietly. 'Don't even go there.'

Glancing over my shoulder to him, I find sheer refusal on William's face. So I take my questioning eyes back to Miller, and though he knows damn well that I'm looking at him in confusion, he doesn't tear his cool impassiveness away from William.

'Don't go all sentimental on me, Anderson. I can see no other way.'

'I'll think of one.' William spells the words out through a tight jaw, revealing his disgust. 'You're thinking the impossible.'

'Nothing is impossible anymore.' Miller moves away from me, leaving me feeling exposed and defenceless, and takes down two glasses. 'I never thought someone could claim me so entirely.' He sets about filling the glasses with scotch. 'I never even thought about it because who wants to consider the impossible?' He turns and slides one of the glasses over to William. 'Who wants to dream about what they can't have?'

I can see with perfect clarity that Miller's words are striking an emotional chord in William. His silence and the slow wrapping of his fingers around his glass say so.

A relationship with Gracie Taylor was impossible.

'I didn't think there was someone out there who was capable of *really* loving me,' Miller goes on. 'I didn't think there was someone out there who defied everything I knew.' He takes a long swig of his drink, keeping his eyes on William, who's shifting uncomfortably on his stool, playing with his glass. 'Then I found Olivia Taylor.'

My heart leaps in my chest and I vaguely register William downing his drink and swallowing hard. 'Is that so?' he asks. He's on the defence.

'That's so.' Miller raises his glass to William and finishes his drink. It's the most sarcastic toast in the history of toasts, because he knows what William is thinking. He's thinking he wishes he could turn back time. I, however, don't. Everything that has happened has led me to Miller. He is my destiny.

All of William's regrets, my regrets, my mother's mistakes, and Miller's dark past have brought me to now. And though this situation is destroying us, it's ultimately making us as well. 'I'll tell you something else that's not impossible for me,' Miller continues, like he's getting a thrill from torturing William, making him live through his regrets. He points a blind finger in my direction. 'Fatherhood. I have no fear because no matter how fucked up I am, no matter how scared I am that some of my screwed-up genes will pass down to my flesh and blood, I know Olivia's beautiful soul will eclipse it.' He looks across at me and steals my breath with his sincerity. 'Our child will be as perfect as she is,' he whispers. 'Soon I'll have two bright beautiful lights in my world, and it's my job to protect them. So, Anderson –' his face hardens and he returns his attention to a silent William – 'are you going to help me, or am I taking on the immoral bastard alone?'

I wait, full of apprehension, for William's answer. He looks just as taken aback by Miller's little speech as I'm feeling. 'Get me another drink.' William sighs heavily, pushing his glass towards Miller. 'I'm going to fucking need it.'

I catch the bar to steady myself, my relief making me dizzy, and Miller gives a sharp nod of respect before pouring William some more scotch, which he knocks back just as fast as the first. They've both fallen into business mode. I know I won't want to hear any of the plotting, and I know Miller won't want me to either, so I step forward to excuse myself before I'm ordered to leave. 'I'm just going to use the toilet.'

Both men turn worried looks onto me and I find myself spilling my desire to remove myself. 'I'd rather not hear how you plan on dealing with Charlie.' I refuse to let my mind go there.

Miller nods, stepping forward to brush my hair off my face. 'Just wait here for two minutes while I make a call. Then I'll take you down to my office.' He kisses my cheek and leaves quickly, not giving me scope for objection. Damn him! The conniving bastard! He knows I don't want to be alone with William, and the resistance it takes not to run after Miller nearly floors me. My legs are twitching, my eyes are darting, and my restless heart has set off on another nervous skip.

'Sit down, Olivia,' William orders gently, gesturing to a stool next to him. I'm not sitting down and getting comfy because I don't plan on being here for long. Two minutes, Miller said. I hope he means it. Thirty seconds have passed already. Another ninety, that's all. It's minimal.

'I'd rather stand.' I remain in place, exuding as much confidence as I can muster. William shakes his head tiredly and goes to speak, but I shut him down with my own question. 'What's impossible?' I ask, standing firm. Even though I don't want to know about their plans to deal with Charlie, I'd still rather talk about that than broach the subject of my mother.

'Charlie is a dangerous man.'

'I've figured that,' I retort shortly.

'Miller Hart is a *very* dangerous man.'

That soon snaps my cocky mouth shut. My mouth opens and closes repeatedly as my brain tries to form words and load them to speak. Nothing. I've seen Miller's temper. It's probably one of the ugliest things I've ever witnessed. And Charlie? Well, he filled me with dread. He exuded nastiness. He carries it around on full display, intimidating anyone he encounters. Miller doesn't. He hides the violence lurking deeply within. Fights it.

'Olivia, a powerful man who is aware of his power is a lethal thing. I know what he's capable of, and so does he, yet he buries that deep down. Unearthing it could be catastrophic.' A million questions burn my brain as I stand like a statue before William, absorbing every little scrap of information. 'Unearthing it *will* be catastrophic.'

'What do you mean?' I question, though I think I already know.

'There's only one way to free himself.'

I struggle to think it, let alone say it, my throat closing off in an attempt to stop me from uttering such an absurd statement. 'You mean Miller has the capability to kill.' I feel sick.

'He's more than capable, Olivia.'

I gulp. I can't add murderer to Miller's ever-growing fucked-up résumé. And now I'm weighing up the merits of a conversation about my mother – anything to try and make me forget what my mind has just been subjected to.

'Olivia, she desperately wants to see you.'

The change of conversation catches me off guard. 'Why didn't you tell me?' I blurt, my fear transforming into anger. 'Why did you lie to me? You had me alone on more than one occasion and instead of doing the decent thing, telling me my mother wasn't dead, that she was back in London, you centred all of your efforts on breaking me and Miller. Why? Because that selfish bitch told you to?'

'Hart insisted you shouldn't know.'

'Oh!' I laugh. 'Yes, so you managed to tell Miller she's back but didn't think that perhaps I ought to know? And since when have you listened to him?' I shout, incensed. My anger is running away with me. I know damn well why Miller held him back, but I'll cling to anything to validate my loathing for William and his reason for sticking around.

'Since he's had your best interests at heart. I might not like it, but he's more than proven how much you mean to him, Olivia. Taking Charlie on spells it out loud and clear. He's making every decision with you at the forefront of his mind.'

I have no counter for that, leaving silence for William to fill.

'Everything your mother did was for a reason, too.'

'But it was you who sent her away,' I remind him, realising the moment the words slip past my lips that I'm wrong. 'Oh my God! You lied, didn't you?'

His pained expression spells a thousand words, and he remains silent, only substantiating my claim.

'You didn't send her away. She left! She left you *and* me!'

'Olivia, it's not—'

'I'm going to the toilet.' My fast response is indicative of my deduction. Speaking of her won't help at all. I speed off, leaving behind a man in clear emotional turmoil. I don't care.

'You can't run away from your mother forever!' he calls, making my angry feet skid to a shocked halt. Run away?

I swing around violently. 'Yes!' I scream. 'Yes, I can! She ran away from me! She chose her life! She can go to hell if she thinks she can step back into mine when I'm finally over it!' I stagger back, my fury making me unstable on my feet, while William regards me carefully, warily. I can see his torment, but I have no compassion for him. Now he's trying to fix things with Gracie Taylor – though I have no idea why he would want that selfish bitch back in his life. 'I have everything I need,' I finish more calmly. 'Why is she here now? After all this time?'

William's lips press together, his eyes hardening. 'She had no choice.'

'Don't you start!' I yell, disgusted. '*You* had no choice; *she* had no choice! Everyone has a choice!' I remember what Gracie said at the Society – *I'll be damned if he's going to strut into her life and toss every painful moment I've endured all these years to shit!* – and suddenly everything comes together. The obviousness of it is almost stupid. 'She only came back because of Miller, didn't she? She's using you! She came back to take away the one true piece of happiness I've found since she abandoned me. But she's got you to do her dirty work!' I almost laugh. 'Does she hate me that much?'

'Don't talk stupid!'

It's not stupid at all. She couldn't have her forever with William, so I shouldn't have mine with Miller? 'She's jealous. She's blinded by jealousy that I have Miller, that he will do anything so we can be together.'

'Olivia, that's—'

'Perfect sense,' I whisper, turning slowly away from my whore of a mother's ex-pimp. 'Tell her she can go back to where she came from. She's not wanted here.' My calmness shocks me, and William's inhale of hurt breath tells me he's just as stunned by my hard-heartedness. It's a shame neither of them considered the hurt and damage *I* would endure all those years ago.

I drag myself across the club, not looking back to assess the hurt I've caused. I plan on curling up on Miller's office couch and shutting out the world.

'Hey.'

I look up as I'm weaving through the corridors below Ice and see Miller walking towards me. Lucky for him, I haven't even the capacity to lob a few choice words at him. 'Hey.'

'What's the matter?'

I manage to give him a *really?* look, and he backs down immediately. Good move. 'You look tired, sweet girl.'

'I am.' I feel like all life has been sucked out of me. I walk straight into him and use what's left of my energy to crawl up his body and cling to him, locking every limb around him. He accepts my need for support willingly, turning and trudging back the way he came.

'I feel like it's been too long since I've heard your laugh,' he says quietly as he lets us into his office and transports me to his couch.

'There's not much to be so over the moon about right now.'

'I beg to differ,' he disagrees, taking us down to the squidgy leather, me beneath him, but I don't release my hold of him. 'I'm fixing things, Olivia. Everything will be all right.'

I smile sadly to myself, admiring his valour but worrying that by fixing problems, he'll be creating others. I also consider the fact that Miller can't make my mother disappear. 'OK,' I breathe, feeling my hair being twisted until it's tugging at my scalp.

'Would you like me to get you anything?' he asks.

I shake my head. I don't need anything. Just Miller. 'I'm fine.'

'Jolly good.' He reaches behind him and starts to push my legs from his back. I don't make it difficult for him, despite wanting to remain attached to him forever. My muscles go limp and I puddle beneath him in a useless heap. 'Take a nap.' His lips meet my forehead and he pushes himself up, immediately pulling his suit into place before he offers a small smile and strides away.

'Miller?'

He stops at the door and pivots slowly on his expensive shoes until his stoic expression greets me.

'Find another way.' I don't need to elaborate.

He nods slowly but unconvincingly. Then he leaves.

My eyes are incredibly heavy. I struggle to keep them open, and as soon as they close, Nan's face pops into my darkness and they're snapping open again. I need to check in. Rolling onto my side, I find my phone and dial, collapsing to my back when it starts to ring.

And ring.

And ring.

'Hello?'

My brow bunches in response to the strange voice on the other end of the line, and I take a quick glimpse of my screen to see if I've accidently called someone else, finding I haven't at all. I take my phone back to my ear. 'Who's this?'

'An old family friend. I'm assuming this must be Olivia?'

I'm sitting up on the couch before I know what's happened, and I'm standing a split second after that. That voice. My mind is attacked by image after image of him. His scarred face, his thin lips, his eyes that harbour all kinds of evil.

Charlie.

Chapter 20

'What are you doing there?' The blood drains from my head, but I don't take my seat and begin breathing exercises, which I know damn well I should do. I'm beginning to feel light-headed.

'Well, our lovely chat was cut short earlier, so I thought I'd drop by.' Iciness oozes from his voice. 'Sadly, you're not here. But your grandmother is keeping me entertained. Quite a woman.'

'You lay a finger on her . . .' I start for the door, energy and purpose blocking my exhaustion. 'You even breathe on her . . .'

He laughs, a cold, evil laugh. 'Why would I ever want to harm such a dear old lady?'

I'm running now, my legs carrying me out of Miller's office and through the winding corridors of Ice's basement. That's a serious question, and it has an answer. 'Because it'll destroy me, and by destroying me, you destroy Miller, too. That's why.'

'You're a smart girl, Olivia,' he says, and then I hear something in the background. Nan. Her chirpy voice stalls my escape and I come to a stop at the top of the stairs, mainly because my pounding feet and heavy breathing are preventing me from hearing what she's saying. 'Excuse me,' Charlie says casually, the line soon becoming muffled. I can only assume he's holding the phone to his chest. 'Two sugars, Mrs Taylor,' he says cheerfully. 'But, please, take a seat. You shouldn't be exerting yourself. I'll see to it.'

He's back on the line, breathing hard, as if to tell me he's there again. Where's Gregory? My eyes close and I beg everything holy to keep them from harm, my gut twisting with guilt. She isn't even aware of the danger I've put her in. There she is, making tea, asking how many sugars the bastard takes, totally oblivious. 'Should I ask her to make it three cups?' Charlie asks, kicking my feet back into action. I run for the exit of Ice. 'I'll see you soon, Olivia.' He hangs up and my dread multiplies by a million.

Adrenaline is sailing through me, and I throw my weight into yanking the doors open . . . and get nowhere. 'Open!' I pull repeatedly, my eyes searching for a lock. 'Fucking open!'

'Olivia!' Miller's worried, stricken tone punches holes in my back, but I don't give up. I yank and pull, my shoulder jarring repeatedly from my constant, dogged attempts to open the stupid doors.

'Why won't they open?' I shout, now shaking them and looking around, not at all averse to throwing something through them in my desperation to get to Nan.

'Damn it, Olivia!' I'm seized from behind and restrained in his hold, but that adrenaline is still working, and it's working well. 'What the hell is wrong with you?'

'Open the door!' I lash out, kicking back.

'Fuck!' Miller yelps, and I expect to be released, but he just increases his hold around my chest, battling with my flailing body parts. 'Calm down!'

I can't see calm. It's nowhere to be found. 'Nan!' I scream, launching myself from his arms and colliding with the glass doors. Pain sears through my head, followed by the sharp curses of Miller and William.

'Enough!' Miller spins me around and pins me to the sheet of glass by my shoulders. Wide blues eyes run a quick scan of my head, then focus on the despairing tears that have now burst from my welling eyes. 'Tell me.'

'Charlie's at our house.' I spit the words out fast, hoping

Miller takes them in fast and then takes me home fast. 'I called to check on Nan and he answered.'

'Fucking hell!' William says, stepping forward urgently. Miller might look stunned, but my broken information has settled perfectly well with William. 'Open the fucking door, Hart.'

Miller seems to shake himself back to life, releasing me to pull some keys from his pocket. The door is opened quickly, I'm guided out quickly, and handed over to William while he locks up. 'Get her in the car.' I have no say in the proceedings that follow, and I don't want any. Both men are working fast and urgently, and I'm good with that.

I'm bundled in the back of Miller's car, ordered to put my belt on and William is in the passenger seat in no time, shifting to look over his shoulder. A serious, almost deadly look is pointing right at me. 'Nothing will happen to her. I won't let it.'

I believe him. It's easy to, because through all of this heartache and torment, one thing is obvious, and that's the feelings both William and Miller have for my grandmother. They love her, too. I swallow and nod, just as the driver's door swings open and Miller falls into the seat.

'You OK to drive?' William asks, giving Miller a wary glance.

'Perfect.' He starts the car, rams it into first, and we're skidding away from the kerb faster than is safe. Miller drives like a demon. Under normal circumstances, I'd be holding on for dear life, maybe even telling him to slow the hell down, but these aren't normal circumstances. Time is of the essence. I know it, William knows it, and Miller knows it. After listening to each man talk about Charlie, plus the added bonus of having had the pleasure of his company myself, there's no element of doubt in my mind that any threats he makes – directly or indirectly – will be seen through. This is a man with no morals, heart, or conscience. And he's currently sipping a good old cup of English tea with my beloved Nan. My bottom lip begins to tremble and Miller's manic driving suddenly isn't fast enough. I look up to the rearview mirror when I feel the familiar sensation of blue eyes burning into me, finding fear reflecting back at me. His brow is a sheen of wet. I can see he's desperately trying to instil some calm into me, but he's fighting a losing battle. He can't conceal his own dread, so trying to ease mine is pointless.

It takes years to weave the streets of London towards home. Miller performs endless illegal manoeuvres – reversing out of traffic-jammed roads and driving up one-way streets, constantly cursing profusely while William points out shortcuts.

When we finally screech to a stop outside my house, my belt is off and I'm running up the path, leaving the car door open behind me. I only vaguely register two pairs of dress shoes pounding after me, but I'm more than aware of strong arms capturing me and lifting me from my feet. 'Olivia, hold your horses.' Miller speaks quietly, and I know why. 'Don't let him see your distress. He feeds off fear.'

I wriggle from Miller's arms and press the tips of my fingers firmly into my forehead, trying to push some sensibility past the fog of panic that's rampant in my mind. 'My keys,' I blurt. 'I haven't got my keys.'

William almost laughs, drawing my attention to him. 'Do your thing, Hart.'

I frown as I look to Miller, seeing him reach into his inside pocket on a roll of his eyes. 'I told you we needed to sort out security here,' he grumbles, producing a credit card.

'Nan probably just invited him in!' I snap, but he doesn't bless me with a disdainful look; he just goes about slipping the card past the wood by the lock and jiggling it slightly, putting some weight behind him. It's two seconds flat before the door is open, and I'm pushing past Miller.

'Whoa!' He catches me again and pins me to the wall in the recess of the front door. 'Damn it, Olivia. You can't just go charging in there like a tank!' He's speaking on a hushed whisper, holding me in place with one hand while slipping his card back into his pocket.

'OK, let's just wait until we hear her screaming, shall we?'

'Just like her mother,' William mutters, pulling my outraged eyes away from Miller. His eyebrows are raised in a *Yes, you heard me right* kind of way; then his head cocks to follow that up with a *You going to argue with that?* look. I hate him.

'Get me to my nan,' I grate, burning through William's powerful presence with fiery eyes.

'Lock down that sass, Livy,' Miller warns. 'Now isn't the time.' He releases me and sets about the ridiculous task of straightening me out, except now I don't let him find the calm he's seeking through perfecting me. I bat him away, hating myself when I take over his stupid ways by finishing what he started. I brush my hair from my face and straighten my dress. Then my hand is claimed and I'm pulled through the front door.

'Kitchen,' I tell him, pushing him down the hallway. 'He was going to make tea.' Just as I utter the information, a loud crash rings out and travels down the corridor towards us. I jump, Miller curses, and William pushes his way past us before I can send the instructions to my legs to move. Miller takes off after him, as do I, every fear amplifying.

I fall into the kitchen, colliding with Miller's back, before putting myself in front of him. Gazing around the open space, I see nothing, only William staring blankly at the floor. My eyes are rooted on him, watching for any further facial expressions or reactions, my mind not prepared to confront what has his attention.

'Drat!' Nan's polite curse creeps past the wall of fear and has my eyes slowly travelling to the floor, where she's on her hands and knees with a dustpan and brush, sweeping up scattered sugar and a broken dish.

'Give it to me!' A pair of hands appear from nowhere, wrestling with her fingers. 'I told you, you silly old woman. I'm in charge!' Gregory snatches the pan from Nan's hand and turns exasperated eyes onto William. 'All right, geezer?'

'Fine,' William replies, looking back and forth between Nan and Gregory. 'What's going on?'

'She –' Gregory points the dustpan's brush at Nan, and she knocks it away – 'won't do as she's told. Get her up, will you?'

'For the love of God!' Nan cries, slapping her palms on her lap. 'Put me back in that prison they call a hospital because you lot are driving me crackers!'

My body feels like it's turned to mush from the overwhelming sense of relief. I cast my eyes to Gregory. He's giving William a look. A serious look. 'You should get her settled.'

William snaps into action, scooting down to collect Nan. 'Come on, Josephine.'

I feel a bit useless as I watch him help Nan from the floor. I'm relieved, confused, worried. It's like he was never here. I didn't imagine that call, and I definitely didn't imagine Nan's chirpy tone in the background. If it wasn't for the telling look that Gregory just chucked at William, I would be questioning my sanity. But I caught that look. He *was* here. But he just left? Gregory looks shaken, so why the hell doesn't Nan look like she's been terrorised?

I flinch when I feel a soft warmth brushing up my arm, and look down to see Miller's perfect hand cupping my bare elbow. It's only now I wonder where the telling signs of internal fireworks have gone. It's been too long since I've felt them. They've been drowned out by too much fretfulness. 'Maybe you should,' Miller says, bringing me back into the kitchen where Nan is now on her feet with William's arm around her shoulder.

I cough the lump from my throat and take over for William, leading Nan away, while I'm sure Gregory will be filling William and Miller in on the events that have recently transpired. As we enter the room and settle on the sofa, I notice the TV on mute. It spikes a clear mental image of her sitting on the couch with the control in her hand, listening when Gregory answered the door to Charlie.

'Nan, was someone else here with you a little bit ago?' I set about tucking blankets in around her, refusing to meet her eyes.

'You must think I'm as daft as a brush.'

'Why's that?' I curse myself for inviting her to tell me exactly why. I'm the daft one here. No one else.

'I might be old, darling girl, but I'm not stupid. All of you think I'm stupid.'

I rest on the edge of the couch and fiddle with my diamond, looking down at it as I do. 'We don't think you're stupid, Nan.'

'You must.'

I look out the corner of my eye and see her joined hands resting in her lap. I don't insult her further by arguing with her. I don't know what she thinks she knows, but I can guarantee the truth is a whole lot worse.

'Those three men in there are talking about my guest. Probably figuring out a way to get rid of him.' She pauses and I know she's waiting for me to face her. But I don't. I can't. Just that little titbit of her conclusion has stunned me and I know she's not done yet. I don't need her to see my wide eyes. I'll only be confirming her thoughts. 'Because he's threatened you.'

I gulp and close my eyes, my ring spinning around and around on my finger.

'Charlie is his name, nasty son of a bitch,' she says.

I turn to Nan, horrified. 'What did he do to you?'

'Nothing.' She reaches forward and takes my hand, squeezing

some reassurance into me. Strangely, it works. 'You know me, Olivia. Ain't anyone who can play the sweet old ignorant lady like me.' She smiles a little, drawing one from me. It's ridiculous that we're smiling, given the awful situation we're in. 'Daft as a brush, me.'

I'm staggered by her coolness. She's bang on the money with her assumptions, and I don't know whether to be thankful or horrified. Yes, there are a few gaps – gaps I'm not about to fill in – but she has the basic outline. She doesn't need to know any more than that. I don't want to do something so stupid as to elaborate on her dotted conclusion, so I remain quiet, contemplating where I go from here.

'I know so much more than I'd like you to believe, my darling girl. I've worked so hard to keep you from the dirt of London, and I'm so very sorry that I've failed.'

My brow creases as she works soothing circles into the top of my hand. 'You know about that world?'

She nods and takes a deep breath. 'The moment I clapped eyes on Miller Hart, I suspected he might be connected. William appearing from nowhere when you ran off to America only confirmed it.' She studies me, and I recoil, shocked at her confession. She pushed Miller and me together. The dinner, everything, she encouraged it all, but she goes on before I can question her motives. 'But for the first time in forever, I saw your eyes come to life, Olivia. He gave you life. I couldn't take that away from you. I'd seen that look in a girl before, and I lived through the devastation when it was taken away from her. I'm not going through that again.'

My heart starts to free-fall into my tummy. I know what she's going to say next and I'm not sure if I can bear to hear it. My eyes begin to fill with painful tears as I silently beg for her to finish right there.

'That girl was your mother, Olivia.'

'Please, stop,' I sob, trying to get to my feet and escape, but

Nan takes a firm hold of my arm and pulls me back down. 'Nan, please.'

'These people have taken all of my family from me. They're not taking you as well.' Her voice is strong and determined. Unwavering. 'Let Miller do what he needs to do.'

'Nan!'

'No!' She yanks me closer and grabs my cheeks, squeezing them harshly. 'Take your head out of the sand, my girl. You have something to fight for! I should have said this to your mother and I didn't. I should have said it to William, but I didn't.'

'You know?' I choke, wondering what she might hit me with next. I'm being bombarded with too much information for my little mind to deal with.

'Of course I know!' She looks frustrated. 'I also know that my baby girl is back and no bleeder has had the decency to tell me!'

I fly back on the couch in shock, my plummeted heart now sprinting up to my throat. 'You . . .' I can't get my words out. I'm utterly gobsmacked. I've grossly underestimated my grandmother. 'How . . .'

She settles back against her pillow, all calm, while I remain stuck to the back of the sofa, searching my mind for something to say. Anything.

Nothing.

'I'm going to take a nap,' she says, beginning to get cosy, like the past five minutes haven't happened. 'And when I wake up, I want everyone to stop treating me like I'm stupid. You can leave me in peace.' Her eyes close and I instantly take the cue – worried of the repercussions if I don't. Gradually lifting my lifeless body from the couch, I start to back out of the lounge, faltering once, twice, three times, thinking maybe we should talk more. But to talk, I need to form words, and none are coming to me. I quietly pull the door closed and stand in the hallway, wiping at my eyes and brushing down my creased dress. I don't know what to do with any of this. One thing is for sure, though. My head has been well and truly yanked from the sand. I'm not sure whether to be thankful or troubled by her awareness.

Hushed whispers from the kitchen draw me from my pondering and my feet take off across the carpet, taking me to a situation I'm certain will only add to my mixed-up state. On entering the kitchen, the first sign isn't good. Miller has his head in his hands at the table and William and Gregory are both leaning against the worktop looking on.

'What is it?' I ask, filling my voice with strength. I'm not sure who I'm trying to kid.

Three heads whip around, but it's Miller who has my attention. 'Olivia.' He stands and comes to me. I don't like that he's sliding his mask into place, quickly concealing his despair. 'How is she?'

His question sends me off into a daze again as I mentally pull together an explanation for how she is. Nothing here is acceptable, except the truth. 'She knows,' I utter, worrying that *that* statement is going to need to be extended. When an inquisitive look jumps onto Miller's face, that worry is confirmed to be warranted.

'Elaborate,' he orders.

I sigh, letting Miller lead me to the kitchen table and sit me down. 'She knew Charlie wasn't good news. She knows he has something to do with you two.' I wave a finger between William and Miller. 'She knows everything.' William's face tells me he already knew that. 'She's going to have a snooze now and when she wakes up, she wants everyone to stop treating her like she's stupid.'

William lets out a nervous bark of laughter, as does Gregory. I know what they're thinking, or at least thinking beyond their initial shock at this news. They're thinking that this is way too much for her to deal with, especially since she's just been discharged from the hospital. I haven't the first idea if they're right. Have I underestimated her? I don't know, but one thing I do know is that I'm about to put their current shock to shame. 'She knows my mum is back.'

Everyone in the room gasps.

'Oh Jesus,' Gregory breathes, rushing across to me, crouching to give me a cuddle. 'Oh, baby girl. Are you OK?'

I nod into his shoulder. 'I'm fine,' I assure him, no matter how *not fine* I am. I let him coo and fuss over me, stroke me and kiss my head repeatedly. And when he pulls away from my seated form, he gazes at me for an age, all fondly. 'I'm here for you.'

'I know.' I take his hands and squeeze, then use the opportunity to gauge the faces of the other two men in the room after my shocking news. William has a strange combination of awe and worry on his. And when I look to Miller, I see . . . nothing. He's poker-faced. His aloofness has fallen into place, but I can see something in his eyes, and I study them forever trying to figure out what it is. I can't.

I stand up, making Gregory sit back on his haunches, and approach Miller. His eyes follow me until I'm before him, nearly touching his chest, looking up at him. But he doesn't take me in his embrace, nor does his straight face crack.

'I need to go home,' he whispers.

'I'm not leaving.' I make myself clear before he starts with the demands. I'm not leaving Nan or this house until this is over.

'I know.' His easy acceptance startles me, yet I keep my composure, not willing to expose any more weakness. 'I need . . .' He pauses, thinking for a moment. 'I need to be at home to think.'

I want to cry for him. He needs his calm and normal to pull his thoughts together. His world has exploded into chaos and he looks like he could give under the pressure. I understand, really, I do, but there's a tiny part of me that's devastated. I want to be the one to settle him – me in his arms, me in his *thing*. Now's not the time to be selfish, though. It isn't just Miller who finds solitude when we're immersed in each other.

He clears his throat and looks across the kitchen. 'Give me the package he left for me.' A brown padded envelope appears to the side of me, and Miller takes it without a thank you. 'Watch her.' Then he turns and walks out. I watch his back disappear down the hallway, followed by the soft closing of the front door. I'm missing him already and he's only been gone for two seconds. My heart feels like it's slowing, and stupid as it might seem, I feel abandoned.

I feel lost.

Chapter 21

A hot shower can only settle my nerves so much. When I get out, the house is quiet. After popping my head around the door to check on Nan and finding she's still sleeping, I follow my feet to the kitchen. Gregory is standing over the stove, stirring something in a pan. 'Where's William?' I ask, joining him by the cooker.

'He's taking a call outside.' The wooden spoon bashes against the side of the pot, flicking some of the contents up the tiles on the wall. 'Shit!'

'What's that?' I screw my nose up at the brown slop being frantically whipped around. It looks disgusting.

'It's supposed to be potato and leek soup.' He drops the spoon and steps back, taking a tea towel up to his brow and wiping it. 'Nan will be horrified.'

I force a strained smile, noticing blobs of goo on both of his cheeks. 'Here.' I take the towel and set about wiping him down. 'How did you manage to get it all over your face?'

He doesn't answer, just lets me do my thing, standing quietly watching me. I take far longer than is necessary, until I'm sure I've rubbed blisters into his cheeks. Anything to avoid the inevitable. 'I think you got it,' he murmurs, taking my wrist to stop my clean-up operation.

My eyes flick warily to soft browns, then drop to the white T-shirt covering his broad chest. 'And here.' I reclaim my hand and start to rub at his chest, but I'm stopped before I can rub him red-raw there, too.

'Baby girl, stop.'

'Don't make me talk about it,' I blurt, keeping my eyes on his hand holding my wrist. 'I will, just not now.'

Gregory flicks the gas off on the stove and leads me to a chair. 'I need your advice.'

'You do?'

'Yes. Willing?'

'Yes.' I nod enthusiastically, loving him for not pressing me. For understanding. 'Tell me.'

'Ben's telling his family this weekend.'

I bite my lip, delighted I'm doing this to stop myself from grinning. A real grin. Not forced or fake. An actual proper grin. 'Really really?'

'Yes, really really.'

'And . . .'

'And what?'

'And you're happy, obviously.'

He finally breaks and grins from ear to ear. 'Obviously.' But his smile fades just as quickly as it appears, making mine fade with it. 'By the sounds of it, this will come out of left field for his parents. It's not going to be easy.'

I take his hand and squeeze hard. 'It'll be OK,' I assure him, nodding when he looks at me dubiously. 'They'll love you. How could they not?'

'Because I'm not a bird,' he laughs, kissing the back of my hand. 'But Ben and I have each other, and that's what counts, right?'

'Right,' I assert without delay, because it really is right.

'He's my someone, baby girl.'

Happiness for my best friend soars. Maybe I should be cautious on his behalf. After all, Ben has been a dick on more than one occasion, but I'm delighted he's finally over what others will think of his sexuality. Anyway, in reality, I'm in no position to pass judgement. Everyone has their demons, some more than others – Miller definitely more than others – but everyone is fixable. Everyone can be forgiven.

'What's up?' Gregory asks, snapping me out of my musings.

'Nothing.' I shake off my wayward thoughts, feeling more alive and awake than I have in . . . hours. Is that all it's been? 'That envelope.'

Gregory's sudden awkward shifting tells me he knows what I'm referring to. He was there, he saw, so of course he knows, yet I have an inkling there's more to it, especially given that he's avoiding my gaze. 'What envelope?'

I roll my eyes. 'Really?'

His face screws up in defeat. 'The evil fucker gave it to me. Told me to give it to Miller. You know it's not the first time I've seen him, right? He was that nasty fucker who turned up when you ran off to New York. I happily left him and William in Miller's flat to their staring standoff. Fuck me, it was like being between two cowboys ready to draw! I nearly passed out when I opened the door to him.'

'You let him in?' I gasp.

'No! Nan did! He said he was an old friend of William's. I didn't know what to do!'

I'm not surprised. Nan's more tuned in than any of us are giving her credit for. 'What was in the envelope?'

He shrugs. 'I don't know.'

'Greg!'

'OK, OK!' He starts with the awkward movements again. 'I only saw the paper.'

'What paper?'

'I don't know. Miller read it and put it back inside.'

'What was his reaction to what he read?' I don't know why I'm asking such a silly question. I saw first-hand what his reaction was when I walked into the kitchen. His head was in his hands.

'He seemed all cool and calm . . .' He pulls up, thoughtful.

'Not so much after giving you a hug, though.'

I snap my eyes to Gregory's. 'What do you mean?'

'Well . . .' He shifts a little, awkward. Or is it worry? 'He asked casually, you know, whether you and I had ever . . .'

'You didn't!' I recoil, fearing all kinds of shit will hit the fan if Miller ever found out about our fumble under the sheets.

'No! But shit, baby girl, I was seriously uncomfortable.'

'I'll never tell him about that,' I promise, knowing exactly what he's getting at. Only Gregory and I know, so unless one of us is stupid enough to mention it, then he will be none the wiser.

'Can I have that in blood?' he asks on a sardonic laugh. He actually shudders, like he's imagining what could happen should Miller find out about our silly little hook-up.

'You're being paranoid,' I tell him. He couldn't possible know. Which reminds me. 'Did he show William the paper?'

'No.'

I press my lips together, wondering if Gregory is working with Miller and William. That letter, whatever was in it, had my part-time gentleman go into emotional lockdown. He needed to *think*. He's gone home to the familiarity and preciseness of his flat to think. And he didn't take me with him – his self-professed source of therapy and de-stressing.

'I think I'll pass on the soup,' William says, strolling into the kitchen. Gregory and I both look across to him, seeing him poking at the contents of the pan with the wooden spoon, his nose wrinkled.

'Good call,' Gregory agrees, flashing me a big smile. I narrow suspicious eyes on him, certain he knows more than he's letting on. And when he coughs and reins in his amusement, getting up from the table to escape my probing eyes, I'm certain of it. 'I'll make something else.'

William's phone begins to ring, and I look over to see him fishing through his inside pocket. I definitely don't imagine the mild wave of agitation on his handsome face as he sees the caller's name on the screen. 'I'll just take this.' He waves his phone at me and strides out of the back door, into our courtyard garden.

As soon as the door closes behind him, I'm up. 'I'm going to Miller's,' I declare, snatching my phone from the table and making my way from the kitchen. I home right in on the certainty that William won't leave Nan, not even with Gregory. She'll be safe. Something isn't sitting right. Everything is telling me so – Gregory's behaviour, William's feigned coolness . . . every internal sense I have.

'No, Olivia!'

I never expected to be allowed to leave with ease, which is why I'm running down the hallway before Gregory can catch me or alert William to my escape. 'Don't you dare leave Nan,' I call, breaking free from the house and sprinting down the street towards the main road.

'For fuck's sake!' Gregory shouts, his frustration travelling down the street with his echo and smacking me in the back. 'I hate you sometimes!'

I'm at the tube station in no time. I ignore the persistent ringing of my phone, Gregory and William both trying to reach me, but once I've been taken down to the tunnels of London by two escalators, my reception dies and I no longer have to reject any more calls.

I find myself in the stairwell of Miller's building, taking the steps fast up to the tenth floor without one thought of using the lift. It feels like forever since I've been here. I let myself in quietly to be immediately greeted by soft music filling the flat. The track sets the tone before I've even closed the door behind me. The deep, powerful notes have me hovering on the edge of worry and peace.

I shut the door without a sound and pad around the table,

through to the kitchen, finding his iPhone docked in its station. The screen tells me what I'm listening to. The National "About Today". My eyes drop as the words leak from the speakers and penetrate my mind.

I wander into the lounge, finding what I knew I would. Everything is Miller-perfect, and I can't deny the settling feeling that engulfs me because of it. But my perfect Miller isn't here. I debate whether I should head for the bedroom or try the studio while I drink in the art that graces the walls of Miller's flat. Miller's art. The beautiful landmarks made to appear almost ugly. Distorted. Beautiful things are mostly noted as beautiful on first sight. Then sometimes you look deeper and discover that they aren't as beautiful as you first thought. Not many things are as beautiful on the inside as they are on the outside. There are some exceptions, though.

Miller is one of those exceptions.

I find myself falling into a bit of a trance, feeling comforted by the tranquil music. I have no intention of giving it up just yet, despite knowing I need to track Miller down and tell him that he's nowhere close to losing me. His flat and everything in it feels like a snuggly blanket closing in on me, wrapping around me to keep me warm and safe. My eyes close and I breathe in deeply, grabbing on to all of the sensations, images, and thoughts that have brought me so much happiness, like the sofa that I can see clearly in my darkness, where he first made his intentions clear. I remember the bowls of huge, ripe strawberries he had in the kitchen. Melted chocolate on the stove, me pinned to the fridge, Miller's tongue licking every part of me. It all catapults me to the very beginning. Then in my dark reflections, I wander into his studio and see the chaotic mess that came as such a surprise. An amazingly wonderful surprise. His hobby. The only thing in Miller's life that's disordered. Or the only thing until he met me.

I'm spread on his table; he's drawing lines across my tummy

with red paint – or, as I now know, writing his declaration of his love for me there. And "Demons" is playing softly in the background. Never have words been so true.

We're entwined on his squidgy couch, wrapped up in each other, stuck together so tightly. And the view. It's almost as beautiful as Miller.

Almost?

I smile to myself. Nowhere close.

My private reflecting couldn't get any better, but then those wonderful misplaced fireworks begin to fizz under my skin and my darkness bursts with light. Bright, powerful, superb light.

'Boom.' His whisper, his voice in my ear, the heat of his mouth engulfing my cheek, it all makes my body feel like it's free-falling into that wonderful light. I'm unable to separate my daydreams from reality, and I really don't want to. If I open my eyes, I'll be alone in his flat. If I open my eyes, every perfect thought of our time together will be lost to our ugly reality.

I can feel the warmth of his hands on my skin now, too, and the strange sensation of moving but . . . not moving. 'Open your eyes, sweet girl.'

I shake my head adamantly, squeezing my eyes tighter shut, not prepared to lose any of my dreams – the feel of him, the sound of him.

'Open.' Soft lips tease me, making me moan. 'Show me.' Teeth nibble in between the tormenting skimming of his mouth on mine. 'Keep me in your light place, Olivia Taylor.'

My breath hitches and my eyes flutter open, revealing the most breathtaking vision I'm ever likely to see.

Miller Hart.

My gaze roams the contours of his face, taking in every perfect detail of him. It's all here – his piercing blue eyes swimming with emotion, his soft lips parted just so, his dark stubble, his wavy hair, the errant lock sitting perfectly in place . . . everything. It's all too good to be true, so I reach up to touch him, the tip of my finger taking its time to feel it all, just to check I'm not imagining things.

'I'm real,' he whispers, taking my fingers gently to stop my quiet exploring. He kisses my knuckles and takes my hand to the back of his neck where my fingers delve into the masses of locks flicking from his nape. 'I'm yours.' His lips drop to mine and I'm hoisted up to his body, held tightly in his arms as we unite – taste each other, feel each other, remind each other of our powerful bond.

My thighs snake around his waist and constrict. I know I'm not imagining anything now. My insides are a riot of heat, sparks, and blazing flames. They are all consuming me, taking over me, rejuvenating me. It's so very needed. For both of us. Right now nothing else exists, only me and Miller.

Us.

The world is shut safely outside.

'Worship me,' I plead between our lapping tongues, pushing his jacket from his shoulders impatiently. I'm desperate to be skin on skin. 'Please.'

He moans, releasing me one arm at a time to rid himself of the expensive material. My hands are at his tie, yanking at the knot frantically, though he doesn't complain. He's as desperate as me to remove everything between us. As he holds me to him with one hand sitting under my bum, he uses the other to help me, pulling hard and taking his silk tie over his head and his waistcoat off. I make a very bold move when I grab the top of his shirt and wrench it open. I brace myself for his gasp of shock, which I've already decided I'll ignore, but it doesn't come. Buttons fly in every direction, the sounds of the tiny pieces meeting the floor around us, and I start pushing at the fine material, yanking it down one arm at a time. The heat of his bare chest against my dress is one step closer to skin. The shirt joins his jacket, waistcoat, and tie on the floor and my hands slap against his shoulders while our kiss becomes more and more urgent. There's not his usual demand. He doesn't try to slow me down or stop me. I'm allowed to kiss him madly and glide my hands everywhere they can reach as I whimper and moan my desperation for him.

I manage to kick off my Converse and push my body higher so he has to drop his head back to maintain our kiss. 'I want to be inside you,' Miller gasps, starting to pace across the lounge. 'Now.' He stops and reaches behind him to push my legs down from his back, all the while going at my mouth like a starved lion. I find my feet and move my hands to his belt, making fast work of removing it and tossing it aside. His trousers are next. They're undone and I work them as far down his thighs as I can manage while keeping my mouth attached to his. Miller does the rest, taking over and pushing his boxers down. Then he kicks everything off – trousers, boxers, shoes, and socks. My desire to remind myself of his full naked perfection doesn't overwhelm me enough to break our kiss, but when the hem of my dress is grabbed and pulled up my body, leaving me no option but to pull away from him, I take the interruption to drink him in. The material of my dress going past my face only hinders my studying momentarily, and I get a little extra time when Miller lazily reaches behind me to unclasp my bra, pulling it slowly down my arms. My nipples harden into tight, sensitive nubs, and my core starts to throb, begging for his touch. My eyes flick to his, my short pants being matched, as my bra is cast aside blindly before warm thumbs slip into the waistband of my knickers. But he doesn't remove them immediately, seeming content with watching me becoming more desperate by the second. He can't start with the torturous control. Not now.

I shake my head a little, watching as the corner of his mouth lifts just the tiniest bit. Then he moves forward, keeping his thumbs in place, encouraging my backward steps until my back's pushed up against the cold paint of a wall. I inhale a shocked rush of air, letting my head fall back. 'Please,' I beg, starting to feel him drawing my knickers down my thighs. The pulsing between my legs moves up a gear, transforming into a consistent thud. My knickers land at my feet.

'Step out of them,' he orders gently, and I do as I'm bid, trying to focus on what's likely to come next. I don't have to wonder for long. Heat meets me between the thighs. The source? Miller's fingers.

'Oh God!' I clench my eyes shut as he strokes up my centre. It makes me push myself farther into the wall in a pointless attempt to escape his teasing tactics.

'So fucking wet,' he growls, taking his finger back down and pushing into me, applying pressure on my front wall. My palms slap into his shoulders and push until my arms are braced at full length between us. 'Turn around.'

I swallow hard and try to filter his instruction, but his fingers are still inside me, motionless, and moving will instigate friction, which will instigate crumbling to the floor in a pile of want and lust. So I stay where I am, frightened to enhance my craving.

'Turn. Around.'

I shake my head obstinately, biting down harshly on my lip, digging my short nails into the flesh around his collarbones. Suddenly, a hand knocks my arms away and his body is flush with mine, putting more force behind his fingers buried inside of me.

'No!' I have nowhere to hide. I'm pinned to the wall, helpless.

'Like this,' he mumbles, biting his way from my chin to my cheek. Miller keeps us as close as possible as he turns me, ensuring his fingers remain submerged. As I feared, the sensations of my movements only heighten my wanton state, and I start to take deep, controlled breaths to stop myself from yelling my heady despair. 'Hands on the wall.'

I comply immediately.

'Back you come.' One hand takes my waist and guides me back, and then his foot taps my ankle, making me widen my stance. I'm wide open, totally at his mercy. 'Comfortable?' He twists his fingers inside of me, making my arse shoot back and collide with his groin.

'Miller!' I shout, letting my heavy head fall to the wall.

'Are you comfortable?'

'Yes!'

'Good.' He releases my waist and a moment later, I feel the hard, broad head of his arousal meet my entrance. I hold my breath. 'Breathe, sweet girl.' It's a warning and all of the air sails from my lungs as his fingers slip from my passage, making way for his hard cock. I'm not left absent of fullness for long. He slides in on a disjointed prayer, robbing me of breath again.

I feel complete. 'Move,' I plead, pushing back onto him, taking him to the hilt. 'Miller, move.' I push into my arms, bringing my head from the wall, letting it roll back on my neck.

My plea is answered. Soft palms rest lightly on my hips, his fingers flexing in preparation. 'I don't want you to come, Olivia.'

'What?' I gasp, beginning to shake just at the thought of restraining my climax. They come out of nowhere, mostly. He's the Special One – talented beyond mine *and* his own comprehension. 'Miller, don't ask the impossible!'

'You can do it,' he pointlessly assures me, grinding into my bum. 'Concentrate.'

I always concentrate. It gets me nowhere, so I have to rely on his expert teasing tactics, where he holds me in limbo. The torture that awaits me lands hard in my desire-saturated mind. I'm going to be screaming my despair, maybe even scratching and biting him. He *always* holds me in no-man's-land, so just the fact that he's warned me is worrying.

I clench my eyes shut and release a broken cry when he

leisurely withdraws until only the very tip of him is submerged. 'Miller.' I'm begging already.

'Tell me how you want me.'

'I need hard,' I confess, stopping myself from firing back and finding that delicious fullness.

'How hard?'

His question surprises me. And so does my answer. 'I want everything you have.'

He stills behind me. He's considering my answer. 'Everything?'

'Everything,' I affirm. His power and energy will strip away so much agony. I know it will.

'As you wish.' He bends, bringing his chest down to my back, and bites into my shoulder. 'I love you,' he murmurs, kissing at his bite mark. 'Do you understand?'

I understand perfectly.

'Yes.' Pushing my cheek into his face, I make the most of the scratchy feel of his stubble before he rises and takes an audible lungful of air. I brace myself.

Yet no amount of bracing stops my yelp of shock when he pounds forward. I half expect him to freeze and panic at my shout, but he doesn't. He swiftly retreats and flies forward on a roar. Those first few drives set the pace. He's relentless, unforgiving. His fingers dig into my flesh and yank me back repeatedly, pushing cry after cry past my lips. I have every faith that he can detect my frame of mind, so I don't try at all to stop my constant yelps. Every crash of his body into mine spikes one, and it's not long before my throat feels raw and dry. It doesn't stop me, though. My body isn't my own. Miller has full control of me and he's making the most of it. He's almost brutal, but the passion and want mingling between us holds me firmly in utter ecstasy.

He keeps up his merciless tempo until it's only him holding me up. There are barely any gaps between his groin slapping against the flesh of my bum, the sound getting louder the sweatier we become. The deep penetration isn't only filling me literally; it's filling me mentally, every thunder forward reminding me of this wonderful place I find myself in each time he takes me – whether controlled and gentle or brutal and unforgiving. There's no control here. At least there doesn't appear to be, yet I suspect it's there. No, I know it's there. I've come to learn that no matter how he chooses to have me, it's all worshipping. It's all undertaken with unremitting love backing it up.

Twinges are starting to stab at the tip of my clitoris. It's the beginning of the end. Oh God, I'm not going to be able to stop this! I try everything – focusing, breathing, but the crashing of his strong body into mine is preventing me from doing anything else but accepting him. Absorbing him. Taking absolutely everything he has to give me. It'll always be this way.

'You're tensing inside, Livy,' he yells, maintaining his ruthless pace, almost panicked, like he knows the internal battle I'm having. I don't have a chance to confirm he's right. He pulls out and spins me around, hoisting me up to his body and slamming back into me.

I scream, wrapping my legs around his waist and fisting my hands in his hair. The sudden loss of friction did nothing to help me. He's working too fast. 'My name, baby,' he pants into my face. 'Scream my name.' On his demand, he jacks me up and yanks me back down.

'Miller!'

'Oh yeah! And again.' He repeats his previous move, this time harder.

'Fuck!' I cry, going dizzy from the depths he's achieving.

'My name!'

I'm getting mad, my looming orgasm and Miller's insistence of controlling it triggering my sass. 'Miller!' I scream, tugging at his hair, throwing my head back as he pounds on.

He's getting thicker and thicker with each strike, has been for a while, yet the bastard refuses to give in.

'No scratching?' he taunts, sending my fingernails on an immediate lashing mission. I shock myself, but my surprise at my own viciousness doesn't stop me. I'm digging right down and then dragging hard through his skin. 'Arhhhhhh!' he roars in pain, tossing his head back. 'Fuck!'

Neither his agonised shout nor his anger-filled curse hold me back. I'm clawing at him like a madwoman, and strangely I think he wants me to.

'Lame, sweet girl,' he puffs, unreasonably incensing me. His eyes drop and lock with mine. They are dark and serious. He wants me to hurt him? His relentless hips pull to an abrupt halt, making my climax retreat.

I lose the plot.

'Move!' I pull at his hair, yanking his head to the side. But he just grins. 'Move, you bastard!' Dark eyebrows rise in interest, but he remains motionless, sending me on a pointless writhe in his hold to try and gain some friction. 'Damn you, Miller!' Without thought, my mouth drops to his shoulder and my teeth sink into his hard muscle.

'Fuck!' His hips piston forward, resurrecting my dying orgasm. 'You . . . fuck!' He's really going for it now, smashing into me like a man possessed.

My jaw locks around his flesh, making him yell, grunt, shout, and my hands are pulling constantly at his waves. I'm being as brutal as Miller. And it feels so good. The pleasure is beyond words, and the pain is replacing other agonies. All of the hurt is being slammed out of me, maybe only temporarily, but it's still going. He's punishing. I'm punishing. My back is being slammed repeatedly against the wall and we're both barking shouts of gratification.

'Time to end this, Olivia,' he pants, nudging my face from his shoulder and tackling my mouth. We kiss like we've never kissed before. It's hungry, fast, and desperate, and in the blink of an eye, I'm suddenly on the floor beneath Miller. He keeps us close and pumps fast until my toes curl and I scream as my release rips through me, drawing him farther into me on long, pulsing constrictions of my internal wall. He groans, his pace slowing, muffled words being mumbled into my neck. I'm milking him dry, relishing in the heat of his cum flooding me.

'Good God,' I gasp, prying my fingers from his back and letting them fall limply above my head.

'I concur,' he wheezes, pulling out of me and rolling onto his back in exhaustion. I drop my heavy head to the side, seeing his arms splayed out haphazardly as he puffs laboured breaths to the ceiling. 'I fucking concur.' His head drops and his eyes meet mine. He's dripping wet, his hair in disarray, his perfect mouth parted more than usual to drink in much-needed air. 'Give me my *thing*.'

'I can't move!' I splutter, astounded by his unreasonable demand. 'You've just fucked me into exhaustion.'

'You can move for me,' he protests, grappling at my waist haphazardly. 'Come to me.'

I'm given little choice. And besides, I want to smother him with my body *and* my mouth, so heaving myself up, I roll onto him until I'm spread limply down the length of his tall body. The only thing working now is my mouth and it's currently stuck to his neck, sucking and biting. 'You taste delicious,' I declare, getting a hit of clean sweat. 'And you smell divine.'

'Suck harder.'

I pause devouring him and bring my face slowly up. I know I'm frowning. Miller Hart is the last person in the world I would expect to want a bruise on his neck. 'Excuse me?'

'Suck . . . harder.' His eyebrows rise a touch, backing up his repeated order. 'Are you going to make me ask a third time?'

Slightly bemused, I fall back to his neck and nibble at him a little, wondering if he'll retract his command, but after a good few minutes of gentle biting, I only get that third time.

'Suck!'

My lips latch on to his neck immediately and suck. Hard.

'Harder, Livy.' His palm meets the back of my head and pushes me to him, making it slightly difficult to breathe. But I do as I'm told, sucking his flesh deeply into my mouth, drawing all of the blood to the surface. This will be seen loud and proud over the collar of his posh shirt. What the hell is wrong with him? I can't stop, though. For one, Miller's locked palm on the back of my head won't allow me to, but two, I'm getting an unreasonable thrill at the thought of everyone seeing such a defacement on my well-mannered gentleman.

I'm not sure how much time passes. The only indication is how sore my lips are and how achy my tongue is. When I'm finally released from his harsh hold, I pull away, a little breathless, and stare down at the monstrosity I've just created on his perfect neck. I flinch. It isn't perfect now. It looks hideous, and I'm sure Miller will agree when he sees it. I can't rip my eyes away from the ugliness.

'Perfect,' he sighs. He yawns and clasps my neck, then rolls us until I'm held snuggly under him and he's straddling my hips, sitting up on me. I'm still dazed and confused, and Miller lightly tracing the contours of my breasts with the tip of his finger doesn't distract me from that.

'It looks horrible,' I confess, wondering at what point he's going to check out the damage I've done.

'Maybe,' he muses, not giving my concern the concern it deserves. He just happily continues to delicately trail his finger all over my torso.

I mentally shrug to myself. I'm certainly not going to get myself all worked up – something Miller does best – if the king of stress isn't even bothering. So instead I ask the question I planned on asking the moment I found him . . . before he laid his hands on me and distracted me with a little Miller-style worshipping, albeit a little harder this time. Little? I smile. That was a proper good fucking, and surprisingly I loved every single moment. 'What was in that envelope?' I begin carefully, knowing this needs to be broached sensitively.

He doesn't even look at me, nor does he falter in his task of drawing invisible lines all over me. 'What happened with you and Gregory?' He looks at me, eyes full of knowing. I can't even breathe. Gregory was right to be worried. 'Gregory didn't look too comfortable when I inquired.'

My eyes close and I remain silent, failing to prevent the guilty signs from charging forward.

'Tell me it meant nothing.'

I swallow hard, furiously debating my best angle. Confess. Or deny. My conscience gets the better of me. 'He was trying to comfort me,' I blurt quietly. 'It went too far.'

'When?'

'After you took me to the hotel.'

He winces, pulling in a calming stretch of air.

'We didn't have sex,' I continue nervously, keen to clear that little bit of suspicion up. I'm not liking the shakes that his body has developed. 'A silly fumble, that's all. We both regret it. Please don't hurt him.'

His nostrils flare, like it's taking every modicum of his waning strength not to explode. It undoubtedly is. 'If I hurt him, I hurt you. I've hurt you enough already.' His teeth clench. 'But it won't happen again.'

That is a statement, not a question or request for confirmation. It won't be happening again. So I remain quiet until I eventually see his chest heaves begin to subside. He's calming, but I still posed a question before we slipped off course, and I want an answer. 'The envelope.'

'What about it?'

I chew on the inside of my mouth, deliberating whether to

continue. He's slipping into detachment. 'What was inside?'

'A note from Charlie.'

I kind of knew that, but his willing reply surprises me. 'What did it say?' The follow-up question slips out without hesitation this time.

'It told me how I can get out of this world.'

My mouth drops open. He has an out? Charlie's going to release him from the invisible shackles? Oh my God! The potential of all this being over, of us getting on with our lives, is suddenly too much to comprehend. No wonder Miller looks so peaceful, but I soon pull up when a small point worms its way past my relief and happiness. Actually, a huge point. He read that letter in the kitchen at my house and looked completely stricken past the cool impassiveness of his mask. He was troubled, so what's changed since then to make him seem so at ease? I steel myself and ask the question I should've asked before I let my excitement run away with me. 'How can you get out of this world?' My instinct to hold my breath worries me. It tells me I'm not going to like the answer.

But my question still doesn't make his finger falter across my skin, and he still isn't looking at me. 'It doesn't matter because I'm not doing it.'

'Is it bad?'

'The worst,' he answers without thought, almost scowling before it drifts into disgust. 'I have another way.'

'Like what?'

'I'll kill him.'

'What?' I wriggle beneath him in a panic, but I don't go anywhere, and I wonder if he positioned himself like this on purpose, knowing damn well I'd start pressing for answers and want to escape when he gave them to me. And I don't know why I'm acting so shocked by his shocking, hateful promise. After what William said and Miller's look, I had a bad feeling he would say that. What Charlie proposed is worse? How?

'Stay where you are.' He's calm. Too calm, and it just makes me all the more freaked. He seizes my wrists and holds them above my head, and I'm now puffing exhausted bursts of air into his face. 'It's the only way.'

'No, it's not!' I argue. 'Charlie's given you another way. Take it!'

He shakes his head adamantly. 'No. And that's the end of it!' His jaw is tight now, eyes darkening in warning. I don't care. Nothing can be worse than killing someone. I won't let him do it.

'It fucking isn't!' I yell. 'Get off me!' I heave and flip myself, all without success.

'Olivia, stop it!' He slams my wrists back to the floor above my head when I manage to fight them up a little. 'Damn it! Stop fighting me!'

I finally relent, but only because of utter exhaustion, and pant in his face, trying to glare through my tiredness. 'Nothing could be worse than killing someone.'

He draws in a deep breath. It's a confidence-boosting breath, and it makes every muscle against him tense. 'If I agree to what he wants, it will destroy you, Olivia. And there's no guarantee that once I do this, he won't ask me to come back and do something else. As long as he's breathing, he's a threat to our happiness.'

I shake my head adamantly. 'It's too dangerous. You'd never be able to pull it off – he must have dozens of heavies watching his back.' My panic is escalating. I heard Gregory mention guns. 'And you can't live with this on your conscience for the rest of your life.'

'It's too dangerous not to. And Charlie himself has given me the perfect opportunity.'

His confounding words hold me silent for a second before realisation slams into me and I gasp. 'Oh God. He wants you to go on a date?'

He nods mildly, choosing to remain quiet and let it settle in my wrought mind. This only gets worse by the minute. There has to be another way.

Something deep and possessive inside of me is stirring at the thought of someone else touching and kissing him. Part of my mind is screaming, *Let him kill Charlie. The world's a better place without him!* And a little devil on my shoulder is nodding his agreement. But I suddenly have a little angel, too, and she's looking at me sorrowfully, not speaking, but I know what she'd say if she did.

Let him go.

Just for one night.

It'll mean nothing to him.

'She's the sister of a Russian drug lord,' he says quietly. 'She's wanted me for years but she disgusts me. She gets off on degrading her partner. All she wants is the power. If Charlie delivers me, he'll get in with the Russians. It would be a very lucrative partnership, and he's wanted it for a long time.'

'Why don't they just join forces anyway?'

'The Russian's sister won't agree to an association unless she gets me.'

'Let go of me,' I whisper quietly, and he does, breaking away from my sprawled body and resting back on his knees. Apprehension is pouring from him. I get to my knees and reach for him, catching him frowning. But he lets me do my thing. I start to tug at his shoulders, encouraging him to turn away from me, and when his back comes into view, I fall apart.

It's a mess. Red lines are crisscrossing his back; some are weeping tiny beads of blood and others are swollen. His back looks like a roadmap. He really did want me to hurt him, but his reasons were far deeper than a pleasure-pain mix. He wanted my marks all over him. He belongs to someone.

Me.

My palms find my face and I push my fingers into my eyes,

unable to stop the constant hitching of my breath from my pain-filled sobs.

'Don't cry,' he whispers, turning and taking me in his arms. He kisses my head repeatedly, stroking my hair and holding me tight. 'Please, don't cry.'

Guilt attacks me and I yell at myself to do the right thing. Miller's willingness to do something so wretched for me is only enhancing it. No matter how much I tell myself that Charlie is the devil in disguise, that he deserves everything he gets, I still can't convince myself to agree. Miller would shoulder the burden for the rest of his life, and now that I know, so will I. I can't let him do that to us. It'll be like a noose around our necks for the rest of our lives together.

'Shhhhh,' he soothes, pulling me onto his lap.

'Let's run away,' I sob. It's the only way. 'We'll take Nan and go far, far away.' My mind is making a mental list of places as he looks at me fondly, like I just don't understand.

'We can't.'

I feel aggravation budding as a result of his simple and final answer. 'Yes, we can.'

'No, Olivia. We can't.'

'We can!' I yell, making him wince and close his eyes. He's trying to gather his patience. 'Stop saying we can't when we can!' We could go now. Pack Nan up and drive off. I don't care where we end up, as long as it's miles from London, away from this vile, cruel world. I'm not sure why Miller has claimed to be on his way to hell, because it feels like he's already there. And I'm with him.

Blue eyes slowly peel open. Haunted blue eyes. They steal my breath and stop my heart, but not in the usual way. 'I cannot leave London,' he says clearly, his look and tone daring me to interrupt him. He's not done yet. He really can't leave London and there's a damn good reason why. 'He has something very damaging on me.'

I hate my body's natural instinct to remove itself from his hold. I sit far back, working up the courage to ask the operative question. 'What?' I barely hear myself.

His Adam's apple protrudes from his throat and settles slowly after his challenging swallow, and his lovely face has drifted into . . . nothing. 'I killed a man.'

The noose I was avoiding is around my neck already, and it's tightening fast. I swallow repeatedly, my eyes wide and rooted to his straight face. My mouth has been zapped of moisture, too, making breathing increasingly hard. 'I . . .' I move back slowly, numbly, feeling the ground around me to check it's still there. I'm falling into hell. 'He can't prove it,' I claim, my tortured mind feeding my mouth words that I have no control over. Maybe it's my subconscious refusing to believe it's true. I don't know. 'No one will believe him.' He's holding Miller to ransom. Blackmailing him.

'He has evidence, Livy. Video evidence.' He's so calm. There's no panic or fear. 'If I don't do what he wants, he'll expose me.'

'Oh God.' My hand rakes through my hair, my eyes darting around the room. Miller will be thrown in prison. Both of our lives will be over. 'Who?' I ask, forcing my eyes to him, all the while hearing Gregory's light sarcasm that time he wanted to add murderer to Miller's long list of flaws.

'That's not important.' His lips press together. I think I need to be angry, but I can't seem to muster the fire in my belly. My boyfriend has just confessed to killing someone and I'm sitting here like an idiot asking calm questions. I don't want to believe that there's an underlying reason for my reaction, but I know for sure there is. I should be running away as far as my legs will carry me, yet I'm still sitting on the floor of his flat, totally naked, looking at him.

'Elaborate,' I grate, squaring my shoulders in a display of strength.

'I don't want to,' he whispers, dropping his eyes. 'I don't

want to pollute your beautiful, pure mind with it, Livy. I've promised myself so many times that I won't tarnish you with my dirty brush.'

'Too late,' I say quietly, whipping his eyes to mine. He must realise. My apparently beautiful and pure mind has long been tarnished with dirt, and not just Miller's. There's plenty of shit I've inflicted on myself, too. 'Tell me.'

'I can't tell you,' he breathes, shame now apparent on his cool face. 'But I can show you.' He slowly rises from the floor and holds his hand out to me. Instinct is working again, because my arm lifts of its own accord and I lay my hand in his. I'm pulled to my feet and our naked bodies meet, the heat of his bare flesh swathing me instantly. I don't pull away. He doesn't have a firm hold of me; he isn't keeping me where I am. I'm choosing to stay. His fingertip meets my chin and pulls my face up to his. 'I want you to promise me that what I show you won't make you run. But I know that's not fair.'

'I promise you,' I murmur, without thought or consideration, for reasons I may never know, but Miller's small smile and then the tender kiss he places on my lips tells me he doesn't believe me.

'You never cease to amaze me.' My hand is clasped and I'm led to the couch, unbothered by my nudity. 'Sit,' he instructs, leaving me to make myself comfortable while he wanders over to a cabinet and opens a drawer. He pulls something out before he slowly strides towards the TV. I can only watch in silence as he takes a DVD from a familiar envelope and loads it into the player. Then my eyes follow his path back to me. He hands me a remote control. 'Press play when you're ready,' he instructs me, thrusting it forward gently until I take it. 'I'll be in my studio. I can't watch . . .'

Again.

He was going to say that he couldn't watch it *again*. He shakes his head and dips, taking each side of my head in his palms and placing his lips on top of my head. The deepest breath is inhaled, like he's trying to siphon off enough of my scent and spirit to last him forever. 'I love you, Olivia Taylor. Always will.' And with that, I watch the distance between us grow as he leaves me alone in the room.

I want to scream for him to come back, to hold my hand, or just hold *me*. The remote control in my hand is burning and the urge to throw it across the room is overwhelming. The screen of the TV is blank. A bit like my mind. Starting to spin the control in my hand, I sit back, widening the distance between me and something that's going to send my already crumbling world into complete obliteration. I know it. Miller has confirmed it. So when I stop spinning the gadget in my hand and my finger pushes down on the Play button, I only stop to wonder what the hell I'm doing for a split second before the image of an empty room stops me from finishing my thought process. I frown and inch forward on the couch, taking in the plush space. It's boasting antique furniture at every corner, including the huge four-poster bed, and there's no question that it's all original. Wood panelling dresses every wall, and detailed paintings of countryside landscapes are hanging randomly, each mounted with intricate gilded frames. It's so posh and I can pretty much see the whole room, which tells me the camera is in a corner. It's empty, quiet, but when the door opposite the camera suddenly opens sharply, I fly back on the sofa, dropping the remote control to the floor.

'Jesus!' My startled heart is racing in my chest as I try to get my erratic breathing under control. I don't have to try for long, though, because my heart practically stops beating when a man appears in the doorway. My pulse slows in my veins and my blood turns to ice. The man is naked – naked except for a blindfold over his eyes. His hands are also held behind his back, and it doesn't take me long to figure out why. He's restrained. My poor eyes feel like they could bleed.

He's young, middle or late teens, perhaps. There's no lean muscle on his chest, his legs don't look powerful and strong, and his stomach is flat – no cut abdominals or shadows from the protruding muscles in sight.

Yet there's no mistaking who this young man is.

Chapter 22

'No!' My eyes flood with tears and my hand covers my mouth. 'No, Miller. No, no, no.' He's pushed into the room and the door shut firmly behind him, and then he just stands there, still and silent. There's no sound whatsoever. Not even when the door closes. I try to force my eyes shut; I don't want to see any more, but it's like a vice is holding them open, denying me any hope of hiding. My mind scrambles. *Find the remote control. Turn it off. Don't watch!*

But I do. I sit like a statue, immobilised by shock, only my eyes and mind functioning. My brain is relentlessly demanding I find a way to stop this – not just now, but stop it back then. He drops to his knees on the floor. I could be having an out-of-body experience. I can see myself standing to the side, screaming my anguish. Miller's head is dropped, and I gasp when a man appears from the bottom corner, his back to the camera. I let out a sob when he grabs Miller by the throat. He looks well dressed, a black suit adorning his tall body, and though I can't see his face, I know with perfect clarity what his facial expression is. Supremacy. Power. Arrogance in the worst possible way.

I continue to torture myself, telling myself that this is a breeze compared to what my love is enduring. The unknown man continues to hold Miller by the throat as he yanks at the belt of his trousers. I know what's coming. 'You bastard,' I whisper, rising to my feet. He takes a hold of himself, shifts his other hand to Miller's cheeks, and squeezes until he's forced to open his mouth. Then he rams himself past Miller's lips and begins to thrust like a deranged madman. I bite my lip as I watch Miller, my strong, powerful man, being violated in the worst possible way. It goes on and on and on. No amount of my tears and gut-wrenching sobs stop the hideousness playing out before me. My stomach turns when the stranger's head drops back a little and he slows down, circling into Miller's mouth like it's so very normal, my tummy twisting further when I actually see Miller swallow. Then like nothing has happened, the guy zips up, pushes Miller roughly to the side, and strolls out.

Every scrap of breath leaves my lungs on a quiet whimper as I watch Miller lie motionless on the floor, not a whistle of his mental state clear. His cautious approach to me taking him in my mouth and his violent reaction when he woke to me pleasuring him in New York is so clear now. I'm shaking with rage, sadness, every emotion possible, and it's all for him. I sniffle and sniff, willing him to get up and leave. 'Run away,' I beg. 'Leave.'

But he doesn't. Not for the longest time. He only moves when another man appears from the same place as man number one. He's back on his knees. 'No!' I yell, watching the new man stalk slowly forward, again in a suit. 'No, Miller, please!' The man follows the same string of sickening movements as the previous guy, except this one strokes Miller's cheek. My hand is back over my mouth, holding back the nausea. He starts to undo his trousers. 'No!' I swing around, searching for the remote control. I can't watch any more. My hands work like demons, throwing pillow after pillow across the room. 'Where are you?' I yell, beginning to sweat – a mixture of exhaustion and desperation to kill what's playing out on the screen behind me. I pull up and scan the floor, spotting it under the table. Dropping to my knees, I grab it and swing around, aiming it at the television, but my finger doesn't stab at the stop button. It just hovers above it, twitching as my wide eyes watch Miller's hands come from behind his back and yank his blindfold from his head.

I choke and heart palpitations send me falling back to my arse. His eyes are revealed. They're hollow. Empty. Dark.

Familiar.

The man staggers back in shock, frantically working at his trousers as Miller rises to his feet, danger coming from every naked pore. He said he killed a man. This man here. My arm goes limp, my finger relaxing as my hand falls to the floor. Now I really know what's going to happen and I can't even be sorry for the sadistic thrill I know I'm going to get from watching it play out. Miller in this footage may not be as physically lean and cut, but it would be foolish to underestimate the sheer violence radiating from him. He starts to stalk slowly forward, his face straight, no hint of anger evident at all. He looks completely composed. He's a robot. A machine. He looks lethal.

I slowly stand, silently willing him on.

The guy's hands come up in defence as every muscle on Miller's body visibly engages, ready to pounce . . .

And then the screen goes blank.

I gasp, frantically stabbing at the play button on the remote control. That can't be it! I need to see him hurt him. I need to see him get revenge. 'Play, damn it!' I yell, but after a lifetime of punching the button, nothing happens. 'Fuck you!' I scream, hurling the remote control across the room with brute force. I don't even flinch when it smashes against the front of one of Miller's paintings, shattering the glass sheet protecting the canvas. I whirl around, heaving and shaking. I feel cheated. 'Miller,' I exhale, bolting across his flat and running like an unhinged nut down the corridor towards his studio.

Bursting through the door clumsily, I pull to a halt and search him out. He's sitting on the edge of his old worn couch, elbows braced on his knees, his face in his palms. But shocked wide blue eyes are revealed quickly. I see life in them. Light and energy, none of which were there in that footage, and none of which were there when we first met. It's all evolved since we've found each other, and I'd rather walk the fiery depths of hell than see it all lost. A painful sob fights past my anger and I start running to him, only vaguely registering him standing through my blurry vision.

'Olivia?' He starts forward tentatively, frowning. He's shocked I'm still here.

I launch myself into his arms. Our naked bodies crash together hard, and would probably hurt if there wasn't another agony consuming every nerve ending. 'I'm so fascinated by you,' I sob, constricting him around the neck, melding myself to him.

Miller accepts my overpowering clinch and holds on just as tightly, maybe even tighter. My rib cage is under incredible pressure, jeopardising my breathing, but I couldn't care less. I'm never letting go. 'I love you, too,' he whispers, sinking his face firmly into my neck. 'So much, Olivia.'

My eyes close and all of the anxiety from the horror scene falls away under his *thing*. 'I wanted to see you do it,' I admit, reasonably or not. I feel like I need that part of the puzzle. Or maybe I just need to be sure he really did kill that wicked arsehole.

'Charlie has it.' He doesn't ease up on his hold, which is fine because I don't want him to. He could squeeze even harder and I wouldn't complain.

My mind settles, allowing me to think clearer. 'He'll take it to the police.'

Miller nods a little into my neck. 'If I don't play ball, then yes.'

'And you're not going to play ball, are you?'

'I'm not doing it, Olivia. Not to you. I couldn't live with myself.'

'But you could live with blood on your hands?'

'Yes.' His answer is swift and decisive before he wrestles me from his arms and gazes down at me. 'Because the alternative is your blood on my hands.' I lose my breath but Miller continues, saving me the trouble of finding any words. There aren't any. And I know now, one hundred per cent, that there's nothing I can do to stop Miller from killing Charlie. 'I have no remorse for what I did to that man. I'll have even less for Charlie. But I would never forgive myself if any harm came to you, Olivia.'

My eyes clench in pain at his honest words and I finally allow myself to take some time and evaluate what they did to him. He was young in the video. Amid all the other shit this poor man has endured, when did that happen? How many times did it happen before he flipped? Did Charlie organise it? Undoubtedly. And now he wants to subject him to some Russian woman who wants to degrade him again. Never.

'I need to get that,' Miller says as the phone rings. He lifts me from my feet and carries me out of the studio into the kitchen. He doesn't release me to take the call, instead holding me just as tightly with one arm and answering his phone with the other. 'Hart,' he greets shortly, resting his bum on the table and dropping me to my feet between his thighs. I'm still stuck to his front, but he doesn't complain or ask for privacy.

'Is she there?' William's irritated tone is perfectly clear to me and likely to be, considering my cheek is welded to one side of Miller's face and his phone to the other.

'She's here.'

'I just took a call,' William tells Miller. He sounds hesitant.

'From?'

'Charlie.' Just the mere mention of his name sets my panic off again. Why is he calling William? They're archenemies.

'So suffice it to say he knows for sure that I'm sleeping with the enemy?' There's a touch of irony tickling the corners of Miller's question.

'Hart, he has copies of the footage.'

My heart slows down. I feel it, and I know Miller feels it, too, because he clings on that little bit tighter. 'Let me guess – if anything happens to Charlie,' Miller says quietly, 'there are two people with instructions on how to find the copies and what to do with them.'

There's a long pause, and I see William in my imagination rubbing stressed circles into his grey temples. 'How'd you know?'

'Sophia told me. And she told me she destroyed all the footage.'

The shocked gasp that travels down the line cools my skin. 'No.' William sounds almost defensive in his counter. 'And you believe her?'

'Yes.'

'Miller,' William goes on carefully, using his Christian name for a change. 'Charlie is untouchable.'

'You almost sound like you don't want me to kill him.'

'Fuck.' William heaves out a sigh.

'Goodbye.' Miller tosses his phone onto the table without care or attention and places his arm around me.

'William knows,' I mumble into his neck, only just comprehending the last few moments' conversation. 'He knows what's in that footage?'

'I guess he suspected. Charlie has only confirmed it. There have always been rumours about a night at the Temple that resulted in the death of a man by my hand, but that's all it was. No one knew the circumstances and no one knew if it was true. It's like the best-kept secret of the London underworld.'

Miller wrestles with me a little, encouraging me away from him. We've been stuck together so hard and for so long, it feels like he's ripping a plaster slowly off my naked skin. I hiss a little, then grumble my protest, but he just smiles fondly. I have no idea what there is to smile about. Reaching up timidly, he gently strokes across my forehead, moving into my hair, pulling it away from my face. 'I'm amazed you've still not turned to dust, sweet girl.'

I smile a little, searching his face. 'I'm amazed you're resting your naked bum on your dinner table.'

He reins in his smile, trying to scowl. 'My table couldn't be any more polluted than it already is, thanks to my beautiful girlfriend.' He stops and seems to consider something for a moment. 'Are you still my girlfriend?'

Albeit insanely inappropriate, I can't help smiling brightly at my beautiful love. 'Are you still my boyfriend?'

'No.' He shakes his head and takes my hands, bringing them to his mouth and kissing each of my rings and my knuckles in between. 'I'm your slave, sweet girl. I live and breathe for no other purpose but you.'

I pout as I look down at his waves, his lush lips making side-to-side brushing motions over the tops of my hands. I don't like the word *slave*. Especially following what I've just witnessed. 'I prefer *boyfriend*. Or *lover*.' Anything but *slave*.

'As you wish.'

'I do.'

He forces his face up to mine and gets nose to nose with me, searching my eyes. I feel like he's feeding off the light he claims to find in them. 'I'd do anything for you,' he whispers. '*Anything*.'

I nod, feeling my irises burning from his concentrated gaze. 'I know.' He's proven that. 'But you can't go to prison.' He can't fight for his freedom and then get locked up. It would be insane to consider that as a potential out. Seeing him once a week for . . . however long it might be won't be enough.

'I couldn't survive a day without losing myself in you, Olivia Taylor. It's not an option.'

Relief makes me dizzy. 'So what now?'

He cuddles me fiercely before roughly releasing me and

wiping at his cheeks. His face takes on an edge of determination, and when I should expect this to settle me, I find it unnerves me. 'I need you to listen to me carefully.' His palms rest on my shoulders, holding me in place. My heartbeat quickens. 'Charlie thinks he has me cornered. He thinks I'm going on that date and trusting he'll hold his end of the deal. And just in case you have any doubt racing through that mind of yours, he would never have upheld his end of the bargain.' He taps my temple gently, giving me high brows.

I don't like where this is heading. Miller looks too determined, and I can see with clarity him trying to inject me with some, too. I'm not sure he can. 'What are you telling me?'

'I'm telling you that I'm going to the Temple. I've accepted Charlie's out, and—'

'No! I hate to think of you with her.' I know that's the least of our problems at the moment, but possessiveness is getting stronger by the second. I can't control it.

'Shhhh,' he hushes me abruptly, placing a finger over my lips. 'I thought I told you to listen carefully.'

'I am!' I'm going to lose my mind. 'And I don't like what I'm hearing!'

'Olivia, please.' He takes my shoulders and shakes me a little. 'I need to go on that date. It's the only way I'll get into the Temple and close to Charlie. I won't be touching that woman.'

Close to Charlie. I withdraw, wide-eyed. 'You really are going to kill him, aren't you?' I don't know why I'm asking. He's told William. I heard it with my own ears, but maybe I thought I'd wake up. This is the longest nightmare ever.

'I need you to be strong for me, Olivia.' His grip increases, almost to the point of pain. He pushes his lips to my forehead and breathes in deeply. 'Trust me.'

Seeing the pleading in Miller's eyes jars something within me, and then the flashbacks from the repulsive footage replay over in my mind. It only takes a second for me to recall the overwhelming need I felt to see Miller hurt that man. To know justice had been done. I want this to be over. I want Miller to be mine now. And then Miller's words. They make perfect sense now.

You possess every part of me, Olivia Taylor. For all of the wrongs I have done and all that I am yet to do, I'm asking for your mercy. Only your love will see me through this hell.

'OK.' I don't even shock myself with my easy acceptance. This is an easy decision. I'm suddenly full to the brim with resolve. I'm sound-minded and determined.

I want to be free of the invisible chains, because I am shackled, too. But more than anything, I want Miller to be free. Wholly free. *He* gets to decide who he belongs to. He chooses me, and that can't happen until this shit is over. He'll never be mine until this is finished. No interferers. No living on the edge. Our histories will be as they should be. History.

'Do it,' I whisper. 'I'll be here for you. Always.' His eyes fill with water and his chin trembles, fuelling my own tears to build. 'Don't cry,' I beg, placing myself into his chest and guiding his arms around my back. 'Please, don't cry.'

'Thank you.' His words are disjointed and gruff as he cuddles me fiercely. 'I don't think I could love you any harder.'

'I'm quite fascinated by you, too.' I smile sadly, already planning what on earth I can do to busy myself when he sees through his promise to kill Charlie.

Can you die for one night and come back to life?

Once we've finally relented and given up our holds of each other, Miller takes his phone and wanders out of the kitchen to make a few calls.

In the meantime, I wander pointlessly around the kitchen, searching for something to do, anything to clean up or tidy. Nothing. I sigh my exasperation and find the dishcloth under the sink, then set about wiping up watermarks around the sink that aren't there. I go over and over the same spots, rubbing at shiny stainless steel until I can see my face in it. It's an awful sight, so I continue with my senseless wiping.

But then I pause.

Boom . . .

I slowly turn, armed with the damp cloth, and rest against the sink, looking across to him at the entrance. He's leaning on the doorframe, spinning the phone slowly in his hand.

'OK?' I ask, folding the cloth and turning away from him to put it in its rightful place, thinking I should try an attempt at normal. I laugh at my stupid endeavour. I have no idea what normal is.

When I get no answer, I pivot slowly, biting my lip nervously.

'Arrangements have been made.' He means for his supposed date.

I nod, my fingers now rotating my ring nervously. 'When?'

'Tonight.'

'Tonight!' I blurt, shocked. That soon?

'There's an event at the Temple. I'm required to accompany her.'

'Right.' I gulp, then nod decisively. 'What's the time?'

'Six.'

'What time . . .' I pull up and take a deep breath. 'What time is your date?' The words make me want to vomit.

'Eight,' he answers tightly, keeping cool blues on my fake brave face.

'So we have two hours to get you ready.'

He frowns. 'We?'

'Yes. I'm going to help you.' I'm going to bathe him, shave him, dress him, and kiss him goodbye, like a woman would who's seeing her boyfriend off for work. Just a day in the office. That's all.

'Olivia, I—'

'Don't try to stop me, Miller,' I warn, approaching him and

taking his hand. He wants me to be strong. 'We do this my way.' I pull him over to the docking station and scroll through the tracks, looking for something a little upbeat. 'Perfect,' I declare, pressing play. Rihanna's "Diamonds" joins us and I turn on a coy smile, delighted when I find a lovely smile gracing Miller's face, too.

'Perfect indeed.'

I start to lead the way to his bedroom, but I'm tugged to a stop.

'Wait.'

Reluctantly, I halt when all I want to do is lose myself in the task of readying him.

'Before we do things your way,' he says, scooping me into his arms. 'We do things my way.' He's moving before I can object, carrying me to his bedroom. I'm placed gently on the bed, like I'm the most delicate object in the universe, before his sits on the edge, one palm resting on the mattress so he can lean over me. 'I need to have you once more.'

I press my lips together and work hard to hold on to my emotions. He means once more before he leaves to murder someone. The pad of his finger lightly settles on my bottom lip as he gazes down at me, and then he slowly walks his fingers over my chin, down my throat, and onto a breast. Every nerve ending ignites under his soft touch, my nipples tingling, begging for some attention. I'm not denied it. He keeps his eyes on me as he slowly drops his mouth to one breast, giving it a little flick of his tongue, before grazing the very tip with his teeth. My back bows and I fight to keep my arms at my sides. My other breast is claimed by his hand, his palm cupping it possessively, squeezing and moulding as he begins swirling his tongue around my other nipple. I shift on the bed, my legs twitching. I give in to their insistence to move and bring my knees up until the soles of my feet find the mattress.

He's being super gentle, a total turnabout from our frantic fucking when I arrived. I sense there is more to it than just having me one more time. He wants to refuel on strength.

'Nice?' he asks, before filling his mouth with my breast, sucking gently.

'Yes.' I hum my pleasure, feeling the heaviness in my lower tummy intensifying. My arms take on a mind of their own and leave my side, my hands searching out the softness of his waves. He laps, licks, and sucks meticulously while my palms rest lightly on the back of his head, following his movements rather than pushing him farther into my chest.

'You taste out of this world, Livy,' he mumbles, kissing his way around my nipple and down to my midriff. I let my lids flutter closed in bliss and absorb every precious second of him feeling me, kissing me, worshipping me. His lips are everywhere on my torso, making me moan and writhe. The delicate bites of my flesh, his lips raining gentle kisses everywhere, it all provides the detachment I need from our imminent future.

I suck in air when his hand drifts close to the apex of my thighs, my tender, sensitive, wet flesh begging him to venture there. 'Hmmmm.' My head falls to the side, my hands now firming up on the back of his head in a silent hint. I want his mouth there.

He circles his thumb lightly over the top of my clit as he continues kissing my stomach. The friction makes me go rigid and hold my breath. 'Always ready for me.'

I sigh, letting him work me up with his tender caresses. The ache in my groin is bubbling as my breath hitches, and I try my hardest not to moan, just so I can hear Miller's pleasure-filled murmurs.

'I want you to come like this first.' His fingers slip into me and every greedy muscle clings on. 'Then I'm going to make serious love to you.'

'You always make serious love to me,' I mumble, transferring my hands to my own hair and gripping hard at my scalp. My hips start thrusting up, matching his tempo.

'And it's the most gratifying feeling.' His fingers flex within me. I gulp. 'Your eyes smoking out as your pleasure builds. The tiny little pants of air as you try to control it.' He circles, putting some weight behind his touch, making me shift up the bed. 'Nothing can come close to watching you shatter beneath me, Olivia.'

I'm going to shatter now.

'Are you nearly there?' he asks softly, moving his face down and blowing a cool stream of air over my quivering centre. It propels me to the edge as I tighten my grip of my hair and clamp onto his fingers as he thrusts and slowly circles.

'Ooooh,' I breathe, my head beginning to slowly shake from side to side. 'Miller, I need to come.' All of my blood rushes to my head as I struggle to regulate my breathing.

I cry out when his mouth encases my clitoris, his fingers still pushing into me gently. I'm beginning to shake uncontrollably. 'Miller!'

He withdraws his fingers and moves fast, lying between my legs and placing his hands on my inner thighs to push them wide apart. I go rigid, probably hampering him, but my climax is taking hold. The wet heat of his mouth suckling at me pushes me gently over the edge as I expel a long controlled rush of breath. I liquefy on the bed. I'm pulsing under his tongue, long and steady, drinking in air and circling my hips into his mouth. 'I love it when you cry my name in desperation.' He laps his tongue around my soaking core, gently easing me down from my subtle release.

'I love it when you make me that desperate.' I spasm when his lips scatter gentle pecks all over my swollen centre, working his way back up my body until he's at eye level with me. Gazing into his burning eyes, he swivels his hips and plunges deeply, catching me a little off guard. His brow is shimmering with sweat, the gorgeous lock of hair skimming his damp skin. 'You're so warm.' He pushes forward some more, his eyes flickering. 'You feel so fucking good.'

I press my lips to his and he responds on a long, low moan, circling my tongue slowly with his. 'Not as good as you,' I mumble against his lips, his long stubble grazing my face.

He breaks our kiss and circles my nose with his. 'We'll agree to disagree.' His hips swing into action, pulling out slowly. 'Olivia,' he whispers my name, and it only serves to increase my heart rate and transform the heat in my veins to flames. 'Olivia Taylor, my most precious possession.' He pushes forward soft and slow and with the utmost control.

My back bows, my hands taking a hold of his shoulders, feeling the flexing muscles as he withdraws again.

'I love taking my time with you.'

I close my eyes on a long moan and let him do exactly that.

'Don't deprive me of your eyes, sweet girl. I need to see them. Show me.'

I can't refuse him. I know he partly survives on the comfort and strength they offer him. Now he really needs that comfort and strength, so I reveal my sapphires to his piercing blues. He's braced on his forearms, watching me carefully as he delivers lazy drives into me. My hips begin to move with him, turning those drives into grinding rotations. The friction is divine and constant, our groins locked together, circling around and around. I begin to pant. 'Please.'

'What do you want?' he asks calmly. I don't know how he does it. It's infuriating. I can feel my body losing control as my pleasure builds.

'I need to come again,' I admit, loving that his cock actually swells in response to my confession. 'I want you to make me scream your name.'

His eyes sparkle wildly, his erection answering again with another expansion. My hips are on autopilot now, which is good because all I can concentrate on is the delicious fire crackling between my thighs.

'No screaming today,' he says, dropping his mouth to mine. 'Today you'll moan into my mouth and I'm going to swallow every second of it.' He notches up a gear with his rotating hips, flinging me back to the brink. I'm going at his mouth too roughly, but I make the most of it because I know what's coming.

'Savour me, Livy,' he orders gently, instantly reining me in. My hands drift down his strong arms and feel their way across to his bum. I moan happily and stroke over the firmness for a short while, then grab on. He's moaning now, too, our collective sounds clashing between our mouths as they duel gently. 'Here it comes.' His tongue speeds up, encouraging me to follow, which I do, my muscles hardening under him. I can feel all of the signs in him. He's breathless, tense, and vibrating against me. 'Oh shit, Olivia.' He bites my lip, then resumes his passionate, hungry kiss. 'Ready?'

'Yes!' I yelp, working hard to capture the peak. It's nearly there. It's . . .

'I'm going!' he shouts into my mouth. 'Come with me, Olivia!'

'Miller!'

'Fuck, yes!' He circles deeply one last time, then withdraws and pushes forward slowly on a broken groan, hurling me skyward. My spine snaps into a violent arch as I crumble into helplessness beneath him, my eyes closing and my head falling to the side in an exhausted heap.

Wet warmth coats my insides and Miller collapses onto me, panting erratically into my neck. In my post-climax haze, I'm vaguely aware of him softening within me.

And there we drift off together, still connected and blanketed in each other.

*

My legs are bent and my thighs parted. My arms are pinned above my head as I feel him shifting above me. I open my eyes sleepily after my brief snooze to find Miller gazing down at me with parted lips, his blues sparkling like diamonds. His arm moves above my head to join his other so that my face is fringed by two lean biceps, but he doesn't pin me down; he just rests his arms over mine.

I whimper when he lifts, letting his erection fall into position before slowly pushing himself into me on a quiet hitch of breath. I shift under him to meet his advance and sigh as he begins an unhurried pace, working himself in and out of me.

'I love you,' he whispers as his mouth falls down to mine. Once again, all woes are drowned out by his worshipping and my aching for him. I soak up the pleasure of him deep inside me and match his languid tongue strokes with my own. He pulls back and rests his forehead against mine as he continues his slow, silent drives. 'You'll be all I see the whole time.' He circles his hips on a delicious deep grind.

I moan.

'Tell me you know that.'

'I do,' I breathe.

He picks up his pace slightly, working in and out on smooth, delicious hits, his damp forehead rocking against mine as he puffs short, harsh breaths. He starts to shake over me. I'm there, too.

'Let me taste you, Olivia.'

I let him have me and kiss him to release, joining him as he tenses and stills above me on a constricted moan, his shakes increasing. The violent shudder that rides through my body has me crying into his mouth, and I pull my arms through his and hold him close to me as we continue kissing, soft and slow, lovingly, long past our float down.

That was his goodbye.

'Now we can do this your way,' he says quietly against my

neck, and takes another inhale of my hair, topping up on my scent.

Having a silent stern word with myself, telling my disturbed mind repeatedly that I can do this, I shift beneath him, forcing him to lift. Our damp skin peels apart slowly and the loss of his softening length inside me rips away at my breaking heart. But I need to be strong. I can't show any signs of hesitance or pain, which is tremendously difficult when I'm very hesitant and I'm in agony at the thought of what he's being pushed to do. He looks down at me, and I can tell there's doubt lingering on the edges of his mind, too, so I force a small smile and lift my lips to kiss him chastely. 'Let's take a shower.'

'As you wish.' He reluctantly detaches himself from me on a deep inhale and helps me to my feet, but prevents me from making my way to the bathroom. 'One moment.'

I stand silently while he makes a long, drawn-out affair of messing with my hair, arranging it just so over my shoulders, and frowning when a new shorter layer refuses to stay where he's placed it. His beautiful face, all bunched in slight annoyance, brings a glimmer of a smile to my face. 'It'll grow back,' I placate him.

His eyes flick to mine and he surrenders the lock of hair. 'I wish you'd never cut it, Olivia.'

My heart sinks. 'You don't like it anymore?'

He shakes his head, frustrated, and takes my neck to lead me into the bathroom. 'I love it. I just hate remembering what drove you to cut it in the first place. I hate that you did that to yourself.'

We arrive in the bathroom and he flicks the shower on before collecting towels and gesturing for me to enter the cubicle. I want to tell Miller how much I hate everything he's done to himself, too, but at the risk of lowering the delicate mood further, I hold my tongue and accept his comment. This time together is precious and the memories we're making now will help me through the night. I don't want any disagreements to tarnish this. So I follow through on his silent order and step into the shower, immediately collecting the shower gel from the shelf and squeezing some into my palm.

'I want to wash you,' he says, taking the bottle from my hand.

I don't stand for it. I need this. 'No,' I retort softly, reclaiming it. 'We do this my way.' I rid myself of the bottle and rub my palms together, working up a lather. Then I spend an age scanning every fine piece of him, trying to figure out the best place to start. It's all calling to me, each perfect bit of him willing me to place my hands there.

'Earth to Olivia,' he whispers, stepping forward, taking my wrists in his grip. 'How about here?' He places my hands on his shoulders delicately. 'We're not leaving this shower until you've felt every part of me.'

I drop my eyes, searching deep in my soul for the lost strength I need to let him walk away from me once I'm done readying him. It's slipping away fast with every word spoken and every touch exchanged.

'Stay with me,' he murmurs, resting his palms over mine. He begins guiding a gentle caress of my hands across his skin, and I watch his chest expand as my eyes climb the planes of his muscles until I'm at deep pools of blue pain. 'Feel me, Olivia. Everywhere.'

I bite back a sob, fighting back tears that are demanding to be freed from my welling eyes. But I find it. That strength I need to get me through this – to get us *both* through this – is found amid the desolation and I step forward, close to his body, and begin massaging my palms gently into his shoulders.

'Good,' he sighs, allowing his heavy eyes to close and his head to drop back a little. He's exhausted. I know he is. Emotionally. Physically. Everything is being taken out of him. I find myself even closer when he rests his hands on my waist and tugs forward a little. 'Better.'

I concentrate on Miller and him alone, not allowing anything else to break down my barriers – no thoughts, no worries . . . nothing. My hands glide lazily everywhere, from his shoulders to his pecs, his stomach, his sharp V, down to his thighs, knees, shins, feet. Then I work my way slowly back up again before turning him to do his back. My face contorts on a wince when I'm confronted by his ravaged flesh. I work fast and gently, then turn the hideous sight away from me so he's facing me again. The water raining down is the only sound. Miller is my only focus. Yet as I find myself at his neck, rubbing the water there to wash away the soap, I see his eyes still closed and I wonder if *I* am *his* only focus. I don't want to consider that maybe he's thinking about the night ahead, about how he's going to see through his plan, how far he needs to go with the Russian woman, how he's going to rid the world of Charlie. But I know that if he was thinking of me, he would be looking at me. And like he's heard my thoughts, his blue eyes slowly appear and he blinks that wonderful lazy blink. I can't quite disguise my sadness quickly enough.

'I love you,' he declares softly, out of nowhere. He can see. There's no fooling him. 'I love you, I love you, I love you.' Moving forward, he encourages my backward steps until my back meets the tiles and I'm swathed in wet, hot skin. 'Tell me you understand.'

'I do.' My voice is low, and though I'm certain of it, I don't sound it. 'I do,' I repeat, attempting to inject some sureness into my tone. I fail on every level.

'She won't get the opportunity to taste me.'

I inwardly shiver, desperate not to let my mind venture there, and nod, reaching for the shampoo. I ignore the worried eyes that I know are currently studying me and set about washing his waves. I'm still slow and soft in my caring for him, but now there's determination behind my tenderness in the form of a consistent mental pep talk. My mind is a whirlwind of silent encouraging words, and I'm going to make sure they continue to play in the background for the entire time he's gone.

Miller is like a statue, only moving when I prompt him with a nudge or a flick of my eyes to his. He can read me through my eyes. He responds to my every thought. He owns my body, mind, and soul. Nothing can change that.

I shut the shower off and step out to collect a towel, drying Miller off and wrapping it around his waist before seeing to myself. I can see with perfect clarity how hard he's finding it to refrain from seizing control and taking care of me.

Opening the cupboard above the sink, I pick out a can of deodorant and hold it up to him. He smiles a little and lifts his arm, giving me access to spray him. Then I move onto his other before putting it neatly away. Next, his wardrobe. Claiming Miller's hand, I pull him through the bedroom, still repeating my mental mantra of positive thoughts.

But the sight when I enter his wardrobe makes them falter and my feet skid to a stop. I drop Miller's hand and run my eyes over the three walls of rails on a slightly gaping mouth. 'You really did replace *all* of your suits?' I ask in disbelief, swinging around to face him.

He doesn't retreat, nor does he look in the slight bit embarrassed. 'Of course,' he says, like I'm utterly daft for thinking he wouldn't. He must have spent a small fortune! 'Which would you have me wear?'

I watch as he casts a hand around the room slowly, and my eyes follow it until I'm faced with a sea of expensive material again. 'I don't know,' I admit, feeling a bit overwhelmed. My fiddling fingers find my ring and start spinning it wildly as I wander the length of each wall, wondering what to put him in. My decision is made easy when I spot a dark navy pinstriped suit. I reach up to feel the material. It's so smooth. Luxurious. His eyes will pop even more. 'This one.' I unhook the hanger and whirl around to face him. 'I love this one.' Because he needs to look perfect when I let him leave me to kill someone. I shake my head, trying to shake my errant thoughts away.

'You should.' He approaches and relieves me of the suit. 'It's a three-thousand-pound suit.'

'How much?' I gasp, horrified. 'Three thousand pounds?'

'Correct.' He's completely unfazed. 'You get what you pay for.'

I muscle in and reclaim the suit, hooking it over the wardrobe runner. Then I fetch some boxers and kneel, holding them open for him to step into with one foot, and then the other.

I work the material up his thighs, being sure to brush my hands across his skin as I do. I definitely don't imagine him flinching each time my touch skims him, and I definitely hear his constant quiet hitches of breath. I just want myself on every piece of him. 'There,' I say, arranging the waist of his boxers just so. I stand back and stare. I shouldn't, but Miller's physique against the crisp white boxer shorts is impossible to ignore. Impossible not to appreciate. Impossible to keep my hands off. Impossible for *anyone* to keep their hands off.

She *won't* be tasting him. My mind is playing tug-of-war, going between the two horrors playing in my mind. Both are unbearable to think about. I'm looking at his ripped torso, seeing stunning, inviting flesh, but I'm also seeing power. Strength. He looked deadly in that footage. There were no cut muscles, no visible signs of danger, only the air of malice behind his empty eyes. Now he has the strength to back up that deadly temper.

Stop!

I fly around and grab his trousers, wanting to reach into my head and snatch that thought right out. 'These,' I blurt abruptly, yanking the button open and crouching at his feet again.

My anxious motions are ignored. Because he knows what I'm thinking. I clench my eyes shut and only re-open them when I hear him shift and feel his trousers move in my hand. He's not going to say anything, and I'm eternally grateful.

Focus. Focus. Focus.

It seems to take me forever to work his trousers up his legs and when I reach his waist, I leave them hanging open, my thumbs tucked into the waist, resting on his skin. My heart is thrumming a consistent, hard beat in my chest, but I can feel my emotion squeezing at my aching muscle. It's going to give soon. My heart is literally breaking.

'Shirt,' I say under my breath, like I'm prompting myself with what should come next. 'We need a shirt.' I reluctantly remove my hands from his body and confront the rails of expensive dress shirts. I don't bother flicking through, instead just taking down one of the dozens of bright white ones and unbuttoning it with care, being sure not to create any creases. His breath kisses my cheeks as I hold it and he threads his arms through. He's silent and co-operative, letting me do my thing at my own pace. I secure the buttons slowly, hiding away the perfection of his chest, until I reach his neck. His chin lifts slightly to make my task easier, the bruise on his neck screaming loud and proud, before I work his cuffs, ignoring my unreasonable mind wondering how he'll cope with blood on his fine threads. Will there be blood?

My eyes clench shut briefly as I fight to halt my train of thought.

Next is his tie. There are so many, and after perusing the rainbow of silk for a few moments, I settle on a silver-grey silk one to match the stripe in his suit. But when I turn towards him again, the difficulty of my next task hits me. I'll never knot it to Miller's high standard. I begin toying with the material as I look up at him, finding lazy blues watching me closely, and I expect that's exactly how he's been looking at me the whole time I've been in my own little world dressing him.

'You'd better take over.' I admit defeat and hold the tie out to him, but he pushes my hand away and moves in fast, picking me up by my hips and sitting me on the counter.

A chaste kiss is placed on my lips before he lifts the collar of his shirt. 'You do it.'

'Me?' I'm wary and it's obvious. 'I'll screw it all up.'

'I don't care.' My hands are taken to the back of his neck. 'I want you to fix my tie.'

Nervous and surprised, I smooth the silver silk around his neck and let the two sides cascade down his front. My hands are hesitant. They are also shaking, but a few deep breaths and a quiet word with myself pulls me around and I start the meticulous task of knotting a tie around Miller Hart's neck – something I know for sure that no one has ever had the privilege of doing in the history of Miller Hart.

I faff and fiddle forever, but I don't care. I feel a ridiculous amount of pressure and despite it being really quite silly, I can't seem to locate the rationality to be unbothered. I'm *really* bothered. I pat the knot a hundred times, my head cocking from side to side, checking it out at every angle. To my naked eye, it looks pretty perfect. To Miller's, it'll look like a train wreck.

'Done,' I declare, finally dropping my busy hands into my lap, but not moving my eyes from the *kinda* perfect tie. I don't want to see the concern on his face.

'Perfect,' he whispers, taking my hands in his and bringing them to his lips. His unusual descriptive, especially when referring to another's handiwork, throws me.

I brave looking up at him, feeling his hot breath heating my knuckles. 'You haven't checked.'

'I don't need to.'

I frown, flicking my eyes back down to the tie. 'It's not Miller-perfect, though.' I'm dumbfounded. Where are his twitching hands, itching to put it right?

'No.' Miller kisses each hand and puts them neatly back in my lap. Then he reaches for his collar and pulls it down, rather haphazardly. 'It's Olivia-perfect.'

I'm quickly looking at him again. His eyes are twinkling a little. 'But Olivia-perfect isn't actually perfect.'

A beautiful smile joins his sparkling eyes and centres my off-kilter world. 'You're wrong.' His answer to that makes me withdraw in surprise, though I don't argue. 'Waistcoat?'

'Right,' I exhale the word slowly and slink down from the unit, watching him as I pad over to the rails again.

He keeps his smile in place. 'Chop-chop.'

I'm scowling now and blindly reaching for the waistcoat after a brief glance tells me where it is. I can't rip my inquisitive eyes away from him. 'Here.' I hold it out.

'We do this your way,' he reminds me, striding over and holding one arm out. 'I like you looking after me.'

I huff a sardonic puff of laughter and remove the waistcoat from the hanger, then proceed to help him into it. His chest is quickly close to mine again and my hands are being lifted to the buttons. I can do nothing more than as I'm bid, fastening up each button, then collecting his socks and tan brogues when I'm done. I kneel and rest my bum on my calves to get him into his socks and shoes, tying the laces before making sure the hems of his trouser legs are straight. And last is his jacket. It completes him. He looks spectacular, and his hair is now damp and the dark waves super wavy.

He looks divine.

Gorgeous.

Devastating.

'You're ready,' I breathe, stepping back and pulling my towel in. 'Oh!' I quickly turn and scoop up his Tom Ford, not resisting a sniff from the bottle before I douse Miller at the neck. He lifts his chin for me again, his eyes boring into me as I spritz him. 'Now you're perfect.'

'Thank you,' he murmurs.

I replace the bottle, avoiding meeting his stare. 'You don't need to thank me.'

'You're right,' he replies softly. 'I need to thank whatever angel sent you to me.'

'No one sent me to you, Miller.' I face unimaginable beauty, my eyes squinting to prevent the image from burning my irises. 'You found me.'

'Give me my *thing*.'

'I'll crease you.' I don't know why I'm searching for excuses when I'm so desperate for him to hold me. Or maybe I do know.

I won't be able to let go.

'I've asked once.' He steps forward gently but threateningly. 'Don't make me ask again, Olivia.'

My lips straighten and I shake my head. 'I can't bear the thought of releasing you. I won't be able to.'

He winces and his blue eyes glaze over. 'Please, I beg you.'

'And I'm begging you not to force me.' I stand firm, knowing I'm doing the right thing. 'I love you. Just go.'

I've never been so challenged in my whole life. Maintaining my front is crippling me, and seeing Miller so unsure of what to do isn't helping. His expensive shoes are rooted to the carpet, his eyes burning into mine, as if he's trying to read past my forced hard exterior. This man can see into my soul. He knows what I'm doing and I'm screaming in my head for him to let me do it. My way. This has to be done my way.

The relief that attacks me when he slowly turns has my hand darting out to steady myself on the unit. He walks away slowly, the hurt building with each step he takes. I'm missing him already and he's not even left the room yet. The urge to scream for him to stop nearly gets the better of me, and my feet are shifting beneath me, willing me to chase him down.

Be strong, Olivia!

Tears pinch the backs of my eyes and my heart slowly beats its way up to my throat. I'm in agony.

He stops at the door.

I hold my breath.

And I hear him draw his. 'Never stop loving me, Olivia Taylor.'

He disappears.

My strength drains from my body and I crumple to the ground, but I don't cry. Not until I hear the front door close. Then it all comes pouring from me like a waterfall. My back finds the unit, my knees meet my chest, and my head meets my knees, my arms wrapping around me, making myself as small as possible.

I cry.

For what seems like forever.

Tonight really is going to be the longest night of my life.

Chapter 23

An hour later, I'm on Miller's squidgy couch after trying his bed, the lounge, the kitchen. The detailed cornice circling the ceiling is imprinted on my mind and I've relived every moment since I've met Miller. Everything. I'm smiling to myself each time I've pictured any one of Miller's spellbinding traits, but then I'm cursing aloud when the image of Gracie Taylor intrudes on my attempts to distract myself. She doesn't have a place in my thoughts *or* my life, so just the mere fact that she's taking up any scrap of my thinking space is infuriating me. I haven't the time or the energy to wallow in the added turmoil she could spike. She's undeserving of any heartache I could allow myself to feel. She's selfish. I hate her, except now I have a clear image – a face etched on my mind to hate.

I toss my body over on the couch, so I'm now staring out across the London skyline, and I'm wondering if my mind is purposely sending me down this line of thought. Am I subconsciously distracting myself from thinking about what's happening right now? Is this anger better than the wretchedness I'm certain to feel if I allow my brain to focus on what Miller is doing right now?

I squeeze my eyes shut, mentally yelling at myself when Gracie is suddenly gone and the perfection of Miller before he left me in his dressing room replaces her. I can't do this. I can't sit here all night waiting for him to return. I'll be certifiably crazy before the night's over.

I jump up from the couch like it's caught fire and hurry from

Miller's studio, being sure not to let my eyes catch sight of his paint table, knowing seeing myself spread on it won't help. Neither will looking at the sofa in his lounge, or his bed, or the shower, or the fridge, or the kitchen floor . . .

'Oh God!' I reach up and tug a little at my hair in frustration as I turn in circles in the middle of the lounge, deliberating on where I should hide. The slight stabbing pain on my scalp only reminds me of Miller's fingers knotted in my hair. I can't escape.

Panic starts to attack me. I clench my eyes shut and start breathing deeply to calm my frantic heartbeats. I count to ten.

One.

All I can offer you is one night.

Two.

And I'm praying that you'll give it to me.

Three.

I've told you, Livy. You fascinate me.

Four.

Are you ready to let me worship you, Olivia Taylor?

Five.

I'll never do anything less than worship you. I'm never going to be a drunken fumble, Livy. Every time I take you, you'll remember it. Each and every moment will be etched on that beautiful mind of yours forever. Every kiss. Every touch. Every word. Because that's how it is for me.

Six.

This beautiful, pure girl has fallen in love with the big bad wolf.

Seven.

Never stop loving me.

Eight.

Accept me as I am, sweet girl. Because it's so much better than what I was.

Nine.

You are my perfect, Olivia Taylor.

Ten.

I fucking love her! I love her. I love everything she stands for and I love how much she loves me. If any fucker tries to take her away from me, then I'll fucking kill them. Slowly.

'Stop!' I dash to his room and seek out my clothes, throwing them on chaotically before snatching up my bag and pelting for the door. I start to dial Sylvie on my way, but my phone rings in my hand before I can call my friend.

Every instinct tells me to reject the call. There's no name. Just a number. I recognise it, though. I pause at Miller's front door, my hand on the handle, and connect the call. 'Sophia,' I breathe down the line, eliminating all caution from my tone.

'I'm on my way to the airport,' she says matter-of-factly, almost business-like.

'And that would interest me because?' It actually does interest me. She's leaving the country? Good!

'It will interest you, *sweet girl*, because Charlie has changed the plan. I need to leave before he finds out I've destroyed that footage and beats me beyond recognition.'

My hand shifts on the doorknob, my interest increasing, but now mixed with fear. She might have a resentful, nasty edge to her smooth voice, but she can't hide the fear that's lacing the edges of it. 'Changed the plan how?' My pulse is suddenly throbbing in my ears.

'I heard him before I left. He's not taking any chances with Miller. He can't risk that jeopardising his deal.'

'What do you mean?'

'Olivia . . .' She pauses, like she's reluctant to give me the information. My stomach performs a full spin, making me feel instantly sick. 'He's planning on drugging Miller and feeding him to that vile Russian woman.'

'What!' I drop the door handle, staggering back. 'Oh God.' I start shaking. He won't be able to kill Charlie. That thought alone has sent my worry into panic, but the added knowledge of what that woman could do to him has just catapulted that panic into terror. She'll undo everything he's worked so hard to fix. It will be like that video happening all over again. My throat starts to close off on me. I can't breathe.

'Livy!' Sophia shouts, snapping me from mental meltdown. 'Two, zero, one, five. Remember that number. You also need to know that I destroyed the pistol. I have a flight to nowhere. Call William. You need to stop Miller before you lose him forever.' She hangs up.

I drop my phone and stare blankly at the screen. Before I can give any amount of reasonable time to consider my next move, I'm on my way to the door, panic flaming.

I need William. I need to know where the Temple is. But first I try Miller, shouting my despair when it goes to voice mail, so I hang up and try again. And again. And again. 'Answer the phone!' I scream, smashing the call button for the lift. He doesn't. It goes to voice mail yet again and I try to gulp down some air to talk, praying he'll pick up the message before accepting a drink at the Temple.

'Miller,' I pant down the line as the doors begin to open. 'Call me, please. I've—' My tongue turns to lead in my mouth and my body stills when the inside of the lift comes into view. 'No,' I whisper, stepping back from the source of my fear. I should turn and run, but my muscles have seized and are ignoring my brain's screaming commands. 'No.' I shake my head.

I could be looking in the mirror.

'Olivia.' My mother's navy eyes widen a little. 'Olivia, baby, what's the matter?'

I'm not sure what's telling her that there's more to my shock than simply finding her in the lift. I back away.

'Olivia, please. Don't run from me.'

'Go away,' I whisper. 'Please, just go.' I don't need this. I don't need her. I have far more important things that need my attention – things that deserve my attention, *need* my attention. My resentment begins to build at the prospect of her delaying me. If time wasn't of the essence, I'd attack her with the sass I inherited from her. But I don't have time for her. Miller needs me. I turn and rush to the stairs.

'Olivia!'

I ignore her desperate cries and barge through the door, taking the concrete stairs two at a time. The loud clicks of her heels on the stone rings out around me, telling me she's in pursuit, but I have Converse on and they win over heels any day of the week, especially when you're in a hurry. I pass floor after floor as I fumble with my phone, trying to dial William as I try to escape my mother.

'Olivia!' She's shouting and obviously short of breath. This only motivates me to sprint faster. 'I know you're pregnant!'

'He had no right to tell you,' I seethe as I rush down the stairs, my fear and worry converting into unrelenting fury. It's eating me from the inside out, and while I'm scaring myself with how fast it's taking over my body, I silently appreciate that it will probably do me a favour once I'm away from this selfish, harlot of a bitch and I make it to Miller. I need some fire in my belly and she's stoking it perfectly.

'He told me everything. Where Miller is, what he's doing, and why he's doing it.'

I skid to a stop and turn, seeing her slump against a wall, exhausted, though her white trouser suit still looks pristine, as does her bouncing, glossy waves. My defences fly up like iron and I curse William and his betraying arse to hell and back. 'Where is the Temple?' I demand. 'Tell me!'

'Not so you can walk into that carnage,' she says, looking adamant.

I bite down on my tongue, praying for some calm. 'Tell me!' I scream, my sanity running away with me. 'You owe me this! Tell me!'

She winces, hurt, but I can't find any compassion for her. 'Don't hate me. I had no choice, Olivia.'

'Everyone has a choice!'

'Did Miller?'

I recoil, disgusted.

She steps forward tentatively. 'Does he have a choice now?'

'Stop it.'

She doesn't. 'Is he willing to do anything to keep you safe?'

'Don't!'

'Would he end a life for you?'

I grip the stair rail, squeezing it until my hand is numb. 'Please.'

'I would.' She moves closer still. 'I *did*.' I'm frozen in place. 'My life ended the day I walked out on you, Olivia. I disappeared off the face of the earth to protect you, baby.' She reaches me and I watch in shocked silence as her hand lifts carefully and comes slowly towards me. 'I sacrificed my life so you could have yours. You weren't safe with me in your life.' Her soft touch rests on my arm, my eyes rooted on it as it drifts down my skin until she reaches my hand and squeezes gently. 'And I'd do it all over again, I promise you.'

I'm immobilised, desperately searching for any insincerity in her voice or words. There's none. All I hear are heartfelt words and a voice quivering with pain. Her fingers entwine with mine softly. We remain quiet. The barren concrete stairwell is cold, but there's warmth spreading across my skin and settling deeply, and it's all coming from her – the woman I've spent the best part of my life hating.

She fiddles with my sapphire ring on the underside of my hand for a few moments, then turns my limp limb over so the gem is sparkling up at us. 'You wear my ring,' she whispers, a certain amount of pride in her soft words. I frown, but I don't withdraw from her touch. I'm confounded by the sense of peace settling over me as a result of it.

'Nan's ring,' I correct her.

Gracie looks up at me, smiling sadly. 'William gave me this ring.'

I swallow and shake my head, thinking of all the times William has toyed with the antique gem on my finger. 'No, Granddad gave it to Nan and Nan gave it to me for my twenty-first.'

'William gave me that ring, baby. I left it behind for you.'

Now I withdraw, and I withdraw fast. 'What?'

Her chin is trembling and she shifts uncomfortably. She's displaying some of the exact reactions William did when speaking of her. 'He said it reminded him of my eyes.'

My eyes dart around the hollow stairwell, my poor mind racing. 'You left me,' I murmur. Gracie's eyes slowly close, like she's fighting off the horrid memories, and now I appreciate that she likely is.

'I really didn't have a choice, Olivia. Everyone I loved – you, William, Nan, and Granddad – was at risk. It wasn't William's fault.' She squeezes my hand gently. 'If I had stayed, so much more damage would have been done. Everyone was better off without me here.'

'That's not true,' I argue weakly, emotion closing my throat. I'm trying so hard to locate the contempt I've maintained for Gracie, trying to inject it into my tone, but it's gone. Lost. I haven't got time to analyse it now. 'Tell me where he is,' I demand.

Her well-dressed body deflates as she casts her eyes over my shoulder. Something's caught her attention, and I pivot to see what it is.

William is standing at the bottom of the stairs, quietly watching us.

'We need to get to Miller,' I say, bracing myself for the resistance I know I'm going to face. 'Tell me where the Temple is.'

'It'll be over before you know it.' His face is awash with reassurance, but it won't work.

'Will,' Gracie says softly.

He throws a warning look past me, shaking his head. He's warning her. He's warning her not to tell me.

I turn to find Gracie with her eyes rooted on him. I don't have to ask again. 'Number eight Park Piazza,' she whispers.

William curses aloud, but I ignore it and make tracks, pushing past him when he doesn't move to let me through. 'Olivia!' He catches my arm and holds me in place.

'Sophia called me.' I grit my teeth. 'Charlie's going to drug Miller. If that woman gets hold of him, we'll lose him completely.'

'What?'

'He's going to drug him! He won't be getting rid of Charlie because he'll be comatose! And that woman is going to make him feel violated again! He'll be ruined!'

He pulls up, flicking his eyes past my shoulders to Gracie. Something passes between them and I find myself glancing back and forth between them, trying to figure out what it is.

I might be challenged in the sanity department, but I know what I heard and I haven't time to convince William. I dash down the remaining flight of stairs and break free of the cold stairwell, hurrying for the exit. Two sets of footsteps are in pursuit of me, but neither will stop me. I scan the street for a cab, shouting my frustration when I see nothing.

'Olivia!' William calls as I hurry across the road.

I round the corner and breathe my relief when I spot a taxi pulling over to the kerb. I barely give the passenger time to pay and jump out before I'm in and pulling the door shut. 'Park Piazza, please.'

I slump back in my seat and spend the journey praying repeatedly that I'm not too late, while shouting my frustration each time he doesn't answer my calls.

*

The grand white building looks ominous beyond the trees lining the street. My stomach is in knots, my breathing challenged. I look down the road, bracing myself for William's Lexus to round the corner. I don't bother trying to convince myself that William didn't know where Miller is. He makes it his business to know everything.

I climb the steps to the double doors, the noises from inside becoming clearer the closer I get. There's laughter, chatter, and classical music playing in the background, but the obvious happy atmosphere within the walls of this building does nothing to lessen my sense of foreboding. I can literally feel the invisible barriers trying to hold me back as I push on, the house seeming to talk to me.

You don't belong here!

Leave now!

I ignore it all.

I see a bell and a doorknocker, but it's the digital keypad that grabs my attention. Four digits are stamping all over my mind.

Two. Zero. One. Five.

I punch it in and hear the mechanical shift of the lock, so I push through gingerly. The noise intensifies, saturating my hearing and cooling my skin.

'You just can't help yourself, can you?'

I gasp and whirl around, finding Tony behind me. He's going to try to stop me, too. My instincts kick in and I push past the heavy door, soon finding myself in a gigantic entrance hall with curved stairs leading up from both sides to a large gallery landing. It's ridiculously ostentatious and I'm momentarily rendered stunned by my surroundings. Then it hits me that I have no idea what to do now that I'm here. My urgency to get to Miller, to stop him from possibly destroying himself beyond my ability to fix him, was all that consumed my mind.

'This way.' Tony's hand wraps around my upper arm and pulls me off to the right aggressively. 'You're the biggest fucking headache, Livy.' I'm hauled into an extravagant study and the door slams behind us. Tony releases me and shoves me up against the wall. 'You're going to get him killed!'

I don't have time to enlighten Tony on the developments because the door flies open on a loud crash and my breath is stolen by the sight of Charlie standing in the doorway.

'Nice to see you again, sweet girl.'

'Fuck,' Tony curses, and rakes a shaking hand over his sweaty, bald head. 'Charlie.'

My eyes bounce back and forth between the two men, my heart beating hard enough for all to hear. The sneer on Charlie's face tells me he can smell my fear. He walks forward casually, keeping his eyes on me, and pats Tony on the back. It's a kind gesture, but I'm under no illusion that it's meant to be friendly, and a quick glance at Tony confirms he knows it, too. He's nervous. 'I give you one job,' Charlie muses as Tony backs up cautiously. 'Keep the girl away.'

Tony's accusing eyes land on me with an almighty bang, making me wilt on the spot. 'I can only apologise,' he murmurs, shaking his head in despair. 'The girl doesn't know what's good for her *or* the boy.'

If I could find my sass amid my fear, I'd be firing it at Tony like bullets from a machine gun.

'Ah,' Charlie laughs. It's a sinister laugh, meant to terrify me. And it does. This man's evil is rampant. 'The Special One.' He takes one step towards me. 'Or *my* special one.' And another step. 'But you want him to be *your* special one.' He's in my face now, breathing down on me. I'm trembling. 'When people try to take what's mine, they pay.'

My eyes close in an attempt to block out his closeness, but my loss of sight has no effect. I can smell him and I can feel him. The Special One. I feel sick, my turning stomach and frantic mind quickly telling me that I was delusional in thinking I could stop this. The few seconds I've spent in the company of Charlie and Tony are enough to make me realise that I'm not escaping this room.

'There's only one person on this planet who has tried to take something from me and come out alive.'

I blink my eyes open, finding his face close to mine. Intuition tells me he wants me to ask who and what, yet my brain isn't loading my mouth with the words to follow through on his silent command.

'Your mother was mine.'

'Oh God,' I breathe, my legs losing solidity, making me wobble. The wall is the only thing holding me up. 'No.' I shake my head.

'Yes,' he counters simply. 'She belonged to me and the only reason I didn't slaughter William Anderson was the satisfaction of knowing he'd suffer a lifetime of torture when she left him.'

His prowling frame is sucking all the air from my lungs. I can't speak. Can't think. I'm blank.

'Death would have put him out of his misery.' His hand comes up and strokes my cheek, but I don't flinch. I'm a statue. A numb statue. 'How does it feel to know she abandoned you to save him?'

It hits me like a sledgehammer. Everything. William didn't send her away. And she didn't abandon me because she never wanted me. Charlie made her leave.

'Step away, Charlie.'

I remain where I am, trapped against the wall by his looming frame, struggling to breathe, but that voice is the most wonderful thing I've ever heard.

'You can leave, Tony.' William's order leaves no room for refusal.

I hear the door close and then the beats of even footsteps,

and though I can't see William yet, his presence is cutting through the thick atmosphere.

'I said step away,' William adds severely.

I see him in my peripheral vision, hovering to the side, but my stare is rooted on Charlie's hollow eyes.

Grey eyes.

I lose my breath.

He gives me a menacing smirk, like he can see that something has just registered. 'Hello, brother,' he drawls, slowly turning to face William.

My mouth drops open and a million words hang from my tongue. Brother? The eyes. Why didn't I see it before? Charlie's are exact replicas of William's, except where William's are soft and sparkling, Charlie's are hard and cold. They're brothers. They're also enemies. My mind is being blitzed with recollections, lots of snippets of information all coming together to form a monumentally complicated picture.

Gracie, William, and Charlie.

Carnage.

William's grey eyes have hardened to match his brother's, taking on an edge of threat. They are traits that I'm familiar with in William, but now they are amplified. He looks as frightening as Charlie. 'You're nothing to me, only a blemish on my life.'

'I love you, too, brother.' Charlie wanders calmly over to William and lifts his arms. It's a condescending act. 'Don't I get a hug this time?'

'No.' William's lip curls and he steps back, away from the imposing presence of Charlie. 'I'll be taking Olivia and leaving.'

'You and I both know that's not going to happen.' He looks over his shoulder to me. 'You couldn't control Gracie, Will. What makes you think you can control her daughter?'

I divert my eyes from his, uncomfortable being the focus of his intense stare. He knows who I am.

William is beginning to shake. 'You sick bastard.'

Charlie raises high eyebrows. He seems interested. 'Sick bastard?'

I don't like the glimmer of worry on William's face when he flicks me a quick glance before returning stone-cold eyes on his brother. But he doesn't speak.

'Sick bastard,' Charlie muses, nodding thoughtfully. 'Would a sick bastard get a cheap thrill from putting this beautiful girl to work?'

I frown, keeping my eyes on William, seeing him fighting to prevent his body from fidgeting. He's uncomfortable. It's a disposition I've seen in him before, and when he looks at me, my heart sinks.

'Would he?' Charlie asks, almost innocently, but I know what he's getting at.

'Don't,' William warns.

'No comment.' Charlie sighs on a menacing smirk. 'OK. Tell me this. Would a sick bastard get a cheap thrill from putting his niece to work?'

'Charlie!' William roars, but I can't be startled by the ferocious bellow. I've just died.

'No,' I whisper, shaking my head furiously. He can't be. My eyes start darting everywhere, my body convulsing from shakes.

'I'm sorry, Olivia.' William sounds defeated. 'I'm so, so sorry. I told you, as soon as I realised who you were, I sent you away. I didn't know.'

I feel sick. My eyes find William and see nothing but torture.

'So you didn't get a sick satisfaction from allowing my daughter to give her body away?'

'We're not cut from the same cloth, Charlie.' William's face contorts in condemnation.

'We're blood, Will.'

'You're nothing to me.'

'You tried to take Gracie away from me,' Charlie grates, but I can see the brimming anger isn't a result of losing a woman he loved. It's principle. He didn't want to lose.

'I didn't want her in this sick world! And you, you poisonous bastard, made her stay!'

'She was clearly a good earner.' Charlie sniffs insolently. 'We were running a business, brother.'

'You couldn't bear the thought of me having her. You couldn't stand the fact that she despised you!' William steps forward, aggression pouring from him, making his suit quiver over his ominous frame. 'She should have been mine!'

'You didn't fight hard enough to keep her!' Charlie roars.

Those words. They make me shiver as the enormity of my mother's story unfolds before my eyes in the form of two bitter brothers. The dynasty split. William left the immoral bastard to be immoral alone.

William practically snarls. 'I tried my damn hardest to fight my feelings for her. I didn't want her in the sickness we immersed ourselves in. You put her in the centre of it. You were willing to share her with your fucking clients!'

'She didn't argue. She loved the attention – thrived on it.'

I wince and so does William before a wave of anger travels across his cool face. He's livid. It's obvious. 'She loved hurting me. You monopolised on it. Turned her to drink and brainwashed her. You took sick satisfaction in watching me die a little bit more each day.'

I begin praying, praying this isn't real, praying that this man's evil blood isn't running through my veins.

Charlie smirks, sending that familiar chill down my spine. 'She had my baby, Will. That made her mine.'

'No.' Gracie's melodic tone drifts into the room, pulling everyone's attention to the doorway, where she's standing, back straight, chin raised high. She steps into the room, and I can see the bravery she's fighting to maintain in Charlie's presence.

He still frightens her. 'Olivia isn't yours and you know it.'

My eyes widen and I look to William, finding him studying my mother, searching for an extension on that statement. 'Gracie?'

She looks at him but quickly backs up when Charlie moves forward threateningly. 'Don't even think about it,' he snarls.

'He sent me away when I told him Olivia wasn't his.'

Charlie visibly starts to shake. 'Gracie!'

She jumps, but William and I are both motionless. 'He threatened to harm her if I told anyone.'

'You fucking bitch!' He lunges for her, but William intercepts, knocking him back a few metres with a swift fist to his cheek.

William roars in anger, heaving and pulsing as Charlie staggers back and my mum screams. 'Never touch her!' he bellows, shaking his fist, eyes enraged.

My mind focuses amid the madness unfolding. Charlie's not my father? I'm too shocked to be delighted at the news that Charlie, in fact, isn't my father. I can't cope with it all. I'm being delivered information at a speed too fast for my fraught mind to cope with.

Gracie pulls William back but soon steps away, like she's frightened of him, too. 'He promised to leave my baby alone if I disappeared.' She glances at him warily. She looks ashamed. And William looks like he's seen a ghost. 'He promised to let you . . .' She takes a long breath. It's a confidence-boosting breath.

'No,' William murmurs, his jaw ticking. 'Gracie, please, no.'

'He promised to let her father live if I disappeared.'

'No!' He throws his head back, shouting to the heavens, his hands diving into his grey hair.

My world implodes. The wall behind me catches me when I stumble back, disoriented, and I push myself into it, like it could swallow me up and remove me from the horrors I'm facing. William's head drops, a million emotions invading his face one at a time – shock, hurt, anger . . . and then guilt when he finally manages to look at me. I can't possibly give him anything. I'm a statue. All he's got to go on are my stunned eyes and frozen form, but he really doesn't need any more than that.

We're both way past stunned.

Charlie chucks my mother a look that would turn iron to ashes. 'You slut. It wasn't good enough that you had ten men a week. You had to have my brother.'

'You forced them on me,' she shrieks. 'You made me write the fucking details!'

'You lied to me!' Charlie fumes. For the first time since he steamrolled his way through that door, I see frightening anger flashing across his face. 'You played me for a fool, Gracie, baby.' He gets up close and personal with my mother, and my trepidation multiplies when she recoils cautiously and William moves in quickly and places himself in front of her.

'Don't make me kill you, Charlie.'

'You just couldn't keep your hands off her,' he rages, pulling at the sleeves of his suit jacket. The action reminds me of Miller, and I suddenly find life, pushing my back from the wall that I've been propped up against all this time. I need to find him.

I dash for the door.

'And where are you going, lovely niece?'

My strides falters, his icy breath hitting my back. But I don't stop. 'I'm going to find Miller.'

'I don't think so,' he declares confidently, making me halt at the door. 'That would be most unwise.'

I slowly turn, finding him way too close for comfort. Not for long, though. William takes my arm and pulls me away from his imposing frame. 'Don't even breathe on her,' William says, taking Gracie in his other grasp and tugging us both to his side. 'My girls. Both of them.'

Charlie laughs. 'I think amid this touching family reunion, you've forgotten a minor detail, dear brother.' He leans forward. 'I can get you and the pretty boy locked up for life with one call to a delivery boy.' He smirks. 'The gun that killed our uncle, Will. I have it and guess whose fingerprints are all over it?'

'You bastard!'

'He doesn't have the gun,' I blurt, suddenly lucid. I remove myself from William and ignore Gracie's worried tone calling me back. I shake off William, too, when he makes a play for my arm. 'Leave me.'

'Olivia,' William warns, making a grab for me again.

'No.' I shake him off and step forward, my bravery accelerating just from the look of utter contempt being lobbed at me from Charlie. This evil arsehole is my uncle. It might be a slight improvement on Dad, but it still makes me want to take a shower. 'Your wife has left you.'

He scoffs, genuinely amused by my news. 'She wouldn't dare.'

'She's on a plane.'

'Rubbish.'

'Escaping you.'

'Never.'

'But before she boarded, she shared something with Miller.' I go on, getting a thrill from the slight falter of his malevolent smirk. 'There is no footage of Miller killing one of your men.' I speak evenly, now hearing Sophia's words before she hung up crisp and clear. 'Because she destroyed it.'

His faltering magnifies.

This immoral bastard has crawled through life on the back of manipulation. Resentment has eaten him alive for years. This evil bastard is on his way to hell and I hope one of the two men I love helps him get there. 'Gracie didn't love you. And neither does Sophia.'

'I said, shut up!' He's beginning to shake, but my fear has fallen away along with my twisted mind.

'She got rid of the gun, too. You have nothing!' I'm suddenly flying back and am pinned to a wall, Charlie's hand around my throat.

I hear screaming, but it's not mine. It's Gracie. 'Don't touch her!'

Charlie's face is up close to mine, his body pressing me into the wall. I gulp repeatedly, trying to breathe. 'You pathetic little slut,' he growls, 'just like your mother.' His breath is crawling across my stunned face.

Only for a split second, though, because his body is suddenly catapulting backwards and William slams him to the ground in one swift motion. I watch in horror as all hell breaks loose.

I don't need to see or hear what happens next. I have a good idea, and finding Miller is my only purpose now. All of this sickness, the web of lies and deceit, it's played too big a part in both of our lives. It ends now.

I steam through the middle of them all, hearing repeated cracks – which I conclude very quickly to be William's fist meeting Charlie's face – followed by torrents of shouted curses. They're on their own. I'm wasting no more time being subjected to the horrors of their fucked-up lives. I've been forced to endure far too much already, and I'm about to pull Miller from Charlie's corrupt clutches. I break free of the study, leaving behind a commotion of epic proportions, and rush towards the sounds of chatter and laughter. I thought I had all the facts. I thought I had the story. I've been mentally processing it all for nothing. Now I have a new version, the updated version, and I hate it more than the original.

I follow my feet to a massive lounge and immediately find myself lost amid a sea of posh gowns and tuxedos, the women holding champagne glasses, the men sipping from tumblers. The money in this room would be enough to blow my mind if it wasn't focused on finding Miller. My eyes dart everywhere, scanning the faces of people, desperately searching for him. I don't see him. Anywhere. My legs kick into action, weaving me through the throngs of people. I catch a few eyes, make a few frown, but most are totally indulged in their company and fine drinks. A waiter passes me with a tray full of champagne flutes, and although I clearly make him pull up on a creased brow, he still offers me the tray.

'No,' I dismiss him rudely, continuing to scan the vast space, shouting my frustration when I still fail to find him.

'Olivia, baby?' A warm palm meets my arm, and I flinch, flying around violently. I find my mum scanning me with worried eyes.

'Where is he?' I shout, drawing a million eyes in my direction. 'I need to find him!' My panic blankets my determination and my emotions take hold, making my body shake and my eyes flood with tears of dread. I've been stalled too long. I might be too late.

'Shhh,' she hushes me like a baby, and pulls my unresponsive body into her side, stroking my hair.

There's only a tiny piece of me allowing myself to register the immense comfort I'm feeling from her warmth surrounding me. It's confusing and bizarre, but so needed. It defies everything, yet feels so right. From my hiding place in the crook of her neck, I feel her head moving around, and I know it's because she's looking for Miller, too.

'Help me,' I whisper pitifully, crumbling under the trauma. 'Please, Mum.'

She stops moving and I feel her heart pick up its pace under my palm resting on her chest. She pulls me from her embrace and spends a few moments drinking in every little piece of my face, finishing at my eyes. I just gaze at sapphires that match mine and let her wipe away the tears trickling down my cheeks. 'We'll find him, baby,' she promises, closing her watery eyes and pushing her lips to my forehead. 'We'll find your love.'

She starts to pull me through the crowd, not caring to be polite or considerate. 'Move,' she orders, making dozens of people jump back, wary. As my feet scurry to keep up with her, I hear the hushed whispers of the people we're leaving behind, and I definitely register the shocked mention of my mother's name from more than one person. It's not only me who feels like she's returned from the dead.

We make it into the huge entrance hall, but Gracie stops, and I watch as she casts her eyes around the area. She doesn't know where to head next.

'He's in the Dolby Suite.' Tony's voice comes from nowhere and I turn to see him holding out a key to me. But my heart plummets. My lungs shut down. He's in a bedroom.

I snatch the key and fly up the stairs like a bullet before I can catch my breath, frantic and shouting his name. 'Miller!' I scream, rounding the landing. 'Miller!' I clock the gold plaque on the door stating THE DOLBY SUITE and fumble to get the key in the lock before crashing through the door like a wrecking ball. The sound of the wood hitting the wall behind it echoes through the entire house, virtually making it shake. My eyes are wild as they dart around the enormous suite, and my hysterical mind is blitzed by panic, not allowing any further instructions to filter through as I stand on the threshold.

Then I see him.

And my heart shatters into a million fragments of devastation.

He's naked, blindfolded, his arms bound to gold rings protruding from the fancy wallpaper. I'm arrested by shock. His chin is dropped to his chest, and it stays that way as I heave and shake on the spot, screaming to myself to go to him. He hasn't moved a muscle. I swallow down my choked sob when I realise I'm too late and let out a scream of frustration, only then noticing a tall blonde woman with a whip in hand prowling towards me.

'How dare you interrupt!' she yells, lashing the whip. The tip catches my cheek, and I recoil, immediately feeling blood trickling down the side of my face. My hand flies to my cheek, my body staggering back in shock. My eyes are pulling, wanting to check on Miller, but her malevolence keeps my wary attention. It's potent and gushing from her like a tidal wave. 'You're interrupting,' she snarls, a tinge of an accent in her tone. Russian. 'Leave!'

There is not a chance in hell I'm leaving him. I see red. 'You can't have him!' I scream, deranged, recoiling when she snaps the whip again. My anger is dominating every fibre of my being, sending my initial fear crashing and burning to the shiny wooden floor.

I scan the room for anything remotely damaging to arm myself with, catching a glimpse of metal on the bed. Miller's belt. I dart over and yank it from his trousers, flying around erratically. I tense everywhere, that red mist thickening, blinding me, as I prepare to strike.

'You little bitch. What do you think you're going to do?' She stalks closer, whip twitching, completely unfazed by my threat.

'He belongs to me.' I grit my teeth, desperately fighting to hold my poise. I won't be whole until I'm out of here and Miller is safely in my arms.

Her lip is curling ferociously, not that it has any impact on the wall of fury taking over me. I find my own lip curling in response, my eyes daring her to come at me. I can see him in my peripheral vision, still hanging lifelessly from the wall. It jerks my anger. My skin tingles from the rampant fury fizzing in my veins, and before I can even contemplate my actions, my arm is flying forward, sending the belt buckle sailing through the air. I don't wait to see where it connects, but her yelp of pain tells me it has. I race over to Miller and lift my hand to his cheek, brushing across his stubble softly. He mumbles some incoherent words and nuzzles sleepily into my palm. His actions and the popping of fireworks under my skin spur me to reach for his restraints. I start to calmly unravel his hands from the fetters.

'Get away from him!' She's suddenly beside me, grabbing at Miller's arm, staking her claim. He flinches on a heart-breaking whimper.

I can't bear the sound.

I tear around, livid, swinging my hand out without stopping to aim. 'Don't touch him!' I scream, the back of my hand colliding with her face on an ear-piercing slap. She staggers back, disorientated, and I take advantage of her stumble, throwing my palms into her chest to push her farther away from Miller. My Miller.

I have no fear. None at all. I slowly return my attention to Miller, but I gasp when my hand is suddenly seized. Not by her hand, though. Pain sears through my flesh and I look down to see the leather of her sick weapon wrapped around my burning wrist.

'Move away,' she repeats, yanking at the whip and hauling me towards her. I cry out in pain, realising quickly that I'm getting way out of my depth. She's not going to give him up.

'*You* move away, Ekaterina.'

My head whips up at the sound of my mother's voice, and I find her at the doorway, heaving, taking a moment to assess the situation. She looks angry, her stance wide, her eyes flicking from me to Miller before settling on the sick bitch who's attached to me by a whip. My mother's face is twisted with contempt.

And she has a gun in her hand.

I'm struck dumb, my eyes rooted on the weapon pointing right at the Russian.

I only have to wait a few seconds before the constricting

leather releases from my wrist, and I begin rubbing the pain away on a wince.

'Gracie Taylor,' she muses, smiling. 'I'm going to pretend you haven't got a gun pointing at my head.' Her accent sounds hypnotising and calm.

'You do that.' Gracie steps forward. 'Then ring your brother and tell him Charlie hasn't delivered.'

Perfectly threaded eyebrows arch in surprise. 'Why would I do that?'

'The deal Charlie and your dear brother struck is void. Miller doesn't belong to Charlie anymore, Ekaterina. He's not Charlie's to give. Look at him. Does he look willing to you? Charlie did that. I'm sure that's not what you were anticipating after everything you've heard about the Special One.' My mum's lips curl, showing a hardness in her I haven't yet seen. 'I know you don't want to tarnish your formidable reputation with the label "rapist", Ekaterina.'

She drops her whip and casts a look over to Miller, pouting, before returning her attention to my mother. 'I like to hear them begging me to stop.' She looks slighted as she slowly wanders over to Gracie, who lowers the gun cautiously. 'And you say Charlie Anderson did this to him? Drugged him? Made him utterly useless to me?'

'Do you want it in blood?'

'Yes,' she sneers, looking my mother up and down. 'Charlie's blood.' She's serious. 'I think I'll call my brother. He doesn't like it when I'm upset.'

'*No one* likes it when you are upset, Ekaterina.'

'Very true.' She almost laughs as she turns a filthy look on me. 'She looks like you, Gracie. Maybe you could teach her some manners.'

'Her manners are just fine in the right company,' she retorts, making Ekaterina smile coldly at my mother's front. 'Charlie's in the drawing room. William has left him breathing for you. Think of it as a thank-you from my daughter.'

She smiles, nodding agreeably. 'You have a brave girl, Gracie. Maybe too brave.' I can see the pleasure filling her immoral bones at the mere thought of revenge. 'I am grateful for your gift.' Her accent rolls beautifully, despite the violent edge to her tone. 'Goodbye, Gracie.' She sashays out of the room, her hips swaying seductively as she drags the whip behind her.

Gracie lets out an audible breath of relief, the gun dropping to the floor, and as soon as the Russian is out of sight, I go straight to Miller, grabbing a towel from the bed on my way. My heart cracks as I wrap the towel around his waist and make quick work of releasing his arms, leaving him falling towards me fast. The best I can do is fold to the floor with him, breaking his fall.

Through his spaced-out state, he manages to cling on to me, and we remain locked together on the floor forever, him mumbling confused words, me humming softly in his ear.

'I'll never stop loving you, Miller Hart,' I whisper, kissing his ear gently and breathing him into me. 'It's over.'

I know he hasn't the capability to utter any words in his current state, but he speaks to me perfectly clearly when he drags his arm from around my back and takes his hand to my tummy. Then he starts circling softly with his heavy palm until I'm certain our baby replies to his touch. A pop of bubbles flutters in my stomach.

'My baby,' he whispers.

I'm disturbed from my contentment by my mother's hand on my shoulder. The heat spreads across my skin and travels directly into my heart, forcing me to break away from Miller, confused, because I know the source of the comfort isn't him. It's an added ease, and when I peel my lids open, my eyes find Gracie kneeling before us, mildly smiling. 'Are you ready to take him home, baby?' she asks, stroking my arm comfortingly.

I nod, hating having to disturb Miller in my arms but eager to take him away from here. 'Miller?' I whisper, gently nudging him, but he doesn't respond, leaving me looking up to Gracie for help.

My attention is pulled to the door when William strides in. I can't retain my shock. My eyes widen as they take in his dishevelled state – his grey hair mussed up, his suit all creased. He's flexing his hand and his anger's still so very apparent. There's only a slight blemish to his jaw, but I get the feeling Charlie isn't in such great shape.

'We need to get out of here,' he mutters, assessing what he's walked in on.

'Miller can't walk.' My throat is almost too tight with grief to speak.

With calm, efficient movements, William strides across the room and hauls Miller into his arms, nodding to Gracie in a silent gesture to help me up, which she does quickly, sensing his silent urgency, despite his calmness.

'I'm good.' Miller's scratchy voice breaks through my worry, and I snap my head up to see him wrestling his way out of William's hold. 'For fuck's sake, let go of me.'

Relief makes me dizzy as I watch him find his feet and then swipe at his hair repeatedly in an attempt to restore his messier than usual waves back to just messy. He pulls the towel in and glances up, hitting me with eyes that are way wider than normal, the black of his pupils nearly cancelling out the blue. They are still very piercing, despite the dilation. I keep still under his intense stare, letting him take me in for a while, refresh his memory of me, until he nods lazily, then follows it up with a drawn out blink of his eyes.

'What's going on?'

He'll hate this. He's the centre of attention, half-naked and vulnerable.

'You were drugged. We can explain more later,' William

tells him, not so calmly now. 'We need to get out of here.'

It doesn't feel like there's much air in this posh suite, but after William's statement, there's none. Miller's already wide eyes have just expanded, almost popping from his head. He doesn't speak, just stands quietly absorbing the news, his jaw ticking violently. I think myself sadistic for wanting to desperately know what's running through his mind. 'Where's Charlie?' His deadly tone tells me it's murder.

William steps forward, holding Miller's glazed eyes with harsh grey. 'It's over, Miller. Walk away a free man, no blood on your hands, no guilt on your conscience.'

'There would be no guilt,' he seethes. 'None.'

'For Olivia.'

He scowls at William, his lip curling. 'Or because he's your brother.'

'No, because we are better men.'

I see William's head cock to the side, and Miller looks at him thoughtfully for a few moments, clearly reading a look. 'Where are my clothes?' he spits, glancing around the room and striding over to the bed when he spots them. 'Some privacy, please.'

'Hart, we haven't got time for you to start getting all fucking particular.'

'Two minutes!' he yells, yanking his shirt over his shoulders.

I wince and watch as William practically bites his tongue to stop himself retaliating. 'You have one.' He grabs Gracie's arm and guides her from the room, slamming the door behind him.

Then I watch as the Miller Hart I know rapidly comes together with each piece of expensive clothing he pulls on. He yanks at his sleeves, straightens his tie, and fiddles with his collar, but it's all done far faster than I've ever seen before, and though he's restored, he's not fully restored. The vacant look in his eyes is still lingering and I suspect it will be for a while.

When he's done, I see his Adam's apple bob in his throat

before he casts his eyes upward to me. 'Are you OK?' he asks, looking down to my tummy. 'Tell me you're both OK.'

My palm meets my stomach without thought. 'We're fine,' I assure him, earning a sharp nod of acknowledgement.

'Excellent,' he breathes, a huge amount of relief apparent through his formal reply. I know what he's doing. He's detaching himself, and I know why. He'll be walking out of this house, oozing his usual aloofness and power, not prepared to let any one of the sinful bastards downstairs see any scrap of weakness. I'm more than happy to let him have that.

He approaches me and when he's nearly touching my chest, he slides his hand onto my nape and massages firmly into my strung muscles. I don't miss the slight wince when he finally registers my cut cheek. 'I'm so incredibly in love with you, Olivia Taylor,' he whispers hoarsely, letting his forehead fall delicately to mine. 'I'm leaving this house my way, but once I'm out that door, I'm yours to do whatever the hell you want with me.' His lips push firmly into my forehead, his hand squeezing my nape.

I know what he's trying to tell me, but I don't want to do whatever the hell I want with him. I just want *him*. I'd never enforce anything on him, not after everything he's endured up to this point in his life. He's free now, and I'm not about to slap conditions, demands, or restrictions on him. *He* can do whatever the hell he likes with *me*. I pull away and smile when I see his wayward curl back and misbehaving. I leave it exactly where it is. 'I'm yours – no conditions attached.'

'Jolly good, Miss Taylor.' He nods agreeably and gives me another kiss, this time on the lips. 'Not that you have any choice in the matter.'

I smile, and he winks. It's beautiful, despite the abnormal darkness of his eyes. 'Go,' I prompt, pushing him away.

His lips tip a little as he takes backward steps, pulling at the lapels of his jacket until he turns and strides out of the room, leaving the door open for Gracie and William, who are waiting cautiously outside. Both look at Miller as he passes, like he's been resurrected. He has. I smile a little on the inside as William follows Miller's perfect form around the galleried landing, shaking his head on a little huff of laughter before he catches up with him and flanks him as he takes the stairs.

I follow on, not even flinching or objecting when I feel an arm settle around my shoulders. I look to see Gracie gazing down at me. 'He's going to be fine, Olivia.'

'Of course he is.' I smile and let her lead me down the stairs behind William as he escorts the Special One away from this sinister place, but as we get to the front hall, my contentment wavers. I see Charlie propped up against the wall outside his office. He's beaten to a pulp, and when one of his men turns to us with a sneer on his face, my contentment slips away completely.

This isn't over – not by a long shot.

I glance to William and Miller, but neither look fazed.

'Evening.' The gruff voice doesn't come from William or Miller or any one of the mean slimeballs flanking Charlie.

Every set of eyes in the room divert to the doors, the atmosphere thickening further. There's a beast of a man filling the doorway. Huge. He's silver-haired, the skin of his face pitted. 'You broke our deal, Charlie.'

The Russian.

I look to Gracie when she settles a shaky hand on my arm, seeing her eyes centred on the ominous being holding everyone's attention.

The unease that creeps over Charlie and his men is visible. I can feel it.

'I'm sure we can renegotiate, Vladimir.' Charlie tries to laugh but it comes out more like a wheeze.

'A deal is a deal.' He smiles, just as he's joined by an army of men, all suited, all as large as Vladimir and all focused on Charlie.

It's quiet.

Charlie's men step away from their boss, leaving him unprotected prey.

Then all hell breaks loose.

William yells and makes a grab for Miller, who's now charging at Charlie, murder etched on every piece of his face. No one will stop him. All of Charlie's men move farther away, clearing the path, giving Miller clear access to the immoral bastard.

I display no shock or worry. Not even when Miller lifts Charlie from his feet by his neck and slams him into the wall, so hard I think the plaster could have cracked behind him. Charlie is showing no fear or shock, his face straight, but that evil glint has disappeared. He expected this.

'See this?' Miller asks, his voice low and dripping with violence, running a finger along the scar on Charlie's cheek, all the way down to the corner of his mouth. 'I'm going to get them to complete this Chelsea smile before they kill you.' He jerks Charlie against the wall, slamming him harder into the plaster. A loud clatter resonates around the hall when a picture jumps off the wall and hits the floor as a result of the vibrations. Yet I still don't move a muscle and Charlie remains straight-faced, taking what Miller is giving. He has no fight in him. He's defeated. 'Slowly,' Miller whispers.

'I'll see you in hell, Hart,' Charlie sneers.

'Been there.' Miller slams him one last, extra powerful time for good measure before dropping his hold. The evil bastard slides down the wall, looking weak and pathetic, while Miller makes an extra-long, precise job of straightening out his suit. 'As much as I'd love the pleasure of killing you myself, our Russian friend here is an expert.' He steps forward, towering over Charlie's slumped body, and draws a long, filthy-sounding cough. He stares at him for a brief moment before spitting what he's collected in his mouth right in Charlie's face. 'And he'll make sure there's nothing left to identify. Goodbye, Charlie.' He turns and strides out, keeping his eyes focused forward, ignoring all of the quiet observers, including me. 'Make it painful,' he says as he passes Vladimir.

The Russian smiles darkly. 'With the greatest of pleasure.'

I'm suddenly on the move, courtesy of Gracie guiding me, looking over my shoulder as Charlie slips all over the floor, trying to get up. I feel nothing . . . until I find William and see him studying Charlie's pathetic form. They both gaze at each other for a long, silent while. It's William who breaks the connection when he eventually looks to Vladimir, nodding mildly. Sadly.

Then he starts to follow us out.

And I have to reason with myself not to stay and watch.

William's driver greets me with a tip of his hat and a warm smile, opening the door for me. 'Thank you.' I nod, sliding into the backseat. I watch for a few moments through the window as William and Miller talk. Or William talks. Miller is just listening, looking down at his feet, nodding every now and then. Every curious part of my brain wants to roll the window down and listen, but my curiosity transforms into panic when I allow the newsflashes of earlier to settle. In the space of a day, I suddenly have a mum *and* a dad. Miller doesn't know. He doesn't know that William Anderson is my father, and something tells me he's going to be even more shocked than I am.

I'm out of the car in a split second, joining them on the pavement. Both men look to me, Miller on a frown, William with a knowing, almost smug, smile. He's going to enjoy this. I know he is. I could think for years about the best way to word this and still be clueless. There's no right way. There's nothing that's going to lessen the shock. Miller's still regarding me closely a few moments later when I still haven't spoken, so I draw the biggest breath I'm ever likely to and gesture towards . . . my father. 'Miller, meet my dad.'

He doesn't give me anything. His face has fallen into complete blankness. Poker-faced. Straight. The most impassive expression I've ever seen on him. All this time I've spent learning how to read him and deciphering his moods, and now I'm lost. I begin worrying my ring on my finger, shifting under his blank face, and I look to William to gauge his mood. His smugness is now full-on amusement.

I shake my head a little in despair and return my cautious eyes to Miller. He looks like he's gone into shock. 'Miller?' I prompt, getting increasingly uncomfortable as the silence extends.

'Hart?' William says, joining me in my attempt to rouse Miller from his daze.

It's another awkward few seconds before he finally shows signs of life. His glazed gaze passes between us a couple of times before he takes in air. Lots of it. And lets it spill slowly out on three familiar words: 'Just . . . fucking . . . perfect.'

William laughs. A proper belly laugh. 'So now you really do have to respect me,' he chuckles, getting a cheap thrill from Miller's reaction.

'Fuck . . . me.'

'Glad you're pleased.'

'Fucking hell.'

'Less of that in front of my daughter.'

Miller coughs his thoughts on that and throws wide eyes my way. 'How . . .' He pauses, pursing his lips . . . and they slowly slink into a mischievous grin as he leisurely returns his focus to William, brushing down the sleeves of his jacket casually as he does.

What's he thinking?

Once he's through fussing over his suit, his hand slowly

extends towards William. 'Nice to meet you.' His grin widens. '*Dad*.'

'You can fuck right off!' William blurts, knocking Miller's offering away. 'Over my dead body, Hart! Just think yourself fucking lucky that I'm even allowing you in her life.' His mouth snaps shut and he looks embarrassed, and I know it's because he's just realised that he has no right to dictate that. 'Just look after her,' he finishes, fidgeting under my bemused eyes. 'Please.'

Miller's palm slides onto my nape and his mouth moves to my ear. 'Will you give us five?' he requests quietly, flexing his hand to turn me towards the car. 'Jump in.'

I don't protest, mainly because no matter how much I try to delay the talk these two men are going to have, it'll happen eventually. So we may as well be done with that today, too.

I slide in and get comfortable, shutting the door softly, and fight the temptation to push my ear up against the window. But I'm distracted from my temptation when the door on the other side opens and Gracie appears, bending a little to get level with me. I shift in my seat, a little self-conscious, feeling under close scrutiny. I am. Her navy eyes are gazing at me fondly.

'I know I have no right to be,' she says quietly, almost reluctantly, 'but I'm so, *so* proud of you for fighting for your love.'

I see her hand twitching by her side, wanting to touch me, but I can see uncertainty now, maybe because Miller's back to his normal self and I seem more stable. I know I feel it. But I'd be lying if I said I didn't need her in there. My mother. She was there for me, and perhaps she was operating on guilt, but when I needed her, she was there. I take her shaking hand and squeeze it, silently telling her that it's OK. 'Thank you,' I murmur, struggling to maintain our eye contact, simply because I might cry if I don't look away. I don't want to cry anymore.

She brings my hand to her lips and pushes them hard to my skin, clenching her eyes shut. 'I love you,' she croaks. It takes every modicum of my remaining strength not to break down on her, and I know she's struggling, too. 'Don't be too hard on your father. Everything that happened, it's my fault, sweetheart.'

I shake my head, angry. 'No, it was Charlie.' And then I have to ask because there's one thing unclear in my mind. 'You met William before Charlie?'

She nods on a frown. 'Yes.'

'And William broke things off?'

She nods again, and I can see it hurts her to think of it. 'I was oblivious to his world. He wanted me out of it, but I slept with Charlie to punish him. I didn't know what I was getting myself into before it was too late. I'm not proud of what I did, Olivia.'

It's me nodding now. I get it. All of it, and despite the horrors my mother and father have endured, I can't help thinking that I wouldn't have my someone if our histories were different. 'Why didn't you just tell William?' I ask. 'About me, about Charlie?'

She smiles fondly. 'I was young . . . stupid . . . scared. He screwed with my mind. It was a simple decision. I hurt or everyone I loved hurt.'

'We hurt anyway.'

She nods, swallowing hard. 'I can't change what happened and how I dealt with it. I wish I could.' She squeezes my hand. 'I just hope you can forgive me for my poor decisions.'

There's no question. I don't need to think about this. I get out of the car and throw my arms around my mum, burying my face in her neck while she sobs relentlessly on me. And I don't let go. Not for a long, long time.

It takes William to sever our contact when he takes Gracie by the hips and gently tries to coax her away from me. 'Let's go, darling,' he soothes, letting her kiss my face a few more times before gently tugging her back.

I smile at William, seeing completeness as he holds on to my mother and looks at me. 'I didn't want you to hate your mother,' he says, telling me without the need to ask why he spun me the story about sending her away. He didn't know she'd been scared away. He thought she'd abandoned us. 'I didn't want you to know who your father was.' He pauses and Gracie squeezes his forearm. 'At least, who I thought was your father.'

'You're my dad.' I smile, drawing one from him, too.

'Are you disappointed?'

I shake my head as I slip into the backseat again, smiling like crazy on the inside. I look across the car when I hear the door open, and Miller slides in, getting comfy in his seat. 'You're coming to mine,' he states matter-of-factly. 'William has spoken to Gregory. Everything is fine.'

I'm abruptly strangled by guilt. I haven't thought about Nan amid the crazy events of the best part of today. 'I need to see her.' She'll be out of her mind, and now I'm remembering all sorts of disturbing things she has said. She knows Gracie is back, and I'm not going to even bother thinking she won't want to see her. I need to get home and prepare her for that.

'No, you don't.' Miller looks to me, his eyebrows high, and while I'm delighted that he's back with an infuriating bang, I'm not so pleased he's insisting on keeping me away from my grandmother.

'Yes, I do,' I retort, throwing my best *try me* look. I'm pleading to God that he doesn't push this. I've only just got him back. I don't want to start off on a disagreement.

'We need some alone time,' he says quietly, yanking at my heartstrings. I screw my face up, feeling defeat muscling past my determination. How can I refuse after what he's been through? 'I need you in my arms, Olivia. Just us. I beg you.' His hand creeps towards me and settles on my knee, flexing and stroking. 'Give me my time, sweet girl.'

My shoulders sag on a sigh. The two people I love most in the world both need me now, and I haven't a clue which one I should centre my attention on. Why not both? 'You can come home with me,' I suggest, solving my predicament instantly, but my satisfaction slips away when he slowly shakes his head.

'I need my home, my things . . . you.' He means his perfect world. His perfect world has been turned up on its head, and now he needs to restore some of it. He won't feel completely settled until he can do that. I get it.

'Miller, I—'

I'm cut short when William leans into the car. 'I'm taking your mother to Josephine's.'

I panic, starting to scramble from the car. 'But—'

'No buts,' William warns, stopping me.

I snap my mouth shut and shoot him an indignant look. Not that it even minutely dents the hard authority he's exuding.

'You'll do as you're told for once and trust we'll do right by your grandmother.'

'She's delicate,' I protest, making to exit the car again. I don't know why. I'm not stupid enough to think I'm going anywhere.

'Back in.' William almost laughs, pushing me down to the seat. Then Miller joins forces with him, pulling me across the seat until I'm a prisoner in his arms.

'Hey,' I gripe, wriggling in a futile effort to escape.

'Really, Olivia?' Miller grumbles tiredly. 'After everything we've been through today, are you honestly going to hit me with your sass?' He squeezes me in. 'There is no choice here. You're coming home and you're going to do it without a fuss, sweet girl. Shut the door, Anderson.'

My stunned eyes look to William, who shrugs on a smile and goes to shut the door, but a well-manicured hand rested on his forearm halts him. He turns to find Gracie's pleading face. He visibly sags and turns a similar pleading face to Miller.

I complete the party and do exactly the same. My poor, exhausted man has three sets of beseeching eyes rooted on him. I can't even feel guilty for the defeated look that replaces his sheer determination to have me to himself. He releases me and flops back in his seat on a sigh. 'Just . . . fucking . . . perfect,' he breathes.

'I need to see her, Miller.' Gracie steps forward and William doesn't stop her. 'And I need Olivia with me. I promise you, I'll never ask for another thing. Just give me this.'

I gulp down my pain and watch as he slowly starts to nod. 'I'm coming, too,' he states, short and sharp, ensuring all involved know it's not up for discussion. 'We'll meet you there. Drive on, Ted.' Miller refuses to look at me.

'Certainly, sir,' Ted confirms, looking at me in the rear-view mirror, smiling brightly. 'With the greatest of pleasure.'

The door closes next to me and as we pull away, I see William escorting a shaky-looking Gracie over to Tony's Audi. I don't waste time trying to prepare for what's to come once we arrive at Nan's. Nothing could possibly work.

I don't want to go in. I know William and Gracie haven't arrived yet. Not even a stunt driver could beat Ted in London traffic. I'm just standing on the pavement, staring at the front door, willing Miller to encourage me onward. I know he won't, though. He'll leave me forever if he has to, unprepared to make me rush something monumental that I thought would never happen. But it *is* going to happen. And I really have no idea how to handle it. Should I go in now? Should I prepare her, let her know Gracie is on her way? Or should I wait and take my mother in to see Nan? I really don't know, but I'm halfway to my decision being made for me when the front door swings open and Gregory appears. It takes a few confused moments to register that he's not alone, and his companion is neither Nan nor George. It's Ben.

'Baby girl.' His greeting rolls out on a gush of relieved air and he moves in fast, taking me in his arms, with not so much as a look at Miller to gain approval or permission. It's not needed anymore. He squeezes me tightly and I look over his shoulder to see Ben smiling fondly. It doesn't even fall away when I watch his eyes cast over our cuddling forms to where Miller is standing. 'Are you OK?' Greg asks, pulling me from his embrace, scanning my face and wincing at the sight of my cut cheek. I try nodding, knowing speech isn't something I'm capable of right now, but even my bodily functions are failing me, so Gregory looks to Miller. 'Is she OK?'

'Perfect,' he answers, the sound of leather soles beating the path getting closer.

'And you?' Gregory asks, his question full of genuine concern. 'Are you OK?'

Miller answers with the exact same word. 'Perfect.'

'I'm glad.' He gives me a small smile and pecks my forehead. 'William called me.'

I don't even flinch. I know that means William has filled Gregory in on . . . everything, my thoughts only confirmed when my best friend lets his eyes slip down to my tummy. He smiles a little but manages to stop himself from saying anything further on that matter. 'She's waiting for you.' He steps to the side, as does Ben, and opens up the route to my grandmother, but I don't get to proceed with caution, as the sound of a car pulling up to the kerb distracts me.

I swing around, knowing what I'll find, and see her tentatively stepping onto the pavement, clutching the top of the open car door. She's doing what I was a few moments ago, gazing up at the house, looking a little lost and overwhelmed. William joins her and slips a comforting arm around her waist, and she looks up at him, forcing a small smile. He speaks no words, just nods encouragingly, and I watch in fascination as Gracie seems to find a bit of strength from their connection, much like how Miller and I work. Her chest rises slowly and her cheeks puff as she exhales, her fingers flexing on the car door.

No one is saying a word. The atmosphere is delicate and thick with nerves, and not just mine. Everyone here loves my grandmother dearly. I won't be silly enough to discount Ben, especially knowing he's obviously spent some time with Nan. Everyone knows the enormity of what is about to happen. But no one seems to be the one who wants to lead. We're all just standing on the pavement, waiting for one of us to make the first move, speak, anything to set the wheels in motion.

But it's none of us out here.

'Let me through!' Nan's demand pulls everybody to face the house. 'Out of my way!' Ben and Gregory are virtually tossed aside as she barrels through and lands on the doorstep.

She's in a dressing gown, but her hair is perfect. *She* is perfect.

She halts on the doorstep, her hand reaching for the wall to offer a little support. I want to run to her, hug her, and tell her everything is OK, but something stops me. She steps forward, her old navy eyes looking past me, down the garden path. 'Gracie?' she whispers, visibly trying to focus harder, like she can't quite believe what she's seeing. 'Gracie, darling, is that you?' She takes another wobbly step forward, her hand now moving to her face where she covers her mouth with her palm.

My teeth clench from my tight jaw and my vision becomes compromised by the onset of tears. I sniffle hopelessly, ignoring Miller's hand around my waist, and turn to see my mother. William is holding her up and she's clinging to him for dear life. 'Mum,' she sobs, tears bursting from her eyes.

A painful weep yanks my attention back to Nan, and I panic when she stutters on her feet, astonishment mixed with happiness rampant on her old face. 'My beautiful girl.' She begins to fold to the floor, her frail body not able to keep her on her feet any longer.

'Nan!' My heart misses too many beats and I rush over to her, but I'm beaten to it.

Gracie intercepts me and seizes Nan, folding slowly to the floor with her. 'Thank you, God, for bringing her back to me,' Nan sobs, throwing her arms around my mother and clinging on tightly. They're locked together, their cries muffled, buried in each other's necks. Everyone leaves them huddled on the ground together, reunited after too many lost years. I spend a few moments casting a look to everyone here, seeing every set of eyes watery. Everyone is choked by the overwhelming reunion. I feel like the final piece of my broken world has just clicked into place.

Finally, I look to Miller and he nods his understanding, taking me gently by the neck. They need their time together. Just them. And truly, deeply, I know my spunky nan will be just fine without me for a little longer.

And truly, deeply, I know that Miller will not.

Chapter 24

'Come here.' Miller stoops to collect me in his arms when we enter the stairwell, but I tenaciously brush him off.

'You're wiped out,' I object, ignoring the hint of irritation that flashes across his face. 'I'll walk.' I begin to take the steps slowly so his tired body can keep up, but I'm soon swiped from my feet on a yelp. 'Miller!'

'You'll let me worship you, Olivia,' he practically snaps. '*That* will make me better.' I relent easily. Anything he needs.

Even footsteps echo around the concrete shaft and I settle my arms around his shoulders, studying his face as he carries me up the ten flights. There's no sign of exertion or strain, only level breathing and his usual impassive beauty. I can't tear my eyes away. I'm reliving the moment in time when he first carried me up these stairs, when I knew nothing about this dark man, yet was taken by him to the point of obsession. Nothing has changed. My fascination will never die, and all of his particular ways are welcome in my life.

Forever.

For eternity.

And beyond that, too.

Miller once told me he was on his way to hell. That only I could save him.

We've been there together.

But we've clawed our way out together.

I smile to myself when he takes a curious glimpse out of the corner of his eye, finding me staring at him intently. 'What are you thinking?' he asks, returning his attention forward as we reach his front door. I'm placed on my feet with the utmost care before he opens the door and gestures me inside. I pad slowly into his flat and soak up the surroundings. I don't question the sense of belonging. 'I'm thinking that I'm glad to be home.' I smile when I hear a quiet hitch of surprised breath from behind me, but remain in position, happily reminding myself of his palatial, perfect flat.

'You don't have a choice in the matter,' he snorts, blatantly forcing indifference when I know it means the world to him.

'We'll need a nursery.' I'm poking him, and I'm going to take a huge amount of pleasure from his reaction when he finally registers that babies equal mess. Now that there's room in his mind for stuff other than depressing heartache, I expect *that* realisation may come soon.

'I concur,' he replies simply, making my smile widen.

'And there will be baby paraphernalia everywhere *all* the time.'

He's not so quick to counter my poke this time. 'Elaborate.'

I surrender to the overwhelming enticement of catching what I know will be mild panic settling on his face and turn to relish in it, ridding my face of all amusement. 'Nappies, romper suits, bottles, powdered milk all over the worktop in your kitchen.' I bite down on my lip when the panic intensifies before my eyes. He rests his hands casually in his trouser pockets and relaxes his standing position, attempting to disguise it. He fails terribly. 'The list is endless,' I add.

He shrugs nonchalantly on a pout. 'They're tiny little things. I can't imagine he or she will cause too much disruption.'

I could squeeze him to death. He clearly needs it. 'Really, Miller?'

'Well there will be no powdered milk because you'll be breast-feeding. And we'll have places for all of the other stuff. You're creating issues.'

'Your perfect world is about to explode into a million pieces, Miller Hart.'

He gives me that glorious dimpled grin, eyes sparkling and all. Then I smile as he stalks towards me and tackles me, carrying me through the lounge with my front pinned against his chest. 'My perfect world has never been more perfect and light, Olivia Taylor.' He hits me with a hard kiss, and I laugh into his mouth. 'And it's only going to get brighter, sweet girl.'

'I concur,' I agree as he takes us into his bedroom, and yelp when he launches me from his arms. I land on his perfect bed, sending his decorative cushions sailing in every direction. I'm a little stunned, even more so when Miller catapults himself towards me, fully dressed. 'What are you doing?' I laugh, accommodating his silent demand and opening up to him when he pushes my thighs apart.

He starts yanking at the sheets around us, pulling them out of position, bunching them into creased balls here and there. I can do no more than watch him in action, squealing in shock and delight when he starts rolling us across the bed, tangling us up in the white cotton.

'Miller!' I laugh, losing sight of him and the rest of the room when I become buried beneath the material. I'm all caught up, the sheets tugging tightly every time I try to move, Miller laughing and cursing as he tries to unravel us but only ending up knotting us more.

I'm being rolled repeatedly. I'm underneath him, then above him. We're bound tightly together by the bedding, blind and laughing.

'I'm stuck!' I chuckle, trying to kick my legs out. 'I can't move!'

'Bollocks,' he curses, spinning us over again, but he goes the wrong way and my stomach drops when there's suddenly no bed under us.

'Oh!' I cry as we hit the floor on an almighty thud. I'm

laughing properly now, feeling Miller tugging and pulling at the sheets as he tries to locate me.

'Where the hell are you?' he grumbles.

All I can see is cotton. Everywhere is brilliant white cotton, but I can smell him and feel him, and when the sheets are whipped from my face on a polite curse, I can see him, too. He takes my breath away.

'Falling out of bed is becoming a habit,' he whispers, circling his nose with mine before saturating my senses with a full-blown kiss that's loaded with a lifetime's worth of love and a ton of exquisite desire. 'You taste divine.'

Our tongues dance delicately together, our hands wander wildly, and our eyes remain open, locked and burning with fiery passion. Once again, it is just me and Miller in our own little bubble of happiness, like so many times before, except this time there's no cruel world to face outside this flat.

It's done with.

Our one night is now one lifetime. And way, *way* beyond that, too.

'I love your bones, Miller Hart,' I mumble into his mouth, smiling when I feel his lips stretch.

'That makes me very happy.' He pulls away and carries out a string of motions, blinking lazily, parting his lips just so, and watching me with hooded, intense eyes. It's like he knows that each and every one of those characteristics contributed to my original fascination and he's reminding me of them. No need. I close my eyes and I see them. I keep my eyes open and I see them. My dreams are my reality, but now it is all good. There's no hiding anymore. I can have him day, night, in dreams, *and* for real. He belongs to me.

'You're creasing my suit, sweet girl.' He's straight-faced. It makes me laugh loudly. Of all the things for him to be concerned about now, it's his fine threads. 'What's got you so tickled?'

'You!' I chuckle. 'Just you.'

'Excellent,' he concludes sharply, pushing himself up. 'That makes me happy, too.' My hands are grasped and I'm pulled up into a sitting position. 'I want to do something.'

'What?'

'Shhh,' he hushes me as he encourages me to my feet, tugging on my hand gently. 'You'll come with me.' He lightly takes my nape and my eyes close, savouring the familiar feel of his touch on my skin, the heat spurting from the source and creeping across my flesh. From my neck to my toes, I'm immersed in the comfort and warmth his touch provokes. 'Earth to Olivia,' he whispers in my ear, opening my eyes.

I smile through my attempted narrowed eyes and let him guide me to his studio. My peace only multiplies by a million when we enter the room. 'What are we doing in here?'

'Someone once told me that it would be more satisfying to paint something I find beautiful in the flesh.' He guides me to his couch and pushes me down, lifting my legs and arranging them the full length of the sofa. 'I'd like to test that theory.'

'You're going to paint *me*?' I'm slightly taken aback. He paints landscapes and architecture.

'Yes,' he answers decisively, leaving me struck dumb on the couch. He wanders over to an easel, pulling it into the centre of the room. 'Remove your clothes, sweet girl.'

'Naked?'

'Correct.' He doesn't look at me.

I shrug to myself. 'Have you ever painted a living object?' I ask, sitting up and reaching down to push my jeans from my legs. What I mean is, has he ever painted a person, and when he flicks smiling eyes to me, I note my question has been decrypted and he knows exactly what I mean.

'I've never painted a person, Olivia.'

I try not to let my relief be known, but my face fails me and

I'm smiling before I can stop it. 'Is it wrong that *that* pleases me immensely?'

'No,' he laughs quietly, taking a blank canvas that's propped against the wall and placing it on the easel.

I'm speaking to him and watching him over the back of the sofa that's facing out towards the view, away from the room. How can he paint me when I'm concealed?

I'm removing my top when he approaches me, and I expect him to turn the couch so it's facing inward, but instead he helps me out of my underwear, slowly, and wrestles with my body until I find my bare bottom resting on the back of the squidgy piece of furniture with my feet on the seat. My naked back is exposed to the room, and I'm looking out across London's beautiful skyline, only the lights of the buildings illuminating the wonderful architecture. 'It would be far better to do this in the daytime,' I say, flicking my hair over my shoulders and placing my hands on the back of the couch, on either side of my hips. 'You'll see the buildings far clearer.'

I shiver when the heat of his breath meets my skin, and soon after that, his lips. He kisses his way across my back, up the centre of my spine, and to the hollow beneath my ear. 'If it was light, you wouldn't be the main subject.' He takes my head and turns it until I'm gazing into sharp blues. 'You are all I see.' He kisses me tenderly, humming as he does, and I relax under the soft motions of his attentive lips. 'Day or night, I see only you.'

I say nothing. I let him shower my face with kisses before he turns my face back towards the window and leaves me sitting on the back of the sofa, naked and completely unbothered by it. I try to admire the glowing landscape of London, something that I can usually lose myself in with ease, but hearing Miller busy behind me is far too distracting. So I take a little peek over my shoulder, finding him collecting an array of brushes and paints, his tall body slightly bent, his disobedient curl tickling his forehead. I smile when he blows it away, unable to brush it with a hand because they're full of artist's tools. He positions everything he needs and removes his suit jacket before rolling up the sleeves of his shirt, but everything else is in place – his waistcoat, his tie.

'You're going to paint in your new suit?' I ask, watching as he pauses mid-arranging of pots and paints. That really would be a huge leap for Miller.

'Let's not make a big deal of it.' He doesn't look at me and quickly resumes readying himself for a painting session. 'Look down at your left shoulder.'

I frown. 'Look at my shoulder?'

'Yes.' He strolls over, dipping a paintbrush in red paint. My eyes follow him until he's standing at my back. Then he takes the thin-tipped brush and brings it to my shoulder. I watch as he writes three words on my flesh.

I LOVE YOU

'I haven't written it on your left shoulder yet. Don't take your eyes off those words.' He kisses my smiling face and leaves me again. But I don't watch him take up position behind his easel. I keep my eyes on those three words. They beat admiring the skyline of London any day of the week.

I only move when I blink. Everything else I find easy to keep deathly still. The direction of my gaze to my shoulder allows me to see his movements, but not his face, which only mildly irritates me. What he's doing now is relaxing him, and I'm more than happy to help. The seconds melt into minutes, and the minutes into hours. I'm a statuette for him, taking the quiet time to allow my settled mind to reflect on everything we've endured and plan ahead for what the future holds.

A future that includes our baby, my mother, and my father. I have no more room for resentment. Our new life will be starting problem-free. Clean and unspoiled. My mind is cleansed and so will our life be. I couldn't feel anything other than totally at peace right now. I inhale on a serene breath and smile to myself.

'Earth to Olivia.' His liquid tone creeps past my contentment and rouses me. Then I feel the prickles of his closeness all over my naked skin. I look over my shoulder and find him standing close behind me, but he looks as pristine as the last time I saw him. There's no evidence of paint on any part of him. 'Were you thinking of me?' His clean hands rest on my hips and his chest pushes to my back, coating me in expensive material.

'I was.' I remove my hands from the back of the couch and place them on his, feeling a little stiff, now I've finally moved. 'How long have I been here?'

'A few hours.'

'My bum's numb.' It's completely dead, and I expect my legs will be, too, if I try to stand.

'Here.' He lifts me over to him and lets me find my feet, keeping hold of me until I'm sure I'm not going to fold to the floor. 'Are you hurting?' His hand slips to my bum and starts massaging life back into my bottom.

'Just a little stiff.' I hold on to his shoulders while he spends time working his firm hands all over me, finishing at my tummy. He pauses circling motions and gazes down, but he doesn't say anything for a long, long time. I let him have his moment, happy to watch him watching me.

'Do you think he'll be perfect?' he asks, genuinely concerned. It makes me smile fondly.

'In every way,' I say, because I know he will be . . . just like Miller. 'He?'

He looks up at me, and I find his eyes gushing with happiness. 'I sense it. It's a boy.'

'How can you be so sure?'

He shakes his head a little, shying away from my curiously amused stare. 'I just sense it.'

He's lying. I take his dark stubbled chin and pull his face up. 'Elaborate.'

He tries to narrow his eyes, but they're sparkling too madly to allow it. 'I dreamt it,' he says, finishing up with his massaging hands and bringing them to my hair. He toys with it, twiddling some strands here and there before fixing it just so. 'I allowed myself to dream the impossible. Like I did with you. And now I have you.'

My shoulders drop from my exhale of contented breath and his face falls to mine.

He's going to worship me.

Soft, slow, Miller Hart-perfect.

'I need to make love to you, Olivia,' he mumbles into my mouth, turning me away from him so his lips drag across my cheek, to my ear, and into my hair. 'Bend.' He grasps my waist lightly and walks back a few paces, taking my hips with him. 'Hands on the couch.'

I hum my acceptance and brace my arms on the back of the old worn sofa, hearing him unfastening his trousers. He's not prepared to waste time undressing, which is fine by me. I'm as naked as the day I was born and Miller is fully dressed, but I feel a certain sense of enhanced power from him with us this way. He needs that power right now.

'Are you wet for me?' he asks, slipping his fingers between my thighs and sinking them into the hot moisture. I'm inviting him in, begging for him. I groan my answer, not that it's needed. I'm saturated. 'She's always ready for me,' he whispers, dipping and kissing the centre of my spine before licking his way up to my neck. 'And she knows how I feel when she deprives me of her face.'

I inhale through my pleasure and do as I'm bid, turning my face to the side so he can see my profile and I can lose myself in him. The absence of his bare chest isn't of concern. My eyes stay glued to his face.

'Better.' He withdraws his fingers, leaving me feeling hollow and denied, but not for long. They are soon replaced by the slippery head of his thick cock, teasing at my entrance, spreading my moisture everywhere. I whimper, shaking my head in a silent plea. He acknowledges it straightaway. 'I have no desire to make you wait for me, sweet girl.' He pushes forward on a deep groan, his head dropping back but his eyes still locked with mine.

My fingers claw into the soft couch, my arms going rigid. I ram back without thought or consideration of the sharp pain it might cause. 'Shit!'

'Shhhhh,' he hushes me on a strangled choke, his hips beginning to shake. 'That feels too fucking good.' He slips from my passage shakily and then immediately circles forward again, grinding hard into my bum.

My breathing is instantly disjointed and strained.

'I love that sound.' He withdraws again and plunges forward, enticing constant and consistent moans and mumbles from me. 'I so love that sound.'

'Miller,' I breathe, working hard to hold my body in place for him, my feet shifting to widen my stance and give him better leverage. 'Oh God, Miller!'

'Feel good, huh?'

'Yes.'

'The best?'

'God yes!'

'I fucking concur, sweet girl.' He's in his flow now, pumping slow, grinding circles repeatedly into me. 'I'm taking my time with you,' he promises. 'All . . . night . . . long.'

I'm fine with that. I want to stay stuck to him forever.

'We're starting here.' He shudders forward, hitting me deeply. I yelp, grabbing on to the tingling sensations inching forward. 'Then I'm taking you up against the fridge.' Pulling back, I see his chest expand beneath his shirt and waistcoat from his deep inhale. 'In the shower.' Forward he drives again. It's taking everything out of me not to close my eyes. 'On my paint table.' His hips grind into my bottom, pushing me up onto my tiptoes on a moan. 'In my bed.'

'Please,' I beg.

'On the couch.'

'Miller!'

'On the kitchen table.'

'I'm coming!'

'On the floor.'

'Oh God!'

'I'm having you everywhere.' *Bang!*

'Arhhhhh!'

'Do you need to come?'

'Yes!' Urgency has taken over. I'm shaking and sweating. I'm gulping down air and tensing – anything to tackle the orgasm that's surging forward at a ridiculous speed. It's going to be an intense one. It's going to make my legs give and my throat sore from my scream. 'It's coming!' I shout, knowing nothing is going to stop it.

'Don't deprive me of those eyes,' he warns, seeing and sensing my frantic movements and thoughts. 'Don't hide them from me, Olivia.'

He's performing rotation after rotation, each one delivered more accurately than before. His skill, pace, and rhythm wouldn't be comprehensible unless you were subjected to it. And I am. I comprehend it fully. It's about to fling me into blissful, mind-blanking euphoria. I'd scream if I could speak. I'm swallowing repeatedly, and when I feel him jerk and swell within me on a gritted curse, I also comprehend how close *he* is.

'I need us to go together,' he pants, increasing his pace slightly, slapping against my bottom, digging his fingers onto my waist. 'OK?'

I nod, watching his eyes smoke and his lids drop as he pulls me onto him constantly, and now with a degree of force.

My mind fogs and a haze of pleasure sweeps through my body like a tornado, nearly knocking me off my feet. 'Miller!' I scream, finally finding my voice. 'Miller, Miller, Miller!'

'Holy fucking shit!' he bellows, yanking me onto him and holding me there, shuddering above me. He's shaking, and his eyes close, prompting me to drop my head in exhaustion, feeling his essence flood me. Warm me. Complete me. 'Jesus, Olivia, you fucking goddess.' He collapses forward, the material of his suit meeting my sweaty back, and breathes erratically into my neck.

We're wiped out, both of us struggling for breath. My eyes are heavy, but I know I'm not going to be allowed to sleep.

'I'm going to worship you all night.' He peels himself away from my naked back and turns me in his arms, then spends a few moments wiping my damp face before kissing every wet piece of it. 'To the fridge,' he whispers.

Chapter 25

I'm aching. I'm deliciously sore between my thighs and spread-eagled in Miller's bed with the sheeting tangled around my waist, my bare back exposed to the cool air of his bedroom. I'm sticky and I've no doubt my hair is a mass of wild blonde, sticking out everywhere. I have no desire to open my eyes. So instead in my darkness, I replay every second from last night over and over. He did, indeed, take me in every available place. Twice over. I could sleep for a year, but the absence of Miller soon registers in my waking brain and I pat across the bed on the off-chance that my Miller-senses have failed me. Of course, they haven't and I fight with the bedding until I'm sitting up and brushing my sweat-infested mane from my sleepy face. He's not here.

'Miller?' I look across to the bathroom, seeing the door wide open, but no noise coming from beyond, so on a crumpled brow, I start to edge my way to the side of the bed, pulling up when something tugs on my wrist. 'What the . . . ?' There's some thin white cotton looped over my wrist, and I take it with my free hand and toy with it, noticing a long length extending from the knot. I follow the cotton with my eyes, seeing it leading to the bedroom door. I half frown, half smile, getting myself to my feet. 'What's he up to?' I ask the empty room, tucking the sheets around me and taking the line with both hands. Keeping hold of the thread, I pad to the door and open it, peeking down the corridor, listening intently.

Nothing.

Pouting to myself, I hold the line and follow it down the hall, smiling as I go, until I find myself in Miller's lounge, but the guide still carries on, and my smile falls away when it takes me across the room and lands me in front of one of Miller's paintings.

Not any of the famous London landmarks.

It's a new one.

Me.

My palm meets my mouth, stunned by what I'm looking at.

My naked back.

My glazed stare traces the curves of my tiny waist, drifting into my seated bottom, and back up again until I'm gazing at my side profile that's looking down at my shoulder.

I look serene.

I look clear.

I look perfect.

There's nothing abstract about me at all. Every detail of my skin, the side of my face, and my hair is impeccably clear. All of me. He hasn't adopted his usual painting style of blurring the image or making it unappealing.

Except with the backdrop. The view beyond my naked body, all of the buildings on the skyline, they're all a wish-wash of colour, mostly blacks and greys with hints of yellow blobs to enhance the glow of lights. He's captured the glass of the window perfectly, and though it defies possibility, my reflection is faultlessly clear, too – my face, my naked chest, my hair . . .

I slowly shake my head and register my lack of breathing when I remove my palm from my mouth, tentatively stepping forward. The oils are shimmering. It's not completely dry, so I refrain from touching, even though my fingertips are being lured towards the picture to trace the lines of me with my eyes *and* my touch.

'God, Miller,' I breathe, awestruck by the beauty of what I'm looking at – not because it's me in the painting, but because my beautifully damaged man created it. He'll never cease to amaze me. His complicated mind, his power, his tenderness . . . his astonishing talent.

I'm painted to perfection, almost lifelike, but I'm framed by a mess of paint. I begin to comprehend something, just as a scrap of paper catches my eye on the bottom left-hand corner of the painting. Reaching forward with only a teeny tiny fraction of uncertainty, because Miller Hart has a history of breaking my heart with his written words, I pull it down and unfold the paper while nibbling on my bottom lip.

There are just four words.

And they choke me.

I see only you.

His message begins to blur as tears collect in my eyes, and I wipe furiously as they release and tumble down my cheeks. I read again on a tiny sob and look to the painting to remind myself of its magnificence. I don't know why. This image and these words are imprinted on my mind already, after only a few sparse minutes absorbing it all. I'm willing the onset of internal fireworks, I need to feel him, see him, but after a few moments of silently begging for him to come to me, it's still just me and the painting.

But then I remember the string attached to my wrist and I seize it, noticing it stemming off from the other side of the painting, so I detach myself from the one connecting me to the artwork and claim the new lead, following it to the kitchen, frowning when I see a line of thread leading back out. It quickly tells me that my hunt isn't over yet, and it also tells me that Miller isn't in the kitchen. But a huge mess on the table is, and I'm suddenly hit by the lingering smell of burning, but it's the very unlike-Miller mess that has me hurrying over where I find scissors, scraps of paper everywhere, and a pot. I look into it, too curious, and gasp when I clock the burned contents.

'Oh . . .' I whisper to myself, returning my attention to the table and absorbing the scattering of ripped and cut pages. Diary pages. I gather a few up and turn them in my hands a few times, searching for anything to confirm what I think I'm looking at. And there it is. Miller's handwriting.

'He burned his date book,' I murmur, letting the scraps of paper float down to the table. And he's left a mess? I'm not sure which I'm most shocked by. I'd give this quandary more thought if I wasn't now staring at a photograph. All of the feelings I felt when I first saw this photo hit me like a sledgehammer – the helplessness, the wretchedness, the sorrow, and I begin to tear up again, yet I still collect the picture of Miller as a boy from the table and regard it for a while. I don't know why, but something makes me turn it over, despite knowing the back is blank.

It's not now, though.

Miller's handwriting is scrolled across the back, and I'm off again, now sobbing like a baby as I run my eyes over his next message.

Dark or light, only you.
Come find me, sweet girl.

I pull myself together fast, now panicked for another reason. I leave the mess and grab the string, following it fast and not giving it much thought when it leads me to the front door. I'm out of his flat, wrestling with the sheets concealing me, and trailing my lead, but I abruptly come to a stop when my trail ends and the string disappears.

Between the doors of the lift.

'Oh my God,' I blurt, smacking the call button like a loon, my aching heart beating a strong staccato against my rib cage. 'Oh my God, oh my God, oh my God.'

Each second feels like centuries as I wait impatiently for the lift to open, persistently smacking the button for no purpose, other than for something to physically hit. 'Open!' I yell.

Ding!

'Oh, thank God!' The string falls from mid-air, down to the ground at my feet when the doors begin to part.

And the fireworks hit me like a charging bull. Flurries or them – all attacking me, making me light-headed and dizzy, challenging my ability to see.

But I see *him*.

My hand shoots out and holds the wall to stop me from collapsing in shock. Or is it relief? He's sitting on the floor of the lift, his back to the wall, his head dropped, and the thread leads to a loop fastened around his own wrist.

What the hell is he doing in here?

'Miller?' I inch forward, wary, wondering what state he might be in and how I might handle it. 'Miller, baby?'

His head lifts. He slowly opens his eyes. And my breath is robbed from me when piercing blue eyes sink into me. 'There's nothing I wouldn't do for you, sweet girl,' he breathes, reaching for me. 'Nothing I *couldn't* do.' A slight cock of his head gestures for me to come to him, which I do without thought, keen to comfort him. Though why he's in the lift is a bloody mystery. Why would he put himself through this? I take his hand and engage my muscles to help him up, but I'm on my way down to his lap and being arranged just so before I can react on instinct and remove him from the monster hole.

'What are you doing?' I ask, resisting the urge to fight with him.

I'm wrestled into position. '*You* are going to give me my *thing*.'

'What?' I'm confused. He wants his *thing* in a scary lift?

'I've asked once,' he snaps impatiently, and he wholeheartedly means it. Why is he doing this?

With nothing else to say and not being permitted to help him from this hellhole, I take my only other option and wrap my arms around him, squeezing him to me. It takes a good few minutes of fierce cuddling before I recognise the lack of shakes coming from him. And it all becomes clear.

'You got in here willingly?' I ask, wondering how else I thought he could have accidently stumbled into the lift.

He doesn't answer. He's breathing into my neck, his heart is beating a nice, calm thrum against my chest, and there are no signs of distress. How long has he been in here? I don't ask. I doubt I'd get an answer anyway, so I let him squeeze me to his heart's content, hearing the doors closing behind me. I definitely detect a stutter of his heart rate now.

'Marry me,' he says quietly.

'What?' I cry, flying back from his lap. I didn't hear him right. I couldn't have. He doesn't *want* to get married. My eyes dart all over his face, noting between my shock that there's a sheen of sweat coating it.

'You heard me,' he replies, remaining impossibly still. His only movements are his lips parting slowly to speak. His wide blue eyes aren't even blinking, just burning holes into my startled face.

'I . . . it . . . I thought . . .'

'Don't make me repeat myself,' he warns evenly, making me snap my mouth shut in shock. I try to form some coherent words. I can't. My mind has shut down on me. So I just stare at his impassive face, waiting for anything that could clue me up on what I think I just heard. 'Olivia . . .'

'Say it again!' I blurt, recoiling as a result of my own abruptness but declining from apologising. I'm too dazed. The mild sign of a twitching lip would usually have my own lips twitching in response. Not today, though. Today I'm useless.

Miller takes a deep breath, reaches forward, grabs the sheets at my chest with his fists, and yanks me to him. We're nose to nose, twinkling bright blues on wide, unsure sapphires. 'Marry me, sweet girl. Be mine forever.'

My lungs burn under the strain of holding my breath. I didn't want any noise when he repeated what I thought he said, including breathing. 'Oooooh,' I exhale it all on that silly gush of comprehension. 'I thought you never wanted to marry officially?' I had got my head around it. His written word and spoken promise are more than enough for me. Like Miller, I don't need witnesses or religion to validate what we have.

Lush lips straighten. 'I've changed my mind and we'll speak no more of it.'

My mouth drops open in shock. Just like that? I would ask what's changed, but I think it's probably obvious, and I'm not going to question it. I'd told myself Miller was right, and I really did believe it. Maybe because he made sense, or maybe because he seemed so adamant. 'But why are you in the lift?' My thoughts spill from my mouth as I sit before him, trying to wrap my mind around what's happening.

Miller's slips into thought and takes a risky peek of his surroundings, but he soon centres his attention back on me. 'I can do anything for you.' He speaks quietly, surely.

I get it.

If he can do this, then he literally *can* do anything for me.

'My life has fallen into place, Olivia Taylor. Now I am who I'm supposed to be. Your lover. Your friend. Your husband.' He drops his gaze to my tummy and I watch in wonder as his eyes take on a peaceful edge. They're smiling eyes. 'Our baby's father.'

I leave him undisturbed while he stares at my stomach for what seems an eternity. It gives me time to let his declaration settle. Miller Hart isn't your average man. He's a man beyond any reasonable ability to describe. I think I have that ability now. Because I know him. Everyone, including me one time, used words they deemed fitting when describing Miller.

Detached. Emotionless. Unloving. And un*lovable*.

He was never any of those things, although he tried his damn hardest to be. And succeeded quite successfully. He repelled positivity and welcomed detriment. Like his paintings, he tarnished his natural beauty. Miller Hart's walls were built so high, there was a risk no one would ever breach them. Because that is how he wanted it to be. I didn't bash those walls down on my own. Brick by brick, he dismantled them with me. He wanted to show me the man he truly wanted to be. For me. There's nothing in this world that could give me greater pleasure or satisfaction than seeing Miller smile. A simple thing, I know, but not in our world. Every smile he gives me is indicative of true happiness, and despite his signature cool impassiveness, I will never live with the worry of reading him. His eyes are a sea of emotion that I'm certain only I can construe. I've completed the Miller Hart induction programme. I've aced that damn course. Yet I'm under no illusion that I did it alone. Our worlds collided and exploded. I deciphered him and he deciphered me.

There was him and there was me.

And now there is only us.

'You can be whoever you want to be,' I whisper, moving forward, needing to be closer to him.

Inconceivable peace reflects back at me when we're looking at each other again. 'I want to be your husband.' He speaks softly and quietly. 'Marry me, Olivia Taylor. I beg you.' His demand steals my breath. 'Please don't make me repeat myself, sweet girl.'

'But—'

'I'm not finished.' His finger meets my lips to hush me. 'I want you to be mine in every way possible, including in the eyes of God.'

'But you're not a religious man,' I remind him stupidly.

'If he accepts you as mine, then I'll be whatever he wants me to be. Marry me.'

I crumble with happiness and throw myself into his arms, feeling overwhelmed by the intensity of my feelings for my perfect gentleman.

He catches me. Holds me tightly. Injects an incredible amount of certainty into me.

'As you wish,' I whisper.

I feel him smile into my neck and constrict me in his grip. 'I'm using my intuition here,' he says quietly, 'and I'm going to suggest that you mean yes.'

'Correct,' I whisper, smiling into his neck.

'Good. Now get me out of this fucking lift.'

Epilogue

Six years later

It's off by at least five millimetres.

And it's bugging the God-loving hell out of me. My damn hands are twitching and my drumming fingers are speeding up by the second.

It's fine. It's fine. It's fine.

'It's not fucking fine,' I bark to myself, diving forward and poking my laptop to the left. I know the sense of released pressure is unreasonable, really, I do, but I just can't figure out why I should leave it so horribly out of place when a split second of my time can put it where it should be. I frown to myself and settle back in my chair, feeling a whole lot better. Therapy is clearly working a treat.

A soft rapping pulls my attention away from my perfectly placed laptop and to my office door. That delicious wave of happiness mixed with a ton of other emotions sails through me like lightning, the fireworks beginning to explode beneath my skin at her known closeness.

My sweet girl. She's here.

I grin and arm myself with my remote control, pressing the button that'll prompt my screens to appear. They take forever, but I don't worry about her walking in, even though she knows the code. She'll wait for me. Like she always does.

The screens kick in and I sigh when she appears on the main centred television, her beautiful petite body dressed in black capri trousers and a crisp white shirt tucked in neatly, her hair cascading all over her shoulders. If I was that way inclined, I'd kick my feet up on my desk, recline in my chair, and just sit here for the rest of the day watching her. But I'm not up for littering my desk with my feet, and no amount of therapy will solve that. So I rest my head against the back of the chair, tapping the remote control on the arm and smiling when my stare drops to her cute feet. Today's colour: coral, and although it kind of takes the edge off the elegant formal style of her work outfit, it doesn't matter. Never has, never will. My girl must have fifty pairs, and I know more will be added. By me. I just can't help it. Every time I see a new colour, I find myself in the store and walking out with another pair, sometimes two, or, on the odd occasion, three. Her face each time I present her with a new hue is beyond the realms of pleasure. In fact, I think I've become mildly obsessed by hunting down every colour on the Converse spectrum. I frown to myself. Mildly? OK, so I search Google every now and then, and maybe reserve a day here and there especially for Converse hunting. That doesn't make me obsessive. Enthusiastic, maybe. Yes, enthusiastic. I'll go with that, and I don't care what my therapist says.

On a silly little agreeable nod of my head, I resume my concentration of the screen, brushing at my forehead when a stray hair tickles my skin. I sigh, rapt by the sheer perfection that is my wife, the side of my index finger rubbing back and forth across my top lip as I think of all the worshipping time I've reserved for tonight. And tomorrow night. And the next night. I smile to myself, wondering what planet I must have been on all those years ago. I knew one night would never be enough. And I know for sure that she knew it, too.

I'm waiting for it.

It's coming.

Any . . . moment . . . now.

'Here we go.' I grin to myself, looking on as she gazes up at the camera and drops her weight casually onto her hip. She's had enough. But I haven't. So I stay exactly where I am, denying her. 'In a minute, sweet girl,' I muse. 'Give me what I want.'

My cock starts to twitch in my trousers when I see her roll her eyes, and I shift in my chair to alleviate the pressure of it pushing against my fly. She begins to turn away from the camera. I release a puff of built-up air and try to regulate my breathing. It doesn't work. 'Oooh Jesus help me.'

She slowly bends, pushing her pert bottom out, and the material of her Ralph Lauren trousers pulls taunt over her cheeks. Then all sorts of frantic activity happens in my trousers when she looks over her shoulder on a diminutive smile. 'Bloody hell!' I'm out of my chair and sprinting to the door in a flash, but I skid to a stop before I make it when something very serious escapes my notice in my urgency. I start pulling at my suit, desperately resisting the powerful urge to look at it. I smooth my collar, my tie, my sleeves – all in a vain attempt to avoid it. 'Bollocks!' I drop my head back and let it slowly fall to the side, my eyes landing on the wayward remote control before travelling across to my chair, which is positioned randomly, the seat still swivelling a little from the brute force of me flying up.

Leave them, leave them, leave them.

I can't. My office is the only sacred place I have left.

I hurry over and swipe the control up, putting it its rightful place in the top drawer. 'Perfect,' I declare to myself, ready to fix my chair.

Knock, knock, knock.

My head whips up and for some unknown reason, I come over all guilty.

Then I hear her silky voice through the door. 'I know what you're doing!' she sings, laughter only a fraction away from her tone. 'Don't forget your chair, baby.'

My eyes clench shut, like I can hide from my crimes. 'There's no need for insolence,' I mutter, loving her and hating her all at once for knowing me so well.

'With you, Miller Hart, there is. Open the door or I'll let myself in.'

'No!' I yell, pushing my chair aggressively under my desk. 'You know I like opening the door for you.'

'Then hurry up. I have studying to do and a job to get to.'

I wander over to the door, pulling my suit into place and raking an annoyed hand through my hair, but when I take the handle, I don't turn it. Something has just come to me. 'Tell me you won't snitch on me,' I say, physically stopping myself from opening the door before she agrees. She's like a magnet and with only a piece of wood between our close bodies, I can feel her luring me closer.

'To your therapist?' she asks, giggling, making my cock resume twitching in my trousers.

'Yes. Promise you won't make a big deal of it.'

'I promise,' she agrees easily. 'Now let me taste you.'

I swing the door open and brace myself for her attack, laughing when her body crashes to mine before I've had the opportunity to absorb her in the flesh. My *thing* is brief before she's kissing her way across my stubbled face and plunges her tongue into my mouth. 'It might slip out accidently,' she mumbles past my lips, nibbling and biting.

I cotton on to her way of thinking fast. I smile. 'What will it cost me for your silence?'

'A whole night of worshipping,' she states with confidence and without delay.

'You really don't have a choice in the matter.' I secure my arm around her tiny waist and carry her to my couch, sitting down and arranging her on my lap, all the while maintaining her wonderful hello kiss.

'I don't want one, so yes, this is a pointless discussion. I agree.'

'Smart girl.' I sound arrogant. I don't care. 'Thank you for stopping by, sweet girl.'

She rips her busy lips away, and I growl lowly, but soon forget my grievance when I'm presented with her flawless face and gorgeous hair. My fingers are instantly delving into the strands and twiddling. 'You thank me every day like it's my choice,' she whispers.

I feel my eyebrows lift. 'I never make you do anything that I know you don't want to do,' I remind her, relishing in that sassy scowl when it's tossed in my direction. 'Do I?'

'Noooo,' she says, drawing the word out on a long exasperated exhale. 'But this one of your obsessive habits kind of interferes with my working day. I might see to it that your therapist tackles it next.'

I scoff. 'She even tries, then I'll no longer utilise her services.' I can't deny it. I have gained some more obsessive little ways, but I've dealt with many, too, so I shouldn't be penalised. I should be rewarded.

She doesn't hit me with her sass this time, though I can see she's dying to. But even my perfect wife has figured out that no amount of her so-called therapy will see me wiping any obsessive habit that relates to her from my life. And anyway, I know she enjoys most of them. I don't know why she tries to pretend she doesn't, that I'm hampering her life.

Her lack of retort leaves silence and me time to absorb her, which I do with the greatest of pleasure. I really haven't laid my eyes on anything so perfect in all of my life. I correct myself on a smile when the most adorable little boy settles at the front of my mind.

'What are you thinking?' she asks on a little cock of her beautiful head.

'I'm thinking you and my little man put perfection to shame.'

Sparkling sapphires send me cross-eyed. 'Speaking of your little man . . .'

My contentment disintegrates quickly. 'What's he done now?' My mind races with a million scenarios, praying he hasn't shown any tell-tale signs of obsessive behaviour.

'He stole Missy's socks.'

My relief is profound. This again? I try to hide my amusement. I really do. 'Why?' I know why.

Olivia looks at me like I'm stupid. 'Because they were odd.' She isn't amused. Not at all.

'I empathise.'

She slaps my shoulder on a scornful look, and I give her a hurt face, rubbing at her target. 'It's not funny.'

I sag beneath her. How many times do we need to go over this? 'I've told them. Tell all the kids to wear matching socks. Simple.' Christ almighty, how hard can it be?

'Miller, he stands at the entrance and makes the other children show him their socks.'

I nod, pouting. 'Very thorough.'

'Or very annoying when he pinches them if they're odd. Are you going to explain to the parents why their children keep going home from school with no socks on their feet?'

'Yes. And I'll tell them how to remedy the problem.' I watch her sigh, exasperated. I don't know why. She overthinks stuff, as always, and I'm not having the parents of my boy's school friends making her think there's something wrong with our son. 'I'll deal with it,' I assure her, glancing at my fingers that are tangled in her locks. I frown, flicking my eyes to Livy's. 'There's something different about you.' I don't know why I didn't notice it before.

Worry kicks in when guilt floods her sapphires and she removes herself from my lap, spending an exceptional amount of time straightening herself out. I push myself up from the couch, my eyes narrowing. 'I know my sweet girl inside out, and right now she's as guilty as sin.'

Her sass rears its ugly head and daggers fire from angry eyes with such force, I'm nearly nailed to the wall behind me. 'I had an inch off!'

I gasp. I knew it! 'You cut your hair!'

'I had split ends!' she argues. 'It was beginning to look tatty!'

'No, it wasn't!' I fire back in disgust, pursing my lips. 'Why would you do that to me?'

'I didn't do it to *you*. I did it to me!'

'Oh,' I laugh, outraged. 'Like that, is it?' I march off to the bathroom, knowing she's in hot pursuit.

'Don't you dare, Miller!'

'I made you a promise. I keep my promises.' I open the cupboard and pull out the clippers, shoving the plug viciously into the socket. She cut her hair!

'An inch, that's all! It's still skimming my arse!'

'My possession!' I bark, taking the clippers to my head with every intention to see my promise through.

'Fine,' she says calmly, throwing me off course. 'Shave your hair off. I'll still love you.'

I pull up and look at her out of the corner of my eye. She's resting up against the doorframe. And she looks cocky. 'I'll do it,' I threaten, jerking the clippers closer to my head.

'Yes, so you say.' She's goading me.

'OK,' I toss back, bringing it nearer still, looking at myself in the mirror as I watch the device creeping closer to my dark waves. The dark waves I love. I'm beginning to get nervous. 'Fuck,' I say calmly, my hand dropping to my side with the clippers. I can't do it. I stare at my reflection for a while, giving myself a mental good talking-to, looking past my defeated face when she appears behind me in the mirror.

'You still fascinate me, Miller Hart.' She reaches up and toys with my earlobe, not making a big deal of her victory. 'A little trim.'

I sigh, knowing I'm being over the top but finding it difficult to reason with myself. 'I love you, too. Let me taste you.'

She obliges, worming her way between me and the sink, and lets me take my time indulging in her. 'I need to get to work.' She disturbs my bliss, pulling back and pecking me on the nose.

'Noted,' I relent dejectedly. 'Me and my boy are going to see Nan after I pick him up from school.'

'Great.'

'Then we're going to that silly therapist's office.'

She smiles brightly and cuddles me fiercely. 'Thank you.'

I don't argue. I might make a fuss of it, but I can't deny that I enjoy my time with my boy while we're there. 'Will you dance with me before you go?'

'Here?'

'No.' I take her hand, loving the curiosity on her face, and lead her up to the club.

'I need to get to work, Miller,' she insists on a laugh, telling me she's in no rush. Not that it matters. She doesn't have a choice. She should know that by now. So I ignore her and place her accurately in the middle of the dance floor when we arrive there, brushing her hair over her shoulders, before making my way to the DJ stand, immediately frowning at the millions of switches and buttons.

'Shit!' I curse under my breath, pressing and flicking everything in sight until the speakers come to life. 'What mood are you in, sweet girl?' I call, scanning the lists of endless tracks on the computer screen.

'Give me something energetic. I have a long day.'

'As you wish,' I say to myself, spotting the perfect track. I smile and load it up, then slowly raise my bent body as MGMT's "Electric Feel" fills the main floor of my club. She's grinning. It's the most beautiful sight, but her mouth is the only thing she's moving, and it will be until I make it to her. She knows.

I hold her breathtaking sapphire eyes as I step down from the booth, then stalk slowly towards her. God bless her, those dainty shoulders are twitching, dying to start pulsing with the music, but she won't. I'm taking my time, as I always do. Her chin drops a little and her lips part, her eyes hooded, her eyelashes fluttering.

She wants to tell me to hurry the hell up, but again, she won't. Savoured. Never rushed. And I'm savouring every nanosecond it takes me to reach her, drinking in pure, raw, exquisite beauty as I do.

'Miller,' she breathes, her voice drenched in sex, want, lust, impatience.

'Let me have my time with you, sweet girl.' I make it to her and push my whole front into hers, feeling her heart beating, steady and strong.

I slide my arm around her tiny waist and tug, sealing us, and nearly explode with happiness when she gives me a coy smile, looking up at me. 'Are you ready to let me worship you on the dance floor?' I ask.

'So ready.'

I return her smile, holding on to her with one arm, letting my other relax by my side. Her arms, though, go straight for my neck, circling and pulling my face closer to hers as I begin to teasingly thrust my groin into her tummy in time to the beat. She'll be naked on the floor by the end of this track. My cock's throbbing, shouting at me to make it happen soon.

I widen my stance and bend my knees a little so I can accommodate the closeness of our faces, and she responds by beginning to follow the grinding of my hips, making sure our groins are touching at all times.

My smile widens as I gaze into her eyes, holding her tightly as we remain on the spot, until I step back and she follows, her upper body falling into a delicious rhythm, swaying with me from side to side. 'Tell me this is worth being late for,' I breathe down on her, thrusting my hips forward harshly when she delays her answer. 'Tell me.'

Her lips slightly purse, her eyes narrowing. 'Are you going to add this to your daily obsessive habits?'

I grin. 'Might do.'

'That means yes.'

I laugh and twirl us around, breaking our joined bodies and claiming her hand. She yelps on a giggle as I yank her into me until we're nose to nose and unmoving, the music still in full swing. 'Correct.' I smash my lips to hers, stealing her breath, and mine, too, for that matter, then throw her out on a spin, her gorgeous blonde hair fanning out and whipping the air around her. She laughs, she smiles, her sapphire eyes glimmer relentlessly, and I once again appreciate how fucking lucky I am. There's not a scrap of darkness in my world anymore. There's nothing but blinding light. And it's all because of this beautiful creature.

My thoughts leave my concentration lacking in the dancing department and I pull her in once more, throwing my arms around her, needing our *thing*. I don't release her for a long, long time, and she doesn't complain. My reality often hits me like an iron bar to the face, quickly having me check everything around me is real and mine. My *thing* is the best way. Problem is, no amount of time with her safe in my arms is long enough. Not even forever. Or an eternity.

The music drifts into nothing, but I remain holding her tightly, still swaying us from side to side. She doesn't complain, and I know she won't prompt me to release her, so I swallow down some strength and break away from her. 'Get to work, sweet girl,' I whisper in her ear, smacking her bottom to send her on her way. It takes all of my strength to remain where I am and not chase her down, as it always does. I try to ignore the ache in my heart that descends quickly as she gets farther and farther away from me. I try. And fail every time. I won't be complete again until she's back in my sight or in my *thing*.

*

I'm looking at every pair of feet that pass me as I wait outside the school entrance, searching for bare ankles. I shake my head to myself, thinking it's really not acceptable for so many kids to go out in public without matching socks. So what if my boy wants to remedy that. He's doing them a favour.

Standing by the door, my hands resting lightly in my trouser pockets, I can't even be bothered to return the smiles of the many women who pass with their kids in tow. Smiling would be engaging with these strangers. It would be inviting them in to talk, ask questions, get to know me. No thank you. So I maintain my stoic expression and only allow my facial muscles to kick in when I see him coming. I smile, watching him traipse out of the doors with his rucksack on his back, his little Ralph shirt tucked haphazardly into his grey shorts and lovely navy striped socks pulled up his shins. His cute little feet are graced in grey Converse high-tops, laces undone and trailing behind him, and his dark waves are a tangle of locks, falling to his ears. My little man.

'Good afternoon, sir,' I say, dropping to my haunches when he makes it to me and tying his laces. 'Have you had a good day?'

His eyes, a carbon copy of the Taylor girls, all navy and sparkling, are irritated. 'Five pairs, Daddy,' he tells me. 'It's unacceptable.'

'Five?' I sound shocked, which is fine because I am. He must have been in a right pickle. I narrow questioning eyes on him as I finish securing his laces. 'And what did you do, Harry?'

'Told them to put socks on their Christmas lists.'

I chuckle to myself, taking his hand. 'We have a date with Great-Nana.'

He squeals his excitement, making me smile.

'Let's go.' I claim his little hand and start leading him away, but I pull up short when I hear the distant calling of my name.

'Mr Hart!'

Looking down at my boy, I cock him a questioning look, but his little face remains deadpan and he shrugs. 'I couldn't concentrate on my drawing.'

'So you told them to put socks on their Christmas list and also made them remove the odd ones they had on?'

'Correct.'

I can't help it. I smile down at my little lad and bright light explodes around me when he returns my amusement.

'Mr Hart!'

I turn, taking my boy with me, and see his teacher scurrying towards us, her floral skirt swishing around her ankles. She's creased beyond creased. 'Ms Phillips,' I sigh, demonstrating my tiredness before she gets into her stride.

'Mr Hart, I know you're a busy man—'

'Correct,' I interrupt, just for clarification.

She shifts nervously. Is she blushing? My probing eyes study her for a few moments, my lips pouting in contemplation. She's definitely blushing, and now she's fidgeting madly. 'Yes, well.' She lifts one of her hands, and I look down to see a bunch of mix-matched material bunched in her grasp. Socks. 'I found these in the boys' bathroom. In the bin.'

Looking down out of the corner of my eye, I catch my boy regarding the pile of material with utter disgust. 'I see,' I muse.

'Mr Hart, this really is becoming quite an issue.'

'I'm being intuitive here,' I begin thoughtfully, ripping my eyes away from Harry's twisted face. 'And I'm going to suggest you mean that it's becoming a nuisance.'

'Yes.' She nods decisively, looking down at my boy. I'm not surprised when her frustration drifts into a tender smile as she regards him. 'Harry, darling, it's not nice to steal the other children's socks.'

Harry's face takes on an edge of sulkiness, but I intervene before he's forced to explain himself . . . again. He has one compulsion. Just one. Matching socks. My relief that there's not so many more refuses to let me take that away from him. It's his thing. I had nothing to fear. Olivia's beautiful soul really has eclipsed all of my darkness.

'Ms Phillips, Harry likes matching socks. I've told you before and despite hating repeating myself, I'll make an exception this one time. Ask their parents to do the decent thing and put their children in a matching pair. It's not hard. And why they're happy to let them leave the house in odd socks is a mystery, anyway. Problem solved.'

'Mr Hart, I'm in no position to dictate what the parents of my children dress them in.'

'No, but you're happy to dictate to me what my son should endure during his school day.'

'But—'

'I'm not finished,' I cut her off with my harsh words and the appearance of a silencing finger. 'Everyone is overthinking this. Matching socks. It's that simple.' I wrap my arm around Harry's shoulder and lead him away. 'And we'll be leaving that line of conversation just there.'

'I concur,' Harry adds, coiling his little arm around the backs of my thighs and hugging into my side. 'Thank you, Daddy.'

'Never thank me, sweet boy,' I say quietly, wondering if Harry's little thing is now becoming my obsession. I often find myself checking out people's ankles on my son's behalf, even when he's not with me. The world needs ridding of odd socks.

'Where's my boy?' Josephine's happy voice creeps down the hallway as I let us in, and I immediately take a glimpse at Harry, seeing him removing his Converse and placing them neatly by the coat stand.

'I'm here, Great-Nana!' he replies, laying his rucksack beside his shoes.

Josephine appears, wiping her hands on a tea towel, her lovely face a joy to see. 'Good evening, Josephine,' I greet, slipping out of my jacket and hanging it on the peg, smoothing it down neatly before returning my attention to Olivia's wonderful grandmother. She grabs my cheeks and assaults me with her lips while Harry waits alongside for his turn.

'How many today?' she asks.

'Five.'

'Five.' She gasps, and I nod my confirmation, making her mutter something about it being a disgrace. She's right. 'I do love it when you're here.' She finishes up, leaving me with a damp face, and turns her old navy eyes onto Harry. He always has a smile for his great-nana. 'And how's my gorgeous boy?'

'Fine and dandy, thank you.' He steps into her open arms and cuddles her fiercely. 'You look exceptionally lovely today, Nana.'

'Oh, you dreamboat.' She laughs, taking Harry's cheeks and squeezing. 'You beautiful, *beautiful* boy.'

Harry maintains his smile as Josephine takes his hand and starts leading him to the kitchen. 'I've made your favourite cake,' she tells him.

'Pineapple upside-down?' Harry's beside himself, and it's quite apparent in his hopeful tone.

'Yes, darling, but it's Uncle George's favourite, too, so you'll have to share.'

I follow behind, smiling like crazy on the inside as she shows Harry to a chair. 'Hello, George,' Harry says, plunging his finger into the side of the cake. I'm not the only one who winces. George looks horrified.

The old boy places his paper down and looks at Josephine, who shrugs it off. She'll let him get away with murder. So I step in. 'Harry, that's rude,' I scold, but find it difficult when his tongue is lapping at his cute little fingers.

'Sorry, Daddy.' He drops his head in shame.

'I've been looking at this cake for twenty minutes.' George takes the serving knife and sets about dishing up a slice for each of them. 'Nana Josephine tells me off, too, if I finger-dip.'

'But it's so yummy! Would you like some, Daddy?' Harry asks me, accepting the plate that's slid across the table. He then lays his napkin across his lap, and his gorgeous blue eyes find mine. He smiles.

I take a seat next to him, gently ruffling his hair. 'I'd love some.'

'Daddy would like some please, George.'

'You've got it, little man.'

I watch as George serves me a slice of Josephine's famous pineapple upside-down cake and accept my plate, resting it in front of me. I tweak its position, just a little, despite my determination not to. It's habit. I can't help it. Looking up to my sweet boy, I find him smiling brightly at me as I lay my napkin across my lap, too.

He's perfect.

My boy is advanced in every aspect of his young life. He's smart, and he has no OCD traits beyond his sock compulsion, but everyone is allowed a thing. Harry's is matching socks. I couldn't be anything but proud of him. I'm so fucking proud of him. I throw him a little wink and burst with happiness when he giggles and attempts to wink back, blinking both eyes instead of one. OK, maybe not advanced in everything.

'So, my handsome young man.' Josephine settles next to Harry and pushes his spoon towards him in a gesture to tuck in, but she immediately slaps her own wrist when he scowls and puts it back in its rightful place.

'Nana Josie!' he tsks. 'Daddy doesn't like it there!'

'I'm sorry!' Josephine casts guilty eyes over to me, and I shrug, thinking she should know better by now. 'I was doing so well.'

'It's fine, mate.' I placate Harry, trying to calm him. 'Daddy's good with the fork there.'

'You sure?'

'One hundred per cent.' I knock the fork off position, making him chuckle. The sweet sound goes some way to curbing my need to put it right back. But I don't. He mustn't see how crippled by obsession I once was. I'm getting better, though. And Harry helps immensely. I probably have the messiest kid on Earth. God's clearly trying to get a balance.

George chuckles, placing his hands in his lap before straightening his face and holding Josephine in place with serious eyes. 'Nana Josie,' he scolds, shaking his head. 'Where's your memory?'

'Up your arse,' she mutters under her breath, apologising immediately when both Harry and I cough. 'Sorry, boys.' She gets up from the table and wanders around to George's side. Josephine's friend looks wary, and so he should. 'Look at that, Harry!' she yells enthusiastically, pointing to a spot across the room. I watch Harry's face stretch into a delighted grin as he glances where indicated, and then I grin, too, as Olivia's spunky grandmother gives old George a cuff around the head.

'Ouch!' He starts rubbing the sore spot as he pouts to himself. 'A bit unnecessary, isn't it?'

I keep my mouth shut. I'm not stupid, unlike George.

'Are you done telling George off, Nana Josie?' Harry asks. His cute question has everyone in the room smiling, even George. 'Because I'm rather hungry.'

'I'm done, Harry.' She gives George an affectionate rub of the shoulder, her way of making friends, and takes her seat.

'That's a relief,' George breathes, his hand now twitching over his spoon. 'Can we start now?'

'No!' Harry shoots his little head back to the table. 'Everyone needs to close their eyes so we can say grace.' We all follow through on his order immediately, and he begins. 'Thank you,

God, for Nana Josephine's cakes. Thank you for giving me the best mummy and daddy in the whole world, and thank you for Nanny Gracie, Pappy William, Nana Josie, Uncle Gregory, Uncle Ben, and old George. Amen.' I smile and open my eyes, but snap them shut in an instant when he shouts, 'Wait!' I inwardly frown, wondering who else he's grateful for, and come up with nothing. So I wait for him to continue. 'And please, God, make the mummies and daddies of all the children in the land wear matching socks.'

I smile and start to peel open my eyes again.

'Amen,' we all sing in unison; then everyone collects their spoons and dives in, me and Harry included, except my boy is more ravenous than me.

'Nana, may I ask you a question?' he asks, mouth full.

'Of course! What would you like to know?'

'Why does Daddy call you a twenty-four-carat gold treasure?'

Josephine chuckles, as do George and I at his genuinely curious question. 'Because I'm special,' she says, flicking fond eyes to me briefly before returning her attention to my boy, 'which makes you a thirty-six-carat gold treasure.'

'Mummy says I'm very special.'

'Mummy is right,' Josephine confirms. 'You're very, very special.'

'I concur,' I interject, observing George working his way quickly through his first helping. There will be no contribution to conversation while he's eating.

A quiet settles around the table as everyone savours Josephine's delicious cake, and I'm aware of the continuous fond smile she has nailed on my perfect boy. His mummy had a strange effect on me, but this little man sent the world that she made light into blinding beauty. Everything seems utterly perfect when he's around, without any need to make it that way. Kind of. OK, so our home looks like a Lego bomb exploded in it, but I'm dealing with that. We lost the nappies, bottles and irritating squeaky toys and gained Legos, plastic crockery, and blunt knives and forks. I'll live. Just.

'Are we too late?'

I look up and see Greg stroll in, Ben in tow, both looking even more cheerful than usual. It gets me thinking.

'Uncle Gregory! Uncle Ben!' Harry's down from the table faster than lightning, running at his honorary uncles.

'Harry, boy!' Gregory catches him and chucks him onto his shoulder, all very neatly. 'We have exciting news,' Gregory tells him, all enthusiastic and tossing a look at his partner, who winks before claiming Harry from Greg. Now I'm *really* thinking. Exciting news? I rest back in my chair and fold my arms.

I don't need to push for enlightenment because my boy does it on my behalf, just as curious as me. 'What? What exciting news?'

'Uncle Ben and I are having a baby!'

I swallow down a choke of shock, glancing at George who *is* actually choking. 'Blimey!' he splutters around his cake as Josephine hurries over and starts smacking him on the back.

I sit up straight and find Harry, my shock turning into pure amusement when I watch him recoil, a little wayward curl falling onto his forehead. He starts shaking his head as Ben sets him on his feet. 'But who will be the mummy, Uncle Gregory?'

I snort all over the table, as do Josephine and George, but Greg and Ben just smile fondly at the cute little sod. 'It won't have a mummy.' Greg drops to his haunches, getting eye level with my boy.

Harry frowns. 'So you'll have a baby growing in your tummy?'

'Harry Hart, you little beauty!' Greg laughs. 'Men can't have babies growing in their tummies. I'm going to let Uncle Ben explain how we're going to have a baby.'

'You are?' Ben blurts, his cheeks flushing crimson, only propelling my laughter into stomach-aching territory.

I get a filthy look thrown at me from Greg, making me pull up and shrug an apology. 'C'mon, Ben,' I pipe up, popping a piece of cake in my mouth and chewing slowly. 'How do two men have a baby?'

He rolls his eyes and looks to Greg, accepting his nod of encouragement and joining him on the floor with Harry. 'There's a lady. She's going to help us.'

'What lady?'

'A nice lady.'

'Does she wear matching socks?'

We're all snorting again, including Greg and Ben this time. 'Yes,' Greg laughs. 'Yes, Harry, she wears matching socks.'

'Oh good. Then your baby will be perfect like me.'

I laugh uncontrollably at his matter-of-fact remark. I should tell him not to be so cocky, but how could I possibly do that when I'm the one who's constantly telling him he's perfect. When he's covered in mud after a day in the park, he's perfect. When he has spaghetti sauce smeared up to his ears, he's perfect. When he's surrounded by the horrific mess of his bedroom, he's perfect.

'Hello!'

I snap out of my hysterics and musings at the sound of the familiar greeting, followed by Harry dashing out of the kitchen, losing all interest in Greg and Ben's exciting news. 'Nan and Pap are here!' he shouts, disappearing down the corridor.

'Congratulations,' I say as Gregory and Ben pull themselves from the floor. 'I'm really happy for you.'

'Wonderful news!' Josephine sings, taking them both in a bear hug. 'Such wonderful news!'

Poor George grunts his happiness before diving back into the cake he's been waiting all day to eat.

'I'm here, my precious boy!' Gracie laughs, and I hear the tell-tale sign of colliding bodies from where Harry has made it to her and performed his usual launch at his nan. 'Oh, I've missed you!'

'I've missed you, too, Nan.'

I roll my eyes. She and William took him out for dinner last night. But knowing her fierce adoration of my boy, I can relate. The school days drag painfully.

'Uncle Gregory and Uncle Ben are having a baby!'

'I know,' Gracie replies, smiling fondly across the room to Greg and Ben as she strides into the room with my boy coiled around her. I'm not surprised she knows. They've formed quite a bond in recent years.

'Hello, Gracie,' I say.

'Miller.' She smiles, sitting herself at the table. 'Hi, Mum.'

'Hello, darling. Would you like cake?'

'God, no! My hips are suffering because of your cake.'

'Your hips are just fine.' William strides in, giving the back of Gracie's head a distasteful look.

'What do *you* know?' she retorts.

'Everything,' he fires back confidently, making me smile and Gracie scoff. William gives a nod in greeting to everyone, then makes a huge fuss over Harry, waving a Harrods bag under his nose. 'Look what I've got,' he teases. 'Mummy called me and said you got a head teacher's award last week for being helpful to the other children! Well done, you!'

I chuckle to myself. Yes, that was before he stole all of their socks.

'I did!' The excitement in Harry's eyes spikes my own. I know what's in that bag. 'Is it for me?'

'Yes, for you.' Gracie pushes the bag away and gives William a warning look that he notes quickly, backing off. 'But first, tell me how your day was.'

'Don't ask!' Josephine yells, collecting some plates. 'Odd socks everywhere!'

Gracie sighs and Harry's little head starts bobbing up and down in agreement. 'Five today, Nan.'

'Five?' Gracie sounds shocked, which is understandable. We've had one or two pairs, but five is a record and it's shaken my poor little boy's world to the core.

'Yes, five.' Harry removes himself from Gracie's lap and puffs his little chest out in exasperation, but he says no more. He doesn't need to. Now everyone is here, he wants proof that five isn't going to increase. George and I stand, joining William, Greg, and Ben, and we all lift our trousers, revealing our socks for inspection. I really don't need to be in the line-up – my boy knows he can depend on his daddy – but I comply anyway, just for the sake of it. Plus, I adore his concentrating face when he does this.

I feel William peek out of the corner of his eye to me and I chance a glance, although I know I won't like what I see. He'll have that tired look on his face.

'He's a kid. Humour him,' I whisper, ignoring William's sardonic puff of laughter. I know what he's thinking. He's thinking that this little quirk has nothing to do with him being a kid and everything to do with him being *my* kid. 'It's just the socks,' I assure him.

My little man walks slowly down the line, pursing his lips, like he's bracing himself for the worst. I know for sure William, Greg, Ben, and I will never let him down, but old George is always a loose cannon. 'Nice choice, George!' Harry sings, dropping to his knees to get a closer look.

I can virtually hear George's chest pumping up with pride. 'Thank you, Harry. Nana Josephine treated me.'

The relief that swoops through me is palpable, and I can sense William's, too. We both look down to George's ankles. He has on a pair of thick navy woollen things. They're vile, but a matching pair so they pass. I look over to Josephine, finding her smiling proudly, and mentally thank her and her forceful ways with the old boy, because the exposure of George's aged feet is not a pleasurable sight when Harry makes him remove his socks. I shudder.

'Nice?' William asks under his breath, nudging me with his elbow. 'We have silk and George's monstrosities get all the praise?'

I chuckle and drop my trousers, now the examination is over, watching as Harry jumps up to his granddad. 'Can I have my present now, Pap?'

William looks to Gracie for permission, who nods her consent. He steps forward and takes a seat, placing Harry next to him. He immediately tries to snatch the bag from William.

'Hey!' he scolds, pulling it away and giving Harry warning eyes. 'Where have those manners gone?'

'Sorry, Pappy.' Harry's tail goes right between his legs.

'Better. You know, there's only one man in this world who I'll allow Nanny to love more than me.'

'Me,' Harry states without delay. 'But you really don't have a choice in the matter.'

I can't help it. I burst into fits of laughter, much to William's disgust, holding my stomach and wiping at my instantly wet eyes. 'I'm sorry,' I laugh, knowing I need to rein it in before he swings at me.

'It freaks me out, I swear,' William grumbles, shaking his head in despair and dodging Gracie's hand when it flies out to smack his shoulder.

'Hey!'

'Well, c'mon!' he argues, clucking Harry's cheek affectionately. 'How is it possible?'

'He's perfect,' I jump in, wiping the crumbs polluting Harry's fingers away with a wet cloth.

'Thank you, Daddy.'

'Most welcome.' I want to scoop him up and squeeze him in my *thing*, but I resist. 'We need to get going.'

'Let me open this,' he says, rummaging through the gift bag and pulling out what we all know is in there. 'Look!'

His excitement over a pair of socks is way past unreasonable. I know that, yet I'll never find the rationale to remedy it. 'Wow!' I join him in his excitement and take the pair when they're thrust at me. 'Very smart.'

'They have horses on them!' He snatches them back and holds them to his chest. 'They match my shirt! Ooooh, this is just too cool!'

I'm beaming. Gracie is beaming. Every damn person in this room is beaming. Don't anyone ever tell me that my boy isn't fucking perfect.

Lifts. There are three of them staring at me. My unreasonable mind believes they are arguing between themselves as to who gets to feel me shaking inside, like it's the highlight of their miserable day. The middle one wins. The doors slide open and my heart rate cranks up twenty gears. But I refuse to let my boy see it. This part of me I never want to burden him with. Never let your child see your fear. Everyone knows that.

Why the fuck does the therapist's office have to be on the eighth floor? I can't make his little legs climb that many stairs and his little ego won't allow me to carry him. So I'm stuck with the poxy lift, and I have been since Olivia insisted on us coming here. My mood plummets.

I feel a little hand flexing in mine, snapping me out of my trance. Shit, I'm hurting him. 'You OK, Daddy?' His navy eyes climb my body until they're locked with mine. They're full of concern, and I immediately detest myself for spiking any worry from him.

'Fine and dandy, sweet boy.' I force myself to step forward, mentally shouting a mantra of encouraging words as we breach the threshold of the horror box.

Focus on Harry. Focus on Harry. Concentrate on my sweet boy.

'Would you like to take the stairs?'

His question shocks me. He's never asked before. 'Why would I want to do that?'

His little shoulders shrug. 'I don't know. Maybe you don't like lifts today.'

I feel like a fool. My five-year-old boy is trying to help me. Have my days of hiding this god-awful fear finally come to an end? Has he figured me out? 'We'll take the lift,' I affirm, reaching over and smacking the button for floor eight, probably harder than is necessary. I'm determined to beat this demon.

The doors close and Harry's little hand starts squeezing mine. I look down, finding him studying me carefully. 'What are you thinking?' I ask, however much I really don't want to know.

He smiles at me. 'I'm thinking you look very dashing today, Daddy. Mummy will like this one.'

'Mummy prefers me in lazy clothes,' I remind him, laughing to myself when he tuts his disapproval. I dread to think how many suits I've bought over the years, all beautiful, yet she still takes a tatty pair of jeans any day of the week.

The lift dings and the doors open onto the reception area of the therapist's office. 'Here we are!' He darts out, pulling me with him. My heartbeat returns to normal quickly and I soon find myself hauled across the room to the receptionist's desk. 'Hello!' Harry chirps.

My boy could bring a smile to the face of the world's most miserable person, I'm sure. And the therapist's receptionist is the world's most miserable person. She's formidable, yet unleashes smiles to my boy like there's no tomorrow. 'Harry Hart! What a pleasure!'

'How are you, Anne?'

'All the better for seeing you. Would you like to take a seat?'

'Certainly. Come on, Dad.'

I'm led to two spare seats, but I'm not graced with an adoring smile from Anne as I nod my greeting. Her cheerful persona slips away the second her stare moves from Harry to me. 'Mr Hart,' she practically growls, leaving no room for further conversation when she focuses on her computer screen and starts tapping at the keyboard. She looks like a Russian weightlifter and behaves like a bulldog. I don't like her.

Pulling the legs of my trousers up, I take a seat next to Harry and spend some time absorbing our surroundings. It's relatively quiet, as it always is when we're here at the end of the day. Our only company is a nervous lady, known as Wendy, who refuses to look anyone in the eye, not even Harry when he's persistently tried to chat with her. He's given up now, and refers to her as Weird Wendy.

'I'll be back in a moment,' Harry tells me, wandering over to the kids' corner, where Lego bricks are all packed neatly away. That will soon change. I relax back in my chair and watch him tip the box over and scatter them everywhere, passing a quick glance to Weird Wendy when Anne barks an order for her to proceed into the doctor's office.

She scurries off quickly, leaving me and my boy the only occupants of the waiting area, Anne aside.

I close my eyes and see sapphires everywhere – bright, brilliant, beautiful sapphires and wild blonde locks. It's a beauty that's so raw and pure, it defies me ever being blessed by it. But she *is* mine. And every fucked-up little piece of me belongs to her. I accept that wholeheartedly now. I smile, hearing the click of Lego bricks from across the room. And so is he.

'Mr Hart?'

I jump in my chair at the sound of an impatient voice, my eyes flying open to find Anne towering above my seated form. I stand quickly, not liking feeling so vulnerable under her narrowed eyes. 'Yes?'

'She's ready for you.' She sniffs and stalks away, snatching her handbag up from behind her desk and disappearing into a waiting lift.

I shudder, then seek out Harry, finding him at the door, his hand resting on the handle waiting to enter. 'Hurry, Daddy! We'll be late.'

I snap into action and follow Harry into the office, grimacing when the sense of a million people's problems hit me like a wrecking ball. It's lingering in the air, and a chill resonates through me as a result. I'm still befuddled as to why this happens every time. The room is plush, with soft furnishings at every turn. It's warm and inviting, but I still feel uncomfortable. I hate coming here. There's one problem, though. Harry loves it and this woman here keeps inviting him. Personally, I think she simply gets a huge power trip out of sitting behind this huge plush desk and watching me squirm.

I groan to myself and drop my arse to the chair opposite her desk, and Harry does the same, but where I'm irritated and pouting, he is grinning madly. It penetrates my foul mood a little and I find my lips twitching at the corners as a result.

'Hello, Harry,' she says. Her voice is like honey, all smooth and calming. I can't see her, I can just hear her voice, but when her swivel chair starts to turn and she comes into view, her sheer beauty renders me stupid for a few moments. And damn if my cock starts dancing in my trousers.

'Hi, Mummy,' Harry sings, his eyes bright and happy now he has his mother to fuss over him. 'We've come to take you home. Have you had a good day?'

She breaks out in the most stunning smile, her navy eyes that match my boy's sparkling like diamonds. 'I've had a wonderful day, made all the better now you're here.' She flicks those delicious eyes in my direction. Her cheeks are flushed. I want to pounce and worship her right now. Her wide smile turns coy and she crosses one leg over the other. 'Good evening, Mr Hart.'

I straighten my lips and shift in my chair, trying to conjure up reasonable thoughts in a vain attempt to remain composed in front of my boy. 'Good evening, Mrs Hart.'

Every blessed shard of light that's engulfed our lives since we met collides across the desk and detonates. It makes my back straighten and my heart race. This woman, pure, raw, and innocently perfect, has given me more pleasure than I ever thought possible. Not just through intimacy, but also from the sheer joy of being the object of her affection. I'm the centre of her world. And she is the absolute core of mine.

I watch Harry jump down from the chair and wander over to the bookshelves. 'How was your day?' I ask.

'Tiring. And I need to study some more when we're home.'

It takes everything out of me to refrain from rolling my eyes, knowing I'll be attacked by her sass if I expose my exasperation. This job is only part time, but she doesn't need to work here. She insists it's good for her studies – gives her a sense of what to expect when she qualifies as a therapist, but all I see is her burning herself out. I can't deny her, though. She wants to help people.

'Will you have an office like this?' I cast my eyes around the partner's office. We hijack it every Wednesday at six.

'Might do.'

I return my eyes to hers, grinning wickedly. 'Can I still call you my therapist when you really are one?'

'No, that would be a massive conflict of interest.'

I scowl. 'But you help me de-stress.'

'Hardly on a professional level!' She laughs, then lowers her voice, leaning over the desk. 'Or are you suggesting I should allow all of my patients to worship me?'

My shock is clear. 'No one else gets to taste you,' I virtually growl, the thought sending me to a maddening place I have avoided for a long time.

But I snap a lid on it when Harry jumps back onto the chair

next to me, looking at me in cute curiosity. 'OK, Daddy?'

I ruffle his hair, ignoring Olivia giggling across the desk. 'Perfect, mate.'

'Are you ready to go home, Mummy?' he asks.

'Not just yet.' She reaches for the remote control and I immediately fear the worst. 'Shall we?' she asks on a wry smile.

I can feel my boy's eyes on my profile as I stare at my love, so I slowly turn to him, finding that familiar exasperated look plaguing his gorgeous face. 'I don't think we have a choice,' I remind him, knowing he already knows this.

'She's mad,' he breathes tiredly.

'I concur.' I can do no more than agree, because he's right, and take his hand when he holds it out to me. 'Are you ready?'

He nods and we both stand together, just as Olivia presses a button that brings the room to life. We remain motionless, despite the instant blast of Pharrell Williams's "Happy", and watch as the woman in our life jumps up, all enthusiastically, and kicks her Converse off. 'Come on, my beautiful boys!' she sings, rounding her desk and seizing our hands. 'Let's de-stress.'

There are too many counters I could make to that, but a quick warning glance from my wife tells me to zip it. My lips purse on a sulky pout. 'I can think . . .' I just can't help myself, but I'm halted when her palm slaps over my face.

She grins and comes closer, keeping her hand exactly where it is. 'I bought Green and Black's earlier.'

My eyes widen and my blood heats. 'Strawberries?' I mumble against her hand, fighting off trembles of anticipation when she nods her head. I match her grin behind her hand and mentally conjure up my plan for later. It'll involve worshipping. Lots and lots of worshipping.

'Can we dance now?' Harry asks, pulling our attention to him waiting impatiently to the side. 'Control yourselves,' he mumbles.

We laugh and each of us claims one of his hands so we form a circle. 'Let's do this,' I say, bracing myself for what I'm about to endure and partake in.

We spend a few moments flicking gazes to each other, smiling, waiting, before Harry makes the first move. My boy breaks out in song, belting out the lyrics as his little body practically goes into spasm. He shakes off our holds and throws his arms into the air, closing his eyes as he starts jumping around the office like a little nut job. I've never seen such a wonderful sight.

'Come on, Daddy!' he yells, jigging his way across to the sofa and jumping onto the cushions. The slight discomfort his carelessness brings isn't something I can help, though I'm getting better, for sure. Plus, we always tidy before we leave.

'Yes –' Olivia nudges me, smiling – 'let loose, Mr Hart.'

My shoulders jump up coolly. 'As you wish.' I hastily shrug off my jacket as a crafty smile slowly forms on my face. It falls to the floor, but I leave it exactly where it is and run to join my boy, dragging Livy behind me. 'Make way!' I yell, catapulting myself up on the couch with him. The sound of his giggles and the look of delight only spur me on. I've lost my mind, shaking my head, spinning Livy on the floor below me and singing along with my boy. God knows what my hair must look like.

'Woooohoooooo!' Harry screeches, springing off the couch. 'The desk, Daddy!'

I'm in action immediately, running across the office again. I lift his little body up and join him on the huge, important-looking workspace. 'Go for it, Harry!'

'Yeaaaahh!' His legs fly out, kicking the piles of paper everywhere.

And I couldn't care less.

It's raining white sheets of paper, we're busting some very questionable moves, and we're laughing in between picking up the lines that we know. It's heaven.

My angels and I are in our own bubble of happiness, except our bubble is now huge. And nothing can pop it.

The music starts to fade, but our energy doesn't. We're still going hell for leather when Goldfrapp's "Happiness" kicks in and Harry screeches his excitement. 'Oh wow!' he gasps, pushing his waves from his forehead. 'My favourite!'

I'm yanked down from the desk and the three of us form a circle again. I know what's about to happen. I'm going to get very dizzy. There's only one thing that can stop the inevitable, so I pin my eyes on Olivia as Harry instigates the spinning of our little circle. He's away with thc fairics again, so he won't notice that my full attention is planted firmly on his mother. And hers is on me.

Around and around we go, over and over, Harry singing and Olivia and I focused solely on each other. 'I love you,' I mouth on a crooked smile.

'Your bones, Miller Hart,' she mouths back, giving me that full-on beam.

Good God, whatever did I do to deserve her?

I'm feeling quite sweaty when the music finally comes to a stop, and continuing to follow our usual tradition, we all collapse to the floor in an exhausted heap. We gasp for breath, our chests heaving, Harry still chuckling with his mum.

I smile up at the ceiling. 'I have a request,' I mumble breathlessly, resisting the urge to meet Harry's cute smiling face at the sound of those words. There's only one right answer to this request.

'We'll never stop loving you, Daddy,' he answers hastily, placing his hand on my arm.

I drop my head to the side to find him. 'Thank you.'

'We have a request, too.'

I take a deep breath and swallow down the lump in my throat that's spiked by pure, undying happiness. 'Until there is no breath left in my lungs, sweet boy.'

My world centres and everything is just perfect once again.

Olivia Taylor sent my meticulous world into fucking chaos. But it was real. *She* was real. What I felt with her was real. Each time I worshipped her, I felt my soul get a little bit cleaner. It was beautiful. It meant something. With the exception of one regrettable time, our lovemaking was never an all-out slamming of one body into another to reach the ultimate aim.

Pleasure.

Release.

Our intimacies were never automatic, either – not in the sense of my body taking over and just . . . doing. But it *was* automatic in the sense that, ultimately, it was natural. Effortless.

This was supposed to happen to me.

One night turned into a lifetime.

And not even that will be enough. *Everything* with Olivia and Harry will never be enough.

My name is Miller Hart.

I am the Special One.

But special because no other man to ever walk this land could ever be as happy as me.

I don't need to elaborate.

I'm free.

About the Author

Jodi Ellen Malpas was born and raised in the Midlands town of Northampton, England, where she lives with her two boys. Working for her father's construction business full time, she tried to ignore the lingering idea of writing until it became impossible. She wrote in secret for a long time before finally finding the courage to unleash her creative streak, and in October 2012 she released *This Man*. She took a chance on a story with some intense characters and sparked incredible reactions from women all over the world. She's now a proud #1 *New York Times* and *Sunday Times* bestselling author.

Writing powerful love stories and creating addictive characters has become her passion – a passion she now shares with her devoted readers.

Learn more at:
JodiEllenMalpas.co.uk
Twitter @JodiEllenMalpas
Facebook.com/JodiEllenMalpas